BEASTS
OF
RUIN

ALSO BY AYANA GRAY

Beasts of Prey

BEASTS OF RUIN

AYANA GRAY

G. P. PUTNAM'S SONS

G. P. PUTNAM'S SONS
An imprint of Penguin Random House LLC, New York

First published in the United States of America by G. P. Putnam's Sons,
an imprint of Penguin Random House LLC, 2022

Visit us online at penguinrandomhouse.com

Library of Congress Cataloging-in-Publication Data
Names: Gray, Ayana, author.
Title: Beasts of ruin / Ayana Gray.
Description: New York: G. P. Putnam's Sons, [2022] | Series: Beasts of prey; book 2 | Summary: Now
separated, sixteen-year-old indentured beastkeeper Koffi and seventeen-year-old warrior candidate
Ekon will have to find their way back to each other as they face off against the god of death.
Identifiers: LCCN 2022013826 (print) | LCCN 2022013827 (ebook) |
ISBN 9780593405710 (hardcover) | ISBN 9780593405727 (ebook)
Subjects: CYAC: Magic—Fiction. | Monsters—Fiction. | Fantasy. | LCGFT: Fantasy fiction.
Classification: LCC PZ7.1.G7326 Bed 2022 (print) |
LCC PZ7.1.G7326 (ebook) | DDC [Fic]—dc23
LC record available at https://lccn.loc.gov/2022013826
LC ebook record available at https://lccn.loc.gov/2022013827

Book manufactured in Canada

ISBN 9780593405710 (hardcover)
1 3 5 7 9 10 8 6 4 2

ISBN 9780593531587 (international edition)
1 3 5 7 9 10 8 6 4 2

FRI

Design by Marikka Tamura
Text set in Arno Pro

For Grandpa Aston—
in the silence, I still hear your trumpet.

THORNKEEP

The Stables

The Forge

THE MISTWOOD

THE FIVE DARAJA ORDERS

ORDER OF MWILI • Order of the Body

ORDER OF AKILI • Order of the Mind

ORDER OF MAISHA • Order of Life

ORDER OF KUPAMBANA • Order of Combat

ORDER OF UFUNDI • Order of Craft

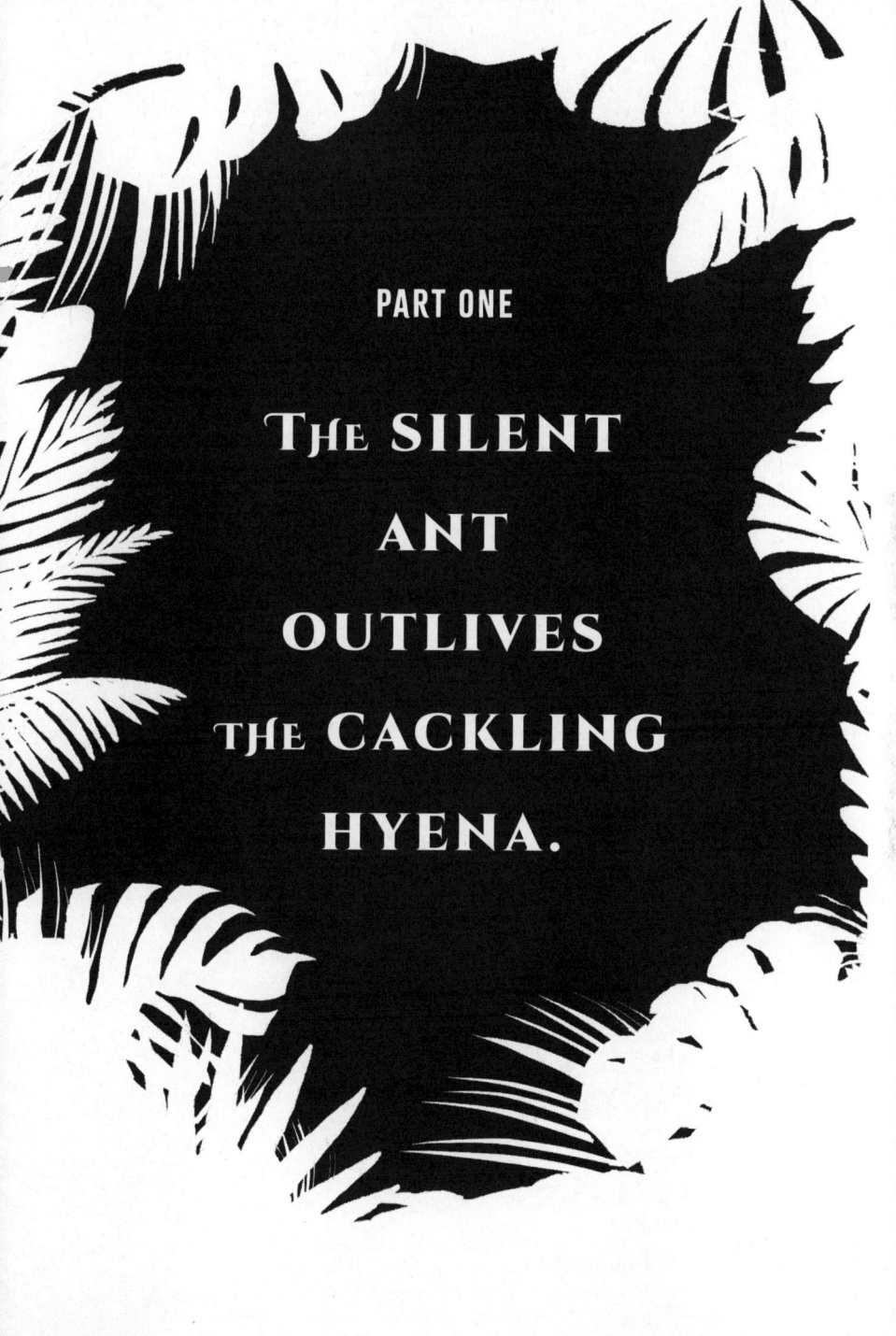

PART ONE

The SILENT ANT OUTLIVES the CACKLING HYENA.

UNSPOKEN THINGS

BINTI

In the fragile hours before dawn, this city belongs to its monsters.

A faltering rhythm beats in my chest like a goatskin drum as I feel for the dagger sheathed at my side. It is only a modest weapon, small and crudely made, but I take some comfort in its weight, in the shape of its carved wooden hilt. The clouds overhead are bruised black and blue, swollen with rain and violence. Among the thunderous rumblings, I hear their discontent. The clouds know what I'm plotting to do.

Beneath their gaze, I am already condemned.

Mud sucks at my sandals as I traverse Lkossa's roads, tempting me to kick them off and continue barefoot, but I resist that urge. These sandals are the only ones I have, and replacing them isn't a luxury I can afford. Each sodden step is weighed with hesitation, and I wonder if I should turn back now before I'm caught and punished, but time is a gluttonous creature this late in the night; it consumes my thoughts and leaves no room for doubt. My strides lengthen.

I need to keep moving.

The mud-brick buildings press in on me from both sides as I

walk, suffocating me in the collective fetor of rotting meat, fermented fruit, and ox dung. They grow more dilapidated the deeper I venture into the bowels of the Chafu District, and I swear their cutout windows follow me like hollow, vacant eyes, watching my progress alongside the clouds. Past them, the soft peaks of evergreen pines rise above the city's tallest buildings, reminding me of my proximity to the notorious Greater Jungle and its legends, but I can't dwell on that either, not now.

I skirt past a flea-ridden cat as I cross one of the district's dimly lit intersections and feel something underfoot: a crumpled piece of parchment covered with words inked in cerulean. That color is distinct, used only for documents that come from the city's temple— a temple *my* people are not permitted to worship within. Some instinct warns me not to read what it says, but I pick it up anyway, unfurling its rolled corners with tentative fingers. Mud has stained it in places, but I can still clearly see the image at its center.

The little girl staring back at me could be eight as easily as she could be twelve; it is impossible to know with certainty. In the rough, blue-lined sketch, her eyes are dark and wary; the rest of her face is emaciated. One single emboldened word is legible above her portrait: REWARD. Below it are more words, smudged and hurriedly scrawled.

FEMALE DARAJA

Description: black hair, brown or black eyes
Age: unknown
Height: approx. 4 ft., 1 in.

Weight: approx. 50–60 lbs.

Wanted for: illicit activity

Additional notes: A reward of 500 shabas will be paid for live capture.

My eyes are immediately drawn to the words *illicit activity*, and a swarm of new emotions begins to collect in the pit of my stomach, buzzing louder as I let the parchment slip from my fingers and flutter back to the ground. I force myself to name each feeling, plucking at them like the flyaway seeds of a dandelion. The anxiety seeps through my pores first, trailed by fear, resentment, and finally guilt. I bite down on the inside of my cheek until I taste the coppery tang of blood.

Guilt is one more luxury I cannot afford.

I reach for my dagger again and run the pad of my thumb along its hilt until I've calmed.

You have to do this, says an imagined voice in my head. It sounds like mine but speaks with more conviction. *Do this one last thing, and you'll finally be free. You'll be safe.* She'll *be safe.*

Safe. I sheathe that word like a second weapon as I square my shoulders and trek deeper into the darkness.

By the time I reach Lkossa's outskirts, there's a chill in my bones.

On the northern front, the Greater Jungle's trees stand as a natural barrier against the monsoon season's winds. Here on the city's western border, though, there are only waist-high lemongrass fields; they do nothing to stop the frigid breeze lashing at my cheeks. My nostrils burn each time I inhale; with every step, the joints in my fingers stiffen. I tug the hood of my tattered brown cloak closer as thunder rumbles from above, and tell myself that the imminent rain is the *real* reason I'm covering my head, not because I'm afraid of being recognized.

The path winds until I come upon an abandoned shop set slightly apart from the others in this area. Louvered wood shutters hang askew from the windows, and decades of chiseled graffiti disfigure its humble face, but that matters little to me. This shop serves a single purpose tonight: It is my hiding place.

I pry its front door open, brushing silken spiderwebs from my face as I enter, and promptly crouch below one of the windowsills. From my vantage point, the entire path is visible, but I am hidden from anyone who might come down it now. My gaze casts to the sky again. The clouds still hang low, but past them I discern the faintest hints of Lkossa's black-veined sky changing hue. Dawn is rapidly approaching, and I am running out of time. My tensed muscles ache as the seconds pass in tiny eternities; within the space of one of them, I dare to hope that, just maybe, I've overestimated her. Perhaps, after all this time, she won't come at my summons.

A sudden movement from the opposite end of the border path renders me immobile.

My breath quickens as the clouds part and a single shaft of pale, glimmering starlight knifes through the dark like a blade. It illuminates the hunched silhouette of an old woman ambling forward on bare feet. Her off-white tunic is stained and frayed, loose on her scarecrow frame. Walnut-brown skin stretches tight over her skull, so that her hollowed face bears an unsettling resemblance to a living corpse. The kinky salt-and-pepper hair atop her head is cropped short and badly matted, as though it hasn't been washed or combed in some time. She runs a tongue over her lips as she looks left and right, searching. I can't quite suppress a shudder at the sight of her. I know who this woman is, and I know what some people call her. In the shop's window, my hand slips to the dagger on my hip for a third and final time. The blade's metal hisses low as I withdraw it from its sheath and count the woman's shuffling footsteps, watching, waiting. Then:

"If you're going to try to kill me, be quick about it. I don't have all night."

I still as the old woman's eyes cut to the shop's window where I'm hiding. Too late, I duck down.

"Come out," she says in a rough voice, "*now.*"

Gods-smite.

An uncomfortable beat passes before, reluctantly, I stand and emerge from the shop. When the old woman sees me, she does a double take.

"Binti?"

I flinch on principle. It's been years since I answered to my old name, but even now, hearing it aloud splits open an old wound. The woman's rheumy eyes widen, and I watch the succession of emotions flit across her face one by one—recognition, confusion, and then joy. It's the joy that makes me angriest. I've learned not to trust the Cobra with things like joy, and I know from experience that what brings her joy rarely bodes well for me. She advances, and I retreat a step. This seems to offend her, but I ignore the pained, impatient look she gives me. The open space between us is a necessary precaution, the designated place for unspoken things to live. The Cobra squints at me.

7

"I don't understand," she says. "The errand boy's message said to come here. *You're* the one who sent him?"

"Yes."

The Cobra's eyes drop from my face to the dagger still clutched in my hand. She doesn't look afraid or upset, only disappointed. Somehow, that's worse. "So," she says with some resignation, "*this* is what you've summoned me for, to kill me? I admit, I'm a little surprised."

"You've left me no choice." My grip on the dagger's hilt tightens, its grooves press into my palm. "I told you to leave us alone."

"And I have."

"You were seen again," I snap, "near the Night Zoo's walls. People are starting to ask questions."

The Cobra pauses a moment, wringing her hands. "I just wanted to make sure . . ." She falters. "I just wanted to make sure you were all right."

I twitch. "We're fine without you."

"*Really?*" The Cobra's brows rise. "So, Baaz Mtombé pays you and Lesego well?"

"It's not about the pay." I can't hide the defensiveness in my voice. "It's about stability."

"Ah, *yes.*" There's a distinct wryness in the Cobra's tone. "Nothing promises stability like indentured servitude. Tell me, if you and Lesego are working all day, who's looking after—?"

"Don't." My teeth audibly click together. "Keep my daughter's name out of your mouth."

The Cobra regards me, assessing. "You cannot keep it from her forever, you know," she murmurs. "What she is, what she will become . . . suppressing it will only make things harder for her. It's in her blood, and there's *nothing* you can do to change that."

I hear a note of satisfaction in her voice, and at once my fear and guilt metamorphose into something else: a vicious, consuming anger that constricts in the hollow of my throat. This wasn't supposed to happen; I wasn't supposed to let her get under my skin. The ghost of a smirk touches the corner of the Cobra's mouth, as though she hears my thoughts.

"It was a brave idea," she says dryly, nodding at the dagger. "But we both know you'd never kill me. You don't have it in you."

I bite down hard on my bottom lip, gnawing until the skin is tender. She's right, and I know it. I hate the Cobra, she frightens me; her presence in my life is like a poisoned thorn pricking at my side and making me sicker all the time, but even that truth isn't enough to give me the courage I need to see this through. I cannot kill her. The Cobra's expression turns haughty as I resheathe the blade, but her show of victory is premature. She doesn't see the last weapon hidden in my arsenal.

"You're right," I murmur. "I can't kill you, but the Sons of the Six can."

Finally, I get the reaction I want. I feel a wicked bite of satisfaction as all amusement slips from the Cobra's face in an instant, as though we're playing a game and now I've shown my hand. She gapes at me. "You . . . you wouldn't."

I stand straighter as, for the first time in a long time, I taste a sweet morsel of power, of leverage.

"I've seen the reward posters," I say quietly, "the prices the Kuhani is willing to pay for a captured daraja. Five hundred shabas for a mere child. Imagine what I could get for turning in the *Cobra*."

"You wouldn't," she repeats. "Not to me." Around us, the air stills, as though even it is waiting for what will come next.

"I will do whatever it takes to protect my family."

At this, the Cobra begins shifting her weight from foot to foot, nervous. She looks frailer, smaller, and older than I remember. The deep creases bracketing her mouth are deceiving; they don't belong on a woman her age, nor does her gray-and-white hair. I watch the way she moves, slow and stiff where she used to be quick and lithe. She reminds me of a once-beautiful tree gone too soon to rot, decaying from within. Her eyes glisten when they meet mine.

"Binti, I—"

"*Stop* calling me that."

She recoils as though I've struck her. "I'm sorry. Just tell me what you want. If you need money—"

"Just stay away from my family, for good."

"I will." The Cobra nods quickly. "You have my word."

"No." I shake my head. "I want more than your word. I want a promise." I hesitate. "I want an eternal vow."

The Cobra's jaw drops at the same time thunder claps above us. "Binti, you can't possibly mean—?"

"That's my condition."

She frowns. "Have you any idea what power such a vow holds?" she asks. "An eternal vow is sacred among darajas, life-binding."

"Exactly."

The Cobra looks around, nervous. "I don't have the proper materials to perform the ritual. I'd need time."

I narrow my eyes. "Liar."

A slow, creeping smile spreads across her face. In that instant, I don't know how anyone could ever mistake this woman for who she is, what she is: a snake curled in a basket, cunning, dangerous. To my discomfort, a hint of pride touches her eyes.

"I taught you well," she says with approval. "Let us begin, then." From her tunic's slightly torn pocket, she produces a tiny pouch, one that rattles when she shakes it. She tips it to the side, and small broken fragments of something white pour from within. I know instinctively what they are, and hot nausea roils in the pit of my stomach.

The Cobra clutches the hand holding the bone fragments in a tight fist, then closes the small gap between us with unnatural speed, filling the air with the smells of earth and cheap palm wine. I lurch back, but she snatches my dagger away, and I suck in a sharp breath.

"Give me your hand," she orders.

"Which one?" With her so close, maintaining my composure is harder.

"It matters not."

I don't know what prompts me to offer my right hand. A streak of silver sails through the air, there's a sting, and then a fine line of blood blooms along the meat of my palm between my thumb and index finger. Before I can react, the Cobra slices her left hand in the same quick motion, then grabs my hand and presses our wounds together. The sensation is revolting—warm, and wet, and sticky—but she holds on as though we're simply shaking hands. When she leans in to speak, her voice is low.

"They're watching now, all of them."

My mouth goes paper dry. She's renowned for her tricks and

deceptions, but something tells me that this time the Cobra isn't lying. We are still alone here on the western border path, but it does feel like we are being watched. By one. By many. I fidget in place. I was taught that darajas sometimes call upon their ancestors during rituals. I didn't believe it to be true until now.

"You're sure you want to do this?" I hear the layers within the Cobra's question as her tired eyes meet mine. "Once I begin, there is no going back." I know well the severity of what I'm asking, the consequences of it. But when I look into the Cobra's eyes, hers aren't the ones I see anymore. Instead, I see my daughter's eyes, alight with childlike innocence. I have to protect that innocence, I have to protect her. I *will* protect her, whatever it costs.

"I'm sure."

The Cobra takes a deep, shuddering breath. "Then, with my foremothers as my witness, I vow not to seek you out again in this life." Tears fill her eyes. "By blood, and bone, and soul, we bind this eternal vow." She nods to me. "Repeat."

The phrase feels strange on my tongue, as though pilfered from a long-dead language. Still, I force myself to say it. "By blood, and bone, and soul, we bind this eternal vow."

A warmth emits from the place our cut hands are adjoined as soon as the words leave me. The hairs on my arms stand on end, but the Cobra doesn't move, nor does she relinquish her grip on me. The bone fragments trapped between us burn hot, their jagged edges and points digging into my skin. With horror and wonder, I watch as a luminescent white vapor seeps from our clasped hands. It slithers up the Cobra's arm, then coils around her neck, weighted by a circular amulet that wasn't there before. My blood runs cold.

"What is that?"

"A mark of the eternal vow," says the Cobra. She drops my hand without ceremony. My palm itches and tingles, yet I don't touch it. There is no trace of the cut that was there only seconds ago, and it takes me a moment to realize that the bone fragments are gone too. My eyes are still drawn to the strange new amulet swinging from the Cobra's neck, but she merely hands my dagger back to me.

"It is done," she whispers. "Goodbye, Binti."

There are a thousand words I want to say in answer—ugly words, beautiful words, desperate words. I settle on just one.

"Goodbye."

An earth-shattering thunderclap crashes overhead; ribbons of lightning dance white-hot across the sky. A seam in the clouds seems to unstitch; in its wake, a sudden deluge of rain soaks through my cloak. I bow my head, trying to cover myself, and when I look up again, the Cobra is gone.

Something else wets my cheeks now, not rain, but I wipe the salted tears away before turning on my heel and running back toward the city. I don't care anymore about the muddied roads or the filth; I don't even notice when my sandals slip loose from my feet. With certainty, I know that I will never see this place again.

With certainty, I know that I will never see my mother again.

CHAPTER 1

THE MASTER OF THORNKEEP

Koffi smelled the blackberries first.

Saccharine, tart, it was their cloying scent that lured her back to consciousness. Slowly, she opened her eyes. A groan began low in her throat, very nearly passing through her lips, but instinct caught the sound before it could escape. In the silence, a realization settled on her skin like motes of dust.

She didn't know where she was.

Life returned to her fingertips, and Koffi let them explore, taking tactile reconnaissance of her surroundings. From them, she gathered that she was lying on something soft—a bed—with linen sheets bunched at her waist. Her head rolled to the left, pressing one cheek against the cool pillow beneath her; she paid for that small movement instantly. A stab of pain throbbed at the base of her skull, and her eyes watered. Seconds passed before her dulled vision sharpened again. Even then, she couldn't make sense of what she was seeing.

She was in a large bedroom, one she'd never been in before. Its walls—at least, those visible in the dimness—were a cool slate

15

gray. Squares of buttery light dappled the vaulted ceiling over-head, which she took to mean it was morning. A glint to her left caught her eye, and she noted a bone-white nightstand beside the bed. There was a gilded serving tray on it, laden with food. Her eyes took in the sliced bread, the tiny bowls of jam, cheese, and fruit, and her mouth watered.

A feast for a king, she mused. She was still staring at the food, considering, when she heard it: the soft rustle of fabric. She stilled.

She was not alone.

At first, she didn't understand how she had not immediately noticed the two people standing on the opposite side of the bed-room and facing a massive bay window with their backs to her. But as the seconds passed, she did understand; she hadn't noticed them because they stood with near-perfect stillness, two statues silhouetted in sunlight. The man was tall, muscled, and lean, with skin like sunbaked clay and cropped black hair. Beside him, the woman was much shorter, with brown skin a shade darker than his and a springy black Afro. His kaftan was river blue, hers was marigold. Without warning, the man spoke.

"How much longer should we let her sleep?" His voice was low.

"We'll wake her soon," the woman murmured. Her voice was lilting. "He's expecting her."

Koffi stiffened on the bed. She was almost certain that these people were talking about her.

Abruptly, the man began to pace. Koffi couldn't see the details of his face, but his movements reminded her of an agitated lion contained in a too-small cage.

"It doesn't make sense," he said between steps. "It's been years

16

since he brought a new one here—why would he start doing it again now?"

"I don't know," the woman replied. She was still facing the window.

The man stopped, and Koffi finally saw his face properly in the light. Every one of his features was smooth and angular, as though carved by a practiced sculptor. He had a long, even nose, ochre eyes framed by thick black brows, and a knife-sharp jawline. Only his scowling mouth looked out of place.

"He said nothing to you?" he asked the woman. "Nothing about where she's from, or what order she belongs to?"

Finally, the woman turned. Even in profile, Koffi knew at once that she was beautiful too. Her face was soft, defined by full pink lips set below a short, rounded nose. She was frowning.

"He tells me as much as he tells you," she said. "All I know is that we're to bring her to the main hall. He didn't say anything else."

Koffi swallowed.

"And how are we supposed to do that?" the man asked. Koffi watched him massage the bridge of his nose. "She's still unconscious."

"We can't take her to him in the clothes she's wearing," said the woman. Koffi noticed she'd lowered her voice. "They're filthy. She'll need to change them."

Koffi's pulse quickened. She'd hoped for more time to form a plan. Her eyes searched the room, desperate. The only other furnishings nearby were a vanity and a divan in the far-left corner, neither of which could be used as a weapon or shield. These people, whoever they were, had the advantage. She'd have to move quickly to catch them off guard.

Think. Think.

A shaft of golden sunlight drew Koffi's eyes back to the serving tray on her left. Just beside it, there was a silver butter knife. She took a slow breath in, bracing herself, then closed her eyes and tried to envision what she was going to do. If she moved over slightly, she could reach the knife. And if she could reach the knife...

"Okay."

Koffi's eyes were still closed, but to her right she heard the man's voice again, closer. She shifted subtly to her left.

"Kena, maybe you should be the one to—"

Koffi lunged, rolling off the bed and snatching the butter knife from the tray in one less-than-graceful motion. She regretted it almost immediately; an explosion of stars erupted in her head and blotted her vision, but her fingers wrapped tight around the knife's tiny handle. She focused on its feel, the cool of its metal against her palm. The room tilted violently from side to side like the deck of an ill-fated ship at sea, and she stumbled. This time, a groan did escape her. She still couldn't see, but she heard a gasp. Then a male voice.

"Oh. You're awake."

Koffi blinked hard, trying to quiet the percussion in her chest as she fought to remain calm. Her ears were ringing, there were still flashing spots in her vision, but she saw that the man and woman who'd been standing at the window were now just on the other side of the bed, looking at her with shared concern. Upright, she realized they were both younger than she'd first thought; not a man and a woman, but a boy and a girl, each about sixteen—her age. It was the former of the two who broke the silence.

"So," he said with one brow raised. "I take it this means you *didn't* like the welcome breakfast?"

Koffi didn't pause to consider the question. "Who are you?" Her voice was a throaty rasp, as though it hadn't been used for days. That scared her. She glanced back and forth, trying to keep her eyes on the boy and the girl at the same time, but the effort was dizzying. Her grip on the knife tightened, but to her faint annoyance, the boy only gave it a cursory glance before smirking.

"Is that really necessary?"

"It is when you're trying to take my clothes off."

"We weren't trying to take your clothes off," said the boy with a note of exasperation. He paused, then smirked. "Well, I mean, technically speaking . . ."

"You have five seconds." Koffi didn't know whether to be irritated or terrified by the boy's nonchalance. "Tell me who you are, where I am, and why I'm here."

"Or what?" The boy's eyes flicked to the knife again, visibly amused. "You'll butter our toast?"

"*Zain.*" Up to this point, the girl hadn't spoken; now she was glaring at the boy. "I think it would be best if you left."

The boy—Zain—considered a moment before he shrugged and headed toward a pair of double doors on the other side of the room. He muttered something that sounded distinctly like "butter knife" before closing them behind him. Koffi exhaled.

"I'm sorry," said the girl. She was looking at Koffi the way one might look at an injured animal, but like the boy, she seemed unfazed by the butter knife. Koffi sighed, then let it clatter to the ground.

"I know this is all probably very overwhelming," the girl continued gently. "But Zain and I aren't here to hurt you, we—"

"Who are you?"

"My name is Makena," she said. "Yours?"

"Koffi."

"Koffi," Makena repeated. "I'm a daraja, like you."

Daraja. Koffi felt the word strike against her like a flint to stone, pulling others to the forefront of her mind. *Daraja. Bridge. Splendor.* They were disjointed, but familiar; she just couldn't remember why.

"What order are you?" Makena asked. "I'm in Ufundi."

Koffi stared back at her, confused. Makena seemed to be asking the question earnestly, but it didn't make sense. "Um . . ."

"That's all right." Makena waved a hand. "We can talk about that later. But for now . . ." She glanced toward the double doors before offering an apologetic look. "You do need to change your clothes."

Koffi looked down at her own body for the first time since she'd woken up. Her burlap tunic was covered in dirt and grime, but she had no recollection of how it'd gotten there.

Why? Why can't I remember?

"I have something for you to wear, actually," said Makena. "If you'd like." She crossed the room and stopped before the divan; Koffi noticed something neatly folded on it. When Makena turned back to her, she was holding up a sleeveless dress. It was long and sweeping, cinched at the waist. A geometric black-and-white pattern covered the wax-print fabric, and golden stitching embroidered its hems.

"I made it," Makena murmured. "I . . . hope you like it."

"I do," said Koffi. "It's really nice." That was an understatement, but they were the only words she could summon. With certainty, she knew that she was awake, and yet this all still seemed like some distorted dream. She felt removed, unfocused, as though she was grasping at spider-silk threads of memory and trying to braid them into something logical.

Makena laid the dress on the bed. "I'll call for a cloth and water basin to be brought up so you can wash," she offered. "But you'll need to be quick, we don't have much time."

"Why?" Koffi tensed. "Where are we going?"

Makena shot a furtive glance over her shoulder as she headed for the bedroom doors. "To take you to the main hall. The master of Thornkeep doesn't like to be kept waiting."

Koffi's heart thundered in her chest as Makena led her down a narrow hall.

Like the bedchamber she'd awoken in, everything around her was carved from the same slate rock, which did nothing to fend off the chill in the air. Around her, a pervading darkness held firm, interrupted only by the cracks of pale light that came from arrow-slit windows. Koffi was tempted to peek out of each one they passed, but she forced her gaze to stay fixed ahead. With each step, more questions filled her mind, and it unnerved her that she had answers to none of them. How had she gotten here? Why was she here? And why couldn't she remember anything from before this morning? Makena's words echoed in her head.

The master of Thornkeep doesn't like to be kept waiting.

This place was called Thornkeep, she had gathered that much at least, but who was its master, and what did he want with her?

They passed into a new corridor, one with a large window on its left that allowed morning light to breach the dark. Makena walked past it without stopping, but this time Koffi stole a glance out of it. Her breath caught.

The lawns outside the window were lush in the extreme, an immaculate expanse of emerald-green grass. Every few feet, tiny ponds trimmed in alabaster stone decorated the grounds, their glass-smooth surfaces reflecting hues of azure and indigo in the sunlight. Her eyes flitted left and right, trying in vain to count the thousands of flowers arranged alongside the arbors and gazebos, but it was impossible. She noted that every single flower, despite its size or arrangement, was some shade of blue, reflecting the sky above.

"Thornkeep's east garden," said Makena. She'd stopped to stand at Koffi's side. "Also called the Blue Garden. There are three others on the grounds, but this one is my favorite."

Koffi nodded, though she barely heard Makena's words. She was still taking in the scene before her. Thornkeep's east garden was unquestionably beautiful, but the longer she studied it, the more acutely she felt an unease. Her gaze drifted past the ponds and plots of flower beds, then stopped at a line of neatly planted trees clearly meant to mark the garden's end. She recognized those trees at once—only acacias had that gnarled, thorny quality about them—but they weren't what held Koffi's eye. It was the wall of heavy mist that hung around them. Most of the acacias' tops were obscured by it, a thick pall of unmoving silver-white.

22

Even from this distance, Koffi imagined she could feel the mist's coolness, the damp that would have clung to everything it touched. She shivered.

"That's the Mistwood," said Makena without prompt. "It marks the border of Thornkeep's grounds."

Koffi didn't respond. She couldn't explain it, but something about that mist, those trees, held her in place, as though daring her to watch a second longer. A beat passed before Makena spoke again.

"We should keep going," she said. "The main hall's not far."

In silence, they left the corridor and continued on. When darkness fell over them once more, Koffi's muscles relaxed. She felt an inexplicable sense of relief the farther she got from the window and the sight of the mist, but she didn't know why.

Makena stopped again a few minutes later, so abruptly that Koffi nearly ran into her back. When she looked up, she realized that they were now standing before two enormous blackwood doors trimmed in a dull gold paint. Directly next to them, Zain was standing at attention. He offered them a cheery wave, and Koffi answered it with a frown before she could stop herself. Zain chuckled.

"Glad you could make it, Butter Knife."

Koffi didn't dignify the comment with a reply, and tried to keep her eyes trained on the double doors, but that was made harder when Zain moved to stand directly beside her, so that she was sandwiched between him and Makena. He was at least a head taller than her, and when he leaned toward her, their shoulders brushed. A smell like freshly laundered linens filled the air.

"A word of advice," he said under his breath. "Try not to threaten anyone with cutlery."

Whatever words Koffi had been planning to say back died in her throat as the doors before them swung open. Makena and Zain moved first, passing through them with an easy grace. Koffi took a steadying breath before she stepped into the room. Almost immediately, she faltered.

The room was the grandest she'd ever seen. A lake of white-veined black marble made up its floor, and a line of towering arched windows on two of its walls flooded the room in rose-gold sunlight. There was little in the way of furnishings here, but Koffi's gaze caught on a single object directly opposite her: a tapestry hung on the wall. It was a massive piece, at least twice her height and many times as wide, and featured at its center a great, swollen hippopotamus. The creature's skin was brown and shiny with wet, its tiny eyes beetle-black. It seemed to be staring right at her as it stood against the backdrop of a faded marshland baring its white tusks, each one longer than her arm. Koffi looked away from it quickly, disturbed. Something about that tapestry, about hippopotamuses specifically, had stirred another memory within her, but it left her as quickly as it'd come.

"Over here." Makena glanced over her shoulder, keeping her voice to a whisper. "I see a place to stand."

Koffi followed until the three of them stopped near the room's center. She turned and, for the first time since entering, realized that they were not alone here. Clusters of people stood together all over the room, and every single person was staring at her. In stolen glances, Koffi took each one of them in. To her right, there was one group of young men and women dressed in blood-dark red; to her left, a second group donned shades of green. She noted one huddle of people swathed in gauzy blue fabrics very similar to

24

Zain's, and still a fourth group who wore pale yellows like Makena. The people farthest from her were dressed in deep violet, and she tried not to think about the fact that—in addition to looking like the most athletic people in the room—they also looked to be the most menacing. One of them openly grimaced at her, and she flinched, immediately annoyed at herself for doing so.

Do not show fear, she commanded her body. *Do not look afraid.*

"It's all right," Makena whispered. "No one here will hurt you."

Koffi didn't take any comfort in those words. She was too busy wading through even more questions. Who were all of these people? Was the master of Thornkeep among them?

Abruptly, the set of double doors she, Makena, and Zain had just walked through opened a second time; at once, every eye that'd been trained on Koffi shot to them instead. On either side of her, Makena and Zain both straightened. Even Koffi found herself watching, waiting.

Several impossibly long seconds passed before a man entered the chamber alone. He was tall, with dark, ochre-brown skin and curly black hair barbered to a low fade. He looked old enough to be Koffi's father. She noticed that, unlike everyone else in the room, he wasn't wearing a colorful garment; rather, his dashiki was a modest black-and-white pattern, not so unlike her own. He said nothing as he moved forward in long, confident strides. One by one, every person in the room bowed their head. There was an unspoken authority about this man, worn like a mantle to which he was well accustomed. Even Koffi found herself lowering her gaze as he approached, his sandaled footfall impossibly soft against the marble. She was staring at her own feet when she heard the words.

"Good morning, Koffi."

An arrow of heat ran the length of Koffi's body, as sudden and quick as a lightning strike. She felt a nudge against her arm, and swallowed hard as her bowed head seemed to rise of its own accord.

Slowly, Koffi lifted her gaze and locked eyes with the master of Thornkeep.

CHAPTER 2

LITTLE MOUSE

Ekon was counting again.

One-two-three. One-two-three. One-two-three.

He stood alone at the window of an old apothecary, its sagging ceiling so low that it nearly brushed the top of his head. Of course, he hadn't known when he'd first arrived that it was an apothecary at all, but now he saw the signs everywhere. He counted *forty-six, forty-seven . . . forty-eight* dusted jars stacked along the built-in shelves, their liquid contents murky and ominous. In one corner of the room there was a small hearth, in another there was a wooden table with two chairs, the kind a couple might have sat at long ago after a hard day's work. It was impossible to know exactly how long it'd been since the shop had been operational, but the sour-sweet blend of old ointments, salves, and dried produce long gone still staled the air. He inhaled, and nearly retched.

One-two-three. One-two-three. One-two-three.

He drummed his fingers against his side, counted the dust motes gathered on the window's mud-brick frame, the spidering cracks that ran along the room's walls like line-thin serpents.

Only when he was finished did he actually look outside, taking in the torrent of rain pouring down just feet away from him. He took in its smell, its sound, tried to find a cadence in its steady patter.

One-two-three. One-two-three. One-two-three.

Between the drops, he envisioned the faces of three people—not six, not nine, but three. Always three.

One. He imagined a girl with chestnut skin. She had a heart-shaped face that framed a small, broad nose and full lips, and there was a mischievous glint in her eyes. That was Koffi, his friend.

Two. He imagined a young man who looked a lot like him, but different. His face was composed of night-sky eyes set even above a long nose with the precise top-fade haircut befitting a warrior. That was Kamau, his older brother.

Three. He imagined an old man, one with unruly white eyebrows and a mouth crinkled with laugh lines. Ekon shivered as that face transformed, as the smile turned wicked and cruel. That was the man who had been his mentor, Brother Ugo.

No. Ekon corrected himself. There was no Brother Ugo. Brother Ugo had never existed.

One-two-three. One-two-three. One-two-three.

He tried to repress what he knew would come next, the threads of new memory knotting themselves in his mind. He caught quick glimpses of imagery, snatched fragments of the words it still hurt for him to recall.

I knew you would be different, knew you wouldn't fail me, whispered the old man. In his head, Ekon saw himself standing in a beautiful garden, watching the flowers wilt and die. The muscles in his throat constricted, and he made himself count until they relaxed again.

One-two-three. One-two-three. One-two-three.

You were the perfect combination. The old man's voice was reed-thin in his ear. *Keen, desperate for approval. It made you easy to mold into what I needed.*

One-two-three. One-two-three. One-two-three.

Brother Ugo hadn't been real.

Ekon screwed his eyes shut and counted faster, focusing on the numbers. Numbers never changed, numbers stayed the same, numbers always made sense—except that now they didn't. Brother Ugo had been an impostor; how many signs had he missed? The old man had been behind everything, and how many clues had been right there all along? Sometimes, Ekon counted none; other times, he counted three thousand. His fingers tapped a faster beat against his thigh. When a clap of thunder boomed overhead, his breath grew shallow, and his vision tunneled.

One-two-three. One-two-three. One-two—

"You shouldn't be near the window."

Ekon turned, his head snapping in the direction of the croaking voice that had just pulled him back to reality. An old woman was standing a few feet away, watching him tentatively. White hair peeked out from her headwrap, and there were deep lines in her face. Even after three days together, Ekon still hadn't gotten used to how quietly she moved.

"It's not safe," she went on, glancing over his shoulder. "Someone could see you."

Ekon took one large step away from the window. "Sorry."

Themba was still looking at him with a shrewd expression. "You're sure you want to go?"

"Yes." The tunnel vision was getting better now. Ekon forced his heartbeat to settle. "I'm ready."

One of Themba's gray brows rose.

"You've healed from the splendor poisoning fast." She tutted. "But you're still recovering from your physical wounds."

Ekon stood straighter. In the last two days, most of his scrapes and cuts had begun to scab—notably, the tender skin under his jaw was almost clear of bruising—but there were other wounds beneath his skin, the ones he couldn't see but felt every time he moved.

"I'm fine," he lied.

Themba's lips pursed like she'd just sucked on a lemon. "It's risky . . ."

"Themba, please. I want to go. I can carry more than you." He wished there was a way to explain the way he was feeling, but he didn't know how to say aloud that, now more than ever in his life, he needed to feel capable, competent, useful. He held her gaze a beat, and perhaps she saw the unspoken words in his eyes, because her expression abruptly softened to one of reluctant resignation.

"Keep your head down and your hood up," she said, "and take this." She withdrew a small coin purse from her tunic's pocket and pressed it into his palm.

"Themba." Ekon looked down at his hand as she curled his fingers over the purse. "I can't take this."

"You can and will," she said sharply. "You've got no way to pay, and we can't risk stealing or bartering, not with the way things are right now."

Ekon swallowed. There was a fierceness in Themba's eyes that he recognized, and he realized they were just like Koffi's eyes. *Of course they are,* he reminded himself. *They're related.* Three days together hadn't been enough time to process that.

"Take your time, and practice caution. Stay hidden if you have to," Themba continued. "And remember, if you even think you've been seen—"

"I won't be," said Ekon. He didn't let her finish the sentence because he knew what the old woman was going to say: *If you even think you've been seen, don't worry about food or supplies or me. Save yourself.*

Except that that wasn't an option, not now. *One-two-three,* Ekon counted. This was technically his third day with Themba, and his presence here had depleted her food supply. They were out of options, and there was no room for error.

He didn't wait for Themba to say more as he grabbed an empty sack and a still slightly damp hooded cloak. It was too small for him, but it would have to do.

"I'll be back," he said over his shoulder. Then, without waiting for a reply, he swung the shop's door open and charged into the torrent.

He was soaked in seconds.

Mud and ankle-deep puddles sloshed around Ekon's feet as he joined the steady flow of people moving purposefully in the rain. Overhead, the pewter-gray sky with its spidering black veins suggested early evening, but in reality it was only midday—another consequence of monsoon season. Ekon slipped in the mud, scrunching his face as he accidentally bit his tongue and drew blood. It was hard to believe it now, but he'd once liked this time of year. Monsoon season in Lkossa was a headache for the brothers of the Temple of Lkossa, thanks to an uptick in beggars seeking

31

refuge in the temple, but Ekon had looked forward to it. Heavy rains meant no drills or sparring practice on the temple's lawns were possible, so those hours had been repurposed for the things he preferred—quiet hours spent in the library, occasional paper-boat races with his brother. Those moments now felt ripped from another life, a life that was gone.

Ekon veered right, taking a sharp turn down one of the narrower roads that fed into the main markets. It wasn't technically the fastest way to get there, but it was safest; he couldn't risk being followed even in the Chafu District. The throngs of people began to thicken as he reached the markets, and he was careful not to walk too fast or too slow. He heard the telltale sounds first—the violent flapping of tents in the wind, intermingled with the cries of peddlers shouting their bargains. He glanced up and counted.

There were sixteen tents arranged, four on each side, to form a square. Earlier Themba had told him what they needed, and Ekon wasted no time moving through the market to procure the items from her list. He bought secondhand water gourds, two cheap burlap sacks, and an assortment of dried meats and fruits. It reminded him that, not so long ago, he and Koffi had been here together in this market, preparing for their hunt in the Greater Jungle. That felt like another life too. He'd just grabbed the last of the items on his list when two voices rose above the din.

"Shame they didn't allow for a stoning." The first weathered voice came from an older-sounding woman. "I've got a good arm for it."

Ekon's ears perked up as he slowed, eyes searching through the crowd. They eventually landed on two women standing beneath a covered stall, clearly waiting for the rain to let up. He'd been right in guessing that the first woman he'd heard was older; gray hairs streaked her waist-length braids. The woman she was standing beside looked slightly younger.

"I think it's better that Father Olufemi destroyed the beast in private," she said, bowing her head with reverence. "It was an evil creature, a *demon*."

They were talking about the Shetani. Ekon looked away but couldn't stop himself from stepping closer to listen. His palms grew clammy as he recalled all that'd happened just days before. Koffi. Brother Ugo. Adiah. The battle in the sky garden.

"I suppose it was," the old woman agreed. When Ekon stole a glance in her direction, he saw she was nodding slowly. "Gods bless the Sons of the Six. I don't know what we would do without them . . ."

Ekon moved away from the women, trying to ignore the fresh anger roiling in his stomach. Of *course* Father Olufemi and the Sons of the Six had found a way to cover everything up. By saying the Shetani had been destroyed privately, their integrity was protected. There was no longer a monster terrorizing the city, and it would be the warriors who received the credit for its demise. Lkossans would never know the real truth, that there had never been a monster at all, only men with horrid secrets.

And you were one of them, whispered a voice in Ekon's head. *For years you trained with them, lived with them. They were your family.*

Ekon felt that churning anger turn into something else, a sudden wave of nausea, sour on his tongue. He knew it wasn't real, the taste of shame, but it was still difficult to swallow. He thought of all the years spent watching and admiring the Sons of the Six, volunteering to clear their plates and clean their weapons. How many nights had he cleaned daggers used to cut down children, cleaned the plates of murderers?

How many signs had he missed?

In the pelting rain, his breath began to grow short, more labored. There was a familiar tightness in his chest that made it harder and harder for his lungs to expand, and his mouth went dry as he recognized the preliminary signs of a panic attack. His hands balled into tight fists as a darkness crept into the corners of his vision, and he ground his teeth together, frustrated.

Not now, not now, this can't happen right now.

He couldn't breathe anymore, there was an old man's laughter in his head, cold and mirthless, the din of the market was fading, he felt as though he was on the verge of falling . . .

And then something caught his eye.

The black fuzziness at the periphery of Ekon's vision receded like a tide as his gaze zeroed in on a girl a few feet away from him. Her skin was the color of a marula tree, her face a composite of two crow-black eyes, a wide nose, and bowlike lips. A cloak covered most of her head, though its hood was pushed back just enough to see a hint of curly black hair. At first, Ekon wondered what about her had caught his attention, but then he understood. There hadn't necessarily been any one thing about the way the girl *looked* that had made him notice her; it was because of the way she moved. Everyone else in the market was milling about, unhurried in their browsing, but this girl walked with purpose, her eyes set straight ahead. She stepped around two textile merchants, and Ekon noted that she was carrying a small satchel on her shoulder, one she seemed intent on shielding from the rain.

She had just passed the place where he was standing when he noticed something else. At once, his gaze narrowed. Some feet behind her, hanging far enough back to avoid detection, two men were following the girl, their eyes fixed steadily on her back. Ekon tensed. He could guess what kinds of men those were and what they had in mind for the girl.

Stay where you can be seen, he wanted to tell her.

His heart sank as the girl did the very opposite, turning onto one of the side streets leading out of the marketplace and disappearing behind a corner. He watched as the men quickened their steps and followed.

It's not your business, said the practical part of his brain, the one still thinking of his groceries. *It doesn't concern you. Get back to Themba.*

That voice in his head was right, the better thing to do—the *smarter* thing to do—was to turn around, but then, without warning, his feet began to move, propelling him in the direction the girl had gone. He walked down it quickly, turned the same corner, and stopped.

"Come on, girl, we're not asking for much," said a gravelly voice. "Just share what's in the bag and we'll be on our way."

Ekon pressed himself against the wall. The alley he was looking down was a dead end, and he could now see that the girl from the market was backed up against it, clutching at the strap of her satchel. Her dark eyes were flinty, but the tremble in her chin gave her away.

"Back off." Her voice was too shrill to have any bite. "I said *no!*"

"Or what?" said one of the men. "You're going to do something, *little mouse?*"

He made a grab at the sack, and the girl swiped, smacking his hand away hard. The man hissed, while the other chuckled.

"Ah, our little mouse has the spirit of a viper," he said. "At least that'll make things interesting."

The other man was not laughing. He lunged, and the girl jumped away, just barely keeping her sack out of his reach. Almost immediately, she had to swivel in the other direction as the first man tried to snatch it. Back and forth, the men began taking turns grabbing at her. Ekon's heart sank. He'd lived in Lkossa long enough to understand what they were doing. There was a reason men like these were called "street hyenas"; they worked the same way real hyenas did, toying with their prey and wearing it down before they made their kill. He had no doubt this girl could hold her own against just one of them, but she was no match for a well-practiced strategy. One of them swiped again, and her dark eyes took on a wild, frantic quality. Ekon's heart seized. She looked more and more like a trapped animal.

He let his own sack slip from his fingers as he stepped forward. *"Leave her alone!"*

All three of them—the two men and the girl—looked up in equal surprise. It was one of the men who spoke first.

"Who are *you*?"

Ekon swallowed. "I *said*, leave her alone."

The second man looked back and forth between Ekon and the girl before cracking a toothy smile. "Looks like the little mouse has a boyfriend." He regarded Ekon with amusement. "This should be entertaining."

"He's scrawny, barely a man," said the first. "We'll make short work of him."

Barely a man. They were only words, but Ekon felt each one like a stab between his ribs. He winced at them and felt something waking in the deepest chamber of his chest. The words echoed in his mind.

Barely a man.

Days ago, Themba had found an old tunic for him to wear. It was clean, plain, and on the whole it fit well. Ekon only now realized, though, what that tunic meant. He wasn't wearing the uniform of a Son of the Six anymore; he was no longer looked at as a man.

One-two-three.

The muscles in his jaw ached and his nostrils flared as he watched the smiles slip from the two men's faces.

"Easy, boy," one of them said, holding up his hands. "We don't want any trouble—"

Ekon didn't give him the chance to finish his sentence. With both hands, he shoved the first man in his chest as hard as he could, watching with satisfaction as he tripped over his feet and then ran. In his periphery, he saw the second man start toward him, but Ekon was faster. Years of training at the Temple of Lkossa returned to him like an old friend, familiar.

Deflect. Disarm. Dismantle.

With ease, he dodged the man's clumsy attempt at a right hook, feinted, then countered with a cross and a series of jabs. Ekon heard the breath leave the man's body, the telling click as his knuckles connected with a jawbone. Pain ricocheted through his hand. The man dropped to the ground, moaning as he curled into a ball and tried to cradle the side of his head, but Ekon still fell upon him, pressing his knee into the man's torso so that he couldn't escape.

"Barely a man," he said through his teeth. "You'll see for

yourself who's *barely a man*." He brought his fist down, and at last he named the monster coming to life in his chest; it was rage, and it roared its approval as his fists rained down on the man, blow after blow.

I trained you well.

Ekon stopped, cringing against the voice that had entered his mind. It sounded like Brother Ugo's.

Young and athletic, smart and meticulous, said the old man. *You were the perfect combination . . . easy to mold into what I needed.*

Ekon reeled, nausea climbing up his throat. He blinked several times, until Brother Ugo's face was gone. He took in his surroundings, then looked down. The man was still pinned beneath him; his face was unrecognizable, his breath shallow. Ekon stared at his own hands; they were bloody, and they ached. A sheen of sweat slicked his brow, followed by a clammy chill. In the darkness, Ekon's eyes wandered. Then they settled on the girl.

She was still standing at the end of the alley a few feet away from him, motionless. Ekon had expected to see some hint of emotion on her face—fear, or perhaps even repulsion—but he saw none there; the girl's expression was utterly neutral. She'd pulled the cloak's hood back over her face and hugged her satchel to her chest. Several seconds passed before Ekon slowly stood. The girl tensed.

"It's okay." Ekon raised his hands quickly, all too aware that he was standing beside a man's unconscious body. "I . . . I won't hurt you. I just wanted to help."

Without warning, the girl sprung to life, moving faster than he could ever hope to. In one moment she was cornered at the end of the alley; in the next she'd turned on her heel and vanished around the corner, leaving Ekon alone in the dark.

CHAPTER 3

A DULL KNIFE

Words formed on Koffi's tongue, but she couldn't speak any of them.

The seconds crept by with a terrible slowness. One by one, she felt the eyes of every person in the room fix on her again, this time with a needle-point focus that made her skin prickle. An anticipation hung heavy in the air; it seemed everyone was waiting for her to say something. But try as she might, Koffi's mouth refused to work. Her heartbeat quickened as she held the master of Thornkeep's gaze, suspended between a consuming fear and undeniable awe. She'd thought before that the man looked old enough to be her father, but . . . the longer she stared at him, the less certain she became. There was an agelessness about him. She studied his eyes; they were impossibly black and rimmed in an earthy red-ochre color. They reminded Koffi of cooling coals in a dying hearth. Something about them felt dangerous but luring, foreign but also familiar. She frowned in frustration as the same unanswered question gnawed at her.

Why can't I remember?

"Welcome to Thornkeep," the man said, apparently unbothered by the uncomfortable pause. "I hope you have found your accommodations here pleasing." He inclined his head. "Tell me, how are you feeling?"

Feeling? Koffi hadn't expected that question, it disarmed her. She didn't want to admit it aloud, but in truth, she wasn't feeling well at all. Her head was still pounding, her empty stomach roiling and twisting. In this chamber's persistent cool, a strange clamminess clung to her skin, dampening the fabric under her arms and along her dress's neckline. None of those things, though, bothered her as much as the nagging feeling that she was still forgetting something vital, an elusive bit of information fluttering on the outskirts of her mind. She steeled herself, then spoke.

"Why am I here?" Her voice was no longer the rasp it had been earlier, but she still hated how small it sounded in comparison to his. In answer to her question, a look of surprise flitted across the master of Thornkeep's face.

"You don't remember." His words were soft. Koffi felt a new unease coil within her, wrapping itself around her rib cage and squeezing. *You don't remember.* She didn't understand what he meant by that. It had been a statement, not a question. Before she could reply, the master of Thornkeep went on.

"You want to know why you are here?" he asked in a louder voice, this time clearly for the benefit of the room. "It is a fair thing to ask, and you are likely not alone in wondering it."

For the first time since he'd entered the room, Koffi's eyes flicked to the other occupants in the chamber. They were all still watching her, but now that she looked at them more closely, she saw that their expressions were not entirely hostile, but uncertain. In some, she saw outright curiosity. It seemed every one of them was waiting, as she was, to see what would happen next. Abruptly, the master of Thornkeep turned with arms extended to address everyone.

"My children." His words carried in a rich timbre. "Some of you have lived at Thornkeep long enough to remember that I once built it with the intention of making it my personal residence." There was a fondness in his smile. "It has, however, become so much more than that. Thornkeep is now a place of learning, fellowship, and above all a haven for those whose gifts and talents might otherwise be destroyed by ignorance." He paused for a moment, letting those words linger in the air. "Thornkeep stands as a beacon of hope for darajas, a sanctuary, a place in which every one of you may always rest in the knowledge that you are safe."

Koffi looked around the room and saw that several people were nodding in agreement. Some were even smiling.

"I have, however, long held on to another hope," he said. "I have dreamed of one day realizing a world in which no daraja need fear persecution or abuse for simply existing as they were born to exist. I dreamed of a better world."

This time, Koffi saw it: the effect those words had on the room. More of the colorfully dressed people began to lean in, as though the closer they were to the master of Thornkeep's words, the closer they could be to the reality of them. Some clasped their hands as though in prayer, while others looked to him with what could only be described as reverence. In the back of her mind, Koffi thought of something Makena had said in the bedchamber.

I'm a daraja, like you.

She panned the room with new appreciation, taking in all the people before her. *They're darajas,* she realized. *All of them.*

"For years, I have searched," the master of Thornkeep went on, "inviting darajas of the highest caliber to reside with me here at Thornkeep in the hopes that I might find one among you with the strength, with the *power,* to aid me in my righteous work." Slowly, he turned to Koffi again. They were standing only a few feet apart, close enough for Koffi to see that something in his face had changed. There was an intense, excited fervor in his gaze. She watched his lips as they formed the words.

"Today, I am pleased to share that my search has ended," he said. "We have, at last, found our chosen one. Her name is . . . Koffi."

A thunderous applause erupted in the chamber at the same time Koffi felt the breath leave her body in a whoosh. Blood pounded in her ears, muting everything around her. In the distance, she heard the sounds of clapping hands, stomping feet, even a whooping cheer. On either side, she felt more than saw Makena's and Zain's eyes on her, though she didn't look at either of them to ascertain what expressions were on their faces. She couldn't. Her mouth had gone paper dry; between each of her heart's frantic drums against her ribs, she heard the echo of the master of Thornkeep's words in her head.

Chosen one. We have, at last, found our chosen one.

Those words didn't make sense to her. She couldn't be these people's "chosen one"—she didn't even know who they were. She still didn't know how she'd gotten here, *why* she was here. Acute panic seized at her throat, making it harder and harder to breathe. Something about this was very wrong.

The room's applause continued as the master of Thornkeep gestured to his right. Koffi watched with growing wariness as a girl emerged from the green-clad group holding something in her arms.

"A gift," said the master of Thornkeep, "in celebration of this momentous occasion."

Koffi watched the girl make her way forward. She looked to be fourteen or so. Her skin was the same dark brown as Koffi's, and golden beads were woven into her box braids. The tunic she wore was pale green, and modestly hemmed below her knees. She made Koffi feel painfully overdressed. When she neared, Koffi saw that in her arms she was cradling a bouquet of long-stemmed roses. They were the largest, reddest flowers she'd ever seen, each one bigger than her fist. The girl stopped before Koffi and offered them with a bowed head.

"For you," she whispered.

Koffi took them, not because she wanted to, but because she wasn't sure what else to do. The girl curtseyed and backed away so that she was standing just behind the master of Thornkeep.

Chosen one. The words seemed to grow larger in Koffi's head, pushing out all other thoughts. That wasn't right, she wasn't these people's chosen anything, so why were they looking at her like she was? Each clapping hand was like a mallet's strike against her temples. The sickly-sweet fragrance of the roses still in her arms made her want to vomit. It was too much, this was all too much. Makena and Zain had moved away to give her space, and she suddenly felt more alone than ever. She looked down. The edges of her vision were beginning to dim, and as she stared at her feet, they blurred. Koffi bit down on her cheek hard, and the sharpness of that pain helped her refocus.

Not here, she told herself fiercely. *Do not pass out here.*

"Koffi."

At the sound of her name softly spoken, she looked up, startled to find the master of Thornkeep had gotten even closer to her. In the room full of people, she felt as though it was only the two of them now. "Be at ease," he said in a soothing voice. "You are free now. You are home."

Home. From the moment she'd woken up in this strange place, Koffi had been looking for the thing that would help her remember. In the end, it was a single word. *Home.* She imagined a light permeating the fog that had filled her mind.

Home.

There was a rush, and then everything came back to her with horrid, vivid clarity. The spider-silk strands of thoughts she'd struggled to grasp before now braided themselves together to repaint images in her mind. *Home. Lkossa.* She remembered it all now: the Night Zoo where she'd spent most of her life working alongside Mama and Jabir; the disastrous fire that had changed everything. She remembered a barter made with the Night Zoo's owner, Baaz, and then a mission, and . . . a jungle. The Greater Jungle.

The images were moving faster in her mind, flipping through her consciousness like pages in a book. When she closed her eyes, she wasn't standing in this beautiful room anymore; she was atop the Temple of Lkossa's highest tower, in a garden with a trapdoor. Pain stabbed through her when she remembered the sounds of Ekon's screams, heard the primal roar of a great beast charging forward. No, not a beast, a girl who'd been turned into one by a power she'd been forced to let consume her, a girl who'd sacrificed her own humanity to save a city from decimation. Koffi knew that girl's name.

Adiah.

She opened her eyes, and her knees threatened to buckle and give out beneath her. All around the room, people were still smiling at her, clapping, and she was still holding the beautiful roses in her arms. She felt a thorn digging into her skin, swallowed bile as she looked at the man before her with new eyes. He was familiar to her, but this man was no man at all. At last, she had the answer to one question.

She knew who the master of Thornkeep really was.

"Koffi?" If Fedu, the god of death, knew what she was thinking, it didn't show as he watched her. "Are you all right?"

"No."

In her periphery, Koffi thought she saw Zain's head swivel in her direction at the same time she heard Makena gasp. She repeated herself, louder.

"No."

This time, her voice carried, and a sudden hush fell over the room. Fedu cocked his head, looking amused.

"No?" he repeated.

"I am not your chosen one," said Koffi. "And I never will be. What you're doing is wrong and I'm not going to help you do it."

A low buzzing filled the room, the sound of voices murmuring among each other. The darajas were now looking at her with concern, worry. Fedu's brows rose, and Koffi hated how frighteningly authentic his own confusion appeared to be. He steepled his fingers.

"I seek to create a safer world for darajas," he said. "You think that is wrong?"

"That is *not* what you want," said Koffi. She fought to keep the tremor out of her voice as she spoke. "You want death and destruction." She gestured wide. "Do these people know what you've done in the name of your better world? Do they know you've forced men to murder for you, that you preyed on an innocent girl?"

An amused smile touched Fedu's lips. "Is that what my songbird told you, that I preyed on her?" He shook his head, visibly disappointed. "Before she ran away, I did nothing but try to help Adiah. My only desire was to see her become the ultimate version of herself. The power I showed her made her stronger, more beautiful, more powerful. She was like a god."

"She was not." Koffi grimaced. "She turned herself into a monster because of you."

Fedu opened his mouth, then closed it. He was looking at Koffi as though she fascinated him. "Is it so simple as that?" he asked softly. "I have lived long enough to know that the only difference between good and evil is perception, and the only distinction between a god and a monster is viewpoint."

"You would kill millions to create your new world," Koffi whispered. "You would obliterate an entire continent."

Fedu shrugged, and the nonchalance of that motion was scarier than anything he'd done yet. "A caterpillar does not complete its metamorphosis without first shedding its cocoon," he said gently. "There can be no great progress without the tithe of sacrifice."

"Say what you want." Koffi spoke through gritted teeth. She was so angry now, she was shaking. "Keep me here as long as you want. But know that I will never help you, ever."

A collective gasp sounded around the room at her words, but Koffi didn't care anymore. She held Fedu's gaze with her own, waiting. She expected anger, rage, even frustration. What she saw instead in the god's expression chilled her blood. He looked amused again.

"It is uncanny." He seemed to be speaking more to himself than to her. "The two of you are so different, and yet . . . you are so much like her." He stroked his chin.

The god moved with sudden, inhuman speed, so fast that Koffi didn't have time to register what was happening. She heard a sharp cry, and then, with horror, locked eyes with the young girl who'd brought her flowers. She was on her toes, suspended only by her beautiful beaded braids, braids now wrapped tight around Fedu's fist as he held her in the air. Fat tears welled in the girl's eyes as she dangled.

"Master!" Her voice was airy, desperate. "Please—"

"Stop!" The roses fell to the floor as Koffi stepped forward. Her eyes were fixed on the girl's scalp; she could see each place the braids were pulling. She imagined she could hear tearing. "Stop, let her go!"

Fedu cast a lazy glance in the girl's direction before dropping her like a sack of yams. Her hands flew to her head as she sobbed. It was a pitiful sight. The longer Koffi watched, the sicker she became.

"So, you are alike in that way, too," Fedu murmured. Then he turned toward Koffi again and cleared his throat. "I am a simple god, Koffi." Gone was the pleasantness in his voice. "And like Adiah once was, you are an intelligent girl. Therefore, I see no need to make veiled threats. You bartered with me. You offered a trade:

47

your life in place of Adiah's; your servitude in place of hers. Let me now clarify the terms of our agreement. *You will obey me.* If and when you do not, others will pay the price for your insolence. Do we understand each other?"

Koffi didn't look at Fedu, but instead to the girl still on the ground. Her arms were wrapped around herself, and the emotion in her eyes was plain: fear. Koffi recognized the look of fear; living in the Night Zoo, she'd grown up under the constant threat of it. In the girl's eyes she saw her mother, Jabir, Ekon.

Others will pay the price for your insolence. The words were double-edged. He had her. Slowly, she felt something within her shrink with defeat.

"Yes," she said as emotionlessly as possible. "We understand each other." Her fingertips dug into the meat of her palms.

"Good," said Fedu. He looked around the room, at the darajas now staring at him. He smiled at them. "You took the splendor from Adiah's body, but it does not seem to affect you the way it affected her. Even now, it rests dormant in your body without destroying or altering it. That is impressive."

Koffi felt the strange urge to cover herself as the god's eyes roamed over her with a hungry look.

"I believe you will prove to be of great use to me, Koffi," he continued, "but first, you must be trained, taught when and how to yield your power. You are a dull knife. But fear not, I will see you sharpened."

Koffi bit down on the words she wanted to say back.

"Makena will see that you are fed, and then you will begin your first lesson," he said. "You are dismissed."

Dismissed. It was all over as abruptly as it'd begun. Koffi was keenly aware that everyone was staring at her. She wanted to scream, to rage, to do something other than simply stand there. Without warning, she felt a gentle touch at her elbow. Makena was at her side again, her face inscrutable.

"Come on," she murmured. "I'll take you back to your bedchamber."

Koffi let her guide them both out of the main hall. Zain did not walk with them. Unease stalked her with each step, but she said nothing. Only when the room's double doors closed behind them did she exhale. In her mind, she heard Fedu's voice, his words.

You are a dull knife. But fear not, I will see you sharpened.

They rounded a corner and entered the corridor they'd passed through before, the same one that offered a view of Thornkeep's east garden. Makena kept walking, but Koffi stopped before it, eyes panning the grounds again. In the morning sunlight, the licks of dew on the garden's grass glittered like so many diamonds, and at its outer edge, the acacia trees still stood silent and stoic and breathing none of their secrets.

The mist was still there too.

Koffi watched as its tendrils snaked up the trees' gray trunks like vines, thickening as it cloaked them in opaque silver and white.

She was so mesmerized by it that she did not immediately notice the lone face, pale and ashen, staring back at her amid the thorns.

CHAPTER 4

The COBRA and the RAT

A lone bolt of lightning knifed through the clouds as Ekon made his way back to the apothecary.

Its stark light illuminated everything before him as he walked: the narrow, mud-sloshed road, the decrepit buildings on either side of him that so clearly distinguished the Chafu District. It illuminated, too, the truths he was not yet ready to face. He held his breath for the inevitable, slowed his footsteps so that they fell in time with his counting while he waited for the thunder.

One-two-three. One-two-three. One-two-three.

In the pause, he remembered a trick Kamau had once taught him when they were small. A storm's distance could be measured in seconds; the higher the count, the farther away it was. He recalled a night in the Temple of Lkossa's library, when a particularly violent storm had come and he'd hidden under one of the tables, gripping its legs so hard, his fingers had numbed. He remembered Kamau finding him there, remembered the sureness in his older brother's eyes.

It's okay, Ekkie, he'd said gently. *The lightning always comes first, and then the thunder. Just wait for it.* He'd joined him under the table, and side by side, they'd watched as new lightning lit up a window. They'd counted together.

One, two, three, four, five.

There'd been a great crash of thunder. Ekon had flinched, but Kamau had taken his hand quickly, squeezing.

Wait for the thunder, he'd whispered. *The storm will pass.*

More lightning, and then another count.

One, two, three, four, five, six, seven, eight, nine.

There'd been a second boom of thunder, but it had sounded softer, farther away. Ekon remembered the relief that had flooded him then, the warmth of Kamau's smile in the darkness.

The storm will always pass, his brother had said, *remember that.*

Ekon started as the bellow of real thunder brought him back to the present. He jumped at the sound, then cursed himself for it. *Grow up,* he told himself, *it's just a storm, nothing to be afraid of.* He flexed his fingers as he quickened his pace, wincing against the new pain in his left hand. He'd almost forgotten, but a glance at his swollen knuckles brought everything back: the street hyenas, the girl, the rage of the imaginary monster in his chest. It was dormant now, but Ekon still felt it within him, waiting; for what, he wasn't sure.

His muscles relaxed slightly as he turned onto the street that led back to the old apothecary. Clouds darkened the black-veined sky now, but even from here, he could discern it, squeezed between two other empty shops. The smallest hint of light flickered in one of its cutout windows, and Ekon felt its warmth. He tightened his grip on the sack slung over his shoulder as his stomach growled. His visit to the market may not have gone exactly as planned, but at least he'd been able to get the supplies they needed. With any luck, Themba would be able to scrounge up some kind of stew. His mouth watered at the possibilities.

He was within mere yards of the apothecary when its front door opened, stopping him in his tracks. He frowned, immediately apprehensive. He was still too far away for Themba to have opened it because she'd seen him, and there was no other reason for her to open that door, especially while he wasn't there. Instinct took over as he lowered, crouching, so that he was partially hidden behind a box of abandoned crates. Waves of anxiety rocked through him, pushing new terrifying possibilities to his mind's forefront. Had he and Themba been discovered? Were the Sons of the Six, even now, inside the apothecary searching for him? Ekon waited a beat, hoping, praying he'd see Themba's silhouette framed in the apothecary's light, but that wasn't what he saw at all. To his surprise, an old man emerged from the shop instead. He was short, frail, with light brown skin and a large bald head that seemed too heavy for his little body. His clothes were modest enough, and his movements were stiffened with age, but something about him set Ekon on edge. He watched as the old man glanced over his shoulder, then carefully closed the apothecary's door behind him. Ekon's eyes narrowed. Who was this man, and why had he been visiting with Themba?

Without warning, another bolt of lightning splintered across the sky. It was the biggest yet, and in its luminance, the whole of the road was visible. Ekon froze. He hadn't made a sound, but in that moment of light, the old man's eyes had come to rest on him. For several seconds, neither one of them spoke; each seemed to be waiting for the other to make his move. Slowly, the old man cocked his head and smiled.

"East and west." The words were a whisper, but they carried. The hairs on the back of Ekon's arms stood on end, goose bumps stippled his skin. The man hadn't come any closer, but he still held Ekon's gaze with an intensity that was uncomfortable.

"Who are you?" The question escaped Ekon before he could stop himself. They were, it seemed, the only people on this street, and in the emptiness, his voice echoed. "What do you want?"

In answer, the man smiled and inclined his head. "One sun rises in the east," he said. "One sun rises in the west."

Ekon felt the skin between his brows pinch as he frowned. Conversely, the old man's smile grew. He nodded, turned, and began to shuffle up the road in the opposite direction.

"Hey!" Ekon stood, shouting at the man's back. "Stop!"

The old man did not falter, did not turn as he ambled into the darkness. Ekon watched until the exact moment he was no longer visible, then charged forward. His breath was shallow by the time he reached the apothecary, and his heart felt as though it'd leaped to his throat as he crashed through its front door.

"Ekon?" Themba, who was on her knees before the shop's tiny hearth, looked up at him in surprise. Ekon noted she'd been in the middle of wrapping one of her hands. He thought he heard an edge in her voice. "You're back sooner than I expected," she said. "Were you able to get everything from the market?"

For several seconds, Ekon stood motionless in the doorframe. His chest rose and fell, and somewhere in his rib cage he felt that imaginary monster raise its head, sniffing the air hopefully. *No,* he told it, *no.* He swallowed until he'd restored some semblance of calm. Only then did he speak.

"I want to know the truth," he said quietly.

Themba's brows knitted. Slowly she rose, still holding the cloth she'd been using to wrap her other hand. In the firelight, Ekon saw that it was stained a dark brownish red. "The truth about what?"

"Everything." Try as he might, the words he bit out were harsher than he'd intended. "I want to know how Koffi is your granddaughter. I spent days with her in the Greater Jungle. She talked about her family, but she never mentioned you."

Something like hurt flashed in Themba's eyes. She fingered the amulet around her neck, the one she never took off. After a pause she said: "Koffi is my daughter's daughter. She doesn't know me because her mother and I are estranged, and have been for some time."

"That's one question answered," said Ekon. "Now I want to know who that man was."

"Man?" Themba's face grew stricken. "What man?"

"The old one who just left."

She shook her head, but it wasn't convincing. "There was no man—"

"I saw him!" Ekon hadn't meant to raise his voice, the sound of it surprised even him, but he couldn't temper it. He was hungry, he was exhausted, and most of all, he was tired of being lied to. Kamau had lied to him. The Kuhani had lied to him. Brother Ugo had lied to him. He couldn't take one more lie.

Themba fixed him with a considering look for several seconds. In her face, Ekon could see the emotions warring with each other, deciding which would be the victor. There was a defiance there, but also a weariness. In the end, the latter won out. She sighed.

"He is called Sigidi," she said quietly.

Sigidi. The name wasn't significant to Ekon in any way, and yet the sound of it sent a shiver down his spine. He remembered all too well the way the old man had looked at him, the familiarity he'd held in his gaze as he'd regarded him. *East and west,* he'd said, but those words meant nothing to Ekon either. He shook his head. "Why was he here?"

"Give me the groceries," said Themba. When Ekon stiffened, she rolled her eyes. "We can have this conversation hungry, or we can have it with food in our bellies. Do you know how to mince?"

"Mince?"

She gave him a wry look and nodded toward a knife placed by the fire. It was slightly dulled, and Ekon noted that another knife lay beside it. There was no mistaking the bits of red wetting its blade. Again, his eyes shot to Themba's bandaged hand, but her expression was impatient. After a moment, he closed the front door, and they both settled before the fire. While he picked up the first knife and began to mince some carrots, Themba poured water into one of the small pots she'd found in the apothecary's old storage room and hung it carefully on a hook above the little fire. She stared into its flames for a long time before she spoke again.

"Sigidi is a daraja." She picked up a stick and poked at one of the fire's coals. "One with a very special affinity."

Daraja. That word held plenty of significance to Ekon. Not so long ago, he hadn't believed that darajas—people with the ability to pull energy from the earth and manipulate it—existed at all. Now, within the span of two weeks, he'd met three, counting Themba.

"What is his affinity?" he asked.

"He has the gift of Sight, the ability to see the things most people can't," Themba explained. "We've known each other a long time, so I asked if he could help me find my granddaughter." She glanced at the blood-specked knife. "He told me he could, but that a payment would be required."

Ekon's eyes widened. "He made you *cut* yourself? That's barbaric."

Themba looked at him as though he'd said something distasteful. "Watch your tongue, boy," she snapped, "particularly when you speak of things you know little about." She gestured to the knife again. "Koffi and I are related, connected through a direct matrilineal line. Our blood is the same, so Sigidi used mine to trace hers. It was not barbaric, it was necessary."

Ekon paused, momentarily chastened. "So, did it work?"

Themba nodded. "I told him what you told me about Fedu, and about the other daraja girl you helped."

"Adiah," Ekon cut in. It felt important to say. "Her name was Adiah."

Themba pursed her lips. "Sigidi saw Koffi with the god of death, in his realm."

Ekon's heart stopped. "Where is that?"

"Somewhere south, in the Kusini Region," she said. "On foot, it's a significant journey from here."

At once, Ekon was on his feet, the knife and the carrots forgotten. "What are we waiting for?" His mouth was dry, and there was a jittery energy in his hands that wouldn't let them be still. He tapped his fingers against his leg. "Let's go."

"Not so fast, boy." Themba hadn't moved. She was staring into the fire again. Slowly, she picked up the carrots he'd minced and deposited them into the simmering pot. "I am a daraja, and you are a wanted man. It would not bode well for either of us to be caught by your brothers."

Ex-brothers, Ekon thought to himself.

"We won't be able to just waltz out of this city," she went on. "We'll need help."

Ekon frowned. "Did you have anyone in mind?"

For the first time since he'd entered the apothecary, Themba smiled. There was a gleam in her eyes. "As a matter of fact, I do."

The air was brisk as Ekon emerged from the apothecary hours later.

His gaze panned the street, appreciating its emptiness. He and Themba had opted to wait until early evening to make their move. For now, it seemed, fortune had favored them; the rains had abated at least temporarily, leaving only a heavy smell of ozone in its wake. The clouds were gone, and in the sky Ekon could just barely see the threads of black strung between the stars. He swallowed a lump in his throat. Not so long ago, he and Koffi had looked at those cracks in the sky together in the Greater Jungle. He'd called the sky's marking's "scars," but he remembered her words about them.

Maybe there's a beauty in the scars. Because they're a reminder of what's been faced, and what's been survived.

Survived. Ekon still remembered the last time he'd seen Koffi's face. She'd looked resolved, but she'd also looked afraid, like someone trying to be brave but only just managing it. He didn't want to think about what could be happening to her now.

We're coming, Koffi. He thought the words, because it was all he could do to make them real. *We're coming to get you. Hang on.*

"Ready?"

Ekon turned. Behind him, Themba was ducking out of the apothecary, her own sack in hand.

"Ready."

"Good," she said. "Now follow me, and stay close."

They traversed the winding backstreets and alleys of the Chafu District together without speaking, Themba leading the way. As he followed, Ekon made himself focus on the gritty crunch of damp earth underfoot instead of the way the buildings here seemed to loom over him. Lkossa was his home, the only city he'd ever known, and yet in places like this it felt like another world. He tried to count his steps, to ease the nagging sense of foreboding roiling in his core, but he couldn't shake it. Even the numbers weren't helping.

Two hundred six, two hundred seven, two hundred—

He swore as his foot caught in a pothole and he tripped, nearly falling to the ground. Themba didn't stop.

"Keep up, boy." Like a wraith, she continued on, her steps making no sound as she darted across a sconce-lit street and then back into the shadows. Ekon copied the move, impressed. He hadn't expected the old woman to be so quick-footed. His eyes settled in the darkness of the alley they'd just entered, and he realized Themba had stopped. She was feeling around, letting her fingers brush the mud-brick walls on either side of her. She turned, and Ekon saw that she was scowling. With exasperation, she reached into her tunic's pocket and withdrew a small coin pouch, shaking it so that its jingle filled the space.

"Mwongo." She shook the purse again. "Come out," she whispered. "I know you're here."

Ekon nearly jumped out of his skin when a figure just a few feet down the alley from them seemed to peel from the wall itself. It moved toward them, and when it was closer, Ekon discerned a young curly-haired man with a dusting of stubble on his jaw. His brown cheeks were hollow, his eyes sunken, but he was grinning.

"How extraordinary." His voice was dry, reed-thin. "The Cobra and the Rat, together in the same alley." He stepped forward, as though to get a better look. "This *is* a surprise."

"Ekon." Themba turned from the young man. "This is an . . . acquaintance of mine, Mwongo."

The young man's grin stretched. "My friends call me the Rat."

Ekon stiffened as Mwongo stepped around Themba. When he was closer, he narrowed his eyes, assessing.

"Is it just me? Or does your face seem familiar?"

"Never mind his face," said Themba sharply. She glanced at Ekon. "Mwongo is going to help us."

"*Am* I?" Mwongo—the Rat—looked back at her in surprise. "And why would I do that?"

Themba rolled her eyes. "Because I speak your language." She tossed him the coin purse, which he snatched from the air and weighed appreciatively.

"You always did have a way with words," he murmured before looking up. "What is it that you need?"

"To leave Lkossa tonight," said Themba. "Undetected."

Mwongo pocketed the coin purse, then stroked his chin a moment, pensive.

"There are warriors patrolling everywhere," he mused. "They're

59

looking for someone, rumor has it, one of their own recently defected." He gave Ekon a meaningful look. "I've heard the reward is . . . substantial."

"Mwongo." Themba glared at the man, and Ekon paused. Something in Themba's eyes had changed in the dark, though he couldn't identify precisely what. Mwongo seemed to sense it too, and straightened.

"All right, all right!" He held up his hands. "The warriors are patrolling, but we can get around them. There are two main roads out of the city."

"One on the west border path," Ekon cut in, "and one in the south."

Mwongo nodded. "The southern route gets you away from Lkossa quicker," he said, "but the western route is closer to here. I've got a friend who drives a fertilizer cart, he takes product out of the city every night." He glanced at the sky. "If we move quickly, we can still catch him, and he could smuggle you out. It won't be a *pleasant* ride, but it'll get the job done."

Ekon looked to Themba, confused, but her expression hadn't changed. She nodded, then turned to him. "This is our way out, boy. Are you in?"

Ekon pressed his lips together, frowning. There was no room in the alley to be discreet, so he looked at Themba and said the words directly.

"I don't like it," he said honestly. "And I don't trust him."

If Mwongo was offended, he didn't show it. His mouth twisted into a nasty smile, and Ekon noted that he was missing several of his teeth. "I've found people rarely like rats," he said, "but I'll tell you something." He leaned closer, and Ekon smelled tobacco on his breath. "Rats are nimble, resourceful, more intelligent than most realize. They know their way around even the filthiest streets. You do not have to like or trust me, boy, but tonight you do need me. Take my offer or leave it. You won't find better for the price."

Ekon's jaw clenched as he sized up Mwongo. The young man had the same build as him, but was several inches shorter. He couldn't have been much older. Still, Ekon couldn't help but feel he was holding the poorer hand in a game of cards. Mwongo leered, as though he agreed. Themba's expression was almost perfectly inscrutable, but she let the mask slip for a fraction of a second, and Ekon saw the real emotion behind it. There was a pleading in her eyes, a desperation. He realized it then. He wanted to find Koffi more than anything else, but so did she. He recognized that desperation because he felt it himself. It was that, above all things, that cemented his decision. It was that, above all things, that made him say the words.

"All right. Let's go."

The fortune that had favored them as they'd left the apothecary seemed to change its course as the three of them emerged from the alley and went down a different road at Mwongo's beckoning. Ekon cast a glance up at the sky and noted that the clouds were returning now, heavy and distended with what he was sure would soon be a downpour. Hopefully they made it to the cart by then. The idea of leaving Lkossa alongside bags of dung wasn't exactly what he'd had in mind, but if it got them out, he'd take it. It was one step closer to Koffi, one step closer to saving her.

We're coming, Koffi. Hang on.

Mwongo glanced left and right, then pointed down one of the market's streets. It was devoid of people, but crammed with empty vendor stalls. Ekon breathed in the smell of hay and dung. Chicken feathers littered the ground along with a few smashed eggs. During the day, this was clearly an area for livestock. He wrinkled his nose. A few feet away, he noted a cart in the middle of the road. Mwongo saw it too, and sucked his teeth.

"Old fool's probably gone to water the mule," he said, shaking his head. "Wait here, I'll find him."

Ekon watched as he turned a corner and disappeared, frowning. Themba shrugged off her sack, taking the moment's rest to lean against a shop's wall. He'd been impressed by her speed before, but now he saw the toll it had taken; she looked exhausted.

"Don't worry about me." She waved a hand when she caught him looking at her. "I'll catch my breath once we're on the cart."

Ekon's eyes cut back to that cart, still sitting in the middle of the road. The gathering clouds had stolen any moonlight from the street, making it impossible to discern its details from afar. He moved closer to it, eyes narrowed.

"Ekon?"

He heard Themba's whisper over his shoulder, but didn't look back as he took another step toward the cart. He realized now what had first drawn his eye to it: There was nothing in its bed. He couldn't remember now what Mwongo had said—was the cart picking up the fertilizer or delivering it? It was within a yard of him now, and he walked around it slowly. His heart beat faster in his chest as he took in its details, the things he hadn't been able to see from afar. The cart's wood was soaked, as though it had been sitting here for some time, not just a few short minutes. The pulling bar's metal was rusted, its wood long since cracked. When he looked down, he noted one of the wheels' spokes had been broken too. This cart hadn't been used in weeks, maybe longer. Ekon looked up as a sudden dread dropped in his core like a stone.

"Themba!" he shouted. "Run, it's a—"

The words died in his throat as he looked past Themba at the same moment new figures entered the street, hanjari daggers on each of their hips. His mouth went dry as he saw one more figure appear behind them. Mwongo. He met Ekon's gaze and shrugged.

"Sorry, kid."

Ekon said nothing as he locked eyes with the Sons of the Six.

A GAME of SURVIVAL

BINTI

I think my mother is a demigod.

There is, of course, no tangible proof of it, only the occasional strands of plausibility that glint golden in just the right light. Sometimes, when I'm bored, I watch my mother from afar and pretend that she is secretly a long-lost daughter of the water goddess Amakoya, with the torso of a woman and a fish's green-scaled tail in place of human legs. Other days, when her temper flares, I imagine Mama could be a child of Tyembu, god and master of the great deserts to the west.

This afternoon, my mother balances a clay-baked vase on her head, one with a long, slender neck and thick handles on each side that remind me of a woman's hands on her hips. The heat is oppressive this time of day, it draws tiny beads of sweat from her brow and glistens on her dark brown skin, but Mama still moves like a practiced dancer, limber and fluid. When she catches me watching her, she smiles.

"Are you all right, Binti?"

I start to nod, then catch myself. I'm trying to balance a vase on my head too. It's smaller than Mama's, but just as difficult to carry. Carefully, I quicken my steps until I'm no longer walking behind her, but beside her, then I adjust my gait to match hers. *Head straight, shoulders back.*

I want to be just like her.

The smell of fresh fruit fills my nose as we continue through the streets of the Kazi District, the small residential area allotted for harvesters and laborers. People in this district are poor, but only to the trained eye. On one of the dust-covered street corners we pass, there's a young man selling jams and preserves, but only a truly discerning person would notice that some of his jars are chipped. Women of all ages sit on the curb chatting among each other. Some are selling cheap trinkets and snacks, and others hold squirming children between their knees while they twist, comb, and braid hair of all textures. The braiders here in the Kazi District are good, but the best ones work in the marketplace.

I love the marketplace.

The air changes as we reach the end of the Kazi District and join the masses of people heading into the city's central hub. Lkossa will never be what it once was, before the Rupture, but she is still a hub of eastern trade and economy. I inhale, and this time not only do I smell the blend of bagged spices stacked in the stalls, I can practically taste cumin, irú, and black cardamom. We stay with the natural current of the crowd until it brings us to the very heart of the market itself. Here there are people of every kind— farmers, potters, and merchants—selling everything under the sun. Its din is like a song of its own, a chorus of shouts, and laughter, and life.

We make our way past the stalls until we reach the city's wells.

Lines of people are queued before them, each waiting for their turn to draw water. A small sigh escapes Mama.

"This shouldn't take long," she promises. "We'll be out of here in no time." In a graceful motion, she uses the heel of her palm to dab more sweat from her brow, and my eyes catch on the bracelet affixed to her arm. In actuality the word *bracelet* is a generous term for the thing. It isn't pretty; the cheap silver it is fashioned from is tarnished, and its edges are crudely cast, but I suppose it's not really worn for beauty. Mama's "bracelet" isn't jewelry, it's a form of identification. People like her, darajas, are required to wear them at all times. In those moments, when I look at her bracelet, I remember that Mama is not a demigod at all. She wears her mortality the way a swallowtail might wear its wings. There is something about her that is wholly of this world, grounded. I am grateful for that. I can't imagine the shape of my life without her.

I don't feel the eyes on me immediately—it happens slowly, the way one might feel a beetle crawling along an arm or neck—but when I turn, I see them: a trio of girls who look to be my age, watching me. Their faces are inscrutable, and the longer they stare, the more uncomfortable I feel. I want to look down at myself so that I can see whatever they're seeing, but the vase is still on my head. Do I have some stain on my clothes, cow dung on my legs?

My heart flutters in my chest when, after a pause, one of the girls starts in my direction. She doesn't necessarily look older as she draws closer to me, but something about the way she walks makes me feel awkward and childish. Her skin is a shade lighter than mine, and her short reddish-brown hair is twisted into little Bantu knots that have been parted and arranged with perfect precision. I already know that this girl doesn't get her hair done in the Kazi District. *She* isn't poor.

"How old are you?" She stops before me and asks the question without preamble. Her expression is still hard to read.

"Fifteen." It feels like the answer to a test I didn't know I was taking. Seconds pass before the girl looks me over.

"Where did you get your dress?" she asks.

I'm so surprised that I nearly forget I have a water vase on my head and look down at myself. The dress I'm wearing is a faded purple color, with small flowers I embroidered around the hem. I hadn't thought it was even worth looking at.

"I . . ." The words on my tongue trip over themselves. "I made it," I say quietly.

A beat passes in which the girl's brows rise. Then, there's no mistaking it, she looks visibly impressed.

"You make your own clothes." It's not a question; she seems to be saying it to herself. "How interesting." After another pause, she looks up. "It's pretty."

My cheeks flush despite the morning heat. "Thank you."

The two other girls are coming forward now, looks of the same intrigue clear on their faces. They both ask me the same questions, and then they both introduce themselves—Nekesa and Chakoya. The first girl tells me her name is Uzoma.

"We have an oware board," she says. "Do you want to play with us?"

A strange thing happens then; for the first time in my entire life, I feel a pull from something, someone, that isn't my mother. More than anything, I want to be just like her, but . . .

But I want to be included too.

I'm afraid to look at Mama, but when I do, she's smiling. With ease, she lifts the vase from my head, and though I'd never admit it, I relish the lightness in its absence. I massage my neck, and Mama nods.

"Go ahead, Binti. I'll be here."

She doesn't know how much her words mean to me, how much power she holds in the mere sound of her approval. A second weight lifts from me, and I am free. Without another word, I run with Uzoma and the other girls across the square. We stoop down together in a huddle, and one of the girls, Nekesa, shows me the oware board. It's a small, flat slab of dark wood with twelve little scoops carved into it in groups of two, six on each side. On either end of the board there are larger cutouts, and each one holds a number of round, brightly painted stones. On the left, the stones are jade green; on the right, they're sapphire blue.

"Do you know how to play?" Nekesa asks. She is taller than Uzoma, with thin, pointed features and black cornrows with white beads on their ends.

My face feels hot again. Oware is a common enough game in Lkossa, played by little children and old men alike, but I've never learned its rules. I shake my head, embarrassed.

"It's easy," she explains. "These little pits on the board are called houses, and four stones go into each one." She takes a fistful of the green stones and begins dropping them into each house in groups. "These bigger pits at the ends of the board are called scores. The goal is to get all of your stones into my score before I get mine into yours. It's a simple game of strategy."

In truth, it doesn't sound simple at all, but the girls are all watching me now, expectant. In their eyes, I feel another test, hear the silent questions. Am I like them, or am I different? Am I still interesting, or have I become boring? I swallow, and when Nekesa finishes dispersing each of our stones, I nod.

"I'm ready."

She makes the first move.

I watch as she picks up four green stones and pauses, studying the board. Then she quickly drops them, one-two-three-four, into new houses, so that the first one is empty. She nods to me.

"Your turn."

I take a deep breath and grab a handful of the sapphire stones. I know, of course, that they're not made from real sapphire—more than likely they're just rocks painted by some local artisan—but in my palm their weight is precious, and I feel a peculiar obligation to place them with care. Like Nekesa, I study the board for a moment, trying to determine where best to put the stones so the fourth won't end up on her side. Then I move, letting each little stone slide from my fingers into its new house. Nekesa purses her lips.

"That was . . . a good move."

We continue on, alternately picking up our stones and designating them into new houses. The other girls say nothing as we conduct our silent war like generals in a battle. Gradually, I begin to find my rhythm. Nekesa was right in saying that oware is a game of strategy, but it's also a game of survival, and I know *that* game all too well. Mama and I play it every day: when we're short on rent, or when food is scarce and the temperature drops. I've been playing that game all my life.

"You've won." I hear the disbelief in Nekesa's voice as she says it, leaning back and examining the board as though it's tricked her.

Slowly, the world returns to focus, and I see Uzoma and Chakoya still sitting around us. They're both beaming at me, clapping, and now in their eyes I can see it—approval touched by envy. My heart is fluttering in my chest again, but this time it's not with fear. No, this feeling is new, and it takes me several seconds to find a name for it: joy. It is not quite the same way I feel when Mama surprises me with a fruit tart from the market. No, this is different. I delight in being, for the first time in my life, someone to be envied. I realize that this is what it's like to be noticed, to be interesting to other people for more than a few seconds.

I love it.

Joy is a fleeting thing, though, as I have since come to learn. It pools in cupped palms, then seeps through the cracks no matter how tightly one might press one's fingers together in the hopes of preserving it.

I feel the precise moment my joy slips away from me.

"Halt!"

My shoulders tense as a voice carries over the market's usual din, loud and sharp as the crack of a whip. When I turn, I find the body it belongs to, a man's. He is dressed in a sky-blue kaftan tied with a golden belt at the waist. His leather sandals are shiny and new, and his dark curly hair has been barbered into a perfect top fade. Even without the golden hanjari dagger on his hip, I know who he is, what he is. This man is a Son of the Six, a holy warrior and an enforcer. Despite the sun still baking overhead, a chill shudders through the length of my body. I don't trust Sons of the

Six. They tout themselves as men of honor and righteousness, but I know better. My teeth clench hard as several more warriors enter the square in the first one's wake, and my entire body goes taut. But those warriors aren't looking at me.

They're looking at my mother.

"Halt!" The assumed leader of the warriors repeats the command again, though my mother has not moved. All around the square, no one is speaking, and all activity has come to a standstill. In that eerie quiet, I sense a foreboding, and my eyes cut to Mama's. She's standing before the well now, still carrying my vase in her arms, and her own on her head. The warrior advances toward her with a hard-set smile full of gleaming white teeth, and I am reminded of a hyena stalking prey.

"Sir." I can't see my mother's face, but I watch her posture change. *Head straight, shoulders back.* She does not cower as the warrior stops before her, and I know from his deepening scowl that he does not like that.

"Is there a problem?" Mama's voice is placid as she asks the question.

The warrior draws himself up to full height, so that he is looking down his nose at my mother when he answers. "Darajas are no longer permitted to use the city's central wells. You will have to go elsewhere for water."

I jump to my feet. That earlier sense of foreboding is now raw anxiety. It pulses within me, and I hear my heart beating all the way in my ears. No one else has spoken a word. I'm sure Uzoma, Nekesa, and Chakoya are still crouched around the oware board, but I don't spare a look at them. I still can't see Mama's face, but I hear the fear in her voice.

"That's . . . I have never heard of such a rule." Her words tremble as they leave her.

"It was enacted yesterday evening, by the Kuhani," says the warrior. "If your kind wants water, you'll have to go to the western border wells."

I make a face. Western Lkossa is where the Chafu District is; it's not a safe or nice place. It's also a significantly longer walk from home. Sending darajas there for water is a punishment.

"I—I—" Mama is stammering now. "But that's . . ."

"Move along," says the warrior. He's no longer smiling, and there's a hard glint in his black eyes. "Unless you want trouble."

Mama straightens. I hear anger in her voice. "Very well, then."

She moves away from the well and the warrior, but he catches her arm. With terrible slowness, I watch as Mama loses her balance. My stomach seizes as the tall vase atop her head wavers once, twice, then slides off her head, shattering into millions of pieces. A small sound escapes my mother, a noise that falls somewhere between a gasp and a cry. She jerks forward, as if to try to salvage those many pieces, but the warrior is still holding her arm. He yanks her back to him.

"Learn to respect your betters, woman, or you'll find yourself in trouble."

I'm still standing across the square watching my mother, waiting. I know what's going to happen next. Mama is going to give this stupid man a piece of her mind. It wouldn't be the first time. I've seen Mama cow men twice her size with a single withering look. I've watched her slice, dice, and cut down boys half her age who've made the mistake of trying to pickpocket her in these streets. I've seen Mama do other things too, things only darajas like her can do, to people who hurt her. I wait for Mama to act, to make this warrior wish he'd never crossed her.

But she does not.

When my mother finally turns around, she does not look anything like the demigod I sometimes imagine her to be. Instead, she looks painfully small, fragile. She's still holding my vase in her hands.

"Binti." She whispers my name, but it carries like a breeze. "Come."

I feel the market's eyes on me as I obey. Just before, when I was running to play with Uzoma and the others, my feet felt featherlight. Now every part of me is heavy. It seems to take centuries for me to close the space between us, and just before I reach my mother, I feel a prick of pain in the arch of my foot. When I look down, I notice a sliver of the shattered vase has slipped past my threadbare sandals and sliced along the soft skin of my sole. I stare at the cut and watch dark blood ooze, pooling in my shoe. I wait for the pain I know should come, but I feel nothing at all.

Mama appears before me, and without a word I take my vase back from her. I do not look at her when I do, nor do I try to balance it on my head again. This little vase, less than half the size of our other one, is the only thing we have to carry water; we cannot risk anything happening to it this season.

The silence holds as we walk together out of the square, Mama with her head held high and me limping slightly from the cut on my foot. I keep my eyes downcast as we go, but even without looking up, I can feel all the eyes on us—the pity, the wariness. When I glance over my shoulder, past the fragmented remains of the vase on the ground, I see Uzoma and the other girls watching me. Their faces are no longer marked by curiosity or intrigue. Instead, they wear expressions of shared disgust, as though all of them have caught a whiff of the same stink.

I know they will not ask me to play oware with them again.

Life returns to the square the moment we leave it. As we turn a corner, I hear the tradesmen calling out their wares again, children laughing and screeching as their games of chase resume. Lkossa moves on, as she always does. I wait until we are far enough away from it to ask my mother the question that has been waiting on the tip of my tongue.

"Mama, why is this happening? Why is the Kuhani making darajas get water from the western wells?"

My mother takes a long time to answer. "Because he can."

"So," I press, "we really can't get our water from the city's central wells anymore?"

"No." My mother sounds remote now, distant. "We cannot."

When the words pass her own lips, they feel more real, more final. Tears fill my eyes, but I don't let them fall. Mama isn't crying, so I won't cry. I want to be just like her.

A thought brushes the borders of my mind then. At first I ignore it, but it wriggles and shines like a single thread in a tapestry, begging to be pulled. It's another question:

"Mama," I ask slowly. "Are we *both* not allowed to use the well?"

For the first time since leaving the square, my mother stops to look at me. "What do you mean?"

"I . . ." Under her gaze, I feel strange saying the words. "The warrior said darajas weren't allowed to use the well, but . . . *I'm* not a daraja, so I could still use it, right?"

I watch as something in my mother's face changes slowly. Her

74

mouth becomes a tightly drawn line, her beautiful brown eyes narrow. She cocks her head and her brows knit together, as though it's the first time she's really seeing me.

"If you wish to keep going to a well where I am not welcomed, you are free to." She speaks softly, but beneath the words I hear the challenge, yet another unspoken test. I shake my head quickly.

"No, Mama. I don't want to. I want to stay with you."

At once my mother's face relaxes. She looks like a demigod again, radiant in the sunlight. When she smiles at me, I relax too.

"Come," she says, starting to walk again, "the wells at the western border aren't too far."

I obey her, not because I have to, but because I want to. I want to be just like my mother, but for the first time in my life, I understand that will be hard because we are not the exact same.

It is the first time I understand that, but not the last.

CHAPTER 5

The FIVE NOBLE ORDERS

The sun was shining. Koffi felt none of its warmth.

She walked through Thornkeep's halls softly, as though trying not to wake them. Ahead of her, Makena's steps offset her own, and together they created a perfect cadence in the silence. Koffi wished there was more sound. This quiet gave her too much time to reflect, too long an opportunity to mentally revisit all she'd seen in the last hour.

Each stride carried her away from the main hall, but when she closed her eyes, she found herself right back in it, watching everything unfold again in excruciating detail. She saw the darajas, gathered in their colors, remembered the way they'd looked at her. The emotions on their faces had ranged from fear to wariness to outright intrigue; the last of those made her more than a little uncomfortable. She remembered one of those darajas—the girl in the green tunic—the one who'd presented her with Fedu's horrible roses. It was all too easy to recall the instant terror that had filled that girl's eyes as Fedu had dangled her by her braids just because he could. He had resorted to violence with an inhuman kind of apathy, a well-practiced ease. Each time she thought of it, her stomach turned.

You are a dull knife. But fear not, I will see you sharpened.

Fedu's promise repeated itself in her mind, playing over and over like a street fiddler's tune. Each time Koffi thought of those words, of the implication behind them, a new shiver crawled over her skin. She'd seen and heard so many terrible things in the course of an hour, but there was still one more that sent a fresh chill up her spine.

A face. She'd just seen a *face* in the Mistwood.

At least, she thought she had; it had vanished as quickly as it had appeared. Koffi tried her best to reconstruct the image. She thought she'd seen an oblong shape between the gnarled trees, a shape the same whitish color as the mist, but distinct. From the window, it had been too far away to know for sure, but she thought she'd seen what looked vaguely like eyes too, a crude slash in place of where a mouth might have been. It had been visible for only a second, too briefly to discern whether it had belonged to a man, woman, or child. The longer Koffi considered it, the less certain she was that what she'd seen had even been a face at all. Her gaze cut to Makena again, still walking a few steps ahead. For a moment, she considered asking the girl if she'd seen the face too, but . . . no. Koffi stopped herself, deciding against it. There was no way to definitively prove she'd actually seen a face in the Mistwood, no way to know if it hadn't simply been a manifestation of exhaustion. In one morning here, she'd already been made into an anomaly; Fedu had told every daraja in the main hall that she was their "chosen one." No need to add kindling to that fire by pointing out one more thing that might make her different.

When they reached the bedchamber, Makena entered first. Koffi stood at its entrance, watching as the girl settled on the divan in the room's corner, neatly tucking her legs beneath her yellow dress. There was a natural grace about her Koffi knew she herself would never have. Her eyes panned the rest of the chamber. The tray of food from before was still on the nightstand beside the bed, and this time when Koffi looked at it, she couldn't stop her stomach from audible rumbling. Makena looked up.

"You should eat."

Koffi considered refusing. She desperately wanted some sense of control in this strange place, even if it was in what and when she ate. But her body had no reserve of energy left for rebellion. The adrenaline that had coursed through her body in the main hall was gone, leaving in its wake fatigue and hunger. It occurred to Koffi now that she had no idea when she'd last eaten. She sighed, defeated, and walked across the room to sit on the bed's edge. After a very quick deliberation, she plucked a slice of bread from the tray. Her mouth watered as she devoured it, and in a moment of vulnerability, she closed her eyes. The face from the Mistwood gave way, yielding so that others filled her mind in its place. She saw Mama's face, then Jabir's, then . . . Ekon's. A stab of pain lanced through her body as she remembered what he'd looked like the last time she'd seen him, on the ground and in excruciating pain. She had no idea what had happened to him, no idea if he, Mama, or Jabir were all right. A sudden stinging filled her eyes, and she screwed them shut until it went away.

"Koffi?"

At once, Koffi opened her eyes again. Makena was still sitting on the divan, watching her. "Are you . . . are you okay?"

Are you okay? Koffi didn't know how to answer that question. She knew she wasn't, but saying so would require her to untangle a snarl of emotions she wasn't quite ready to face. The idea of doing something like that right now made her brain hurt, so instead she deflected with her own question.

"Makena, can I ask you something?"

From her spot on the divan, Makena sat up straighter. "Of course."

"Why did you come here?" Koffi hadn't meant to ask so bluntly, but once asked, the words tumbled from her in a rush. "I mean, you, Zain, those darajas in the main hall, you all have to know Fedu's whole speech about 'a better world' is a lie. How did he convince you to come to this place?"

Koffi watched as, slowly, something slipped from the girl's face. When she spoke, her voice was different. The cheer was gone, replaced by something frail.

"Fedu didn't 'convince' any of us to come here," she whispered, "and believe me, plenty of us don't support the things he wants to do."

Koffi frowned. Whatever she'd been expecting to hear, this wasn't it. "I . . . don't understand."

Makena's face changed again. This time, the frailty was replaced with anger. "He stole us from our homes," she said through her teeth, strained. "All of us, one by one. This place, Thornkeep, is no haven. It's a prison, a place for Fedu to keep darajas whose affinities interest him. All of us are part of his collection."

Koffi felt suddenly sick.

"He did tell one truth in the main hall," Makena went on bitterly. "He does test each daraja that he brings here; we've all been evaluated to determine if we were strong enough to help. None of us were until you." She threw Koffi a sidelong glance. "You must have really impressed him."

Koffi made herself breathe. In a rush, everything that had happened in the sky garden flooded her memory, washing over her in a deluge.

"I didn't impress him," she said quietly. "But there was another daraja who did; her name was Adiah. He really wanted to use her power." Saying the words made Koffi shudder. "But she didn't want to. She resisted for a long time, and in the end, I took the splendor she was holding in her body so that he couldn't hurt her anymore." She sagged a little on the bed. "So he took me instead."

Makena's eyes widened. For several seconds, she seemed at a loss for words. "That was . . . really selfless of you."

Koffi dropped her gaze. To someone else, perhaps what she had done for Adiah seemed selfless, but the word made her uncomfortable. Could she call what she'd done truly selfless if a part of her regretted it? She wasn't sure. When she looked up, Makena was still looking at her, though with new appreciation in her eyes.

"I made assumptions about you," she murmured after a moment. "I'm sorry."

"It's okay, I did too," said Koffi. It was surprisingly nice to say it aloud. "About you, about Zain . . ."

Makena rolled her eyes. "Most of the assumptions you made about Zain are probably true," she said, with all the exasperation a sister might have for an annoying brother. She crossed the room so that she was sitting on the bed.

"So, what's your order, anyway?" she asked, returning to her cheery disposition. "When Fedu brings in a new daraja, he usually announces their order in the main hall, but he didn't share yours."

Koffi frowned. This was the second time Makena had asked about her order, and she understood the question no more now than she had before. She shrugged. "I . . . don't know what you mean," she said honestly.

Makena's brows knitted, a perfect mirror of the confusion Koffi was sure she had on her own face. "You don't know your order?"

Koffi shook her head. Makena probably didn't mean it, but she was making her feel increasingly more awkward.

"But how could you—*oh*." A look of understanding dawned on Makena's face. "Now that makes sense."

"What?"

"When Fedu asked me to make your dress," she said, nodding to Koffi's garment. "He specifically asked me to pick a fabric without colors."

Makena seemed to be getting at something, but Koffi was more confused than ever. "Why would the colors of my clothes matter?"

Makena cocked a brow. "Didn't you notice that the darajas in the main hall were all standing together based on the color of their clothes?"

Koffi nodded.

"It's because, traditionally, darajas are grouped together based on their affinity. Those groups are collectively called the Five Noble Orders." She used her fingers to tick them off. "Order of Akili, Order of Mwili, Order of Kupambana, Order of Maisha—"

"Which order are you in?" Koffi asked, interrupting.

"Order of Ufundi," said Makena with a smile. "Darajas like me

81

make things, though our talents can vary. For example, my obvious specialty is in creating beautiful gowns." She brushed her shoulders. "But there are other darajas in my order who can cook, paint, build things; some even know how to make weapons." She pinched at her own dress. "We wear yellow. Order of Akili—that is, the Order of the Mind—wears blue, which is why you saw Zain wearing it."

Koffi nodded. "So, Fedu told you to make a dress for me without colors. Why?" She was dreading the answer to that question, but she knew she had to ask it.

Makena faltered. "Historically, a daraja without colors doesn't have a specific affinity," she said.

Koffi's stomach dropped, but she kept her voice even. "How common is that?"

"Not very." Makena sounded uncomfortable. "Usually, it happens when a daraja comes into their power late, sort of like . . . when a child's growth is stunted early on." She gave Koffi an apologetic look. "Did your parents not tell you any of this?"

Koffi dropped her gaze again, glad the heat in her cheeks didn't show. She knew the sudden wave of shame she felt was unfounded, but she still felt it. Not for the first time, a single unanswered question pricked at her side. Why hadn't Mama told her that she was a daraja? Why had she kept all of this from her?

"No," Koffi finally said. "They didn't."

Makena paused, then: "It's okay. You're not the first daraja not to have an official affinity. You won't be the last. The specific nature of your power isn't as important as what you do with it."

They were simple words, but kind. Koffi looked at Makena then, abruptly overwhelmed. She drew her knees to her chest, and

Makena seemed to understand that this particular moment called for quiet. Neither one of them spoke. Koffi let her gaze wander to the bedroom window. Without anyone standing there, she could see most of a garden below; the majority of its flowers were yellow. She stood, moving closer to the window to get a better view. The sun was much higher in the sky than before, shining golden light onto the flowers and neatly manicured grass. She looked toward the back of the lawns and noted the Mistwood. It appeared just as it had before, an opaque white wall of curling tendrils and fog, but in this light it seemed less ominous.

"Makena," she asked, "if the Mistwood's the only thing keeping the darajas at Thornkeep, why hasn't anyone tried to leave it?"

Makena's gaze darkened. "They *have* tried."

Koffi waited for her to say more, but abruptly Makena rose.

"We should get going," she said. "Your first lesson is in the south garden, and we don't want to be late."

Koffi didn't ask Makena about the Mistwood again.

She'd had every intention to at first, tried to find opportunities to bring it up as they made their way out of Thornkeep and onto its south lawns. But once they were outside, thoughts of Mistwood were forgotten. She turned and took in Thornkeep in its entirety for the first time. It was a great, hulking sort of building— something about its black stones and many towers reminded her of a cross between a temple and a fortress. Perhaps that was appropriate. She took several steps back and looked up, trying to take in the very scope of it. Thornkeep was bigger even than the Temple of Lkossa, and she couldn't help but be a little impressed by it.

"Imagine having phenomenal cosmic power and choosing to live in this." Makena threw a nasty look at the building, as though it had done something distasteful.

"You don't like it?" Koffi asked.

"It's *gauche*," said Makena. She wrinkled her nose. "I mean, gods, you've got the continent's most talented darajas on the property and nobody helped with the décor? Couldn't be me."

Koffi laughed. "Do they make nice houses where you're from?"

Makena smirked, as though enjoying some sort of joke. "Yes and no. My people are travelers, our whole life fits in a wagon." She nodded to Koffi. "What about you? Where are you from?"

"Lkossa," said Koffi, and she was surprised by how much it hurt to say her city's name. "I miss it."

Makena nodded with some sympathy before they continued on. When they finally reached the south garden—distinguishable by its white flowers—Koffi saw a girl was already there, waiting. Like Makena and Zain, she looked to be about sixteen. She was tall, with brown skin and long black Fulani braids styled with knife-sharp precision. She wore a sleeveless purple tunic, and Koffi noted her bare arms were muscled. Every inch of the girl exuded power, strength, confidence. She nodded at them both as they approached.

"Koffi, this is Njeri," said Makena. "She's in the Order of Kupambana, the Order of Combat."

"Nice to meet you." Njeri offered a hand. Her alto voice was accented, and Koffi placed it.

"You're from the Baridi Region, in the north."

Surprise flickered across Njeri's face. "I am. Have you been?"

"Er, no." Koffi cringed. "I just had an unfortunate experience with a Baridian merchant and his wife once."

"Really?" Njeri looked genuinely interested.

"It's not a great story," said Koffi quickly. "And it ended with a lot of trouble."

"I like trouble," said Njeri with a wink. "It can be fun." She exchanged a coy look with Makena that Koffi didn't understand. "I think I've got it from here."

"I'm sure you do." Makena smiled at them both before turning to Koffi. "I'll come back for you in a bit," she said, "just meet me here."

"Okay."

When she was gone, Njeri turned to Koffi. "So," she said ruefully. "Do you know how to fight?"

"Yes." Koffi immediately regretted saying that. She'd learned exactly one move from Ekon in the Greater Jungle, and even her execution of that had been iffy. While they'd trained, Badwa had tried showing her some basic maneuvers with the splendor, but that hardly counted as real training. She started to clarify herself, but it was too late. Njeri was already beaming.

"Great, so we can skip the basics and get straight into some sparring exercises." She sounded entirely too excited as she picked up the two staffs on the ground. "We're going to play a game I like to call Skins."

Koffi tensed. *That* didn't sound fun at all.

"The goal is for us to practice defensive and offensive movement," she explained. "We're both going to try to hit each other while also blocking the other's moves. The person whose staff hits skin first wins the bout."

Koffi hesitated. "Uh, no offense, but how does this help me figure out my affinity?"

Njeri grinned. "When darajas in my order summon the splendor, it manifests when we fight—in our hands, feet, weapons, et cetera. As you try to block my hits and land your own, try to summon and direct the splendor into the staff. If you're in the Order of Kupambana, that should feel pretty natural."

Koffi tried not to grimace. Absolutely nothing about this felt natural.

"We'll do best three out of five, okay?"

Koffi nodded, taking the staff from Njeri. Its wood was a deep reddish brown, and it was heavy, despite its slender cut.

"We'll start easy to warm up," said Njeri. "On my count. One . . . two . . . three."

Koffi sucked in a breath as Njeri charged forward, much faster than she'd anticipated. She brought her staff down, and Koffi thought she saw tiny golden speckles of light—the splendor—near the business end. She tried to jump out of the way, but it was too late; the staff's tip smacked her shoulder, hard. Pain ricocheted down Koffi's arm.

"I win," said Njeri brightly. "Let's go again."

Their second and third bouts ended the same way as the first. Koffi gritted her teeth. She'd tried to summon the splendor, tried to draw it into the staff as she moved, but it was to no avail. Njeri, meanwhile, was fast, strong, and seemed to specialize in finding an opponent's weak points to exploit them. Koffi doubted even a Son of the Six would fare well against her in a fight.

"Maybe we should try something else," said Njeri after the fourth bout; it had ended with her putting Koffi on her back, and there was a bit of pity in her voice now.

"No." Koffi shook her head. "We have one more bout, let's finish it."

Njeri's brow rose, clearly hesitant, but after a moment she inclined her head and stepped back. "All right, positions."

Koffi ignored the pain in her arms and legs as she stood and raised her staff. The last few bouts hadn't ended well for her, but they hadn't been a complete waste. She'd been taking mental notes. Njeri was tall, and her long arms gave her more reach. Koffi took a deep breath as they circled each other, and tried to imagine what Ekon might say if he was here.

Watch for patterns. Watch for weaknesses.

Njeri shifted her weight from foot to foot, as though dancing to an inaudible song. She'd done it each time they began, and Koffi realized she was trying to figure out which direction to move in. An idea came to her. She didn't know if she could pull it off, but she could try.

She feels bad for you, thinks you're weak, pretend-Ekon's voice said. *That's an advantage you can exploit.*

Koffi leaned left and watched Njeri's eyes follow the movement like a cat watching a mouse. This time, she moved first, stepping left, then quickly changing course. Njeri fell for it. The girl lunged just as Koffi veered away, so that she only swung at air. At the same time, Koffi planted her foot and spun, trying to recall everything Ekon had taught her about the duara. Her execution wasn't flawless, but her arm cut through the air in a perfect arc and smacked against Njeri's rib, hard. The girl cried out in surprise and made to strike back, but Koffi quickly backed away.

"My bout."

Njeri grinned. "Nice move." She smirked. "I've heard you're good with butter knives too."

Koffi grimaced, the joy of her victory slightly sullied. She didn't know if and when she would see Zain again, but she made a mental note to give him a good kick the next time she did.

"I think we can call it a day," said Njeri.

"What? But I thought we were just warming up?" Koffi surprised herself saying the words. The truth was, while she hadn't necessarily enjoyed sparring with Njeri, it had felt good to move, to do something that made her feel like she was at least in control of herself.

Njeri shook her head. "Best not to overdo it," she said. "We'll train again another time." She nodded to Thornkeep. "Want me to walk you back inside?"

"No," said Koffi quickly. "I'll stay here and wait for Makena, maybe look around a bit."

"Okay." Njeri nodded. "I'll see you around, then. It was nice to meet you."

Koffi watched Njeri head down one of the south garden's stone paths, realizing once she was gone that, for the first time since she'd woken up, she was alone. She took in the garden around her slowly. There were clusters of white daisies arranged sporadically near stone benches, blooming dahlias and bunches of baby's breath; every flower within reach was white. She looked past them and noticed something else: the Mistwood. It was several yards away, but even from this distance she could see that the acacia trees were much taller than she'd first imagined; even the smallest among them was twice her size. Her eyes traced along their trunks, which were gray like ash, and the thorns that protruded from their gnarly branches, the color of bone. Even the grass at the trees' roots had a brittle, deadened look about it. Makena's words came back to her.

They have tried.

Koffi reflected on those words. If darajas had tried to leave Thornkeep without success, what had stopped them? She looked toward the Mistwood again. Its telltale mist seemed less opaque from here; she could make out the start of the trees within. She felt a brush by her ear and jumped, startled, but it was only two birds with wings the color of the sky. They fluttered past her, twirling together in the air, before flying toward the Mistwood and disappearing into its fog. Koffi steeled herself.

Her feet seemed to move of their accord as she began to walk closer to the woods' edge. With each step, she expected someone to stop her, but the garden was empty and no one did. Her heartbeat quickened as the looming trees seemed to grow taller right before her eyes, alongside an anticipation. She stopped again, now only a few feet from the trees, and drew in a breath.

A quiet fell over everything as Koffi extended her hand, letting the mist's curling tendrils wrap around her fingers in ribbons of white. They were silken to the touch, soft, as the cool mist encircled her wrist. A smell like freesia suffused the air and she breathed in, feeling an odd sense of calm.

"Koffi!" A voice cracked through the silence like the snap of a dry branch, ripping Koffi from that calm. She turned in time to see Makena racing toward her. Her eyes were wild with terror.

"Get away from it!" she screamed. "Get away before it—"

Koffi turned back to the mist, but it was too late. The curling tendrils of mist that had encircled her wrist turned ice-cold, constricting. She tried to pull away, but like fingers, the mist fettered around her wrists. She felt hands snatching at her ankles, her dress, her hair, each touch chilling her blood. Panic clawed its way through her as she thrashed, trying to free herself to no avail. It was clear now: The Mistwood was pulling her in.

"Koffi, hold on!" Warm arms wrapped tight around her waist, tugging her away from the trees. Makena. She heard the strain as the girl pulled with all her might, pulled until Koffi's arms felt as though they might be ripped away. A dull roar filled her ears. The chill in her arms was snaking through her body now, and it was getting harder and harder to fight the Mistwood's pull.

"No!" Makena screamed again, and there was a desperation in her voice. Koffi felt it happen all at once, in a kind of slow motion. Makena turned her body so that both of their sides were facing the Mistwood. Koffi's eyes squeezed shut as a sudden blast of its cold air grazed her cheek. There was a pause, and she felt the mist's grip on her arm loosen at the same time Makena's did. Koffi opened her eyes, relieved for only a second, before she was doused in a new horror.

The mist had taken hold of Makena.

Koffi commanded her body to move, but it wouldn't listen. She could only watch as sinuous ropes of translucent white wrapped around Makena's body—like vines, like snakes. She saw the raw fear in Makena's eyes, the tears.

"Koffi!" Her voice was tight and strangled. "Help me!"

Koffi made to grab at her, but it was too late. She could only watch as the mist dragged Makena into the woods and out of sight.

CHAPTER 6

BLOOD TRAITOR

Ekon's breath hitched as he took in each of the warriors.

His eyes flitted back and forth, from their faces to their blades. A panic set in slowly. He watched, with some detachment, as one of them tossed Mwongo a coin purse twice the size of the one Themba had given him. The young man took it and nodded before disappearing into the dark. Ekon felt the distant burn of anger, of betrayal, but the situation at present didn't allow him to linger on either emotion long. He counted the warriors—one, two, three—and realized almost instantly that he knew all of them. Chiteno and Fumbe were two years his senior; they'd been initiated into the Sons of the Six the same year as his brother. He'd last seen them in the temple's prisons, when he'd helped Koffi escape right under their noses. Judging by the identical sneers on their faces, they remembered that, but he didn't care. Beside them stood another young warrior, the smallest of the trio. Ekon felt a stab of pain as he met Fahim's eyes.

"Ekon?" Lightning flashed overhead as his former co-candidate stepped forward in the dark. He wore the full attire of an anointed

Son of the Six tonight: a knee-length blue kaftan, a golden belt, and an embroidered cloak. His hanjari dagger was sheathed at his hip, and his topknot of braids was neatly tied up. He looked every part the warrior, except for the horror on his face.

Ekon reacted instinctively, reaching for his own dagger, and felt his stomach sink when he grasped at air instead. Of course. Two days later, he still wasn't used to his hanjari's absence. He'd given it to Koffi, which meant he was without a weapon now.

"Stay back." He said the words with as much menace as he could, but kept his voice low. Chiteno and Fumbe tensed, but Fahim's eyes widened.

"Ekon, what are you doing?"

Ekon opened his mouth, then closed it. He'd been prepared for aggression, accusation, but not this. His old friend sounded genuinely confused. Ekon took a deep breath, steeling himself.

"I'm leaving, Fahim. It's for the best."

"Ekon." Fahim sounded hesitant. "You've been summoned by the Kuhani. He wants to speak with you, wants to know if you've heard from Brother Ugo. No one's seen him in days."

At the mention of Brother Ugo's name, Ekon flinched, then shook his head. "I'm not coming back to the temple."

Chiteno and Fumbe bared their teeth, but Fahim's face reflected nothing but shock. Ekon understood why. For years, they'd been trained to obey authority. The Kuhani was the city's highest authority, and defying him was a transgression of the highest order.

"But . . ." Fahim's voice was small. He looked less like a warrior now and more like a young man full of uncertainty. "Ekon, y-you have to. You need to come home."

"I don't, and I'm not." Ekon prayed his voice sounded stronger than he felt. "I'm sorry, Fahim."

"Enough of this!" Chiteno was advancing now, his hand on the hilt of his hanjari. There was no confusion or reserve in his gaze, only irritation. "If he won't come willingly, he will come by force."

Fumbe was advancing now too, and something in Ekon's chest fell when even Fahim withdrew his blade. He shook his head.

"Please don't do this." He raised his hands as the three warriors neared. "Don't come any closer, or I'll—"

"Or you'll *what*, Okojo?"

Ekon started as another voice permeated the darkness from his left, a voice he knew well. As if cued, Shomari, his second co-candidate, appeared from the shadows with a leer.

"Or you'll *what*?" he repeated, a goading in his voice. "You'd raise a hand against your own brothers, men you swore loyalty to before gods?" He spat on the ground and shook his head in disgust. "I always knew you were a coward, but I didn't think you were a *blood traitor* too."

Ekon winced. The Yabahari people had few insults more grievous than *blood traitor*. To be called one meant you'd done the worst thing: betrayed your people, your heritage, your *kin*. Shomari watched his words find their mark and grinned, though it didn't reach his eyes. Ekon shook his head.

"Shomari—"

"You're just lucky the Kuhani and the brothers of the temple ordered us to bring you in alive." He spoke over Ekon with gritted teeth. "Because I'd kill you where you stand, if I was permitted it. You deserve it, and I'm not the only one who thinks so."

Another ribbon of lightning streaked across the sky, followed almost immediately by a clap of thunder; the deluge of rain Ekon had predicted fell in a sudden torrent. The drops blurred his vision, but he kept his gaze trained on Shomari. In his periphery, he sensed more than saw Fahim and the other two warriors closing in on him. His fingers tapped his thigh frantically, trying to think of a plan.

One-two-three. One-two-three. One-two-three.

"But no," Shomari continued, his voice soft. "I think, in the end, it's more just to let you live. There are so many people who want to see you: the Kuhani, the brothers of the temple . . ." His eyes gleamed. "Kamau."

He hadn't laid a hand on him, but Ekon felt the sting of that name, the instantaneous pain. *Kamau.* In his mind, he recalled everything: fighting with Kamau like he'd never fought with him before, the manic look in his older brother's eyes brought on by the hallucinogenic leaf he'd been poisoned with. He remembered knocking his brother out cold, leaving his unconscious body in the temple. Guilt twisted in Ekon's side like a knife.

Thunder rumbled, and Shomari's eyes danced with new malice. "It's good your father died all those years ago," he said in a voice only Ekon could hear. "Better that he didn't live long enough to see the disgrace you've become."

He's goading you. He wants you to react. A rational part of Ekon understood that, but it felt further and further away. The downpour of rain soaked through his clothes, a chill seeped into his pores, but at the mention of Baba, Ekon felt something catch fire within him. The anger burned through him in a blaze, only stopping when it reached the imaginary monster in his chest, the one that wanted blood. He did not try to temper the creature as it awoke in a howl of rage, and he did not mind when his vision turned red.

Tear them apart. Three words. *Tear them apart.*

The warriors were closing in on him now—Chiteno and Fumbe moving so that they were at his three and six, Shomari and Fahim at his twelve and nine. It was a maneuver he recognized well, one he'd practiced many times. They were going to try to surround him, trap him. In unison, all four warriors took a step forward, tightening their perimeter. Ekon braced himself, balling his hands into fists, readying himself to let loose the imaginary monster at last. He tensed, then:

"STOP!"

Ekon jumped, and the warriors stopped their advance to look over his shoulder. Themba was now standing in the middle of the street with her hands raised. Her headwrap was slightly askew, revealing white hair beneath. With her wet clothes, she looked even smaller than normal, exhausted. Ekon stiffened. He'd entirely forgotten about her in his distraction. From the looks on the warriors' faces, they had too.

"Let us go," she called above the rain, "and no one will get hurt."

A beat passed in which no one spoke, and then Fumbe and Chiteno sniggered. Fahim looked to her, confused, and Shomari's brows rose.

"What's this?" His voice trembled as he began to laugh. His eyes cut back to Ekon. "First you run off with that Gede girl, now you've hired an old woman to be your bodyguard?"

It wasn't true, but Ekon's face burned anyway. He tried to meet Themba's eye, imagined he'd see some mirror of the fear he felt himself. Instead, he saw a steel in her gaze, a determination he realized was familiar to him. Themba looked the same way Koffi did when she was about to do something reckless.

"Last chance," said Themba. She was eyeing the warriors now. "Let—us—go."

Shomari waved a dismissive hand and kept walking. He was within a few yards of Ekon now; he'd soon be at arm's reach. Ekon counted his steps, planning out exactly when he would lunge. A surprise attack was the only option now, but it had to be perfectly timed. His gaze dropped to Shomari's feet.

Twelve steps away. Eleven . . . ten . . .

Without warning, Shomari stopped short, rocking his head back as though he'd been struck by something. Slowly, his eyes rolled into the back of his head. His face grew slack. Startled, Ekon looked to the other warriors. Whatever was happening to Shomari seemed to be happening to them too; each one of them appeared to be frozen still, gazes vacant. Ekon felt the waves of a new terror.

"Ekon!"

He looked past the warriors and did a double take. Themba's hands were raised higher; she was still getting drenched by the rain, but something about her had changed. He was too far away to discern what.

"Ekon!" When she said his name again, her voice was shrill. Ekon watched her chest rise and fall. "I can't hold all four of them for long, go!"

Can't hold all four of them? The truth made Ekon's stomach lurch. He looked back and forth, from Themba to the warriors, with new understanding.

It's her. She'd doing this to them.

"Go!" she shouted again. "It's you they want, I'll catch up!"

Ekon hesitated a second longer, then took off. His steps were unsteady in the mud, he sucked the breath he took in sharp gasps. Behind him he heard someone yell, and then more footsteps behind him.

"Go!" He didn't dare look over his shoulder, but he knew that was Themba's voice. "Turn up ahead!"

Ekon's eyes searched the darkness until he saw it: a narrow backstreet filled with empty laundry lines. He ducked beneath them, and when he looked back, Themba was doing the same. He breathed relief as they fell into the alley's shadows and crouched.

"Did we lose—?"

Themba clapped a hand over his mouth. Seconds later, footsteps sounded just outside the alley. Ekon heard the metallic scrape of daggers being unsheathed. Blood pounded in his ears.

"Which way did they go?" He heard a voice, Chiteno's, ask the question.

"I didn't see," said Fahim.

"Head south," said Shomari's voice. "If they're trying to leave the city, that's the direction they're most likely to go in. Send word to the Kuhani as well."

Ekon listened until their footfalls had faded. Almost immediately, Themba stood.

"What are you doing?" he whispered.

"We have to keep moving," said Themba, but her voice was thin, weak.

Ekon looked up and down the alley. As far as he could see, they were alone. "No." He tried to sound forceful, and when he caught

Themba by her wrist, she did not resist as he helped lower her to the ground. She sighed.

"You need to catch your breath," said Ekon.

"Bad luck." Themba let her head gently thud against the wall behind her. She closed her eyes. "I haven't worked with that much splendor in a long time. I forgot how exhausting it is."

Ekon fidgeted a moment, uncertain, then asked the question he'd been thinking. "What exactly did you do back there?"

Themba cracked one eye in answer, and the ghost of a smile touched her lips. "When the splendor moves through my body, I can use it to manipulate the minds—and by extension, bodies—of other people. I can suppress pain receptors, make it so that you don't feel anything. I'm particularly good at temporary paralysis." She smirked. "It's how I earned my nickname the Cobra."

For a long pause, Ekon didn't know what to say.

"We need to figure out a new way to get out of here," Themba continued. "Quickly."

"We'll come up with something," Ekon said, hoping his voice held more ease than he felt. "I know we—" He suddenly stilled, tense. The downpour had lessened to a drizzle, and in the new quiet, he thought . . .

"Themba," he whispered, rising to his feet. "Do you smell—?"

His words were cut off as a blade came to rest at the hollow of his throat.

CHAPTER 7

THε MISTWOOD

For several seconds, Koffi was immobile.

She stared, unmoving, into the white tendrils of the mist, watching as they spiraled and curled in the silence. One would never have known that, just seconds ago, Makena had been dragged into that very mist writhing, screaming. The world had returned to silence with an unsettling indifference.

Koffi! Help me!

Each time she saw Makena's face, heard her plea, a stab of pain twisted between Koffi's ribs. It was illogical to feel this way, to grieve someone she'd only known for the space of an hour or so. But when she was honest with herself, she knew why she did. Makena had been nothing but kind to her. She'd been patient, understanding, encouraging. Koffi looked down at herself. Makena had made the very clothes on her back.

She tried to prepare herself for the singular thought rising in her consciousness, the one she'd known would inevitably come the moment Makena disappeared, but that made it no easier to face when the words finally took shape.

This is your fault. Your *fault.*

Koffi flinched against that truth. Makena was gone, and it *was* her fault. She thought of the way she'd looked back in the bed-chamber, when she'd first brought up the Mistwood. Makena hadn't simply been afraid—she'd looked terrified. That should have been enough to make any person with common sense steer clear, but it hadn't. Why? Koffi tried to rationalize her decision to approach the Mistwood. Every reason she came up with now seemed unbelievably foolish. The simplest answer was brief; she'd gone to the Mistwood because she'd felt drawn to it, because she'd been curious.

And now your curiosity has cost Makena her life.

Another truth crept into her mind, quieter, uglier. Makena was yet another person paying for her mistakes. It'd been Mama and Jabir first, when she'd gambled their freedom on a foolhardy bet without their consent. Then there'd been Ekon; in the Greater Jungle, he'd paid for her mistakes too. Now Makena was another name on that list.

People around you get hurt, a voice in her head said. *People around you end up worse off for knowing you.*

Tears pricked in Koffi's eyes as the words set in, branding themselves to her with a terrible sting. A part of her agreed with that voice. Maybe people were better off for not knowing her. Maybe it was easier to accept that, to give up.

No. She was surprised to feel the word reverberating through her like a struck chord, humming. *No. I will not accept that.*

She had failed Mama and Jabir, and she had failed Ekon, but this time would be different. She would not fail Makena. Makena, who'd been kind to her. Makena, who'd she'd only just met.

No, I will not give up.

Koffi lifted her chin as she stared into the Mistwood again. The acacia trees were still draped in mist, only visible for a foot or so. She listened. There was no sound around them, no sign of Makena at all, but a thought snagged on her and held fast.

She couldn't just stand here anymore. She had to do something.

She glanced over her shoulder, wary, as an idea began to take shape. No one else was in the garden, she was alone, which meant no one would see what she was about to do. She took a deep, steadying breath as she turned to face the trees again.

You have to try, she told herself. *For Makena, you have to try.*

A chill passed over her as she took another step toward those trees, then another. She'd expected the mist to reach for her the closer she got them, as it had before, but nothing happened as she drew nearer for a second time. The opaque wall of white was inches from her now, stretching in both directions for what seemed like an eternity. She sucked in a breath as she took another step forward, and it began to envelop her.

For Makena. Do it for Makena.

That was her last thought before she stepped into the Mistwood.

A hush fell over everything at once.

Koffi had expected that, but she still shivered as she plunged into the darkness. She'd only taken one small step to enter the Mistwood, but the change had been instantaneous; the sun had vanished. Around her, the mist coiled, reminding her of so many snakes twisting through the air. She held out her hands, feeling her way forward, and without warning a sharp pain lanced through one of them. She snatched it back quickly and watched as a line of bright red blood bloomed along the back of it. When she looked closer, she saw that she had sliced it on one of the acacia tree's thorns. They stood silent around her and seemed to be watching, waiting. Koffi blotted the blood with her dress and kept walking, taking care to be more mindful. Already the mist's chill was beginning to settle over her, to draw goose bumps from her skin.

"Makena?" Her voice echoed, sounding strange. She thought she heard the patter of feet, a movement directly to her right, but when she turned, she saw nothing but trees. Her pulse leaped. It was all too easy to think about the face she thought she'd seen from the window now, the way the mist had wrapped itself about Makena and pulled at her so viciously. She swallowed hard.

"Makena?" No answer.

Koffi picked up her pace, trying to temper the feeling of dread skittering up her legs. She tried to walk in a straight line, to maintain some vague sense of direction, but it was getting harder and harder to differentiate one tree from another. She heard a chirping sound above and jumped, waiting to see birds, but there was nothing. Her hands began to tremble. There'd been a mist in the Greater Jungle too, but that one had been different. That one had been confined to one place, and she'd had Ekon when she'd gotten caught in it. She hadn't been alone, and the gravity of that difference seemed to grow heavier with every step she took.

You're alone here, a voice in her head reminded her. *All alone.*

"Makena?" She called the girl's name a third, desperate time, and in response something screeched in the distance. The sound was shrill, long, inhuman. The hairs on the back of her arms stood on end, and she stopped short. What had that been? It hadn't sounded like Makena at all. She quickened her steps, flinching when another thorn snagged on one of the twists in her hair.

Don't stop, she told herself. *Don't stop.*

Another screech tore through the air, closer, and she broke into an outright run. Some distant part of her realized she was getting lost, losing any semblance of direction she'd had. Another thorn sliced through the sleeve of her dress, cutting her upper arm and drawing blood. Her throat went dry; panic fluttered in her chest. New thoughts began to descend. What if she never found Makena? What if she got stuck in here? What if—?

Child.

Koffi stopped as a new voice filled her consciousness. It took her a moment to recognize it as Badwa's. The goddess of the jungle's voice sounded gentle in her mind, but firm.

Take a deep breath, child, said imaginary Badwa. *Calm yourself.*

That command felt impossible, but Koffi tried. She inhaled and exhaled, once, twice, and then a third time. Her heartbeat slowed.

Do not run from your emotions, imaginary Badwa went on. *Acknowledge them.*

Acknowledge them. Koffi took a fourth breath, in and out. In the Greater Jungle, Badwa had tried to teach her the basic rules of using the splendor as a daraja. She'd learned that the splendor was an energy, one that could only be channeled properly when one was emotionally sound. Back then, she'd only worked with a small amount of it, but now ... Koffi closed her eyes. Already, she could feel the difference. She'd taken the splendor that Adiah had held in her body for more than ninety-nine years. Her choice to do so had gone against a natural order; darajas were only meant to channel the splendor, not keep it within their bodies. She felt a sudden, sharp throb at the base of her skull, a pressure in her chest. She was doing what Adiah had done, retaining a power she had no business retaining. For Adiah, doing so had turned her into the Shetani, a monster; Koffi wondered what holding on to this amount of the splendor would do to her.

She shook the thought from her mind, trying to refocus on the matter at hand. Fedu had wanted Adiah to use the splendor to destroy, and because of that she'd kept all of it in. But a new thought came to her. What if she could use a small bit of the splendor in her body for something else? There was a risk in that, but . . .

Makena. For Makena, you have to try.

Koffi planted her feet on the ground, trying to keep herself as anchored to the earth as she could. She knew what she had to do now, and that it wasn't going to be easy. Earlier, Makena had asked her if she was all right, and she hadn't been ready to talk about it. Now she made herself identify every emotion one by one.

I'm not all right. She forced herself to reckon with that truth. *I'm not all right at all. I'm sad.* There was a strange freedom in that word. *I miss my home, my mama. I miss Jabir, and I miss Ekon.*

What else? imaginary Badwa asked.

I am angry. Koffi felt something come to life in her bones. She was tempted to wrangle it back to her as she felt it burn through her core, but she let it free, felt its truth. *I am angry at Fedu, for what he did to Adiah, for what he's done to the darajas here. I'm angry at* ... She stopped.

Go on.

I'm angry that, deep down, I'm scared. Koffi exhaled. *I'm scared of what he can do to me, scared of what he can do to the people I care about. I'm scared that his plans are going to succeed and that I won't be able to stop them.* Koffi's eyes were still closed, but beneath their lids she felt the sting of tears. This time she did not try to stop them as they fell. After a beat, imaginary Badwa spoke.

Good. Now, reach.

Koffi needed no further instruction; she reached for the splendor like an instinct. Her balled fists unclenched as she turned her hands so that their palms were facing upward. A new heat burgeoned in her chest, and she felt a lifting sensation though she knew she was still on the ground. In the end, she felt the splendor before she saw it. She felt the magnitude of it, the new level of power coursing through her. Koffi understood now. Fedu had always equated the splendor with destruction, a power to be taken and weaponized. But that was a choice, a choice Koffi had all the power to make for herself. It wasn't safe to use all the splendor stored in her body, but she could use a tiny fraction of it, if she was careful. It required tremendous restraint. She remembered the analogy Badwa had once used to describe it: like pouring only drops of water from a vase full to the brim. Koffi felt the rest of the energy building like a dam, but she released only a little, just enough. Slowly, she opened her eyes.

Tiny speckles of golden light floated around her, bobbing and twinkling like stars in a night sky. Relief flooded her at the sight of them. The speckles of light emitted no sound, but hung close to her, as though waiting.

"I'm trying to find my friend." This time Koffi spoke aloud. "Show me where she is."

She watched as, at once, the speckles of light grew brighter, rose higher. In the brilliance, they illuminated everything, pushed the mist back. Koffi looked around. The acacias were easier to see now, and from a distance her eye caught something. Her heart stuttered in her chest. There were several people gathered around the base of one of the trees, their backs to her as they stooped.

"Hey!" she called out, taking a step toward them. "Hey, are you—?" The words died in her throat as one of the people turned toward her, and a chill skittered up her frame. The face she was staring back at was human, but only just. Its skin was brown like hers, but touched with a grayish tinge, translucent. She met the place where its eyes should have been, and saw two hollow cavities, then the gaping, overlarge hole where a mouth should've been. The others turned, and Koffi saw their faces were the same.

"Who . . . who are—?" Her gaze shifted down to the thing the figures were huddled around. Her heart jolted in her chest as she caught a glimpse of yellow, a head of springy black hair.

"Get away from her!" Koffi's voice cracked as she screamed, but the people—if they could be called that—only continued to stare at her. Their empty eyes betrayed no expression, but one of them slowly stood and let its head tilt to one side.

"Leave her alone." Koffi's voice was raw. "Please!"

But the figures remained still, unbothered. Koffi glanced again at Makena's body. From here, she couldn't tell if Makena's eyes were open, if she was breathing. She looked up to the speckles of light still hovering above. Another idea came to her. She focused on those speckles of light, poured a tiny bit more splendor into each of them. They grew brighter, almost impossible to look at. She heard a low moan and looked down. Another one of the figures had stood more quickly, raising a hand to shield its face from the onslaught of light. Koffi grimaced and directed more of the splendor into the lights. She felt their heat even from afar as they blazed, felt the satisfaction as the third figure stood, and all three of them began to move away from Makena's body, their eerie mouths still agape.

"Go!" Koffi commanded. "GO!"

The figures continued to back away from the light, horrible rasps and screeches escaping them. Koffi pushed the speckles of light toward them, and they began to limp away. She waited until she could see them no more, then ran to the place where Makena lay. She saw now that the girl was on her side, hugging her knees with a ducked head so that her face was obscured. Her eyes were open, but she didn't appear to have seen Koffi.

"Don't hurt her," Makena said in a small voice, staring at the ground. "Please don't hurt her. No, no, no, please, please, please . . ."

"Makena." Koffi grabbed the girl by her shoulders, trying to lift her so that she was upright. "Makena, wake up. It's me."

But if Makena had heard her, she gave no indication of it. Her head lifted; her eyes were open, but they were blank, unseeing. "Make it stop," she moaned. "Please don't hurt her."

A shiver passed through Koffi. Her? Whatever Makena was seeing now, it wasn't real. She pressed a hand to the girl's cheek.

"Makena," she said softly. "It's all right. You're all right. Come back."

One second passed, and then another. Makena's eyes began to flutter. She blinked several times, then shook her head. When she looked at Koffi, her confusion was plain.

"Koffi? What are you doing here?"

"I came to get you." Fresh tears welled in Koffi's eyes. "I'm so sorry. I'm so sorry I let them take you."

"I . . . I remember." Makena looked around them, at the looming mist and surrounding trees. "We were in the garden, and I saw the Mistwood take you. I tried to stop it . . ."

"You saved my life, Makena." The truth in the words felt solemn when Koffi them aloud. "You saved me. Now it's my turn to save you."

Makena's eyes were still widening, as something appeared to be dawning on her. "Koffi, we shouldn't be here." She shook her head. "We can't be here. There are things in the Mistwood, things that—"

"We're going to find a way out," Koffi assured her. "I promise." She hoped she sounded more confident than she felt. In truth, she had no idea how they were going to get out.

"But—"

"Trust me." As she said it, Koffi's eyes lifted to the speckles of light one more time. She prayed with all her might that this would work.

We need to get out. She thought the words instead of saying them this time. *Please help me. Help us.*

For several long, terrible seconds, she wondered if it wouldn't work. Her breath grew shallow as she waited, and even Makena stopped looking around. Then Koffi watched as the speckles of light slowly fell again, dimming so that it didn't hurt to look at them anymore. They descended and began to split and multiply, over and over, until they'd formed what was unmistakably a lit path hovering inches from the ground.

"There!" Koffi was on her feet at once. "We need to follow that trail of lights." She turned to Makena again. "Can you stand?"

Makena nodded, trying to rise. Koffi helped her to her feet. The girl looked wary as they both watched the speckles of light continue breaking into smaller pieces, as the path seemed to disappear into the mist.

"Koffi, are you sure?" Makena's voice was weak. "Are you sure this will take us back?"

No. That was the honest answer, but Koffi didn't say it aloud. Instead, she looped her arm under Makena's waist to steady her. "It's the only chance we have. Come on."

Koffi kept her eyes trained on the speckles of light as they made their way through the maze.

With every passing second, she was sure that they would dim, abandon them. But the light held like a candle, only flickering sporadically as they walked. The silence held until Makena spoke.

"Thank you," she whispered. "For coming to get me."

"It was nothing." Koffi braved a smile. "Honestly, it was the least I could do. I should never have gotten so close to the Mistwood."

Makena shook her head. "I was vague when you asked me about it earlier. I should have told you what happens to people who come here."

Koffi shifted, slightly uncomfortable, but she asked the

question on her mind anyway. "When I found you, you were talking about someone. You . . . you said 'don't hurt her.'"

Makena's jaw clenched. She looked as though she might cry again. "Before you came, I was having a nightmare," she said softly. "Or at least it felt like one. Except, I wasn't asleep." She dropped her gaze. "But it was like . . . I was trapped in my mind, seeing all the worst things my imagination could come up with, all the bad memories, all of my worst fears." She looked at Koffi again. "I saw my sister, Ife. She was the last member of my family that I saw before Fedu stole me. In the nightmare, Fedu was hurting her. I knew it wasn't possible, wasn't real, but I couldn't wake myself up. I felt like I was losing my mind. I've never felt so bad before in my life."

"I'm sorry," said Koffi softly.

"What did *you* see?" Makena asked. "When you came into the Mistwood?"

"What do you mean?"

"What was your nightmare? How did you break yourself out of it?"

Koffi frowned. "I didn't have a nightmare when I came into the Mistwood."

"But . . ." Now it was Makena's turn to frown. "How could that be? Why wouldn't the Mistwood affect you the way it affected me?"

Koffi considered the question, trying to come up with an answer, but in truth she was finding it harder and harder to focus. A sudden wave of fatigue was seeping into her body and seemed to grow more overwhelming with each step.

"Koffi?" She heard Makena's voice now, concerned. "Koffi, what's wrong?"

Koffi opened her mouth to try to speak, but found that she could not. The dull throbbing in her head had returned, a pounding in her temples.

Too much. Koffi heard the words, but they sounded farther away. *Too much,* said a voice in her head. *You've used too much of the splendor.*

"Koffi!" She heard Makena's voice now, frantic. "I can see the garden!"

The words sounded even farther now. Koffi stumbled, and several of the light speckles flickered. Up ahead, she thought she saw a new light, an opening in the mist. If she could just hold on a bit longer, follow those lights . . .

"Koffi, we're almost there!" said Makena. "Hang on!"

There was a tremble in Koffi's legs now. Her eyelids were growing heavier, and there seemed to be an increasing weight with every step. The speckles of light were dimming now, disappearing along with the last reserves of her energy. She'd used so much of the splendor. *Too much . . .*

"Koffi, we're here!" said Makena. "We made it."

There was a sudden burst of light and warmth that brought Koffi to her knees; it took her a moment to recognize it as the sun. She collapsed on her back and heard a soft thud as Makena did too, feeling the prickle of the garden's grass on the backs of her arms and legs. In the distance, she heard birds chirping again, someone laughing. She exhaled in relief. They'd made it back. They were safe. For several seconds, neither of them said anything. Finally, Makena broke the silence.

"Koffi," she whispered. "How did you summon those lights, the ones that led us back here?"

"I don't know." Koffi was still trying to catch her breath. The edges of her vision were still slightly blurred, and she felt as though she'd just spent the last hour running. Every muscle in her body ached. "I'd never done it before."

Makena sat up, propping herself on an elbow. She looked uncertain, as though she was trying to search for the right words. "Koffi, what you just did has never been done before. It defies every rule we've ever known about the Mistwood, it should have been—"

"Impossible."

At once, both of them turned. Koffi's heart plummeted as her eyes met Zain's. He was standing several yards away, watching them. Perhaps he'd been there the whole time. His expression was inscrutable except for his eyes; they were wide with horror. He stepped forward, his gaze trained on them.

"You two need to come with me. Now."

CHAPTER 8

The ENTERPRISE

"Don't move."

Ekon obeyed, even as his pulse quickened. He didn't recognize the voice that had just spoken, and he wasn't sure if that made this situation better or worse.

The knife at his throat was withdrawn momentarily, and his eyes automatically shut as something rough—a strip of burlap cloth, more than likely—was tied around his eyes so that he couldn't see. To his left, he heard a scuffle, and then the blade returned, its press cool against his skin. He thought he felt something warm trickle down his neck.

"Up, old woman. Or I'll cut his throat."

Ekon couldn't see, but he heard the sound of Themba slowly rising to her feet. In the stilted silence, her breaths were short, shallow.

"Please." Ekon didn't dare turn around. "She needs to sit down, we just—"

"Silence, boy."

Ekon clamped his mouth shut as the blade dug deeper into his flesh. He tried to stay calm, but it was to no avail.

"Both of you, hands on your heads," said his captor. The voice was deep, slightly rugged, male.

Ekon forced his tapping fingers to still as he complied. He heard the rustle of fabric, footsteps, and then felt someone beside him, likely Themba.

"We're going to take a walk," said the voice. "Don't try anything funny."

Ekon swallowed. The knife's tip lowered to his back, and next to him he heard Themba's sharp intake of breath. Panic constricted in his chest.

"Move."

A sharp nudge prompted Ekon forward, and he heard Themba start walking too. With the blindfold on, it was more difficult to navigate the alley's uneven grounds, but he did his best to keep from stumbling. Beside him, Themba's breaths were still labored, and he prayed with all his might that she didn't pass out. She'd looked so exhausted before, and he didn't know what their captor would do if she fell.

He shifted focus, listening to and counting the crunch of feet in the dirt.

One-two-three. Three.

There were three sets of footsteps here—his, Themba's, and their captor's. In normal circumstances, those odds might have been favorable, but not when two of the three were blindfolded and without decent weapons.

Gods-smite.

Ekon tried to steady his breathing as they walked down the

alleyway, tried to imagine who their captor was. Clearly, he wasn't a Son of the Six; Ekon had never heard the man's voice before, and if he had been a warrior, he would have called the others by now. He could have been a street hyena, desperate for some coin, but if that'd been the case, he would have just taken their bags and run. A sudden thought came to Ekon, and a chill broke out across his skin.

Bounty hunter.

It made sense. Bounty hunters weren't common in Lkossa, but it wasn't unheard of to see one in the city, particularly if there was an unusually high bounty posted. He thought of what Mwongo had said before, about how much the Kuhani wanted him. No doubt the old man had posted a sizable amount of money for his capture. He would have announced that Ekon was still in the city. For someone whose job was to capture fugitives, it was easy money.

"Sir." Ekon knew he wasn't supposed to be talking, but he couldn't stop himself. "Please, if it's money you're after—" He winced as the knife cut through his tunic, pierced skin.

"I said, *be quiet.*" There was a real menace in his captor's voice now. "You're in enough trouble."

He heard Themba wheeze, and a stab of new panic ran through him. There hadn't been time for him to look down the alley when he and Themba had run into it, and he couldn't remember now what was at the end of it. A hard lump rose in his throat, impossible to swallow.

"Turn left here," said the captor.

Ekon stopped short, surprised. They'd only walked a few feet, so there was no way they were even out of the alley.

"Now."

He felt Themba move away from him as she obeyed, and after a pause, he did too. A door audibly creaked, and Ekon jumped when a large hand forced his head down. He stumbled slightly as the ground beneath him softened, and without warning the air around him changed. A sharp smell filled his lungs, so intense it brought tears to his eyes. He heard Themba, still beside him, begin to cough.

What's happening? His mind was racing now. *Are we being poisoned?*

Another nudge made Ekon keep walking, though his steps felt much heavier now. He was surprised to hear—in the not-so-far distance—the sounds of people talking, laughing. Despite his blindfold, he frowned. Clearly, they were inside some kind of building, but where, why?

He heard his captor clear his throat and push past him without a word. There was a sound like another door being opened, and then, without warning, he was grabbed by the front of his tunic and hauled forward. At once, the buzz of conversation he'd heard before died. There was a long silence, and then:

"Thabo, what is this?"

Ekon turned his head, confused. The voice that had just spoken was new, a woman's. He had no sense of direction, but he thought her words had come from his right. He swiveled, but before he could do anything else, his captor's voice thundered through the air.

"Thieves," he said irritably. "I caught them on my way in. They were hiding, more than likely planning to break in, and—"

"Wait!" Ekon's hands were still raised as he turned. "Wait,

that's not true!" When no one spoke, he added, "We weren't trying to steal anything. We were only hiding!"

There was a long pause. Then he heard the woman's voice again.
"Remove their blindfolds."

Ekon heard heavy footsteps behind him, felt a scratching sensation, and then the blindfold was yanked off his head. He blinked
several times as his eyes adjusted, taking in his new surroundings. Themba was next to him, as he'd guessed, and they were
both standing in the center of a room he'd never seen before. The
mud-brick walls reminded him of the apothecary, but this room
was much smaller and shabbier, windowless. The floor was well
worn in several places, and the ceiling was patched in its middle.
Its only light came from a single oil lamp set in the corner, which
just barely illuminated the people sitting on the floor around
him. Every one of them was wearing a hooded cloak to obscure
their face. His eyes cast to a rickety table, pushed to one corner of
the room. On it was what looked like a scale, and several small
cloth bags, neatly tied. His brow furrowed. Those kinds of bags
were familiar—he saw them all the time in Lkossa's markets. Those
were the bags merchants used for herbs and spices, which ratio-
nalized the smell in the room, but . . .

"Explain yourselves."

Ekon turned at the same time Themba did. Behind them
stood a man so tall, the top of his head nearly brushed the room's
ceiling. His curly black hair was thinning, but that was somewhat
compensated for by his woolly beard. When he spoke, Ekon felt
the hum of the man's voice in his bones. He knew immediately
that *he* had been the one who'd captured them.

"It's . . . it's like I said." He hated the stammer in his voice, but it couldn't be helped. "We weren't trying to steal from you, we didn't even know you were here. We were hiding."

The man's black eyes narrowed. "Hiding from *who*?"

"The Sons of the Six." It was Themba who interjected now. To Ekon's surprise, she sounded highly irritated. When he looked at her, her eyes were trained on the man. "Now, what *I* want to know," she said between her teeth, "is why this boy and I have been accosted and harassed by the likes of you."

"Yes, I'd like to know that too."

Ekon's eyes jumped from the man to a woman sitting on the floor. He recognized her voice as the one who'd spoken before. It was difficult to discern much of her in the dark, but he could see, even in this light, that her skin was the same dark brown as his. Her eyes appeared to be rimmed in black kohl, and her ebony hair was tied up in a headwrap similar to Themba's, so that only a fraction of her hairline was visible. She was looking up now at the man with a skeptical look.

"Thabo," she said softly. "Did you have any *proof* that these two people are actually thieves?"

Ekon looked back at the man in time to see him shift his weight from foot to foot uncomfortably. He looked less and less formidable by the second. "Well, no . . . but—"

The woman pinched the bridge of her nose, looking tired. "Thabo," she said with audible exasperation, "if I've said it once, I've said it a thousand times: You've got to use more discretion. These incidents are bad for business, word will get around if you continue to—"

"Wait a minute," said Ekon. "*Business*? You're *not* bounty hunters?"

Several of the cloaked people around the room chuckled. Even the man—Thabo—scoffed. For her part, the woman cracked a small smile.

"We are no more bounty hunters than you are apparently a thief, boy."

"But . . ." Ekon looked around the room. "If you're not bounty hunters, who are you?" His eyes fixed on the scale and the bags in the corner. He felt the blood drain from his face. "Wait, are you drug dealers?"

This time, there was no subtlety; everyone in the room except for him and Themba laughed openly. Ekon squirmed, uncomfortable, and his fingers began to tap against his leg. He didn't like this feeling, like he was missing the punch line of a very obvious joke. After a moment, Thabo dabbed at his eyes and grinned.

"We're not drug dealers, kid." He chuckled. "Our business is strictly in herbs."

"Uh . . ." Ekon gave him a dubious look. "Herbs, like . . . ?"

"*Lavender,*" Thabo said slowly. "Devil's claw, aloe, occasionally rooibos and bergamot."

"You're talking about real herbs," said Themba. She appeared to be as confused as Ekon. She gestured toward the tied bags in the corner. "These are the kinds of things you can get at the market."

"That's correct." The woman nodded.

"Then . . ." Themba's frown deepened. "Why do you keep your product here, hidden?"

Thabo looked uncomfortable again, but the woman's gaze stayed measured. "Normally, I would not disclose that sort of information," she said, folding her hands. "But if what you say is true, you two are on the run. You're as likely to go to the authorities as we are." She sat back a moment before she continued. "Our herbs are entirely legal, but our means of transporting them are not strictly aboveboard."

"What do you mean?" Ekon asked.

"Our business is not just in growing and selling eastern herbs and spices. We move them too," said Thabo. "Primarily south, to cities like Bandari, sometimes as far as Chini."

"Southern Eshōza is mostly marshlands," the woman explained. "Most of the spices and herbs that grow well here aren't suited to be farmed in that climate. That creates a high demand. People want herbs and spices for their food, medicine, cosmetics."

Ekon shook his head. "I still don't understand why you're holed up here, then. There are well-established merchant routes up and down eastern Eshōza. There's no reason to sneak the herbs south."

"Spoken like someone who's never paid Lkossan tax."

Ekon jumped. A heavyset figure to his right, another woman, had lowered her cloak's hood. She had light chestnut skin, iron-gray Bantu knots, and a cheeky glint in her dark eyes. Ekon noticed that she was surrounded by papers that looked to be covered with different numbers. "The Kuhani charges a hefty fee to anyone who takes Lkossan products out of the city." She made a face. "He calls it an 'export tax.'"

Ekon frowned. "Well, yeah, to make sure that some profit for Lkossan products always stays in Lkossa."

The woman in Bantu knots snorted. "That tax was levied to line the temple's pockets, and nothing more."

Ekon opened his mouth to argue—as a general rule, this sort of law-breaking made him itchy—but . . . but . . . a troubling thought had just occurred to him. He recalled the nice uniforms the Sons of the Six and brothers of the temple were permitted to wear, the fine meals they enjoyed. When he was honest with himself, he realized he'd never truly scrutinized how those things were paid for. He'd always assumed the people's tithes covered most of the temple's costs, but the more he considered it, the less likely that seemed.

"Fortunately, we have found an alternate solution to that particular problem," said the first woman. "My name is Ano, by the way." She nodded to the rest of the room. "You are looking at the founders of the East Eshōza Trading Enterprise."

"Also called the Enterprise," Thabo added helpfully.

"Very clever," said Themba curtly. Her arms were still crossed, her lips pursed.

"We apologize again for accosting you," said Ano. "But hopefully now you can understand why we're cautious."

"What *I* want to know," asked the woman in Bantu knots, "is why the two of you were hiding from the Sons of the Six in our alley in the first place."

Ekon exchanged a look with Themba. In truth, he wasn't sure how much was safe to say. In the end, she spoke before he could.

"The warriors intercepted us as we were trying to leave the city," she said. "We're headed south."

Ano's brows rose. "People don't normally go south by choice unless it's for trade. It's sparse terrain."

"My granddaughter was kidnapped," said Themba. Ekon noticed she omitted saying by who. "We believe that's where she was taken."

Ano's expression changed, and Thabo's eyes darkened. "My

sincere apologies," she said, sounding genuine. "Human trafficking along the eastern merchant roads is rare but, sadly, not entirely unheard of. I hope you are able to find her and bring her home."

The idea that occurred to Ekon hit him suddenly. "Could we ride south with you?" The words tumbled from him in a rush.

Ano raised one brow. "Excuse me?"

"We need to get south," Ekon said quickly. "It'll take us twice as long to travel on foot. But if we could ride with you—"

"I'm sorry, boy." Ano was already shaking her head. "I sympathize with your plight, but unfortunately, we are not in a position to help you."

"Wait!"

Everyone in the room looked up at once. One of the cloaked figures who'd been sitting in the shadows had just stood and was making their way forward. They stopped a few feet from Ekon, and when they pulled their hood back, he startled. The girl standing before him looked to be sixteen or seventeen. Her black hair was practically braided down her back, and she looked uneasy. It took him seconds to determine why she was familiar.

The market, he realized. *She's the girl from the market.*

"Safiyah?" Ano's brows were pinched in confusion. "What's wrong?"

The girl—Safiyah—looked around the room a moment before she spoke. "Earlier today, on my way back from one of my runs, two street hyenas started following me," she said quietly. "They cornered me in an alley, and they were going to take the herbs I was carrying." She looked to Ekon. "This boy . . . intervened."

Ekon almost laughed. *Intervened* was a polite word for what he'd done. Murmurs filled the room as some of the still-hooded people turned to each other, speaking in low voices. For her part, Ano looked at Ekon with new scrutiny.

"Is this true?" she asked Ekon.

"*Yes*, Ekon," Themba said under her breath. "*Is* this true?"

Ekon suddenly felt every eye in the room turn to him. He fidgeted, tapping his fingers. "Well, I didn't mean to." He flinched when the girl, who'd been watching, threw him a dirty look. "Uh, this is to say . . ." He stammered. "I *did* want to help, but not because I knew who she was or what she was carrying."

"But you did help her?" It was the Bantu-knot woman who asked this time. She seemed to be calculating something the longer she stared at him. A silence fell over the room as everyone waited for Ekon's answer.

"Yes," he said quietly. "I did."

"What are your names?" Thabo asked. "What are you called?"

"This is Themba," Ekon offered. "My name is Ekon Okojo."

Something flashed in Ano's eyes, so briefly he wasn't sure if it was real. At once, she sat up straighter on the ground, a new reserve in her gaze.

"We sincerely appreciate your help, Ekon." She sounded uncomfortable. "But that does not change my answer. Our trips south are carefully planned. We do not have the resources or the space to take on two additional—"

"Hold on."

Ekon looked up in time to see Thabo's expression changing to one of incredulity. His eyes were widening by the second; he looked shocked. To Ekon's surprise, he was looking right at Themba. "I know you."

In response, Themba jutted her chin. "I seriously doubt that, young man." Ekon wondered if he was the only one who heard the uneasiness in her voice.

"No." Thabo was shaking his head. "I mean, I don't know you, but I know *of* you. It took me a minute to remember, but then I saw the amulet."

Ekon's gaze dropped to Themba's hand. In fact, she was rubbing one of her thumbs along the amulet that hung from her neck. It was something she did all the time that he'd never paid much notice to, but Thabo was staring now with new comprehension.

"I recognize that amulet," he went on. "It's worn by the Cobra."

A new, excited buzzing filled the room that Ekon didn't understand. More people on the floor were pulling down their hoods, looking at Themba with interest. For her part, Themba's expression remained inscrutable, but Ekon thought she looked markedly uncomfortable. After a moment, she nodded in resignation.

"That's right. I am the Cobra."

Thabo stepped forward. "So it's true, then?" he asked. His eyes were alight, like a child who'd just discovered a secret kind of magic. "I've heard you can make a grown man stop moving, render someone completely immobile."

"She can." Ekon jumped in quickly, without thinking. Themba threw him a withering look, but he ignored it. "I saw her do it with my own eyes, just tonight. She took down four trained Sons of the Six on her own, without even laying a finger on them."

"Ooh." Thabo clapped his hands. "Would you be willing to try it on—?"

He stopped when Ano held up a hand, and Ekon recognized at once that there was a command in that simple gesture. The room quieted as, slowly, she stood. Upright, she was taller than Ekon had guessed.

"Themba." There was a new reverence in Ano's voice, and the woman offered a small bow of her head. "Your name and your powers are well known within certain circles of this city. It is an honor to meet you. As I mentioned before, however, we are a small operation. Our meals are rationed exactly for each trip we make to the south; the storage in our caravans is finite. We are neither outfitted nor equipped to take on extra—"

"That isn't entirely true, Ano." Bantu Knots spoke up again. She was now looking at the papers before her, a quill in hand. "If we reallocate five percent of the food portioned for breakfast each day, and increase our travel speed slightly, they could both join us at little to no additional cost."

Ekon looked to the woman appreciatively. He'd always had a fondness for people who understood the beauty in numbers.

"The Cobra's abilities are distinct," Thabo added. "Having her with us for the journey south could be useful."

"I don't know." A reedy, balding man toward the back of the room who hadn't spoken before shook his head. "I think I'm with Ano on this. We're risking enough as it is with the transport, taking two wanted fugitives with us just adds to our trouble."

Ano looked between the members of the Enterprise. "If we are not in agreement, then—per our company's bylaws—we will bring the matter to a vote. All opposed to allowing Themba and Ekon with us, indicate with a raised hand now."

Ekon had expected it, but he still felt a small stab of disappointment as Ano raised her hand, along with two other people in the room. Automatically, he counted them.

One-two-three.

"Very well," said Ano, lowering her hand. "Now all in favor, indicate by raising your hand."

Ekon felt a surge of gratitude as Thabo's hand went up first, followed by Bantu Knots. Another member of the Enterprise raised their hand too. He counted again.

One-two-three.

"Three to three, a tie," Ano announced. "We will need to break it. Safiyah." She looked to the girl. "You did not vote."

All eyes went to Safiyah as she straightened. "I . . . want to abstain."

Ano shook her head. "Normally that would be permitted, but your vote is the deciding one. You must choose."

Safiyah looked around the room, and Ekon noted that she was careful not to look at him. A beat passed before she spoke.

"The Sons of the Six will be looking for them," she said. "It's not going to be easy to get them out of the city."

Ekon felt something in the pit of his stomach drop.

"But . . ." Safiyah hesitated. "I think we—*I*—owe it to them. So, I vote to let them come."

Ekon's heart leaped at the same time Ano made a face at Safiyah that implied she'd been betrayed. Several seconds passed before she looked back at Ekon.

"The vote is decided, then," she said with resignation. "It seems you two are now probationary members of the East Eshōza Trading Enterprise. Welcome. We leave Lkossa tomorrow."

PART TWO

WHEN THE LION KILLS, THE JACKALS REJOICE.

A Noble Lineage

BINTI

There is nothing so unpleasant to the mouth as the taste of hunger.

It rests in one's belly, chalky and bitter, until it rises to consume the senses. Even when I close my eyes at night to sleep, I cannot escape it; like a monster, it waits for me on the jagged edges of my dreams, in the darkest corners of my mind.

These days, I am always hungry.

Tonight, like so many nights in Lkossa's monsoon season, the wind bares all her teeth. No matter how tightly I hug my knees, there is no fending off the merciless bites of the cold. I flex my fingers, willing blood back to my veins, but it is no use. Beside me, Mama shivers.

The pair of us are camped in an alley several blocks south of Lkossa's central markets, watching the end of the Bonding Day celebrations from afar. I cannot help but notice what a difference even the short distance between myself and the night's revelers makes. They are enwrapped in a bliss that cannot reach me.

"Mama." My teeth chatter so hard, I can barely speak. "It's late. We should call it a night."

"Not yet." My mother's answer is immediate, though she doesn't look at me. Her eyes are fixed ahead. "Just a bit longer."

Outside the alley, the streets are littered with the remnants of festivity: empty glass bottles and discarded bags of throwing rice, shredded pieces of confetti, even tattered streamers of blue, green, and gold. This morning, brothers of the temple ambled through the streets, gifting sacks of grain to beggars and widows—Mama refused to take anything from them. I listened as their footfalls faded, and in their place the cheery jingle of a tambourine filled the air. For most of the day, little ones have run wild through these streets, but now the sun is down. This is an hour for older children, the ones like me who stand on the precarious line between adolescence and adulthood. Already, the black-veined sky is interrupted by intermittent columns of smoke, the consequence of bonfires. I can't see them from here, but I can imagine the girls dancing around them, the boys clustered in groups deciding which among them is prettiest.

I know, even now, that I will not participate in any dances tonight.

"Binti, look!"

At the sound of hope in my mother's voice, I look up, brought back to the present. Her eyes are wide and she's grinning, holding up a leather satchel by its strap. No doubt, she found it on the ground; its seams are worn, and it looks like at least one or two rats have already gotten to whatever was once inside of it. My mother brandishes it like a treasure.

"Mama, what is that?"

"A lucky find!" she exclaims. "Imagine what we could barter this for!"

"Mama." My voice comes out with a sharpness I did not plan to wield. "No one will barter for that."

Mama shakes her head emphatically. She's still examining the bag, inspecting its condition. "We won't get much, of course, but it's still worth—"

"Mama, it's garbage. Worthless."

My mother flinches, and I watch some of the light leave her eyes. Beneath the anger, I feel a stab of guilt. A year ago, I saw my mother differently. I still imagined her as a demigod. Things have changed. Mama is still beautiful, but her body is thinner; missed meals and a life on the move have sharpened the details of her face. She looks slightly hollowed now. We eat less since our move from the Kazi District, but it can't be helped. Last season, a daraja child on our old street was run over by a careless merchant's cart. The Kuhani did not levy charges against the merchant, and in the aftermath, Lkossa's darajas stormed the streets in protest. The merchant in question was eventually forced to pay a fine, but in the end, the daraja community paid much more. Shortly after the protest, the Kuhani decreed that no darajas or their kin could live in the Kazi District anymore. We have been in the Chafu District ever since.

Abruptly, my stomach seizes, sending hunger pangs through my body that are so sharp, I want to double over and scream. I know that Mama could use her affinity to numb that pain, but I don't ask; it isn't a good use of her already finite energy. I inhale, trying to calm myself, and instead take in a waft of the alley's refuse. It stinks, just like everything else in this part of the city. The pangs eventually subside, but they give way to more anger. These days, I'm always angry too.

"We should go, Mama," I finally say, clutching at my ribs. "No one else is going to come, we might as well—"

"Shh!" Mama puts a finger to her lips. "Look."

I turn again, expecting to see another of my mother's "finds," but what my eyes land on instead is very different. A man is making his way toward us on unsteady feet. He is young, perhaps my senior by only a few years, and dressed in a red wax-print dashiki that immediately informs me of what kind of family he must come from. His skin is oakwood-dark, sharp cheekbones define his face, and a chin touched by stubble tells me that if he didn't shave for a few days, he'd likely have a formidable beard. I surprise myself when I realize I find him handsome.

Mama tenses, and I clamp my mouth shut, bracing myself. We haven't had any foot traffic in hours, so this is likely our last shot for the night.

"Remember, let me do the talking," Mama says between her teeth. Neither of us moves as the young man continues his approach. Mama waits until he is within a few feet before she calls out her usual line.

"Excuse me, sir!" she says. "Spare some food or coin?"

The young man stops short, clearly startled, before his gaze settles on us in the dark. I can tell within seconds that, though he holds it well, he has been drinking. The smell of banana beer is pungent in the air around him. Those eyes, the ones I imagine might be sharp under normal circumstances, have a slightly unfocused look about them.

"Sorry?" the young man asks, frowning. There's a slight slur to his speech, but he is at least able to stand without wavering.

Still sitting beside me on the ground, Mama turns her palms

upward, which has the very convenient effect of making her look frail and helpless. "Please, kind sir," she says in a feeble voice that is entirely put on, "our Bonding Day has not been so fortunate. My daughter and I are hungry, if you happen to have coin or food."

I say nothing as we wait, though I am uncomfortable in the silence. After a moment, the young man's confused frown disappears.

"Oh." He smiles. "Sure, I'm happy to help." He reaches into the pocket of his dashiki and withdraws a small coin purse, but he doesn't give it to Mama. Instead, he turns to me, dropping to one knee so that our eyes are almost level. He puts the purse into my hands, then inclines his head.

"For a beautiful girl on a beautiful night."

Despite the evening's chill, a sudden heat rises in my face. There's nothing suggestive or lewd in the young man's eyes as he looks at me, only kindness. For several seconds, I'm not even sure what to say.

"Go on," he says, "open it."

Slowly, I lower my gaze and pull the purse's drawstring open. I can feel Mama's eyes on me as I do. Both of us exclaim when I look inside and see the bright golden gleam of dhabus, the most highly valued coins in the city. My heart skips a beat.

"Sir!" Even Mama seems at a loss for words. She takes the coin purse from me and weighs it in her hand. "This . . . this is generous."

The young man rises to his feet, albeit a bit unsteadily. A small smile still plays on his face. "It's nothing. Happy Bonding Day."

"What's your name?" Mama asks. "We can't possibly accept a gift like this without knowing the name of the man who's given it."

The young man inclines his head. "My name's Asafa. Asafa Okojo."

"Asafa." Mama repeats the name, still staring at the purse in disbelief. "We will never be able to repay this kindness."

Asafa waves a hand. "It's nothing," he says, "really."

"Still . . ." Mama suddenly exchanges a look with me, a look I unfortunately recognize. "You must allow us to show you our appreciation." It's her turn to grin. "Have you ever had your palm read?"

At once, I stiffen. Mama has deviated from the usual routine, and I no longer know what she's planning to do. My eyes cut from Asafa to her, then back again. To my dismay, he's looking at her with clear intrigue.

"I haven't," he says. "How does it work?"

"Sit, sit." Mama gestures toward the ground. Asafa considers a moment, then settles across from her, so close their knees are almost touching.

"Your dominant hand, please."

Asafa offers his right hand, and Mama takes it in her own. A strange, inexplicable jealousy pricks at me as she holds his hand, which is large and looks slightly calloused. Mama traces her index finger over the lines of his palm a moment, then looks up at him.

"You see this line?" she says. "It's long, which means you will have sons."

Asafa's brows shoot up. "Really?"

Mama nods solemnly. In actuality, I seriously doubt she has any idea what kind of children Asafa may have someday, but her acting is convincing. She points to another line. "And this one," she says, "this one means you will marry soon, to a beautiful woman."

There's no other word for it; Asafa looks a bit sheepish now. "I am courting a girl," he admits after a moment. "But I haven't asked her family's permission to marry."

Mama nods sagely. "The time to act will soon be at hand," she says. "But beware, she may break your heart, in the end."

Asafa leans forward. "Is there anything else?" There's a keenness in his voice. "Can you see anything else?"

Dread pools in my stomach as I watch my mother's smile change. There is a hard, flinty quality to it now, though I doubt Asafa can tell the difference in the dark. I watch as Mama draws his hand closer to her, tracing little circles in his palm.

"Oh yes," she says softly. "There is one more thing. But for this, you'll need to *look into my eyes*."

I realize a second too late what's about to happen. A cry rises in my throat, but it's not quick enough. I look on in horror as my mother's eyes change from brown to green, as her pupils slit. The moment Asafa meets her gaze, his own eyes roll back in his head. He slumps over with a heavy thud, and he does not move again.

"No!" I'm on my feet at once. "Mama, what did you do?"

"Calm yourself." Mama is already stowing the coin purse in her satchel, rising. "He's only unconscious." There's a disturbing hunger in her eyes now. "Come, help me check his pockets." When I don't move, she sucks her teeth and stoops down beside Asafa's limp body. She begins patting him down, feeling along the linings of his beautiful clothes. I shudder as she unclasps a golden chain from his neck, pulls a beautiful golden signet ring from his pinkie finger. I can't help but wonder if these things are precious to Asafa, family heirlooms perhaps. The longer I watch my mother, the sicker I feel.

"I don't understand," I whisper. "He was kind to us, he gave us money, and you're still stealing from him."

Mama remains crouched beside Asafa. She pinches a piece of his dashiki, looking almost wistful. "Judging by the quality of his clothes, I think he'll be just fine."

"But . . ." The words I want to say stick in my throat. I struggle to reconcile the emotions running rampant through my heart. I realize I'm angry, I'm sad, and . . . above all, I am embarrassed. Slowly, Mama rises again to look directly at me.

"His face is handsome, but don't be fooled, Binti," she says quietly. "He will change. He is young now, but he will grow up to become yet another person who hates and persecutes our people. There is us, and there is them, nothing in between. We have to take our wins where and when we can get them."

I remember the first time I heard someone call my mother by her other name, the Cobra. It seemed, back then, so categorically wrong for her. I used to think my mother was a demigod, a down-to-earth woman who wore her mortality like a swallowtail wears its wings. But I see something else now when I look at my mother. There is an edge to her that feels sometimes dangerous, predatory. I steel myself as the words pressing against my teeth escape me.

"This does nothing to change the way people look at darajas," I say, trying to keep the whine from my voice. "They think we're nothing but criminals who steal, and cheat, and hurt people.

When you do this . . ." I hate that there are tears in my eyes. "When you do this, all it does is prove those people right."

"What would you have me do instead, then, Binti?" Mama's gaze is hard now. "Would you have me clean rich men's homes, be a wet nurse to the children of the people who hate us?" She spits on the ground, and it's a strangely violent act. "We come from a noble lineage of darajas, a powerful one. Our foremothers would weep blood and tear their hair to see us in such subservience. I will not dishonor them that way."

"So you honor them as a thief?" I can't bite down those words as they rise from me. "I'll bet they're really proud."

Mama's expression hardens. "Don't you dare speak to me that way."

For several seconds, we glare at each other, matched in our anger. It's me who breaks first.

"I'm sorry, Mama." I press the heels of my palms into my eyes, trying to stop the tears from falling. "I'm sorry."

When I move my hands, Mama's expression has softened too. "I'm doing the very best I can, Binti," my mother murmurs. "I will do whatever it takes to protect my family."

It's not enough. I don't have the heart to say the words aloud, but that doesn't make them any less true. *No matter how hard you try, it'll never be enough.* And I know that's true. This is what it means to be a daraja in Lkossa. My mother's kind were once revered and praised—not anymore. Lkossa will never accept people like her.

Which means that, by default, they'll never accept me.

CHAPTER 9

THE KEY

Koffi walked alongside Zain through Thornkeep's halls, trying to keep up with his strides.

It had happened quickly. In one moment, she and Makena had been on the ground just outside the Mistwood, staring back at Zain with the same confusion with which he stared at them. Then, in a sudden lunge, Zain had grabbed Koffi with surprising strength and hauled her to her feet, saying nothing as he frog-marched her none too gently toward Thornkeep. Koffi had thought to run, to fight, even to plead as the boy's eyes fixed ahead, but each idea had flitted out her mind in the fashion with which it had come. The truth settled over her with dead weight.

She was caught.

It was clear—from the face he'd made to the way he was acting now—that Zain had seen *something*. Perhaps he'd seen it all, from Koffi's solo entrance into the Mistwood to her exit from it with Makena in tow. Maybe he thought he'd seen something else. Regardless, the farther and faster they walked, the more acutely the panic in Koffi's chest constricted, making it harder for her to breathe.

"Zain, stop." Behind them, Makena was following, nearly out of breath as she fought to keep up with them. "Where are you taking her?"

Zain didn't answer. Koffi glanced over her shoulder and met Makena's eyes, grateful. She was glad Makena was there, glad to have someone else fighting for her, but in truth she was scared. It was all too easy to cast her thoughts back to what had happened to that little girl this morning in the main hall. Fedu had harmed her just to make a point to Koffi; what would he do to Makena if he thought she'd actually helped her do something that displeased him?

Zain's head snapped left and right, and without warning, he steered Koffi down another hall. Unlike most of Thornkeep, there were no windows here, and in this darkness, Koffi felt a new stab of fear. He was taking her to Fedu, she was sure of it. Perhaps they would go to one of his personal chambers, a place with no audience. That scared her even more. What if the god wanted to know how she'd gone in and out of the Mistwood unscathed? It was a question she couldn't have answered even if she wanted to. Maybe he would get angry, maybe he would punish Makena if Koffi couldn't tell him. More thoughts skittered into the walls of her mind like so many spiders, each one bigger and more terrifying. She was afraid of what would happen if she couldn't replicate what she'd done with the splendor, but she was even more afraid of what would happen if she found she could. For what felt like the thousandth time, Fedu's words touched her mind like a poison.

You are a dull knife. But fear not, I will see you sharpened.

She had to do something, she decided. In the same way that she hadn't resigned Makena to her fate in the Mistwood, she couldn't resign herself to whatever Zain and Fedu had planned for her. She looked up at the boy as they walked, trying to summon as much strength as she could put into her voice.

"Zain," she started, but almost immediately she stopped. She'd been so lost in her thoughts, so distracted by the fear of what might happen next, that she'd stopped paying attention to her surroundings. Now she realized that they were at the end of a corridor, staring at a tapestry. Like the one in the main hall, this one was of a hippo, rendered a wet gray color and positioned among water reeds so that only the top half of its body was visible. The weaver had oriented it so that no matter which direction she moved in, the creature always seemed to be staring at her. Still in Zain's grip, she fidgeted.

"Zain, what are you—?"

"Keep your voice down," Zain said between his teeth. "Or we will be caught."

At once, Koffi's mind started to race. She didn't know what had caught her off guard more: the fact that Zain had actually spoken as though he didn't want Fedu to know what he was doing, or the words he had used to expression that wish.

We will be caught. We.

"I don't understand." Koffi shook her head. "What's—?"

Zain let go of her and took a step toward the tapestry. He surveyed it a moment, made a face, then pulled it slightly to the left. Koffi was surprised to see that behind it was a small wooden door.

140

"Inside," he said, "quickly."

Makena had moved to stand beside her. Koffi shot her a questioning look, but the girl seemed just as confused as she was now. Zain opened the door with a hard tug. He bent his head, taking one step in, then looked back at them.

"Come on, hurry!"

Koffi took a deep breath, then followed him in, Makena on her heels. Once inside, Zain shut the door behind them, and they were cast in total darkness.

"Just walk forward," she heard him say. "You'll be able to see in a minute."

Koffi swallowed. Ahead, she could hear Zain's footsteps, soft and careful on the stone. Anticipation thundered in her chest as she tried to mimic the movement, tried to understand what was happening. Where was he taking them?

Abruptly, Koffi heard a click, the sound of a door being unlocked. She shielded her eyes as a square of new light appeared, but after a moment, they settled. Zain was going through another door. Blood pounded in Koffi's ears as she followed. She straightened, and then went very still.

She was standing in some sort of den—she could think of no other word for it. It was a cramped, circular room, mostly furnished by old armchairs and well-worn divans. Initially, she'd thought it was windowless, but when she raised her gaze, she saw the tiniest slivers of windows were positioned several feet up the wall. The ceiling of the room was vaulted. She frowned. Were they in one of Thornkeep's towers? Her gaze lowered, and then she froze. There were two other people in this room.

She recognized Njeri at once; the girl had been sitting in one of the chairs, but was now sitting up, eyes alert. Koffi didn't recognize the boy lounged on the divan beside her. He was unnervingly beautiful, with impossibly smooth brown skin, and a full mouth curved like an archer's bow. Wavy black hair framed his face, and his eyes seemed unable to determine whether they were green or brown.

"Zain." Njeri's eyes darted between Koffi and Makena. "What is this? Why would you bring them here?"

"We need to talk," said Zain. He closed the door he'd just led them through, and Koffi swallowed as she heard its lock click in place again. "Right now."

The boy on the divan slowly sat up and, to Koffi's surprise, offered her a smile. Her heart fluttered in her chest of its own accord.

"Well, this isn't the way I thought we'd be meeting." He nodded to her. "Hi there, I'm Amun."

"Koffi."

Amun acknowledged Makena with a familiar nod, which she returned despite still looking uneasy. Koffi looked from them back to Njeri.

"Zain." The girl's voice was more tense now. "What's going on?"

Zain didn't immediately answer, but began pacing in small circles back and forth. Koffi noted that the pattern of his steps mirrored the ones he'd taken this morning when she'd first seen him in her bedchamber. Five steps in one direction, then a sharp turn on his heel, followed by another five steps and another turn. A minute passed before he stopped and looked directly at Koffi.

"How did you do it?" he asked. He sounded bewildered, as

though he was waking from a dream he didn't understand. "How did you get out of the Mistwood?"

Immediately, Amun's and Njeri's heads snapped in Koffi's direction, an identical shock registering clear on both of their faces. Koffi's own face grew warm as they gaped at her.

"You did what?"

"How?"

"It was because of me!" Makena held up her hands as she stepped in front of Koffi, shielding her. Koffi was grateful when she offered to speak first. "I saw Koffi near the Mistwood a little earlier today," she explained. "I tried to pull her away from it, but the mist pulled me in instead."

"What?" Njeri's expression changed to one of horror. "Makena, how could you? You know what the Mistwood—"

"Koffi just got here, and she was in trouble." Makena straightened, visibly trying to hold her head high. "I wanted to help her, and I'm not sorry for trying."

In spite of everything, Koffi felt an overwhelming warmth, a gratitude for Makena.

"What happened next?" Amun didn't look quite as alarmed as Njeri, but his eyes still held concern as he looked between them. "What happened after the mist pulled you in?"

Makena wrapped her arms around herself then, as though fending off a sudden chill. She closed her eyes and took a deep breath in and out before she spoke again.

"I don't remember very much," she said in a small voice. "It was really cold, and really dark—the mist was everywhere. I couldn't tell up from down as it pulled me in, and eventually, I ended up on my back near some trees. Then they came."

"Who?" asked Zain. He'd been standing statue-still as Makena recounted her story, but now he seemed unable to stop himself. "Who came?"

"The . . . the strange people," said Makena. "At least, that's sort of what they looked like. They were grayish, and they didn't talk or have eyes, but . . . but they stared at me."

"How could they stare at you if they didn't have eyes?" Njeri asked, frowning.

"I know what she means," Koffi volunteered. "I saw them too. They didn't have eyes, but they still seemed capable of seeing. They looked dead, like . . . like . . ."

"The Untethered," Zain said under his breath. He seemed lost in thought for a moment, then nodded to Makena. "Sorry, go on."

"The gray people wouldn't leave me alone," said Makena. "They just kept touching me all over, pinching my skin and my hair and trying to poke my eyes." She shuddered. "So I closed them and tried to cover myself. That's when the nightmares began."

"Nightmares?" Amun's brows rose.

"I started seeing all of my worst memories," Makena explained. "It was like all of my worst fears, playing in my mind in this never-ending loop. I felt trapped in my own brain, and I was sure I was going to lose my mind. But then . . . Koffi was there."

Again, Koffi felt Zain's, Amun's, and Njeri's eyes on her. This time, she was ready for their questioning looks. "I followed Makena into the Mistwood after it took her," she said. "When I found her, those gray things were attacking her, so I chased them away."

"How?" Zain asked.

"With the splendor," said Koffi. "I called for it, then asked it to show me where Makena was. It illuminated everything, like a light, so I could see her. Then I used that same light to push the gray people back."

"The lights were really pretty," Makena offered. "Like little fireflies."

"After I got Makena, I asked the splendor to show us the way out." Koffi felt ridiculous saying the words aloud, but she forced herself to continue. "That's when we saw you."

Zain looked to Amun and Njeri. "Now do you understand?"

"I can't believe it," Njeri said quietly. Her expression was caught between sheer disbelief and another emotion Koffi couldn't name. "I just can't believe it."

"But it makes sense." Amun was still watching her. "You don't belong to an order, do you?"

"Not that I know of." Koffi's face warmed again. "But—"

"Don't you both see?" asked Zain. There was gleam in his eyes. "After all this time, all this searching, it's her. She's the key, she could—"

"Wait!" Koffi held up her hand. She hadn't planned to say the word as loudly as she had, but it got the attention of everyone in the room, so she took advantage of it. "One of you needs to explain this. What are you talking about? What am I the 'key' to?"

For a long moment, Zain only stared at her. "You're the key to helping us leave Thornkeep, once and for all."

Koffi blinked. Whatever she'd expected Zain to say, it hadn't been that. "What?"

"Unless you'd prefer to stay here?" said Amun. Mirth twinkled in his eyes.

"No." Koffi shook her head with slightly more emphasis than necessary. "I don't want to stay here, but . . ." She looked to Makena. "I thought we were all trapped here. I thought there was no way out."

Zain and Makena exchanged a look before the boy spoke. "You might want to sit down now," he said gently. "This is going to be a lot."

Koffi didn't need to be told twice. Most of her muscles still ached from her excursion in the Mistwood. She picked one of the cushier-looking chairs and sank into it, barely suppressing a sigh, then looked up at Zain again.

"Okay. I'm ready."

"You're right," he said. "There is no natural way to get out of Thornkeep, because the Mistwood surrounds it."

"Which was always Fedu's intention," said Njeri. "The Mistwood serves a twofold purpose. It keeps us darajas trapped here within Thornkeep, and it's also where he keeps the Untethered."

"The Untethered?" Koffi repeated.

"The souls of people who don't pass to the godlands," said Zain. "There are all kinds of names for them."

Koffi stiffened. As a little girl, Mama had taught her all manner of Gede traditions. Few were as important as the traditions around burial. In Gede culture, the dead had to be buried with a coin in each hand to pay their way into the godlands. She'd always been told that souls without payment were damned to wander the earth aimlessly as ghosts, but if this was true . . . if this was what really happened to the dead who couldn't afford to pay . . .

"Those beings were barely human," she whispered.

Zain nodded. "It's incredibly dangerous for any mortal, living person to go into the Mistwood for that reason. Above all things, what the Untethered want is life, and they'll do anything to try to take it from those who they believe have it."

Koffi thought of what Makena had just said about the Untethered. *They just kept touching me all over, pinching my skin and my hair and trying to poke my eyes.* Revulsion shuddered through her.

"You understand now the problem we have faced," said Zain. "There are plenty of darajas who've wanted to leave Thornkeep, plenty who have tried, but they've all come back or perished."

"It's impossible to get through the Mistwood without encountering the Untethered," said Njeri. "There are thousands in there, maybe more, and they're extremely sensitive to the presence of mortals."

"Not to mention the mist itself," Amun added. "Which makes it almost impossible to navigate safely."

"A few darajas have tried to run," said Zain. "Some have even tried to map possible escape routes. Every attempt has ended the same way." He looked grim.

"Which is where you come in," said Amun.

Koffi's brows shot up. "Me?"

"If what you and Makena just told us is true—"

"It *is* true."

"Then what that means is that your affinity with the splendor is unlike any other daraja in Thornkeep," he said. "It means you belong in the sixth daraja order."

"The *sixth* order?" Koffi frowned. "I thought there were only five."

"There is a sixth," said Amun, "but it's rare, so rare that the daraja scholars who first classified the noble orders didn't want to include it. It's called the Order of Vivuli, the Order of Shadows."

"The . . . the Order of Shadows?" Koffi tried to hide her grimace. Of the six orders she'd now learned about thus far, this one sounded silliest in her mind.

"Darajas who belong to the Order of Shadows can use the splendor to do intangible things," said Zain. "I've never met one, but I've read about them in books. There have been darajas who can use the splendor to see glimpses of the future, or speak with stars about things that have already happened. Some can even leave their bodies and occupy the minds of creatures hundreds of miles away. In your case," he said, inclining his head, "I think your affinity allows you to use the splendor as some sort of compass. It obeys you, illuminates the path for you to find what you most want."

A memory suddenly returned to Koffi, a moment from back in Lkossa. She'd been in the temple's stables trying to find Adiah in a short amount of time, and she'd been worried that she wouldn't be able to find her. She'd reached for the splendor then too, asked it to help her, and it had. In fact, the splendor had formed a chain of light that had led her right to Adiah. All she'd had to do was ask. She frowned.

"I thought . . . I thought that was normal," she said. "I thought plenty of darajas could do that."

Zain shook his head. "I assure you, *no one* can do what you just did with the splendor, Koffi. And the fact that you're able to command it, that it does your bidding, confirms what Fedu already knows. You are more powerful than any other daraja here."

Koffi felt the weight of those words as they landed. She was glad now to be sitting, because she wasn't sure she could have handled them standing. *You are more powerful than any other daraja here.* She took a deep breath as she tried to process that, tried to believe that.

"Are you telling me," she said slowly, "that this means . . . there's a way for me to leave Thornkeep, a way for me to go home?"

"Yes," said Zain, "but not immediately. You'll need to train, to build up the strength to ensure that, when you are ready to leave, you have a clear understanding of how your affinity works. You and Makena were only in there for a short while this time, and you're already exhausted. You're going to need a lot more endurance . . ."

His words grew faint as Koffi's mind began to race.

Home. There was a way to go home.

Her heart began to pound again, but this time it was not with fear, but joy. Joy. She thought she'd never feel that again. Tears filled her eyes as the possibilities crowded in her mind. She could leave this place, return to Lkossa. She could get back to Mama and Jabir, to Ekon.

Home. There was chance. She could go home.

"Wait." It pained her to say the words, but she knew she had to. "There's something else, something you need to know about me." The darajas stared at her, immediately tense again, but she didn't give them the chance to speak before she recounted the entire story of Adiah, what had happened to her, and what Koffi had done with the splendor from the girl's body. When she was finished, she expected them to immediately assail her with questions, but for several seconds, all four of them only stared.

"You mean to tell me," Njeri said slowly, "that you're just holding all of that splendor *in your body*?"

Koffi shifted her weight, uncomfortable. "Yeah."

"It doesn't hurt you?" asked Amun. Even he seemed perturbed.

"No." Koffi shook her head. "Right now, at least, I can sort of control it. When I use it, I have to be really careful to hold most of it back. But that's really, *really* draining. I don't want to find out what will happen if I lose that self-control. It's what Fedu wants me to do, to release that splendor and use it to upend the world as we know it."

It was Makena who spoke after a pause. "Are you stuck like that forever?"

Koffi shook her head. "Before I took Adiah's power, my friend Ekon and I were planning to take her to the Kusonga Plains, somewhere far away from everyone, to deposit her power safely during the Bonding. Now that I have her power, I guess I would have to do that, if I can get out of here in time."

"The next Bonding is in less than two months," said Amun. "That's not much time."

Koffi swallowed. "It's why I want to get out of here," she said. "And it's why I'll help you all get out too."

Amun, Makena, and Njeri looked up, a visible hope—a longing—in each of their gazes. Koffi took a deep breath before she spoke again.

"All of you are trained darajas," she said. "You know way more about how to be one than I do. There's no way I'm going to be able to learn how to use this affinity without help, so . . ." The words felt familiar. "I'll make you a barter, a deal. You all train me, teach me how to do this right, and when the time comes, I'll get us all out. I promise."

For several seconds, no one spoke; every daraja in the room seemed to be considering. In the end, it was Njeri who finally broke the silence.

"That's . . . that's an incredibly generous offer, Koffi." She sounded genuine. "But before you make it, I want you to understand something." Her eyes filled with a steeliness, a reserve. "If you agree to do this, to help us get out, you need to understand the risks involved. The training will be easy enough to hide from Fedu—it's in line with what he already wants for you—but when the time comes to actually leave . . ." She trailed off. "It's going to be dangerous. You saw what he did to Jiri this morning in the main hall, just to make a point with you. That's nothing compared to what he'll do if he finds out you're trying to leave this place, leave *him*. You are the most precious jewel in his collection, the centerpiece to his righteous work. He would kill you before he let you leave."

Koffi steadied herself as the words rose in her throat. "I would rather live a single day free than a century in bondage."

Something flickered in Njeri's eyes. Koffi saw within the girl's gaze a sadness, and then an understanding. Slowly, a small smile touched her lips.

"We have a deal."

"Great." Koffi stood as she answered the girl's smile with one of her own, the most honest smile she'd felt in a very long time. "So, when do we get started?"

CHAPTER 10

An ABRIDGED EDUCATION in BOTANY

Ekon had trouble falling asleep that night.

He listened to the rain on the roof of the Enterprise's hideout, imagining he could count the thousands of drops as they fell. It was, of course, as futile an effort as ever, one that made him more frustrated than anything else, but it was also a coping mechanism, the only one he had. Counting raindrops distracted him from thinking about what he was about to do, what he was *doing*.

One-two-three. One-two-three. One-two-three.

Ano had said that they'd leave Lkossa the next day, but Ekon still had no idea how the Enterprise was going to manage it. He and Themba were now likely the city's most wanted fugitives. Every time he thought of it, he was doused with a fresh wave of anxiety.

One-two-three. One-two-three. One-two-three.

He was surprised to find, when he woke in the morning, that most of the members of the Enterprise had already packed their things. In the morning light, now that they were no longer worried about hiding their identities from him with their hoods, he saw them more clearly. Bantu Knots—Ekon had since learned her real name was Abeke—sat before the same neat spread of papers, a quill twirling in her hand as she read something to herself. Thabo sat in one of the room's corner counting the tiny sacks of herbs and spices over and over, as though he needed something to do with his hands. Ekon looked up as Themba rose from her bed pallet too, rubbing at her eyes.

"How are you feeling?" he asked.

She offered him a small smile. "I've been better." In a lower voice, she added, "When Sigidi said we needed to go south, this wasn't what I was picturing."

"It's a good deal," said Ekon. "Probably the best we'd have gotten."

After their vote last night, Ano had added stipulations to the Enterprise's agreement with them. Ekon and Themba would be permitted to ride south with them, but with the condition that they would earn their keep like everyone else in the caravan. Ekon still wasn't sure what sort of work Ano had in mind.

As though summoned by the mere thought of her name, the door to the Enterprise's hideout suddenly opened and Ano ducked inside. She shrugged out of her soaked traveling cloak and pulled a paper from one of her bags, holding it up for the group's benefit.

"I've got the documents, we're ready to go."

A small cheer went up around the room, though Ekon didn't understand why. Ano pointed to Thabo.

"Fetch the mules from our stable," she commanded. "And get ready to move the product to our caravans. I've done my checks, and everything seems to be in good order. We'll leave in an hour."

"An hour?" Ekon couldn't entirely stave off the sudden panic that'd lanced through him. At his outburst, Ano turned to him, brows knitted.

"Is that a problem?" She hadn't raised her voice, but there was a challenge in the question, an inflection in her tone that reminded Ekon that she was the authority here, not him. He tapped his fingers against his side, trying to calm himself.

"It's just . . ." He faltered. "The morning rush." He'd lived in Lkossa long enough to know the best and worst times to try to leave the city. "Won't we get caught in all of the outbound traffic?"

Several members of the Enterprise chuckled, Thabo the loudest of all.

"Probably for the best that you didn't pick a life of crime for yourself, boy," he said. "You do *not* have an instinct for it."

Ano's eyes were cooler as she regarded Ekon. "We'll leave in an hour because the morning rush is the precise time it's best for us to try to depart," she said. "More traffic means the Sons of the Six will be more occupied, and hopefully less likely to scrutinize us as carefully as they would if we were one of only a few caravans leaving."

"Oh," said Ekon. He suddenly felt very foolish. That *was* a better strategy. "Sorry."

"If you're finished questioning the way I run my business," said Ano, "Safiyah needs to speak with you."

"Safiyah?" Ekon couldn't quite explain the jolt that went through his body at the mention of the girl's name. "She . . . she wants to speak with me?"

Ano looked bored. "I believe it has to do with her plan for

smuggling you and Themba out of the city," she said. "I put her in charge of its coordination."

Ekon nodded. "I'll go see her. Where is she?"

"In the back room, I believe."

Ekon stood, nodding to Themba when she told him she'd meet him there once she was finished getting ready. For her part, Ano turned her back on them both without another word. Ekon frowned. She'd made no secret of the fact that she hadn't wanted them to join the Enterprise on their trip south, but he couldn't help but feel the woman was being a bit over the top about her displeasure now. He shook his head as he ducked into the back room. According to Thabo, who'd given him a brief tour the night before, the back room was the space for the Enterprise's extra product. The moment he walked into it, the blended smell of herbs filled his lungs, and he coughed. Like most of the Enterprise's hideout, this room was small, dim.

"Uh, Safiyah?"

"I'm here."

Ekon looked down, surprised to see that Safiyah was, in fact, sitting cross-legged on the floor. She'd placed a folded cloth before her, and when Ekon caught her eye, she gave a small wave.

"Hey."

"Uh, hi."

"Please sit."

Ekon crossed the room and sat directly across from Safiyah. After a moment of uncomfortable silence, he spoke again.

"We're leaving in an hour," he offered. "Ano said you had a plan to smuggle Themba and me out?"

The look on Safiyah's face was hard to read. "I do," she said with a nod. "But . . . it's not going to be comfortable."

Ekon stiffened on principle. "What do you mean?"

Safiyah's gaze dropped to the cloth before her. Very carefully, and using only the tips of her fingers, she pinched its corners to unfold it. Ekon saw that, within the cloth's creases, there was a handful of flower petals. They were dried, and slightly browned now, but they looked to have once been a delicate shade of purple or blue. Safiyah looked back up at him.

"Ever heard of plumbago?"

"No," Ekon said honestly. "But I'm assuming that's what these are?"

Safiyah nodded. "I was looking through our extra inventory this morning when I found them," she explained. "They gave me an idea. You're about to get an abridged education in botany."

"I do like to learn."

"As you can see, plumbagoes are quite pretty, even when dried," said Safiyah. "They also have a nice smell, which can make them an attractive décor item for southern noblewomen." She raised a finger. "Unfortunately, plumbagoes have another characteristic: They are highly poisonous—touching one will give you a rash, one that usually spreads throughout the body."

Ekon withdrew his hand quickly. It had been hovering inches from one of the flowers' petals.

"Oh, you might as well go ahead and touch it," said Safiyah, grinning. "I'm about to cover you with it."

"What?" Ekon stared. "You just said it causes rashes!"

"And pockmarks," said Safiyah with a grin. "Which is precisely what we're after this morning." When Ekon continued gaping at her in horror, she went on. "You and Themba are going to be coming down with a severe case of leopard pox."

"Leopard pox?" Ekon repeated.

"It's an illness common in more rural parts of the Zamani Region," said Safiyah. "Named for the leopard-like spots it leaves on the skin of the infected. It's known to be highly contagious."

Ekon pursed his lips together. "Sorry, I'm not following you."

"After we put the plumbago on you, we're going to put you and Themba in one of the wagons of our caravan," said Safiyah. "We'll wrap you in bandages, and when the Sons of the Six come to investigate, we'll tell them that you're sick."

One of Ekon's brows rose. "And you think that'll be enough to keep them from checking us?"

Safiyah's grin widened. "I don't think so. I know so."

"How?"

A wicked glint shone in the girl's eyes. "Because we're going to make sure to mention that, in addition to the markings, leopard pox also causes some rather unfortunate things to happen to certain parts of the body." She gave him a meaningful look. "Parts of the body that would make a man very nervous."

"Oh. *Oh.*" Ekon's expression darkened. "Wait, is that true?"

"Hopefully, you never have to find out," said Safiyah with too much cheer for Ekon's comfort. "And I'm betting the Sons of the Six won't want to take that gamble either."

Ekon leaned back. He was both annoyed and impressed. Admittedly, it was a good plan. "Sons of the Six value masculinity," he said. "They wouldn't do anything to, uh . . . jeopardize that."

"Precisely."

"All right," Ekon sighed. "So, how do we do this?"

Themba joined Ekon and Safiyah in the back room a short while later, and Safiyah reexplained their plan to her. The old woman laughed when Safiyah mentioned the effects of leopard pox, but seemed to like the idea. When Thabo popped his head into the room to tell them the mules and wagons for their caravan were ready, Ekon tensed.

"Okay, we'd better get the plumbago on you," said Safiyah. She'd taken the dried petals she'd shown Ekon before and ground them up in a mortar until they'd become a grayish paste. "I promise it won't be that bad. A little uncomfortable, but as soon as we get out of Lkossa and put the counter ointment on you, the itching will go away."

"I'll go first." Themba rolled up her tunic's sleeves and sat down before Safiyah. Ekon watched as Safiyah dipped a small brush into the mortar, then, one by one, carefully painted tiny dots on Themba's arms, legs, and face.

"How does it feel?" he asked as Safiyah worked.

"Oh, it's definitely unpleasant," said Themba with a frown. "But not intolerable."

Safiyah handed Themba a cloth, then turned to Ekon. "Your turn."

Themba left to finish getting ready, while Ekon took the spot on the floor she'd just occupied. He tried to keep still as Safiyah began applying the paste to his face, but the minute it touched skin, he wanted to squirm. Themba's description of the paste being unpleasant was a gross understatement; it felt like ants crossing his skin.

"Sorry," said Safiyah, not looking very apologetic.

"It's fine." Ekon tapped his fingers against his knees, trying to focus on numbers instead of the increasing discomfort spreading across his body.

One-two-three. One-two-three. One-two-three.

"I need you to stand so I can do your legs," said Safiyah once she'd finished his face. Ekon stood. His fingers continued tapping, this time on his thigh, as the itching intensified. Safiyah was adding spots to his knee when she looked up.

"Do you always tap your fingers like that?"

Ekon flushed. "Uh. Yeah. Sorry."

The skin between Safiyah's brows pinched. "Why would you apologize for that?"

"It's . . ." It took everything Ekon had not to fidget, and this discomfort had nothing to do with the plumbago. "It's just, I know it's strange."

Safiyah stopped her dotting for a moment to look at Ekon. Her expression was wry. "Every morning, when I wake up, the first thing I do is braid my hair twice. Twice. It doesn't matter if I do it perfectly the first time. I always have to redo it. When I don't, I feel . . ." She trailed off. "Strange is relative, Okojo."

Ekon didn't know how best to respond to that, and by the time he opened his mouth to, Safiyah was on her feet. She handed him a cloth like the one she'd handed Themba.

"Wait a few more minutes, then wipe the paste off," she said. "It'll come off, but the rashes will be there."

Ekon nodded. He still felt like he should say something in

answer to what she'd told him about her braids, but he couldn't find the words.

"Um, I—"

"I'll see you outside." Without another word, she was gone.

✦

Ekon had never been so itchy in his life.

By the time the Enterprise's caravan was ready, he was ready to crawl out of his own skin, literally. Safiyah has been right about the cloth, the plumbago's paste had come off without issue, but the rashes left in the spots she'd applied it to his skin were unbearable. Add to that the bandages they'd used to make it look like he was being treated, and he wanted to scream.

"Come." Ano gestured to him, Themba, and Abeke. "You three will be in the last wagon of our caravan."

Ekon winced with every step as he followed Ano outside. They walked down the same alley Thabo had found them in the previous night, then turned onto a slightly larger side street. Three covered wagons were arranged there, all hitched together, and led by a team of four large mules.

"The first wagon holds our spices," she explained. "The second one is for our herbs, and the third one is where we usually keep food, water, and personal items. That's the one you three will be going into."

Ekon followed as Abeke and Themba climbed into the third wagon, as directed. A few more minutes passed in relative quiet before he heard Ano give the order to start moving. Ekon felt a jolt in his stomach as the caravan lurched forward. His fingers tapped.

One-two-three. One-two-three. One-two-three.

"Easy, boy." Abeke was sitting across from him in the wagon, looking amused. "It's going to be fine."

"How does the Enterprise leave Lkossa each time without paying the tax?" Ekon asked, trying to distract himself from the itching. "It's not like three hitched wagons are subtle."

"Ano takes care of that," Abeke explained. "She has a connection with a forger, and he writes up the tax export documents for our trips in exchange for a cut of the profit. Today's papers will say that we're a group of nine travelers instead of our normal seven. If everything runs smoothly, she'll just present those papers to the sentries at the southern gate, and we'll be on our way."

"Sounds easy," said Ekon. To himself, he added: *Almost too easy.*

The ride through Lkossa to the front gates was more comfortable than Ekon had expected, but not by much. Downpours of rain had softened and muddied the roads, which meant he felt every bump and dip as the wagon rolled through the streets. He peeked through a crack in its canvas when they finally came to a stop.

It was clear they'd reached Lkossa's gates; the roads were packed tight with people. Already Ekon could smell the unpleasant blend of odors—old produce, animal dung, and sweat from those who'd been standing there for a while waiting. At least it gave him something to count. He started with the wagons, and moments later he'd counted thirty-two, at least that he could see. He was counting mules when he noticed someone moving in the crowd, a thin bald man. Unlike everyone else, he was moving away from the gates instead of toward them. Ekon realized why the man had caught his eye; he was a member of the Enterprise, coming their way. Ekon thought his name might be Boseda. Ekon watched as he stopped at the first wagon in the caravan, presumably to talk to Ano, then made his way to theirs. Ekon only just had time to turn around before Boseda climbed in.

"Bad news," he said. "There's been an accident, two farmers' wagons crashed right at the gate. It's created a huge mess of traffic. The Sons are rerouting everyone toward the secondary gate, half a mile from here."

Ekon sat up straight now. "What does that mean?"

"Nothing, hopefully," said Boseda. "We'll continue to follow our original plan, but at a different location. For now, we'll just turn the wagons and start to make our way in that direction. Stay here." He disappeared without another word, and a few minutes later, the wagon started to move again. Abeke sighed, settling in her seat, but Ekon exchanged a look with Themba.

It's going to work, he told himself. *It's a good plan. It's going to work. It has to.*

He chanced another peek out of the wagon's canvas and saw that they were nearing the city's second entry gate. Even from here he could see the bright blue of the Sons' uniforms; there looked to be two stationed on either side of the entrance. They came to a stop again, and—ignoring the cautioning look Themba threw him—he stood and moved to the front of the wagon, trying to see what was happening. His mouth went dry.

Two men were walking toward the caravan, and Ekon knew them both well. One was round and short, the other taller and muscular; one man wore a long blue robe, the other a standard

162

blue Son of the Six tunic. Ice-cold fear constricted in Ekon's lungs as he watched the Kuhani and Kamau, his older brother, stop before the Enterprise's first wagon. He was too far away to hear them above the din; he could only watch as Thabo—not Ano—descended from the first caravan and held out the export documents. Ekon had to admire that particular attention to detail; the temple was far less likely to scrutinize a group of travelers led by a man. Kamau took the paper without much interest and gave it a cursory look before nodding. The Kuhani didn't even seem to be interested. He walked with Thabo as the man pulled back the covering of the first wagon, then the second. When he pointed at the third, Kamau's face twisted in disgust. The seconds seemed to pass in centuries as Ekon waited, then . . .

Kamau stepped back and waved them on.

Relief flooded Ekon as Thabo gave Kamau and the Kuhani a neat bob of his head before climbing onto the first wagon. He urged the mules forward, and the caravan began to move again.

"That was unusual." Like Ekon, Abeke had peeked through some of the wagon's covering to watch the exchange. "The Kuhani doesn't usually frequent the city's gates."

Ekon pressed his lips together tightly. He had a feeling that he knew why the Kuhani was here. *Me. They're here because of me.*

He'd known he was wanted by the Sons of the Six, but he hadn't guessed it was serious enough for the Kuhani to come to the city's gates. Kamau had let them pass without much fuss, but adrenaline still coursed through Ekon's veins. That'd been close, too close.

"We're almost to the gates," said Abeke. "Thank the gods, then you can take that paste—"

"Halt!"

Ekon froze at the same moment Themba stiffened, and Abeke's eyes went wide. This time, all three of them pried apart pieces of the wagon's covering to see what was going on. Ekon's eyes searched, then his heart plummeted.

A part of him wasn't surprised to see Shomari standing in front of the Enterprise's first cart with his hand raised, and yet another part of Ekon was terrified. His co-candidate held himself with all the confidence and swagger of a newly minted Son of the Six—his chest was puffed out, and he jutted his chin importantly as Thabo descended from the first wagon again. Ekon strained to hear the two men's conversation.

"Sir, is there a problem?"

"I need to see your papers." There was a hard glint in Shomari's eyes. "Your caravan is considered large, and I'll need to verify that you have the right documents."

"Of course." Once again, Thabo produced the export papers, the same ones Ano had brandished this morning. Shomari examined them with far more scrutiny than Kamau had. He looked up.

"What's in that third wagon? Your document says 'miscellaneous.'"

Ekon's blood went cold. *Not good, not good, not good.* This was not good at all.

"Some members of our party are in there," said Thabo. "They are unwell, and have to be separated from the group."

Shomari's brows rose. "Unwell?"

"Leopard pox," Thabo said in a hushed voice. "Don't know if you've ever had it, but it's not pretty. Leaves rashes, along with some, uh . . . less pleasant symptoms."

Ekon watched from the sliver of the wagon's covering as Shomari's frown deepened.

"That's unfortunate," he said. "But all the same, I'll need to check it."

Raw panic shuddered along the length of Ekon's body. They had nowhere to go, no way to get out other than through the wagon's front. If they tried it now, they would be seen. Beside him, he heard Themba's gasp. Abeke's hand disappeared into the folds of her tunic.

"What are you doing?" Ekon whispered.

"Silence, boy."

Ekon's eyes cut back to Shomari. He was walking toward them now with that same deep frown. A few feet away, he saw someone else jump down from the second wagon to intercept him. Safiyah.

"Sir," she said in an artificially sweet voice. "Please have some compassion, these people are very ill—"

Shomari brushed right past her. Terror climbed up Ekon's throat. He was still watching as Shomari drew closer. Twelve feet, eleven feet, ten—

Someone snatched the sleeve of his tunic, hauling him back. Themba. There was a ferocity in her eyes.

"Lie down and turn your head away from the front of the wagon. Now."

Ekon's heart thundered in his chest as he obeyed. He felt someone throw a blanket over his legs, adjust the bandages on his arms. Seconds later, the wagon's front canvas was ripped open.

Ekon lay perfectly still, willing his eyes to stay closed. He couldn't see what was happening, but he felt Shomari's eyes on him. His face was fairly mottled by the rashes, but would that be enough if Shomari forced him to turn his head? Next to him, someone—Themba or Abeke—gave a shuddering cough, an exaggerated moan of pain. There was a stilted silence, then:

"All right."

The wagon's covering was closed up again; Ekon felt the whole thing dip as someone jumped off it. He sat up and looked through one of its cracks. He couldn't believe it. Shomari was walking away with hands over his nose and mouth, back toward Safiyah. Her face was impassive as he stopped before her.

"That was disgusting," said Shomari.

Safiyah dipped her head. "If you're done checking our wagons," she said, "we'll be on our way." The words themselves were soft, but even from here, Ekon heard the slight edge to them. Something hot unfurled in his chest as he watched the way Shomari's eyes wandered over Safiyah's body. He leered.

"Sorry, sweetheart," he said in an altogether different voice. "I don't think I caught your name before."

Safiyah's eyes narrowed to slits.

"Aw." His hand struck out without warning, taking hold of Safiyah's chin between his thumb and index finger. He forced her head up so that their gazes met. "You know, you really shouldn't make faces like that, it's not attractive."

White-hot rage burned through Ekon, but Safiyah didn't move or speak. Eventually, Shomari let go of her.

"Be on your way."

Safiyah needed no other prompt as she turned on her heel and started to climb back into the second wagon. Ekon relaxed.

And then several things happened at once.

Shomari's hand brushed Safiyah's bottom as she bent over the wagon's edge. He made it look subtle, careless, but she whirled around immediately. Shomari raised two hands, feigning innocence.

"Sorry about that—"

The words were cut off as Safiyah rounded on him, delivering a slap across his cheek that was so hard, it sent him reeling.

Everyone in the immediate vicinity froze.

"Arrest her!" Shomari shouted, rage bright in his eyes as he held his cheek. In an instant, two more Sons of the Six were emerging from the crowd. Ekon watched in horror as they grabbed Safiyah's arms.

"Let go of me," she shouted. "Let go!" It was no use. A lump rose in Ekon's throat as he watched her struggle in the warriors' grasp. Shomari's hand was still on his cheek, but at the sight of her, he leered.

"Stupid girl," he spat. "You really thought you could strike an anointed Son of the Six without consequence? You'll pay for that mistake dearly." His lips curled. "What do you have to say now?"

Ekon watched as Safiyah opened her mouth and uttered a single word.

"Fireroot."

There was no sound in response, but Ekon saw it: something small, hurtling through the air. At first glance, he thought it was a bird, but no . . . When he squinted, he saw it was a tiny burlap pouch, no bigger than his own fist. He had seconds to wonder at that, to wonder why someone would be throwing something like that through the air, before the pouch hit the ground and exploded in a cloud of red-brown dust.

A scream tore through the air, and another. Ekon felt the hairs on the back of his neck stand on end. He tried to back away, but it was too late; the air inside the wagon was beginning to change, to take on a rancid smell like old pepper sauce. It clung to his throat, hot, drawing involuntary tears from his eyes. Beside him, he saw Themba and Abeke both double over in a fit of coughs.

"What's happening?" Ekon could barely speak between his own gasps.

"Fireroot," said Abeke. "It's a . . . spice."

Alarm bells sounded in Ekon's mind as more screams filled the air outside the wagon. Abeke and Themba were still coughing, but he dragged himself by the elbows, trying to stay low, until he'd reached the wagon's front. He forced open its canvas door to look out, and the breath left his body.

The entire street was in pandemonium.

It seemed several more pouches of the fireroot spice had been thrown into the crowd; everywhere people were screaming, rubbing their eyes, on their knees. Ekon's eyes cut left and right, trying without success to find any familiar face in the mayhem. Sons of the Six were on the ground too, just as disoriented as everyone else who'd been touched by the fireroot. He looked toward the first wagon in the Enterprise's caravan, and a new panic lanced though him. No one was manning it anymore, and while the mules didn't seem to be affected by the red powder still suffusing the air, they were definitely irritated by all the chaos around them. Ekon could see what would happen if they stayed there much longer—they'd bolt from the wagons entirely. He turned back to Themba.

"I'm going out to the first wagon."

"What?" Themba's eyes watered as she looked up. Beside her, Abeke was still coughing. "Ekon, no. You and I have to stay hidden, we—"

"The mules will bolt if someone doesn't get up there," said Ekon. "I have to go."

Themba opened her mouth as if to say more, but seemed unable to, with the powder still in her lungs. Ekon threw one more glance at her over his shoulder before he ducked out of the wagon.

The situation on the street seemed to be getting worse by the second. Storm clouds were gathering now, bringing with them a breeze that spread the red-brown dust far and wide. Ekon looked toward the caravan's first wagon again. Past it, he saw that all of the warriors who'd been standing at the gate were gone, likely summoned to help control the crowd. His pulse quickened. If he could get the wagons to the gate, they had a clear path out.

He shot forward, trying to ignore the sting in his eyes as another wave of the dust flew into them. With every inhale, it seemed to coat his lungs, to make breathing even harder. The mules jumped when he climbed atop the wagon's driver bench. He grabbed the reins without waiting and steered them forward.

Come on, he pleaded as they began to move. *Faster, faster . . .*

Around him, the street was still in chaos; people were running into each other as they tried to get the red dust out of their eyes. Ekon maneuvered the mules around them as quickly as he could manage to without accidentally trampling someone. The city's gates drew nearer, and his breath quickened.

Almost there. He leaned forward, urged the mules on. *Almost there, almost there . . .*

"Ekon!"

Ekon stopped, pulling on the mules' reins just in time. A figure had stepped directly in front of the wagons' path, blocking his way forward. His blood chilled as he saw who it was.

He knew the tears in his brother's eyes were likely from the powder in the air; that made them no easier to see. Ekon met Kamau's gaze and counted the emotions he saw in his face—confusion, sadness, anger. Worst of all, he saw hope. Kamau still had hope that this might all be some mistake. That Ekon could go back to who he'd been. It was too close, too similar to the last time he'd seen his brother, at the Temple of Lkossa. He'd been trying his hardest to forget that moment, but now he felt as though he'd been thrown right back to it all over again. Once again, he needed to get away, and once again, his brother was standing in his path.

"Ekon."

Ekon didn't hear his brother say his name the second time, though he watched Kamau's lips form the shape of it. For a moment, time seemed to stand absolutely still, neither one of them moving an inch. Then Kamau's expression changed. The confusion, the grief, and the hope all fell from his face, replaced by another emotion: fury.

"Ekon!" This time Ekon heard his brother's roar as he charged toward him, already reaching for his hanjari dagger. Ekon found he couldn't move. Around him, the noise seemed to fade to nothing as he watched Kamau drawing nearer. He counted that distance, watching it grow smaller.

Nine feet. Six feet. Three feet.

"ARRGH!"

Ekon didn't understand what he was seeing. Kamau had stopped short just feet away from him and keeled backward. A red stain was spreading across the front of his blue kaftan. For one terrible second, Ekon thought it was blood, but then . . . no, the shade of red wasn't right, it wasn't darkening the right way. In fact, the longer Ekon stared, the more he realized that the red wasn't really staining his clothes at all—it was fireroot. Kamau's hands flew to his eyes as he screamed in pain.

"Ekon!"

Ekon's head snapped right. Safiyah was running toward him. She held one of the Sons' slingshots in one hand and another small burlap sack of the red powder in the other. In one graceful leap, she was on the second wagon. "Go!"

Like that, Ekon was ripped back into the present again. His grip on the mules' reins tightened as he urged them forward again, careering toward the city's gates. He could still hear the din of people, but over the noise one person's voice seemed louder than the rest. Kamau. His brother was still screaming.

"Go!" shouted Safiyah. "Go!"

They emerged on the other side of the gates just as a clap of thunder overhead shook the ground. The mules brayed, and this time, Ekon let them run at a full gallop.

He did not look back as Lkossa disappeared in a cloud of dust.

CHAPTER 11

The HUNTER and the LIONESS

When Koffi woke the next morning, she felt different.

It took her a moment to remember why, to separate her dreams from the reality of what had happened the day before. When it all came back to her again, she beamed.

Home. I'm going home.

Every time she said those simple words in her mind, she felt a part of herself thawing, coming back to life. She had, for the first time in a long time, a plan, a path forward, hope. She hadn't realized how powerful a thing hope could be until she'd almost lost it.

Makena came to her room a short while later with clothes for her to wear, and after Koffi was dressed, she led the way down to the west garden. They had stayed with Amun, Njeri, and Zain for the better part of the day yesterday, deciding how best to divvy up Koffi's daraja training, and it was decided that the simplest plan was to do exactly what Fedu expected. Koffi would continue learning from the other darajas of Thornkeep, exploring the finer points of how her own affinity worked. She would just be having a secondary lesson to accompany the first.

Thornkeep's forge was at the far end of the west garden; Koffi hadn't immediately recognized what it was as she and Makena approached the building. It was a simple enough structure: small, modest, and masoned from the same black stonework as the rest of Thornkeep. Even several feet away from it, Koffi could feel the heat emanating from it, smell the sulfurous coal and metalworks that suffused the air. Makena didn't bother to knock when they reached the forge's front door. Instead she walked right in, gesturing for Koffi to follow.

The room before them was large and dark. Long stone worktables were pushed directly up against two of its four walls, and both of those tables were almost entirely cluttered with tools, wood shavings, and odd scraps of carved metal. The setup reminded Koffi of an old man's workshop, which was why she was more than a little surprised when a petite girl emerged from a door in the back of the room. She had muscled arms, shoulder-length dreadlocks pinned away from her face, and big rounded cheeks that gave her the look of someone always on the verge of smiling. She gave Koffi a cheery wave.

"This is Zola," said Makena. "Zola, Koffi."

"Hi!" Zola's voice reminded Koffi of an atenteben flute, high-noted and musical. "It's nice to meet you." She extended a hand in greeting, and Koffi felt calluses on her palm.

"And you."

"Zola is in the Order of Ufundi, like me," Makena explained. "But her affinity is . . ." She cast a look around the disorganized workshop. "Different from mine."

Zola laughed. It was a hearty, full sound that Koffi found she instantly liked. "That's one way of putting it," she said ruefully.

She turned back to Koffi. "I'm a blacksmith. I like to make things with the splendor."

Koffi started. "You can do that?"

"Yep!" Zola looked pleased. "Come on, I'll show you a few pieces." She gestured, then led them into one of the workshop's back rooms. They passed a larger room that housed the actual forge, another one that appeared to be used for storage, then stopped at a small one in the room's very back. It was furnished only with a workbench, several drawers, and a table, but like the rest of the forge, the floor was littered with knickknacks.

"Watch your feet," said Zola pleasantly.

Makena picked the hems of her dress up and made a face, making no effort to hide her discomfort. Koffi barely suppressed a chuckle. She hadn't known Makena long, but it was already abundantly clear that this kind of place was the stuff of her personal nightmares. If Zola noticed, she didn't indicate it as she sat at the workbench, swung her legs over, and ducked her head under the desk. When she emerged a moment later, she was holding something.

"Here," she said. "Some of my early work."

Koffi opened her palm as Zola dropped something weighted into her hand: a statuette of a heron, wrought in cast iron. Its legs were long, and its beak was spindly. Every one of the fine feathers on its back had been ornately carved. Koffi held it up in wonder. "It's incredible," she said in awe. "How'd you do this?"

"I'll show you," she said. She searched the floor a moment, then picked up what looked to be a small black lump of iron. Makena and Koffi watched as Zola was silent a moment, pinching her brows in concentration. Slowly, the iron began to transform, to smooth in places and take a sharper form. Moments later, it was a perfectly even cube.

"Whoa."

Zola smiled. "When I summon the splendor, I direct it into my hands," she explained. "The energy then moves into what I'm holding, and I can manipulate it from there the way a blacksmith can manipulate heat. Obviously, the more complicated the shape, the more time it takes."

"That is an extremely useful affinity."

Something twinkled in Zola's eyes. She held up the cube, smirking. "This is just a parlor trick." In a lower voice, she said, "I can do way cooler things."

"She's with us," Makena whispered when she saw Koffi's confusion. "She wants to leave Thornkeep too."

"Oh." Koffi felt a new jolt of excitement. Makena's grin widened.

"Zain came to me last night, after you all talked," Zola said. She was whispering too now. "I got to work right away." She opened one of her drawers and fished around a moment before withdrawing what looked to be a sword hilt with no blade. Zola weighed it in her hands as she stood.

"When I was a little girl, my father told me stories about the darajas of old," she said. "He told me that they used to have weapons made from the splendor, entire blades made from it." She rotated the hilt carefully. "I've been experimenting, trying to figure out how to re-create them." She looked at Koffi. "I figure they'd be helpful to have in the Mistwood, in case we come up against the Untethered."

"That's . . . really smart," said Koffi.

"You're supposed to be having a lesson with me to try to determine what your affinity is," said Zola. "But since we already know that, I thought we might try something else." She handed the metal hilt to Koffi. "Take it."

Koffi hesitated, then accepted the hilt from Zola. It was far heavier than she'd expected.

"I want you to try to summon the splendor," said Zola. "Carefully. And try to focus it in the shape of a blade. If I've done this right, your splendor will create a sword."

Koffi swallowed as she eyed the hilt. Vaguely, she remembered doing something similar inside the Temple of Lkossa as she'd been trying to help free Adiah, but that had been different. She'd been putting splendor into a blade that already existed, not creating one from nothing. She looked between the girls, nervous.

"It's okay, Koffi," Makena encouraged. "You can do this."

Koffi stared at the hilt a second longer, then closed her eyes. She tried not to think about the way she must look; in the dark, she felt incredibly foolish. Instead, she tried to replicate the techniques Badwa had taught her in the Greater Jungle, to repeat exactly what she'd done yesterday in the Mistwood.

Focus. Focus.

She wasn't sad or angry; there was no emotional block in her way. Slowly, she drew the splendor resting in her body and pushed it into her arms. There was a swoop in her belly as she felt it come alive.

Imagine a blade, she told herself. *Imagine a very long, very pointy blade.*

Koffi felt the splendor humming in her bones. Not for the first time, she remembered, distantly, the warning Badwa had once given about holding this kind of energy in her body for too long. Adiah had done it, and it had altered her, but . . . nothing bad seemed to be happening now. She felt warm, as though she was standing in direct sunlight. The idea of creating a blade didn't seem hard now. She imagined its shape and pushed that splendor toward the hilt between her hands, imagining its feel, its weight. When she opened her eyes, she was disappointed to find nothing was there. She looked up just as Makena and Zola exchanged a look.

"I . . . I don't understand." The words escaped her before she could stop them. "I felt it."

"It's okay, Koffi," said Makena gently. "That was your first try."

"It's a complex bit of splendor work," Zola added. "And it requires a lot of control. Even I haven't really mastered it."

Koffi tried to ignore the flush of embarrassment creeping into her cheeks. For just a single moment, she'd been confident in herself, confident in what she could do with the splendor. Now she felt like she was back at square one.

"I want to show you something," said Zola. She seemed eager to break the awkward silence that'd filled the room. "I haven't shown this to anyone, and it might make you feel better."

Koffi doubted it, but she was intrigued as Zola riffled through the drawer again. After a moment she pulled out a thin box and held it in her lap. When she opened it, Koffi's heart stuttered. The box was filled with drawings.

Some of them were rough sketches, drawn on scraps no bigger than her hand, but then Zola pulled one folded paper out that detailed an elaborate-looking spear. She looked from the papers to Koffi and smiled.

"I draw in my spare time," she explained. "A lot of these are just drafts of things I've imagined in my head or remember from my father's forge. But . . ." She looked down at them again. "I think I could really make a few of them, redesign them so that they're true splendor weapons that we can use when we go into the Mistwood."

Koffi found herself lost for words. When she'd spoken with Zain, Njeri, and Amun yesterday about leaving Thornkeep, it had still felt like a concept, a hypothetical. But looking at Zola's sketches of weapons made everything feel real, and that much more feasible. She was surprised to feel a tight lump rise in her throat the longer she thought about it, and was embarrassed to feel tears stinging her eyes.

"I'm working on something else for you," Zola added. "It's not quite ready yet, though, so it'll be a surprise."

"Thank you," Koffi said, choking on the words. "Thank you for . . . for doing this."

Zola dismissed her with a wave of her hand. "No, Koffi. Thank *you*."

"But—"

"I'm serious." Zola's expression changed, her cheeriness replaced by something more stoic. "Thank you. For helping us, for caring about us, for being our hope."

Koffi opened her mouth but couldn't think of any answer to that. Zola's truth felt heavy on her shoulders, almost overwhelming. The only hope. Not so long ago, she'd been nothing, an indentured beastkeeper with nothing to her name. Now these people—these incredibly powerful people—were looking at her with a faith that almost made her uncomfortable.

"I . . . I won't let you down." Her voice sounded hollow in her throat, but Makena and Zola both seemed to be convinced by them, because they smiled.

"I know you won't," said Zola. "Now, have a seat. You may not be in the Order of Ufundi, but there are still some things I can show you."

Koffi and Makena spent the rest of the morning in Zola's workshop. Koffi tried a few more times to master the splendor blade, but after a while she gave up on it. By the time she and Makena left, she was sweaty and sore, but for the first time in a long time, she felt like she'd really worked at something useful, something that'd made her happy. Makena left Koffi to her own affairs when they returned to Thornkeep, and admittedly, Koffi was glad for the time alone. After she'd agreed to help them yesterday, Zain had mentioned that there were some books about the daraja orders in Thornkeep's library. She decided to head there. Makena had pointed it out to her before, and Koffi hoped she was right as she retraced her steps to find it. She was relieved when she reached a set of double doors, not quite as large as the ones that led to the main hall. A carved scroll hung over them, but Koffi couldn't read the words written on it—they weren't in any language she knew. She crossed her fingers, hoping no one was inside the library as she gently nudged the doors open, and breathed a sigh of relief at her continued fortune.

Thornkeep's library was small but orderly. Tomes of all sizes lined its curving walls, and from the room's shape Koffi guessed that this was one of the turrets she'd seen from outside. It was empty for now, and she took advantage, at once dropping to the ground to begin searching the book's aged spines. She found almanacs, encyclopedias, a particularly tattered book covered in more words Koffi couldn't decipher. Her heart began to race, but she wasn't sure why. What was she hoping to find in one of these books? A part of her knew, even if she didn't fully admit it to herself. She wanted more information about the sixth order, the one Zain had told her about last night, the one he'd said she probably belonged to.

The Order of Vivuli, the Order of Shadows.

She was still trying to get used to the name, to the idea of it. Recently learning that she was a daraja had been jarring enough; learning that she belonged to an order within the darajas so rare that scholars disputed whether it should be named felt akin to being told she'd been going by the wrong name all her life.

She traced a finger along the spines of the library's books, skimming their titles briefly. There were books here about the Order of Ufundi's variations, several books on the history of the Order of Kupambana, but she didn't see any that even mentioned the Order of Vivuli. A rather old book had just caught her eye, when—

"Looking for something?"

Koffi whirled around, her heart leaping to her throat. She hadn't heard Fedu enter the library, hadn't noticed him until he stood there before her. Perhaps that'd been deliberate. The god of death was wearing a plain white linen dashiki, immaculately pressed, and a single golden chain about his neck. Had she not known better, Koffi might have mistaken him for a wealthy merchant.

"I . . . I am," she said. Subtly, she moved toward a shelf of books on the history of textiles and away from the books about the daraja orders. Fedu didn't seem to notice.

"I'm told you spent your morning with Zola, in the forge," he said, his tone light. "Was your lesson with her beneficial?"

He can't read minds, Koffi reminded herself. *He doesn't know what you talked about with Zola. He doesn't know anything except for where you were. Lie.*

"Yes." Koffi was careful to keep her tone neutral, to not sound too happy or too perturbed. "Zola's a talented daraja."

"She is." Fedu inclined his head, agreeing.

An uncomfortable silence fell between them then, and Koffi fidgeted. To break it, she added: "I'm no closer to figuring out what my affinity is." *Yes. Good.* Better to let him think she still had no idea which order she belonged to; the more time she could buy, the better.

"It will come to you," said Fedu breezily. His eyes skimmed the bookshelves. "I've found that, often, the best things take time."

"Right." Koffi crossed her arms and said nothing else.

Fedu rubbed his hands together, still taking in the rows of books around the library. After a moment, he spoke again. "This is one of my favorite places in Thornkeep," he said softly. "I've always had a fondness for libraries, for places of learning."

Koffi barely resisted making a face. Fedu took a step forward, then nodded toward one of the armchairs.

"Do you mind if I sit?"

"It's your home." Koffi made herself sound as nonchalant as she could manage. "Do what you want."

Fedu gave her an indulgent look before easing into the chair with a sigh. He crossed his legs and steepled his fingers, watching her for a second longer than was comfortable. Then he said, "Let us be forthright, if only just for a moment, Koffi. I know that your feelings toward me are . . . less than warm."

Koffi hid her response, digging her fingernails into her palm. She hadn't expected their conversation to go in this direction. She tried to think of words to say back, but fortunately, the god went on.

"It is disappointing, but not surprising," he said. "I've always struggled to feel truly understood, even among my own immortal brethren and sistren. Perhaps you can relate to that." He looked up, holding her gaze. "Would you believe me if I told you that I've spent decades considering the finite points of my endeavor, and that I truly think it would make this world better for darajas?"

Koffi grimaced. "I don't believe anyone who hurts innocent children to further their ambitions."

Fedu studied her for a moment, then shrugged. "Drastic change requires drastic measures," he said.

"What you're doing isn't drastic," said Koffi. "It's wrong, evil."

Fedu paused and Koffi waited, sure that he was going to admonish her. She was surprised by what he said next.

"Have you ever heard the old tale of the hunter and the lioness?" he asked.

Koffi didn't admit aloud that she hadn't. In truth, she didn't want to hear the story. Spending any more time than she had to with the god of death was about as appealing as cold warthog stew. But he seemed able to read her silence. He nodded.

"The story goes that, once upon a time, there was a hunter who ventured into a nearby jungle in pursuit of a lioness," he said. "All day he searched, following her tracks through the hours. Just when he thought to give up, he found her, and the two battled. He had only a spear, she had only her claws. Their fight was a well-matched one, both drew blood. But in the end, it was the hunter who emerged from their contest victorious." Fedu's eyes gleamed. "He killed the lioness with a blow to her heart, then he skinned her and took her hide back to his village. Now . . ." Fedu leaned forward. "Tell me, in that story, who is the villain?"

Koffi stiffened. The question felt like a trap, but Fedu was looking at her expectantly, waiting. She took a deep breath before she answered.

"The hunter. The hunter was the villain."

"Why?"

"He entered the lioness's home," she said, unable to keep a hint of defensiveness from her voice. "He sought her out, and then he killed her."

Fedu sat back and nodded, as though considering the merits of that argument. "Now, allow me to slightly alter the parameters of that story," he said. "What if I told you that the hunter who went into that jungle to hunt down the lioness did so because, the night before, she'd crept into his village and slain his firstborn son? Who would you call the villain of the story then?"

Koffi didn't answer. A lump had risen in her throat, and she wasn't sure how to swallow it.

"Or," Fedu went on, "I will take things one step further. If I told you that the reason the lioness went into the village and killed the hunter's son was that she needed food for her own young cubs, would she be the story's hero, or its villain?"

Still, Koffi said nothing. Fedu offered her a small smile.

"Pretentious old men with white in their beards will asseverate that the notions of good and evil are simple," he murmured. "You should know that those old men are nothing but fools and cowards. Good and evil are never simple. They are capricious beasts, ever shifting in their shape, and rarely beautiful." He stared off into the distance then, so long that Koffi wondered if he'd forgotten she was there. He didn't look at her when he spoke again. "You may not agree with my method of choice right now," he said, "but someday, my dearest hope is that you will come to understand it. When, one day, Eshōza is a better, richer land for what we are going to do, I don't expect that you will thank me for it, but I hope that you will, at least, find the prudence to see the truth in it." Slowly he rose from his chair. "Have a good afternoon, Koffi." He headed for the library's doors without another word. Koffi watched him go, unable to temper the unease coiling in her stomach like a snake.

CHAPTER 12

A FRIENDLY WAGER

Ekon had been certain the Sons of the Six would hunt him down.

In the first hour, as the Enterprise's caravan had careered away from the city, he'd waited for the inevitable. In his head, he heard the war cries, saw the telltale splashes of blue in the distance. But by the third hour, as morning had approached noon, he'd become less sure they were coming. Shortly after leaving Lkossa, he'd pulled off to the side of the main road to let Thabo drive the mules, and after taking a few strategic forks in the road, Ekon was beginning to wonder if maybe—just maybe—they might actually be in the clear.

The hours passed in relative quiet; it seemed most members of the Enterprise were as exhausted as they looked. Several were now sporting cuts and scrapes, and almost every single one of them had some remnant of fireroot powder still sprinkled on their clothes. By midday, Ano asked Thabo to stop the caravan for lunch, and Ekon was more than a little grateful for a chance to stretch his legs. The members of the Enterprise set up lunch with the same efficiency with which they'd packed up this morning; blankets were unfolded and neatly packed boxes were laid in their centers for everyone to share. To Ekon's surprise, he saw the expected dried fruits and nuts, but also carefully stored cheeses and wrapped meats. His mouth watered as Themba settled beside him to eat. She wasn't coughing anymore, but she looked fatigued. She handed Ekon a basket of bread, and when Ekon reached to grab one of them, he noticed one of the fireroot pouches had found its way into it. He pinched it between his fingers and addressed the group.

"So . . . does anyone want to tell me what this stuff actually is?"

One of the members of the Enterprise held out a hand. When Ekon offered the pouch to him, he held it to his nose and whiffed.

"Eugh!" Ekon made a face.

"Fireroot is a combination of several different spices and dried vegetables ground together," the man explained, seeming unbothered by Ekon's reaction to him. "It's considered a key ingredient in several southern delicacies."

"People put that in their food?" Ekon didn't even try to keep the judgment out of his voice.

"In much smaller amounts, yes." The man looked amused. "On their own, each of the individual spices that make up fireroot is quite tasty." His eyes danced. "But when it's packed and preserved for long amounts of time . . ."

"It becomes a lachrymatory agent," Ekon finished. Now he was staring at the pouch with new interest. "So, you guys are telling me that you've basically developed your own plant-based weapon?"

Thabo shrugged. "We're environmentally conscious."

"I have a question." Next to him, Themba was still nibbling on a corner of bread, but she nodded now to the first man, the one who'd taken the fireroot pouch from Ekon. "How long do the effects of that stuff last for those afflicted?"

"Most of the people on that street should be fine by now," he said. "The intense burning only lasts an hour or two at most, less if you have the sense to use milk to neutralize it instead of plain water."

"But the watery eyes last for much longer," said Thabo. "It's not comfortable."

Ekon couldn't stop the shudder that went through his body. He now had an entirely new appreciation for the word *uncomfortable.* As soon as he'd pulled the caravan over to let Thabo resume driving it, he'd found Safiyah and gotten the counter ointment that took away the plumbago flower's itch. All remnants of the flower's rash were gone, but Ekon still felt the occasional phantom itch on his skin and had to resist scratching viciously.

"It's good most of the Sons of the Six got hit with the fireroot, then," he said as he reached for one of the apple slices and took a bite. "We would have been done for if they hadn't been disabled by it."

For the first time since they'd sat down, Safiyah looked up and scoffed. "Please. We would have been fine with or without fireroot. The Sons of the Six can't fight."

Ekon nearly choked on his apple slice. "I'm sorry, what?"

Safiyah gave him a pitying look. "They walk around with their fancy clothes and shiny knives, but they'd be useless in a real fight, one without their oh-so-precious rules of conduct."

Ekon opened his mouth, then closed it. He was surprised at

the sudden defensiveness he felt for his former brothers. "Sons of the Six train for years," he said, trying to keep his voice neutral. "I know, from personal experience, that the selection process for candidates is highly competitive."

Safiyah's smile was haughty. "I know for a fact that, in one-to-one combat, I could take on any Son of the Six and win."

"I seriously doubt that," Ekon muttered into his water gourd. When he lowered it, there was a wicked glint in Safiyah's eyes he didn't like at all. She jutted her chin at him, challenging.

"Do you want to bet on that?"

"Bet?" Ekon frowned. "What are you talking about?"

"Just a friendly wager," said Safiyah. She steepled her fingers and let her chin rest on them. "Ten fedhas says I can beat you in a sparring match. Right now."

Ekon waited for her to say that she was joking, and when she didn't, his eyes widened. He would have been more prepared for Safiyah to grow another head or confess that she was actually a tree.

"You . . . want to fight me?"

"Not fight," said Safiyah sweetly. "Spar. Isn't that how warriors train?"

"It is, but . . ." His words trailed off. Several members of the Enterprise were now looking between him and Safiyah with interest. But surely they weren't serious. Surely they didn't think it was a good idea for the two of them to . . .

"Are you *afraid* of me?" Safiyah asked the question in that same sweet voice.

"No." Ekon cheeks started to warm. "Of course not."

"Then why won't you spar with me?" she pressed. "It's just a casual bet."

Ekon swallowed. "We don't have any weapons. Per the rules of a proper spar, each participant must have—"

"Okay, so no weapons."

Ekon threw his hands up. "Then it's not a true spar."

"That's okay." Safiyah's grin widened. "We can just do hand-to-hand combat."

"Hand-to—?" *No.* Ekon began to tap his fingers against his knees. *No. No. No.* "I can't do that."

"Why, exactly?" Safiyah asked, raising one of her brows.

Ekon sputtered. "Because you're a . . . and I'm a . . . and we . . ." He sighed. "It wouldn't be a fair match," he finally said. "Not for you."

Safiyah smirked and rose to her feet. "I'm sure I'll be fine. C'mon, Okojo, what have you got to lose?"

Plenty.

"Come on." She turned to Thabo. "You'd referee for us, wouldn't you?"

"Absolutely," said Thabo. "I'm intrigued."

"I think we all are, but if Ekon isn't *comfortable . . .*"

Ekon now saw what she was doing. He was in a corner. If he fought Safiyah and won—which he would—he would be a jerk. But if he flat-out refused to . . .

They'll think you're afraid of her.

"Fine." Ekon got to his feet too. "I'll do it."

At that moment, Themba also joined them on her feet. She looked between Ekon and Safiyah, shaking her head. "On that note, I'm going to take a nap."

"What?" Ekon was surprised. "You're not going to stay and watch?"

"I think not," said Themba with pursed lips. "In my experience, bought sense is better than any given."

She turned on her heel after that, and Ekon redirected his attention to Safiyah. She was still smiling.

"Where shall we do it?"

Ekon searched around, then pointed to a spot of grass some feet away from the caravan. "Over there."

He, Safiyah, and Thabo moved to stand in the spot he indicated, with some members of the Enterprise coming to join them. Using a stick, Thabo drew a crude circle with a circumference of about twelve feet.

"Standard rules," he said. "First one to be pushed out of the circle or pinned to the ground loses. Other than that, anything goes."

Ekon moved to stand in the circle, flexing his fingers. Already he could feel his body priming itself—he planted his feet and steadied his heart rate. He couldn't remember the last time he'd had a proper spar, it would have been weeks ago, well before his final rites to become a Son of the Six. He didn't want to admit a small bit of excitement was coursing through him.

Safiyah did not stretch as she moved to join him in the circle. Instead she looked him over, amused. "Anything goes," she repeated. "This won't be like your prim little practice matches at the temple."

Ekon didn't answer. He had fallen back into the mindset years of training instilled in him. He focused on Safiyah, stopped seeing her as anything other than his target. He narrowed his eyes, focused.

"On my count," said Thabo. He moved between them and held up his hands. "One, two—"

"Three." Safiyah lunged with unexpected speed. Thabo barely moved out of the way as she charged at Ekon, her face full of nothing but new fury as she punched and kicked at any spot on Ekon she could find. Her left hand swung around, ready for a roundhouse, but he dodged her easily, and again when she tried for an uppercut. She was fast, he could admit that, but it was obvious she was also self-taught. There was no strategy to the way Safiyah fought, no precision. A tiny smile pulled at Ekon's lips.

This would be easy.

He moved backward slightly, keeping an eye on the edge of the sparring circle. Safiyah saw how close he was and rushed him, and he neatly sidestepped her, causing her to have to pivot sharply to stop herself from falling. She tried another punch, and when he blocked it with ease, she gritted her teeth.

"Is this your plan?" she snapped. "Just keep running from me so you don't actually have to fight? I didn't think the Sons of the Six were cowards."

She's goading you. Ekon almost found it funny. It was a predictable, common tactic; she was hoping he'd get sloppy. He considered a moment as he moved around the edge of the circle, her on its opposite end, mirroring his steps. Ekon counted, finding the cadence in their dance.

One-two-three. One-two-three. One-two-three.

He attacked without warning, and he was satisfied to see the suddenness of his movements had caught Safiyah off guard. He was careful not to actually punch or kick Safiyah, but he directed them so that now she was the one forced backward. She glanced back as one of her heels neared the circle's edge.

"Not bad," she panted, "for a Son of the Six."

But Ekon wasn't finished. He didn't need the monster in his chest as he continued pushing Safiyah back. Then he caught her ankle with a heel hook that threw her off balance. She yelled as she fell to the ground, but Ekon caught her upper arm just before she hit the dirt. She looked up at him, eyes blazing.

"You forget," he murmured, tightening his grip. "I'm not a Son of the Six."

Safiyah's expression changed abruptly. He'd expected to see defeat in her eyes, but instead her gaze dropped, so that he could count the eyelashes fanned across her cheeks. Ekon became suddenly hyperaware of how close they were. His own gaze fell, only for a second, then—

Whoosh.

He felt the air get knocked out of his body as Safiyah kneed his inner thigh, too close for comfort. She spun, and Ekon felt himself falling as she bore down on him. They landed in the dirt together, her knees on either side of his waist, and when she leaned in, so that her chest hovered inches from his, something hitched low in his stomach.

"I *didn't* forget."

The words barely registered in Ekon's mind as she sprang to her feet and stepped back. He tried to speak, but the words were choked.

"I—you . . ."

"Safiyah wins," Thabo declared unnecessarily. Ekon started.

He'd almost forgotten Thabo and some of the other members of the Enterprise had come to watch. Heat rose in his cheeks.

"Wait a minute, you—"

Safiyah raised a brow as she held her hand out. "I won. Pay up, Okojo."

The other members of the Enterprise chortled, and the heat in Ekon's face grew. He shifted his weight from foot to foot for a moment. "Uh, I don't actually have any money to give you," he said. "Sorry."

Safiyah narrowed her eyes. "You mean to tell me you've been walking around with no money at all?"

Ekon shrugged. "I spent most of what I had. What's left is back in the temple. I didn't exactly have time to pack my things."

She was openly frowning at him. "You mean to tell me you're not even carrying mugger money?"

"Mugger money?" It was Ekon's turn to frown. "What's that?"

"I—" Safiyah opened her mouth, then closed it just as quickly, shaking her head in disbelief. "You've got a lot to learn about survival, Okojo."

Ekon stayed in a sour mood for the better part of the next hour.

His tailbone hurt from the way he'd fallen with Safiyah, but when he was honest, he knew the thing that was really bruised was his ego. He could imagine what Shomari and the other Sons of the Six would say, what Kamau would say. Thinking of his brother made him recall the way his brother had looked back in Lkossa, and he felt even worse.

"This seat taken?"

Ekon looked up. Abeke was ambling over to him, carrying a raffia basket in her arms. He shook his head and she sat beside him, smiling.

"Don't be too put out about Safiyah," she said wryly. "That girl's wily as a jackal."

"What's that?" asked Ekon, nodding toward her basket. He was eager to change the subject. Abeke's basket was filled with quills and tightly rolled scrolls.

"Ah, these are the Enterprise's accounts," she explained. "It's my job to review them." She pulled out one of the scrolls and showed him. The document showed a complicated spreadsheet of figures, numbers concerning how much the Enterprise earned for each of their products, how much they lost, how much money was spent on operational costs. Ekon was embarrassed to admit to himself that he thought it was cool.

"And this is your job?" he asked. "Just messing with numbers all day?"

Abeke smiled. "It's a bit more complicated than that, but at essence, yes."

Ekon thought on that. All his life, he'd wanted—no, no, he'd been *told* that he wanted—to be a warrior, like every other male member of his family. He'd never considered doing anything else for a job, but . . . he turned something over in his thoughts. What if he had a job like Abeke's, a job where he got to mess with numbers all day? To himself, he shook his head before he could even let the idea take off.

"If you like numbers, you'll be interested in this," said Abeke, reaching into the basket again. "It's a calculation of—"

Ekon knew instantly that something was wrong. Abeke's eyes grew wide, her mouth slack.

"Abeke?" He frowned. "Are you okay?"

Abeke withdrew her hand from the basket slowly, too slowly. She stared down at her hand, and when Ekon followed her gaze, he started. There was a bright red dot on the back of her hand. It took him a moment to understand what he was seeing. He looked back toward the basket again, and a chill went through his body.

A yellow scorpion was sitting at the bottom of the basket, its telson glinting in the sun. Ekon's heart plummeted.

"Abeke!" He turned back to the woman. Her breath was already shallowing. Drops of sweat were forming on her brow. She wavered once, twice, then keeled forward.

"HELP!" Ekon yelled. "Someone, help!" He felt more than heard the other members of the Enterprise running his way, standing over him.

"What happened?" asked Thabo.

"She was stung," said Ekon. "Help me turn her over. Someone get water."

Together he and Thabo rolled the woman to her side while one of the other members of the Enterprise ran to fetch water and a compress. Ekon's heart thundered in his chest. Abeke's eyes were fluttering, and he could barely hear her breathing at all.

"What got her?" asked Safiyah. Gone was any of the cheekiness or laughter in her eyes. She looked to be on the verge of tears.

"It was a deathstalker scorpion, hiding in her scrolls." Ekon had known as soon as he'd seen the creature's coloring that it was true. "I've read about them. They're highly venomous."

A terrible shudder went through Abeke's entire frame,

followed by a long, dry rasp. The tears Safiyah had been trying to hold on to fell and streaked her face. "Is there anything we can do?"

No. Ekon didn't want to say it aloud. Deathstalkers were among the most toxic creatures in all the Zamani Region, maybe in all of Eshōza. "The only thing that counters its venom is—" He stopped short, glancing over at one of the wagons. "Wait. Do you all have any eucalyptus?"

Safiyah looked up at him. "Of course."

"Grab it, now!"

Safiyah moved without another word, darting to the wagon and coming back within seconds. She held an entire clove of it in her hand. "What do I do?"

Ekon could feel other members of the Enterprise standing around them, watching. "Back up, she needs air!" he said. "Safiyah, try to force her to eat it. It doesn't have to be a lot, but make sure she swallows."

Safiyah pried Abeke's mouth open and forced some of the eucalyptus into the woman's mouth. Abeke gagged instantly, but carefully Safiyah used a finger to push it down, then immediately gave her water.

"Come on, Abeke," she pleaded. "Swallow."

A moment that felt like a lifetime passed as they both watched, waited. Then Abeke's jaw began to move. Ekon kept his eyes on her throat as it bobbed, as she swallowed both the water and the eucalyptus. Another few seconds passed, and her eyes fluttered open. She sat up and began to cough.

"Abeke!" Safiyah was kneeling by her, her hands fluttering uselessly over the woman's body. "Are you okay?"

"Water?" Abeke croaked. "I need water."

Safiyah held the gourd up for her while the woman took several greedy gulps. Her body shuddered again, but her breathing had slowed. When she was finished, she lay back down on the grass.

"I thought I was done for," she said weakly.

"You would have been," said Thabo. He was standing a few feet back. One of his hands was on his head in sheer disbelief. "If Ekon hadn't saved you."

Ekon's cheeks warmed as Safiyah's eyes cut to him. "How did you do that?"

"What?"

"How did you know eucalyptus would work?"

"It's . . . it's basic venom theory," said Ekon. When Safiyah's eyes narrowed, he added, "Normally, eucalyptus is poisonous, but when combined with the venom from the scorpion, the two neutralize each other."

"And you just knew that?"

"I may not know about mugger money, but I do read a lot."

"Abeke needs rest," one of the other members of the Enterprise said. "We need to get her into the wagon."

Ekon and Safiyah both helped bring Abeke to her feet, then walked her into the wagon so she could lie down. Once they'd left her to sleep, Safiyah turned to Ekon. She looked uncomfortable.

"That's the second time you've saved a member of our crew," she said quietly. "I'm sorry for being unkind earlier."

Ekon didn't know exactly what to say back to that. *I'm sorry.* He hadn't grown up in a place where apologies were given so freely. "Um, that's okay," he said. "Really, it's no big—"

"Ekon."

They both looked up. Ano was standing a few feet from them, next to Abeke's basket, with her eyes trained on him. In the midst of everything, Ekon had forgotten about her, but he saw now the woman was frowning.

"I'd like a word with you, alone."

Safiyah looked back and forth between them, visibly surprised. But when Ano nodded, she left, going to join Thabo and the other members of the Enterprise as they continued eating lunch. Ekon swallowed as he approached Ano. His eyes flitted to Abeke's basket. He wanted to tell Ano that the deathstalker scorpion might still be in there, but he didn't dare. A long pause passed between them before she spoke first.

"I appreciate what you did for Abeke."

Ekon nodded.

"It's curious, though," she said in a cool voice. "I've operated the Enterprise for several years now with virtually no issues whatsoever. The very first day I let you join us, and we have our most ill-fortuned day yet."

Ekon frowned. It hardly seemed fair to blame him for what had happened back in Lkossa, and it seemed even less reasonable to blame him for the scorpion. He opened his mouth to argue, but before he could speak, Ano took a step closer, her own dark gaze narrowed.

"I saw you hesitate," she said in a low voice.

"What?"

"*I saw you hesitate,*" she repeated. "When we were leaving the market, and the warrior stepped in front of you."

Kamau. Ekon didn't think anyone but Safiyah had seen that

moment. Knowing she'd watched that tiny, intimate moment felt strangely intrusive.

"You knew him," Ano went on. "Didn't you?"

"Yes." Ekon saw no point in lying. "He's my brother."

A look Ekon didn't understand passed over Ano's face, so brief he wasn't sure he'd seen it at all. For several seconds, the woman didn't say anything. Her gaze bored into him before she spoke again. "We don't get to choose our family." She said the words with surprising softness. "But you do get to choose where your loyalties lie."

It took Ekon a moment to understand what she was implying. "Ano." He shook his head. "Themba and I are grateful for all you've done to help us get south. If you think we're going to betray the Enterprise—"

"What?" Ano's brow rose, her face the picture of skepticism. "Will you make some impressive oath and promise that you'd never betray me because we've known each other for a whole day and a half? Please excuse me if such a vow does not move me, as you would have made the very same kind to the Sons of the Six, before you left them."

He was surprised to feel the real sting in those words, but they were true. He had made vows to the Sons of the Six. He'd vowed to uphold the tenets of his people, to act with courage, honor, and integrity, to obey. In a matter of hours after making those vows, in a temple no less, he'd gone back on his word.

"Ano, you don't know me," he said slowly. "But for however much it's worth, I give you my word that, on my honor, I'll never betray you, or the Enterprise. Ever."

One of Ano's brows rose as she stooped down beside Abeke's

basket. She stared at it for several seconds, as though looking for something. Then, with uncanny speed, she snatched something from it. It was the deathstalker scorpion. Its legs wriggled as she held it up, and Ekon watched with a slightly nauseated feeling as its telson flexed between Ano's pinched fingers. She lowered the scorpion to the ground, picked up a rock, and brought it down on the creature. The scorpion did not move again.

"A word of advice, Ekon?" she said. Her gaze met his and held it. "Mind that your honor doesn't get you killed."

A SPRAWLING SECRET

BINTI

DANAH.

From the street, I read the crude white sign nailed to the door of the shop immediately before me.

Its corners are bent and slightly torn, but those five letters are painted prominently in bold blue temple ink. There is no mistaking their meaning or their origins.

DANAH.

To an unknowing eye, it might look like a woman's name, but it is not. DANAH. *Darajas Are Not Allowed Here.* It is an efficient acronym.

I can still remember when the first of those signs cropped up in the city. There was one and then there were many, cropping up among the vendor stalls like weeds in the night. Now I've grown used to them. Of course, non-darajas do not care what the DANAH signs mean for those they apply to; they don't care that we have even fewer places to buy our food from these days. No, they only care that the line between us is made clear and visible, that we are segregated as totally as possible.

"Binti!"

I look up and see my mother waving me over. She's standing next to a woman I've never seen before with short, thin twists dyed a reddish-brown hue with what looks like cheap henna. The woman gives me a toothy smile.

"Binti, this is Ola," my mother says. "I've just met her. She's a daraja too."

I fake a small smile. "Hello, Auntie." This woman is decidedly *not* my auntie, but at seventeen, I know better than to say otherwise.

"Ola was just telling me she has a girl your age," Mama continues. "I thought it would be nice if you two could make friends."

I barely suppress the urge to roll my eyes. Mama still thinks she can orchestrate my friendships by simply placing me next to someone else my age. Judging by Ola's broadening smile, she's in agreement with my mama. I watch as she glances over her shoulder.

"Nyah," she calls. "Come here, girl!"

My eyes widen as I look over Auntie Ola's shoulder in time to see the young woman coming toward us. She is dressed in a modest brown kaftan, no fancier or more expensive than my own, but something about the way she's wearing it—the way she's walking in it—catches the eye of every young man in the market. Slight curves hug her body subtly in all the places where my clothes still hang loose, and her hair is coiffed into long, perfect black twists down her back. Her lips are even colored the distinct shade of red that I know comes from the dye they sell in the more expensive parts of the market. She stops before us and smiles.

"Hello," she says with a cheery wave.

"Nyah," says Auntie Ola. "This is Binti. Her mother is daraja-born too."

"Oh!" Instantly, Nyah's eyes light up. She embraces me, and I'm surprised to find that the gesture feels genuine. Over her shoulder, my mama is practically misty-eyed. When Nyah pulls back, she holds me at arm's length. "It's so lovely to meet you."

"Nyah is starved for friends who share her heritage," Auntie Ola explains.

At this, Nyah looks over her shoulder, slightly exasperated. *"Mama!"*

I smile in spite of myself. There's something familiar, even comfortable about the way Nyah and her mother act. It reminds me of how Mama and I are, but it's the first time I get to observe the dynamic in someone else. I suddenly feel a bit more normal, like maybe Mama and I are not as strange and different as I usually feel.

"Themba and I are going to do some shopping," says Auntie Ola. "Why don't you girls spend some time together, get to know each other?"

"That sounds like a wonderful idea!" Nyah claps her hands with more excitement than I feel is strictly necessary, given the situation, but admittedly, I'm looking forward to the prospect of spending time with someone other than my mother. As it is, Mama already looks nervous.

"I don't know . . ." Her lips are pursed. "I don't usually let Binti wander the markets by herself."

"Nonsense, Themba!" Auntie Ola waves a dismissive hand. "She won't be alone, Nyah will be with her. They're sensible girls, and Nyah knows this market like the back of her hand. I'm sure Binti does too."

"I'll be fine, Mama," I add quickly. "Promise."

Mama shifts her weight a moment longer, still looking unsure, before saying, "All right, then, I suppose you can go for half an hour."

"You have nothing to worry about, Auntie." Nyah is still beaming, and I'm wondering how a person can look so radiant in the thick of a farmers market. "We'll meet you right back here in thirty minutes' time."

Auntie Ola steers my mother away, already chatting to her about some new tax the Kuhani has just levied against the darajas. In her absence, my muscles relax just slightly, and when I look over at Nyah, I'm surprised to find her smirking.

"So, first time?" Her voice is slightly lower, and there's a knowing look in her eye. It catches me off guard.

"What do you mean?"

One of Nyah's perfectly painted brows rises. "Have you ever gotten to shop in the markets without your mother, Binti?"

"Well . . ." I stare at my feet. "Um, no." When I look up again, I expect to see mocking in Nyah's eyes. Instead, there's kindness.

"Don't worry," she says breezily. "You'll get the hang of it, and you have one of the city's best to show you around. Do you have money?"

My hands dig into the pocket of my kaftan before I nod. "A few fedhas I've been saving up."

Nyah nods. "That'll be enough. Come on." She starts in the opposite direction that our mothers went in, and I follow.

"Where are we going?" I ask, trying to stay on her heels as she picks up the pace.

"To my favorite store," Nyah says over her shoulder. "Trust me, you're going to love it."

If I owe my mother thanks for anything, it is for my friendship with Nyah.

The first time we roamed the markets together, Mama was cautious, but eventually, I grew accustomed to spending whole afternoons with Nyah, wandering the stalls of the market and memorizing the craft behind her cleverest tricks. I learned how to find affordable clothes even in Lkossa's most expensive shops by looking at the bargain items in the back; how to ask for sample sizes of the paints and cosmetics sold at the apothecary instead of paying for the much pricier full-size amounts. I learned other things from Nyah too.

"So, have you ever done it?" Her eyes are full of mischief the day she asks me. "Kissed a boy?"

"I . . ." As usual, Nyah catches me off guard. "Well, no, I've never . . ."

"Or a girl." Her eyes dance. "If that's what you prefer."

"It's not that . . ." I fidget in place. "It's just . . . I haven't really had the opportunity . . ."

"You see that boy over there?" She nods subtly to a young man standing behind one of the fruit stalls. "He wants to kiss you."

"What?" I choke out the word a touch too loudly. "How do you know?"

"You can just *tell*," she says with a smile. "It's all in the way they look at you. Plus, everyone knows that every time a man adjusts his pants, he's thinking about kissing a girl."

I sneak a second glance at the young man. He *is* handsome. His hair is curly and black, though he's slightly overdue for a haircut, and the faintest hint of a dimple touches one side of his mouth. We wait a minute, watching, and sure enough, he glances at us, then adjusts his pants. We double over in fits of laughter.

"I *told* you." Nyah's holding her sides, laughing so hard there are tears in her eyes.

"You're lying," I say between gasps. "That boy doesn't even know me."

"Not yet." Suddenly, Nyah lights up. "But maybe that could be arranged."

At once, I stiffen. "What are you talking about?"

"First, we have to pick out an outfit for you, yes, I think a full makeover is due." She says these things more to herself than me. "Come with me."

Nyah leads me through the city until we reach the Tajiri District, the second-wealthiest district, only behind the district where the Temple of Lkossa is housed. I know immediately when we've crossed into it because, here, there is no dirt on the cobbled streets; sweepers are paid to keep the place pristine. Nyah doesn't falter as she leads me down the street.

"Nyah," I whisper. "Are you sure we're supposed to be—?"

"Relax, Binti," she says under her breath. "And trust me."

She walks on until we've reached a shop near the district's edge, one of the largest on the entire street. Its size alone catches my eye—the building must be at least three stories—but I'm also captivated by the gleaming white of its bricks, the metallic gold trim of its massive windows. The women who walk in and out of it are all finely dressed, with beaded Fulani braids falling down their backs, and tailored wax-print dresses that look more expensive than what Mama and I see in a month.

"This shop has the most beautiful jewelry," Nyah says dreamily, "and you can always find something good in their bargain bins." She makes to go up the stairs, but I catch her arm before she can. My eye has just fixed on the small white sign propped against the front window's lower right corner. It has the telltale letters, the cerulean ink.

"Nyah," I murmur. "It says we're not allowed."

"No." Nyah gives me a coy look. "It says *darajas* aren't allowed."

I frown, confused. "But you and I . . . our mothers . . . there are heritage laws—"

"We don't *have* to tell anyone that our mothers are darajas, Binti," says Nyah. "I mean, it's not like they ask to see papers."

"You mean . . ." I falter. "You're saying we should lie?"

"Not lie." Nyah waves a casual hand, as though this is all the simplest thing in the world. "We just . . . omit the entire truth. No one asks, no one tells."

I stare at her in horror until she offers me a distinctly pitying look.

"Oh, Binti." She takes my hand and squeezes it gently, but I recognize the glint of mischief in her eyes. "Don't tell me that you've never passed before."

"Passed?" I repeat the word. It sounds strange to me, like the door to a sprawling secret.

"Come on." Now Nyah tugs on my hand. "It'll be fine. Besides, how else are we going to find a cute outfit for you?"

"But—"

Nyah doesn't give me any more time to argue; she's already

leading me through the shop's front door. My heart hammers in my chest as its tiny golden bell rings to announce our entrance. I hold my breath, and we cross its threshold.

The shop's interior is even more beautiful than its exterior. Polished wooden floors gleam bright against the light, and the long tables on either wall are laden with dresses and headwraps of every fabric and color. There are wooden boxes full of glittering jewelry—earrings, brooches, and bracelets. I notice a display of massive hand-painted fans, each one longer than my arm. A glance at the price tag sends a chill up my spine.

"Nyah," I whisper as loudly as I can manage. She's already examining a dress of scarlet silk. "Come on, let's go. We shouldn't be—"

"Can I help you girls with anything?"

A jolt of sheer panic runs the length of me as I whirl around and face one of the shop's associates. She looks only a few years older than me and is dressed in a modest white dress and has a small smile. She looks at me, expectant.

"Um . . ." I can't find the words to speak. "I . . . we . . ."

"Good afternoon." Nyah has appeared by my side without warning. "My friend is looking for a dress and accessories. She has a *suitor*."

I glare at Nyah, but she only beams in answer. The shop attendant nods enthusiastically.

"How exciting," she says warmly, "and I can see why—you're stunning."

I don't know how to name the feeling blooming in my chest. It occurs to me that this is the first time someone other than Mama has ever paid me a compliment about the way I look. *Stunning*. It's not a word I'm accustomed to hearing, let alone in relation to me.

Is she just saying it to make me feel better, or is it possible that she means it?

"Isn't she?" Nyah grins. "I was just telling her that pink and green are her best colors."

"I agree," says the attendant. "I'm sure we can find something for you. What did you say your name was?"

"Uh . . ." Once again I don't know what to say; the words trip on themselves as I try to speak them. Fortunately, Nyah comes to my aid.

"Her name's Rashida," she says quickly. "I'm Daya."

Rashida. The name reverberates through me and I listen to its rhythm, memorize the ebb and flow of its syllables. Rashida seems a fitting name for a girl rich enough to shop in stores like this.

"It's lovely to meet you both," says the attendant. "If you'll follow me, we have some more options on our second floor . . ."

We spend the rest of the afternoon in the dress shop, trying on dresses and jewels we know we could never really afford. Each time the attendant comes with more things for us to try, I brace myself for the inevitable eruption, the moment in which she catches on and realizes who we are. I imagine the screaming, the embarrassment of being kicked out the store. I've heard horror stories of darajas who were forced into indentured servitude to pay for goods they or their daraja relations contaminated with their touch. I've seen darajas hauled through the streets for disobeying the DANAH laws. I think of my mother's face if she saw me like that, and I can't imagine which would hurt her more: watching that happen to her daughter, or understanding the reason it was happening—because her daughter pretended not to be of daraja blood, because she lied about who she was.

209

In the end, my fears are in vain; the attendant never catches on at all. We leave the shop hours later without a dress, and relief settles over me as we reenter more familiar streets.

"Sorry we couldn't find you anything after all," says Nyah.

"It's okay." In truth, I'm just glad to be out of the shop. "You tried."

"Still . . ." Nyah has that look in her eyes again, the one that makes me nervous. "I thought you deserved a present." She reaches down the neckline of her dress and pulls out a silver bracelet. The chain is silver, and a twinkling amethyst jewel carved in the shape of a heart dangles from it. The breath leaves my body.

"How did you—?"

"I swiped it while you and the attendant were talking about colors. I was still right, by the way—pink and green *are* your best colors."

She's grinning, but all I can do is gape at the bracelet. In the eventide light, it glitters every time it moves. I don't even want to think about how much a thing like that is worth. My eyes fill with tears.

"Oh, don't *cry*." Nyah pushes the jewelry into my hand and folds my fingers over it. "Call it a friendship bracelet, a token of thanks for putting up with me all the time."

We walk together down the road, neither one of us saying a word. I don't know what thoughts are with Nyah tonight, but in my mind all I can think of is the bracelet. Every few feet, I open my palm and stare at it in awe, in wonder, in fear.

In the same moment that I know it is my dearest possession, I know too that I can never, *ever* show this bracelet to my mother.

CHAPTER 13

KONGAMATO

Koffi didn't shake her unease for the rest of the day.

Her dreams that night were filled with images, hunter and lioness locked in battle. She imagined the blistering cracks of a lightning that came with no storm, the glint of a spear's blade as it buried itself in warm golden fur. She saw Fedu's face in her mind, heard his laugh, his words.

Good and evil are never simple. They are capricious beasts, ever shifting in their shape, and rarely beautiful.

Fedu truly believed that what he was doing was right, which scared her. When it became impossible to sleep any longer, Koffi opened her eyes, tossing and turning in her bed as the first hints of light bled through the chamber's window. Not for the first time, a chilling question floated to the top of her mind. What if Fedu figured out what they were doing? What if he already knew? She shook her head. No. If Fedu already knew what they were planning, he would have put a stop to it, and he certainly wouldn't have let Koffi continue her training. As for what would happen if he found out . . . she shivered, not wanting to think about that possibility.

An hour later, when Makena entered her bedroom, she stopped short at the sight of her. "Uh . . . you okay?"

"Yeah," said Koffi quickly, swinging her legs over the bed's edge as she sat up. She'd decided almost as soon as Fedu had left her yesterday that she wouldn't say anything about his visit to the other darajas. It wouldn't do any good to.

"I've got a new outfit for you," said Makena, beaming. "If I do say so myself, this one is among my best pieces." She unfolded the garment on her arm and held up a black tunic and matching pants covered in an array of white wax-print leaves. "What do you think?"

Koffi's brow rose. "Pants?"

"I figured they would be more practical," Makena explained. "Your lesson today is with Amun, in the stables."

"The stables?" Koffi repeated. "There are stables at Thornkeep?"

Makena frowned. "Of course there are." She said it like it was the most obvious thing in the world. "They're in the north garden. Hurry and get dressed, we don't want to be late."

The air warmed as they reached the stables. Koffi couldn't help but draw the obvious comparisons to both the Night Zoo's grounds and the Temple of Lkossa's lower stable. After a moment, she decided this reminded her of a combination of both. The scents—wood, hay, and manure—were right, but there was also something inexplicably magical about the place. The stalls themselves were large, even for a big ox or horse, and Koffi wondered what creatures were housed here. She heard chirps, snorts, even a distant roar that made her instinctively crane her neck. She was still gazing around the room when Amun came around one of the stalls' corners.

"Koffi, hey!" His smile was warm as he offered a cheery wave. "It's good to see you."

"And you," said Koffi. She meant it.

"I'll leave you to it," said Makena before heading off. Koffi closed her eyes a moment and breathed in. When she opened them, Amun was looking at her with a peculiar expression.

"That's not the reaction most girls have to the stables."

"I used to work in a sort of zoo with my family," Koffi admitted. "This is the first thing here that's felt kind of familiar to me, though the zoo where I worked wasn't nearly as nice as this."

"Ah." Amun nodded with understanding. "In that case, let me give you the grand tour."

Amun spent the better part of an hour leading Koffi through the various sections of Thornkeep's stables. Initially, Koffi had expected to only see the normal livestock—sheep, cows, and pigs—but she was pleasantly surprised to see that Fedu kept other creatures on the grounds too. To her surprise, one of the larger paddocks held a handful of black-pronged impalas; in a smaller one, two fennec foxes with fur the color of sun-bleached sand tumbled and played with each other. Koffi couldn't hold back the smile that pulled at her face.

"This is incredible," she said, casting around the endless stalls and pens.

Amun nodded. "If not for the whole entrapment part of this situation, it would be nice," he said. "Fedu has really tried to make it the perfect place for a daraja in the Order of Maisha."

"Maisha," Koffi repeated. "That's the Order of Life."

"It is," said Amun. "Generally speaking, darajas in my order are split into two categories—those who deal in plant life, and those who prefer to work with animals. Obviously, you can tell from the state of Thornkeep's gardens that there are some pretty talented darajas in my order." He smiled. "But I prefer to work with things that have faces."

A sudden bang made them both jump. Koffi looked over Amun's shoulder and noticed a shadowed part of the stables. There were no animals there, just a single large stall. There was another bang, and its door shuddered violently. Amun put his hand on her shoulder and moved them both slightly away from it. She heard what sounded like a low bellow from within, the splintering of wood.

"What's in there?" she asked quietly.

Amun's expression sombered. "Something you hopefully never have to see."

Koffi stared a moment longer, before Amun steered them down a different hall of stables. This one was primarily filled with small mammals—meerkats, civets, and an aardwolf.

"So, how do affinities actually work for darajas in the Order of Maisha?" Koffi asked.

"It can vary," he explained. "The most unskilled of us might have a gift for finding animals from a specific species. At the other end of the spectrum, some legends say that, in days of old, there were darajas in the Order of Maisha who could change their bodies, actually transform into the animal of their choosing."

Koffi's eyes widened. "Could you do that, if you wanted to?"

"No." Amun laughed. "Communications are my specialty."

It took Koffi several seconds to fully appreciate what he'd just said. "You can talk to animals?"

He shook his head. "Not exactly, but . . ." He paused, thoughtful. "Actually, maybe I'd do better to show you. Normally, I wouldn't, but since you've worked with animals before . . ." He seemed to be convincing himself. "I think it'll be fine." He gestured, leading her to the back of the stables. Koffi noted that there were fewer animals here, and it was quieter. A massive set of sliding doors took up most of the stables' back wall; when they approached it, Amun held up a hand.

"I'd ask you to keep your voice down," he whispered. "And don't make any sudden moves."

Both fear and anticipation coursed through Koffi now. Amun nodded, then turned to the sliding doors. He shifted one of them just slightly, and gestured. Koffi took the cue to squeeze between them, and behind her she heard Amun do the same. She turned once they were through the doors, and her breath caught in her lungs.

She was staring at a massive open paddock, its grass hued a rich emerald green. The white fences marking its parameters stretched several yards in all directions, and directly adjacent to her, she could see that one of them even backed up to what had to be the northernmost edge of Thornkeep. Her eyes had exactly one second to process this before she heard it.

A long, shrill shriek.

The sound was unlike anything Koffi had ever heard before; it set her teeth on edge and raised the hair on her arms. At once, she tensed. She'd been so taken by the sheer size of this enclosure that she hadn't immediately thought to question why it was so massive, but she had her answer now.

The beasts sprawled across the paddock had a reptilian look about them, and their scales glittered an array of colors in the sunlight. Each one of them was huge, easily twice the size of any horse she'd ever seen, and coils of muscle flexed along their sinewy bodies as they moved. Koffi had to remind herself to keep breathing. There was only word she knew to describe creatures like this.

"Are these . . . ?"" She hesitated. "Are these dragons?"

Beside her, Amun chuckled. "Not quite." He took a careful step forward. "If you'll look closely, you'll notice some key differences."

Koffi forced herself to blink several times, though she didn't want to. It seemed like these creatures would vanish if she even looked away from them for a second.

"What are they called?"

"Kongamatos," he said softly. "There, look." He pointed. A kongamato a few feet from them, one with scales of brilliant red, was rising. "You see the beak? They're made from a metal like no other on the entire continent. It can cut through just about anything."

Koffi forced herself not to step back as the red kongamato turned in their direction. Amun had been right; now that the initial shock had faded, she saw that—despite what she'd initially thought—this creature was not a dragon. Its body certainly resembled a lizard, but its head was more birdlike. A long, slender beak protruded from its head, cast a color caught between copper and rose-gold. She noted the sharp point at the end of it and swallowed.

"I've . . . never heard of kongamatos before."

"No," said Amun, a new sadness in his voice. "You wouldn't have. Kongamatos used to live throughout the continent, albeit in different species. They were undomesticated at first, but as rulers realized how powerful they were, they began to breed them for war."

Koffi's gaze cut to another kongamato, one who'd just risen to stretch its legs. Its scales were a deep blue-green that reminded her of a peacock's feathers. It opened its beak, and she noted that it had not one, but two rows of pointed teeth.

"I can see why," she said to Amun. "I wouldn't want to see one of them on a battlefield."

"It worked for a while," said Amun. "But when the kings realized they could simply take the kongamatos' beaks and make their own weapons, they nearly hunted them into extinction. It's only because Fedu brought some of them here that they exist at all."

An unexpected sadness lanced through Koffi's body. She looked around at the paddock again. There had to be less than thirty kongamatos here in total. To realize that this was what was left of a species that had once probably populated the entire continent was devastating.

"The good news is, some of them are breeding here," said Amun. "See that little one? She was born a few seasons ago, so she's not fully grown yet."

Koffi found the one he was indicating, a notably smaller kongamato with scales colored a pearlescent gray. She startled when the creature tossed her head, unfurling the wings that'd been neatly folded against her sides.

"They can fly?"

"They can, but rarely do," said Amun. "Since these were raised here and have no real sense of the outside world, they mostly like to stay in their paddock. Sometimes they'll fly around the perimeter of Thornkeep. Hopefully you get to see when one of them does it. They're brilliant in the sky."

"Could you ride one?"

"Technically, yes, but I wouldn't try it," said Amun. His eyes turned serious for a moment. "Kongamatos aren't known for their mild, predictable temperaments, even the ones here who are pretty used to seeing humans."

"You said you were going to show me your affinity," Koffi reminded him.

"Ah yes." His grin returned instantly. "Here, I'll show you. Stay here." He walked toward the gray kongamato. Some of the others raised their heads as he passed them, but most seemed perfectly unbothered. When he reached the creature, he offered a hand.

"Nyeupe," he said gently. "How are we feeling today?"

To Koffi's surprise, the kongamato made a small, keening sound—high-pitched, but not as shrill as what she'd heard before. She watched as the kongamato circled Amun lightly on her clawed feet, almost as though she was dancing. She lowered her head and nudged Amun gently.

"I have someone I want you to meet," he murmured to her. Abruptly, he looked up. "Koffi, come on over!"

Koffi paused. She'd spent her whole life working with and

caring for dangerous animals, which had given her a healthy dose of caution when it came to animals she was unfamiliar with. She hesitated.

"It's okay," Amun encouraged. "I promise, she won't hurt you. Just walk slowly."

Koffi took a deep breath, then started across the paddock. Her breath shallowed as she passed some of the bigger kongamatos, as she felt their piercing yellow gazes on her skin, following her footsteps with mild interest. She focused on Amun and didn't stop walking until she was standing next to him again. Up close, the baby kongamato seemed much bigger.

"Nyeupe," said Amun. "This is my friend Koffi. Say hello?"

Koffi stilled as the creature turned her full attention to her. Nyeupe had eyes colored the deep orange of a sunset, and Koffi found herself mesmerized as she stared into them. The seconds slowed, and a peculiar thing happened as her gaze and the creature's stayed locked: she saw understanding in her eyes. Nyeupe cocked her head, visibly curious, then bowed her head so that it pressed into Koffi's. The sensation nearly knocked her off her feet, but Koffi held her ground, smiling.

"Thank you," she said. "It's nice to meet you."

"When I channel the splendor, I'm able to connect with Nyeupe in a special way," Amun explained. "I can't speak to her, but I can hear her thoughts, and she can hear mine. Sorry if that doesn't make sense."

"No." Koffi shook head. "It does."

"Obviously, you're not in the Order of Maisha," he continued. "But I thought we could try something, if you're up to it?"

"Sure."

"I want you to try to summon the splendor," he said. "The same way you did . . . before." Koffi knew he had stopped just short of saying *in the Mistwood.*

"Okay," said Koffi. She adjusted, anchoring her feet to the ground, and breathed in, then out. It was strange, doing this with an audience, but she tried to ignore the fact that Amun was there, to focus on her emotions.

I am excited. I am scared. I am hopeful.

She felt the splendor resting dormant within her spring to life, warming her arms and legs as it coursed through her. The longer it stayed within her, the more acutely she felt the difference in its strength. A pressure built behind her eyes as she worked to restrain it, to use only the smallest amount she needed. She opened her palms, and a handful of small twinkling lights appeared in the air. They swirled around her like a breeze, and without speaking she directed them so that they danced around Nyeupe. For her part, the kongamato seemed transfixed. Koffi let the light dance around her a few more times before she called it back to her and exhaled. Beside her, Amun clapped.

"That was pretty good."

"Thanks."

"How do you feel?" he asked.

"Honestly, a little tired."

He nodded. "That's to be expected. The more you practice, the easier it'll feel, and the less exhausting those small spurts will be." They watched together as a butterfly fluttered by Nyeupe and the kongamato turned to go after it with a series of delighted shrieks. Koffi sighed.

"They're really beautiful creatures," she said.

"They are," Amun agreed. "In all honesty, I feel badly for them. People look at them and see monsters, beasts of ruin and destruction, but kongamatos are intelligent, complex, powerful."

Another stab of pain struck Koffi unexpectedly. Amun's words reminded her of something Mama had once said to her at the Night Zoo.

Sometimes things that seem dangerous are just misunderstood.

Tears suddenly welled in Koffi's eyes. Her mother loved animals, and it occurred to Koffi now how much Mama would have loved this place.

"Hey." Amun's brows rose. "Are you all right?"

"Oh, I'm fine." Koffi wiped the tears away, embarrassed. "I just—"

They both turned around as the stables' sliding doors opened behind them. Koffi was surprised—and not sure if she was happy—to see Zain stick his head between the doors.

"Ah, Butter Knife," he said. "Hello."

"Good morning, Zain."

Zain's eyes went to Amun. "Sorry to intrude, but I've just come from Thornkeep's kitchens," he said. "You're needed there, something about a mouse issue . . ."

"I can only imagine." Amun was already pinching the bridge of his nose. "Sorry, Koffi, we'll have to postpone the rest of this."

"It's okay," said Koffi. "Thanks for what you did show me."

"Zain will walk you out," he said, pushing the doors open wide. "I'll see you." He was gone without another word, leaving Koffi and Zain alone. He inclined his head, and she answered it with a frown.

"Butter Knife?"

"I like it, actually," said Zain. His grin was widening. "Rolls off the tongue."

Koffi suddenly remembered Njeri's comment. "Stop telling people about that."

"Why?" Zain stepped fully into the paddock. If he was at all nervous about the kongamatos, he didn't show it. "Personally, I think it's a great story—"

"Zain."

"Fine, fine, I won't tell anyone else."

"Thank you."

An uncomfortable silence fell over them then. Zain waited a beat before he broke it.

"So," he said slowly. "How have your lessons been going?"

"Fine." Koffi was relieved to have something else to talk about. "This is technically my third one, but Makena's been working with me too. I think I'm getting the hang of things." She lowered her voice. "I really do think I'll be able to get us out of here."

At this Zain's brows went up. For the first time since he'd entered the paddock, he looked visibly uncomfortable. "Uh, as a rule, we don't really talk about that kind of stuff out in the open."

Heat rose in Koffi's cheeks. "Oh."

"There are just too many opportunities to be overheard."

"Um, got it. Okay." She shifted her weight a moment, feeling awkward, but then she frowned. No. She decided it then. No, she wouldn't let Zain—or anyone else for that matter—make her feel embarrassed. She jutted her chin at him.

"Do you always follow the rules?"

It was Zain's turn to frown. "Psh. No."

Got him. Koffi barely suppressed a smile. "Mm, I don't know. I'm not convinced."

Zain smirked. "I could change your mind."

"How?"

"Take a ride with me," he said, nodding. "On one of the kongamatos."

"What?" All thoughts of their little game immediately abandoned Koffi as his words sank in. "Are you serious?"

"Unless you're scared." There was an insufferable glint in Zain's eyes now, a delight in his voice.

"But . . ." Koffi looked over her shoulder at the kongamatos still in the paddock. Amun had just said that these kongamatos' tempers were unpredictable, that only a fool would dare ride them.

"C'mon," Zain coaxed. To Koffi's surprise, he almost sounded sincere now, like he really wanted her to do this. "I've done it before. As long as we're respectful, they don't mind."

"I . . ." Koffi didn't know what to say. On the one hand, she very seriously doubted climbing aboard a highly intelligent, metal-beaked creature that had once been bred for war was the wisest thing to do this morning, but on the other hand . . . Zain held her gaze now. He seemed to be waiting for her answer, daring her. Was he daring her to say no, though, or yes?

"If, hypothetically, we were going to do this," said Koffi, "which kongamato would we be riding?"

Zain grinned. "Mjane."

As though she heard her name, another kongamato approached them. Her scales were night-sky black, and a jagged set of long, pointed spikes decorated the top of her head. Koffi couldn't put her fingers on it, but something about the creature demanded respect. The kongamato stopped before them and raised her head to the sky imperiously.

"Mjane is one of the most senior kongamatos at Thornkeep," said Zain. "She's great, aren't you, old girl?"

Koffi had expected the creature to snap her massive beak at Zain, and was surprised when, instead, the kongamato lowered her head the same way Nyeupe had before. Zain gave Mjane a pat on her long beak before turning to Koffi again. "What's it going to be, Butter Knife?" he asked. "Amun will be back soon. It's now or never."

Koffi pressed her lips into a tight line. "Will anyone see us?"

Zain shook his head. "Even if they do, no one will give us a second look. We'll be way too high up."

Koffi swallowed. The idea of being hundreds of feet off the ground on a highly intelligent, metal-beaked creature that had once been bred for war sounded even more foolish. But she'd be lying if she said that she wasn't tempted, that the idea of doing something reckless didn't also sound fun. She made a face, shifted from foot to foot, then said:

"Fine."

"Yes!" Zain clapped, albeit quietly, so as not to disturb the other kongamatos. "Okay, come on. I'll help you up."

Koffi tried to keep her breathing steady as Zain led her around the other side of Mjane. The kongamato seemed to understand what was happening, because she lowered herself down so that she was lying on her belly. Even at that height, her back came up to Koffi's torso.

"Here."

A jolt went through Koffi as Zain's hands found her waist and hoisted her onto Mjane's back. She didn't know what she'd been expecting, but the kongamato's black scales were sun-warmed, slick to the touch. Suddenly she was very grateful Makena had suggested pants. Zain pushed himself onto Mjane and settled behind Koffi. Once again his hands found her waist.

"I've got you," he said. Koffi could practically hear the excitement in his voice. "Ready?"

"Ready."

"Mjane, *kapunda*!"

Koffi felt a lurch, a pull somewhere around her navel, as the kongamato soared into the air. Her body slid back into Zain's as they careered higher and higher, but his arms wrapped around her and held her steady.

"It's all right!" he shouted. Koffi could barely hear him over the rush of wind. "You're not going to fall!"

Mjane veered left, and Koffi's knees instinctively tightened around the kongamato's waist. They leveled, and for the first time, she dared to glance down. The sight below her was wondrous.

From this vantage point, they were high enough to see Thornkeep in its entirety. Koffi saw the outlines of each cardinal garden, the way the uniform colors of each one created blocks of color as they flew over them. Like the rose of a compass, Thornkeep itself was situated exactly in the middle of it all. She'd hated this place the minute she'd woken up in it, but when she was honest with herself, from here it was beautiful.

"We're going to land now!" said Zain. "Hang on!"

Koffi almost regretted that. They'd only done one lap around Thornkeep's perimeter. Zain leaned just slightly, pushing both of their bodies forward, and the kongamato responded, dipping sharply. Koffi threw her hands out to catch herself as they slid even farther down, so that Koffi's knees pressed into the place where Mjane's wings met her back. The kongamato plummeted, flying toward the grass with a speed that made the air tear through her hair. Mjane was descending fast, too fast. Zain's grip on her tightened as the ground rose to meet them, but they were still sliding. Koffi understood what was about to happen a second too late.

"Zain—"

She gasped as they both slid off Mjane's back, falling through the air. For one blissful second, Koffi felt like she was flying, and then she met the ground with a hard thud. It took a moment for the explosion of stars clouding her vision to clear; even when they did, she just lay on her back for a moment. Nothing felt broken, but something warm was trickling down her chin. She sat up and winced.

"Koffi!"

She turned her head in time to see Zain running toward her. How he'd managed to get up so quickly was beyond her. He dropped to his knees. She was surprised by the level of concern in his eyes, the panic. "Are you all right? Are you hurt anywhere?"

"I'm fine." Koffi dragged an arm across her mouth. She'd busted her lip, it seemed, but other than that, she really did feel okay. "Honestly."

Zain shook his head. "I'm so, so sorry. I thought it would be fine, but Mjane—"

"Koffi!"

They both looked up to see Amun and Makena running toward them across the grass, both their faces pictures of pure horror. Amun pushed Zain aside as he fell to his knees too and grabbed Koffi by both shoulders to look her over. "She doesn't appear to have any broken bones," he said, more to himself than to anyone else. "Just a cut lip—"

"OW!"

Koffi and Amun both looked up. Zain had jumped to his feet quite suddenly, and Koffi saw why. Makena was running after him across the lawns, jabbing him with what looked like one of her sewing pins. He kept trying to escape, but Makena was fast, even in her dress.

"WHAT—WERE—YOU—THINKING?"

"Ouch!" Zain leaped away from her in a sort of graceful pirouette. "I thought it would be fun!"

"Fun? FUN?" Makena stopped chasing him. Her eyes were wild with rage. "You thought it would be *fun* to take the one person who might be able to help us get out of this place several hundred feet in the air, and then drop her?"

To Koffi's surprise, Zain looked properly chastened.

Makena threw Zain one more look of disgust before turning to Koffi. "Come on," she said gently. "I'll take you to a healer. They'll be able to patch up your lip and check for other injuries."

Koffi didn't think that was entirely necessary, but she let Amun help her up anyway and nodded. Makena slipped an arm around her to help her walk as they headed back toward Thornkeep. Koffi went with her willingly, but as she looked over at her shoulder, Zain offered a small salute. She couldn't quite stop herself from smiling.

CHAPTER 14

BLOOD AND GOLD

In the following days, Ekon fell into step with the Enterprise surprisingly quickly.

It didn't take long for him to figure out the group's rhythm, the tempo with which they traveled. Days started and ended early, which he didn't mind because it meant they were always packed and ready to head off by sunrise, and prepared to go to sleep by sunset. Breakfasts and dinners were short and efficient affairs, but Ano permitted lunch to last a bit longer. It took several days—three, to be precise—but gradually, Ekon started to understand the group's structure. It seemed each member of the Enterprise had both official and unofficial duties.

Safiyah, for example, was usually the Enterprise's runner, delegated to deliver spices and collect monies from clientele, but she was also responsible for looking after the mules. Kontar—the man who'd explained what fireroot was to Ekon—acted as one of the group's herbal specialists, able to assess the quality of the spices and herbs they worked with; he was also a decent cook. In time, Ekon and Themba found their own roles within the group. His love of counting meant that, more times than not, he helped Abeke with the inventory, a task no one was sorry to relinquish to him. Themba, meanwhile, did the group's washing, and used her splendor to offer relief to those with sore backs and feet. It was, Ekon found with some surprise, almost a pleasant way of life. No two days looked exactly the same, but there was a routine built around each one that brought Ekon some comfort. At the temple, life had been regimented by the hour—patrols, study of scripture, and then training. But with the members of the Enterprise, he was permitted to do the things that made him happy. Sometimes, a quiet part of his imagination let him wonder, just briefly, what it might be like to live this sort of life all the time, on the road among people who—for the most part—didn't judge him for being himself, but every time a thought like that flitted into his mind, so too did another one.

Koffi.

She was still being imprisoned by the god of death somewhere in the south, and he couldn't forget his mission, the real reason he was traveling with the Enterprise. It'd been decided that once they reached Bandari—one of the south's major port cities—Ekon and Themba and the Enterprise would go their separate ways. That destination was getting closer by the day.

There's no point in getting attached, he reminded himself. *You have a job to do, stay focused.*

The words made sense. Ekon just didn't know why, the more times he said them to himself, the sadder he began to feel.

They continued south, making slow headway each day.

Ekon thought he felt the air getting cooler, but he couldn't be sure. He'd never been to the Kusini Region, the Eshōzan south, and his knowledge of it only went as far as what was in the books that had been available to him in the Temple of Lkossa's vast library. Scholars had written that the Kusini Region was mostly marshlands, inhabited by a people who relied heavily on fishing as their main source of industry. Weather there wasn't like the Zamani Region's, where the seasons were exact. Rather, the south was best known for the unpredictable fogs that roamed the land, moving in any which way they pleased. Ekon had once read a tale about a fog that had fallen in love with a human girl, and so lingered over her village for fifty years waiting for her unrequited love. Back then, he'd dismissed the story as ridiculous, but now... well, he'd learned to examine myths and fables a bit more carefully.

Ano called for the caravan to be stopped early that night, and no one was sorry for it. The particular stretch of road Thabo had driven throughout the day had not been well maintained, which had made for a bumpy, less-than-pleasant ride. Ekon resisted the urge to massage his backside as he dismounted the wagon. Dusk was fast approaching, and most members of the Enterprise seemed more than happy to eat their dinners quickly and set up bed pallets by the fire. Ekon had just begun to unroll his own when he felt eyes on his back. Ano was standing behind him.

"I'd ask you to keep watch tonight," she murmured. "This particular area can sometimes be troublesome."

"Troublesome?" Ekon repeated.

Ano nodded to their right, and Ekon followed her gaze. In the fading light it was difficult to see, but he could just discern the outlines of trees in the distance. The Lesser Jungle. Little differentiated it from its counterpart slightly to the north.

"Have you ever been to the jungle?" Ano asked.

"Unfortunately, yes."

Ano's eyes glinted. "Then you know that it can be fraught with dangers," she said. "From here on, we'll do night-watch shifts every two hours. You'll take the first tonight. Safiyah will relieve you."

Ekon suppressed a groan. After the day of travel they'd just had, he wanted nothing more than to close his eyes and go to sleep. Ano seemed to be able to read his mind, because one of her brows rose.

"Unless you aren't feeling up to it?"

"No, no," said Ekon quickly. It was all too easy to remember the last substantive conversation they'd had about loyalty, to remember the disturbing way she'd killed that scorpion. "I'll do it."

Ano nodded. "Ring the kettle bell if you hear or see any trouble."

Ekon watched as, one by one, the other members of the Enterprise went to bed. He felt a touch of envy as he saw them settle into their bed pallets and close their eyes, but he also found that, as the camp quieted, there was a peacefulness about the world around him. In the distance, he could heard cicadas in the Lesser Jungle's swaying trees, serenading the moon as it rose higher in the star-speckled sky. The camp's small fire crackled merrily as it burned, and Ekon found himself remembering—with some sadness—another night like this. He thought of Koffi, of the wonder he'd seen in her eyes as she stared up into the stars, marveled at the stories he'd once told her about those constellations.

Ekon found himself wondering if, wherever she was now, she could see those same stars.

His thoughts were interrupted by a noise, faint but distinct. At first he thought he might be imagining it, but then he was sure: Footsteps were padding toward him in the darkness. At once, every muscle in his body tensed. He stood, gripping one of the camp's small cooking knives tight. The footsteps appeared to be getting closer, and the person they belonged to was walking more slowly. Ekon clenched his jaw, ready for an attack when—

"*Please* tell me that's not your fighting stance."

Ekon paused. Safiyah was emerging from the darkness, grinning. Ekon frowned.

"What are you doing?"

"What does it look like I'm doing?" she whispered, settling directly across from him. "I'm staying up for night watch."

Ekon shook his head. "You're supposed to relieve me in two hours."

Safiyah shrugged. "I couldn't sleep."

Ekon opened his mouth to argue, then thought better of it. If Safiyah wanted to waste a night's sleep for no reason, that was up to her. He sat down beside the fire, hoping to return to enjoying the night's quiet, when a rough metal scraping sound filled the air, and his eyes shot back to Safiyah. She now had a small blade in one hand and a whetstone in the other.

"*What are you doing?*"

Now Safiyah glared. She held up the knife. "I'm sharpening my blade."

Ekon felt a touch of annoyance. "I can see that. But do you have to do that now?"

Safiyah didn't look up as she continued her work. "There's no time during the day."

Ekon didn't answer, but watched Safiyah continue to sharpen the dagger. He hated to admit it to himself, but he was intrigued.

Safiyah was sharpening her blade with the ease of someone who'd done it many times, yet her knife had obviously seen better days. The blade itself, despite being sharp, had speckles of rust near its base, and it looked as though the leather on its hilt had had to be rewrapped several times. Finally, curiosity got the best of him.

"Where did you get that dagger?"

"None of your business," Safiyah snapped.

At first, Ekon planned to leave it at that, but when the minutes continued to pass in awkward silence, he pressed.

"Come on, tell me. You know I'll just keep asking, and we've got at least a few more hours ahead of us."

Safiyah threw him a scathing look. "Do you really think you can just annoy me into telling you?"

"I can certainly give it my best effort."

When Safiyah said nothing, Ekon yawned. "You know, I grew up in the Temple of Lkossa."

Safiyah glared.

"Part of my training to become a Son of the Six involved a *very* rigorous study of the Book of the Six, our religious text. To be eligible for warrior candidacy, I had to memorize the whole thing, word for word. It takes me about two hours to recite from start to finish, but when I'm *tired*—"

"Fine." Safiyah stopped sharpening the blade long enough to glower. "I got this knife from my father. Happy?"

"Really?" said Ekon. He was almost enjoying this. Almost. "And did your father give it to you *willingly*, or . . . ?"

"Don't insult me," Safiyah snapped. "I would never steal from him. This blade was a gift, the *last* gift he ever gave me before I ran away from home." Something in her voice had changed, there was a sharper bite to it, and behind that an emotion Ekon hadn't heard in Safiyah before. He held his hands up.

"Hey, I'm sorry," he said in earnest. "I wanted to know about the knife, but . . . I didn't mean to pry."

Safiyah's glower slipped for a moment before hardening again. She moved the whetstone along the blade faster, and Ekon grew increasingly worried that she was going to slice off her own fingers. "I don't expect you to understand," she said. "Boys like you are raised to be warriors from the time you can walk. *Your* father probably made sure you knew everything there is to know about how to fight, how to protect yourself."

Ekon chose not to mention that, in fact, this wasn't true at all. His father had died when he was seven, and it had been his brother and the man he'd once called a mentor who'd both raised him and prepared him for a warriorship. He thought of telling her as much, but decided against it. Safiyah went on.

"Not all of us have the support to do the things we want to do in life," she said. "You should count yourself lucky to have been given such an opportunity."

Ekon started to say something, then tried a different tactic. "You weren't?"

Safiyah made a face. "No. Girls weren't allowed to learn combat in my village. My father didn't care, though; he taught me everything he could and gave me this knife for my birthday. But my mother . . ." She grimaced. "My mother just wanted me to secure a good marriage, to become a proper *lady*. She used to make me sit with her for hours and do nothing but *read*—"

"Sounds like the perfect life to me," Ekon muttered, not bothering to lower his voice.

"Of course it does!" Safiyah threw her whetstone to the ground, frustrated. "Because you're not the one living it. Do you have any idea what it's like to be good at something, *really* good at something, and then be told you can't do it because of some arbitrary rules that make no sense?"

Yes. Ekon thought it, but didn't say it.

"You have no idea what I would have given up to have the childhood you did," said Safiyah. "To get to live in a temple and spend my days training, learning, *doing*."

"I don't know," Ekon said mildly. "I think the grass is always greener on the other side of the temple."

Safiyah rolled her eyes. "Maybe my mother should adopt you," she said. "Then she can take *you* to some crusty matchmaker, and—"

"Safiyah." Ekon suddenly sat up straight. "Be quiet."

Safiyah scrunched up her face. "Excuse me?"

He held up a finger and saw the exact moment Safiyah realized what he already had. It wasn't just quiet anymore around the camp; there was no sound at all. The cicadas in the trees had gone still.

Ekon's eyes panned slowly. He couldn't see anyone, but in the night, he didn't trust his eyes. Carefully, he rose, and Safiyah mirrored his movements until she was standing at his side. In as low a whisper as possible, he said, "You go left, I'll go right. If you hear or see anything off, yell, make as much noise as you can. Even if it turns out to be nothing, it's better to be wrong."

Safiyah nodded, holding the dagger close as she stalked off into the darkness. Ekon went in the opposite direction. He moved on the balls of his feet so as to make as little noise as possible as he edged around the sleeping members of the Enterprise. They were arranged in a circle, with their three wagons set up in the middle. Anyone who wanted to get to their supplies would have to step through sleeping bodies to get to them. He couldn't see Safiyah anymore, which meant she had to be exactly opposite him, on the other side of the circle. A few more steps, and he would see her.

Without warning, he felt the cold press of metal at the base of his throat. He tried to move, but someone clapped a hand over his mouth and dragged him to his knees before he could yell or make any sort of warning noise. A few feet away, he heard a scuffle and a whimper and knew Safiyah was down too. He couldn't see his assailant, but he heard his low chuckle.

"Drop the knife, easy does it." It was a male voice that wheezed in Ekon's ear; his breath reeked of chewing tobacco. "There's no reason to make this difficult."

The man held the blade against Ekon's throat until he'd dropped his knife, then he walked him all the way back around the wagons and to the campfire again before raising his voice.

"Attention, everyone! Your attention, please!"

One by one, the members of the Enterprise sat up, groggy and confused at first, then horrified as they laid eyes on the person Ekon could not see. He watched Themba sit up, saw her start to raise her hands. As subtly as he could, he shook his head until she lowered them. They didn't yet know exactly what and who they were dealing with. At the moment, they didn't have many advantages, but Ekon figured that if Themba's power was going to be one of them, it would be best to keep that secret for as long as possible.

"Bind him, Rahid," said Wheezy Voice.

Ekon felt someone else come up behind him and bind his wrists none too gently with what felt like leather cord. Once he was restrained, the knife was removed from his throat, and he was shifted slightly to the side. For the first time, he got a proper look at his attacker.

The man's head was completely shaved, and his clothes, though nice, looked worn. A single golden hoop earring was stuck through his right ear, and it danced in the dying firelight. When he flashed a smile, Ekon saw his two front teeth had been replaced with golden caps to match, and gold chains hung about his neck.

"Apologies for the rude awakening," said Wheezy Voice. "But I'm afraid the matter was urgent. You see, you all don't look like you're local to this area, which means you're unaware of its perils. Fortunately for you, I have come to offer my services. My name is Damu Kanumba, and with me is one of my many associates, Rahid." He gestured over his shoulder. "Now, as an entrepreneur, I'm committed to creating businesses that serve this community. I founded Kanumba and Company with the aim to provide a unique service to the travelers of this region."

For the first time, Ano stood up. Ekon almost couldn't bear to look at her, to see the disappointment he knew he'd find in the woman's eyes. But when he did make himself look, he saw no disappointment, just caution as she met Damu's gaze.

"And just what *service* might that be?" she asked pleasantly. The warmth in her voice didn't reach her eyes.

"Protection," said Damu. "From this area's . . . less savory characters. Our fees are reasonable: a mere tenth of the goods you're traveling with, in exchange for the promise that you will not come to any harm from here to Bandari. You see, I am well respected on these roads, and once you have my friendship, you will find no troubles. For your convenience, I accept payments in the form of either coin or valuable goods—"

"What a generous offer," said Ano. She didn't return his smile. "Fortunately, as you can see, our group is large enough in number that we are able to look after ourselves. So, I would very much appreciate it if you could ask your *associate* to release the boy."

There was an uncomfortably long pause before Damu's eyes cut to Ekon. Slowly he circled him, looking him up and down with every step. He was still smiling, but Ekon didn't miss the flinty quality behind his brown eyes.

"*Auntie*," Damu said slowly, "forgive me, perhaps I should have been clearer—"

"She said *no*." Ekon tried to muster as much confidence as he could manage. Now more than ever, he wished he had his hanjari dagger. "So let me go, and be on your way."

Damu stopped midway through his second circle so that he was right in front of Ekon. He leaned in, so close the tips of their noses were almost touching, before he spoke again in a low, deadly voice.

"And what are *you* going to do if I don't, little boy?"

"Enough." There was no trace of pleasantry in Ano's voice now. "Thank you again for your offer, but as I said, we don't need—"

"Oh, I *really* don't think you're understanding me, Auntie." Like Ano, Damu's tone had changed too. "Our service is both generous, and obligatory." He signaled, and a troop of men emerged from the shadows. Like him, they wore gold chains and rings, but they had a rough, hungry look about them. Each of the men carried a machete longer than Ekon's arm. He swore.

"Everyone on your feet!" Damu ordered. "Move *away* from the wagons."

Ekon's heart thundered in his chest as the members of the Enterprise rose. Thabo, who was the largest among them, tensed, but several of the bandits moved so that their knives were pointed at his chest.

"This doesn't have to be difficult," Damu said. He swatted a fly from his face. "All we want is our fair share here." He pointed to Ano. "She's the leader. Bring her to me."

The men shoved Ano forward, but to her credit, the woman kept her head held high as she faced Damu.

"First things first," he said. "Tell us where you keep your gold."

"We don't travel with gold," Ano said simply. "We're herbalists, our profit is in our produce."

Damu eyed her a moment before nodding to one of the bandits. "Check the wagons."

They all waited as one of the men climbed into each wagon and began audibly rummaging through the carefully packed supplies. With every second that passed, Ekon grew angrier, but he still didn't have any sort of plan. Themba was out of his line of sight now, so he couldn't communicate anything to her, which meant he just had to wait. Everyone at the campsite watched as the bandit jumped down from the last wagon holding a few small coin purses.

"They don't have very much," he conceded. "Mostly spices and some smelly herbs. I did find a bit of coin, though . . . only shabas by the looks of it."

"Mm." Damu didn't look overly impressed. "Less than I would have expected from a group of nine, but I suppose it'll have to do. Take the coin and anything else you see of value." He turned back to Ano, and his eyes were much cooler. "You *lied* to me."

"I did not." Ano held her head up higher. "I told you that we did not travel with gold, and we do not. We cannot afford it."

"Eugh!" Damu made a disgusted sound, swatting again at something in the air. His eyes cut back to the man standing by the last wagon, frowning. "What's wrong with you?"

But the bandit didn't appear to have heard him. He was staring off into the distance now with a blank look Ekon thought he recognized; the other bandits were staring blankly too. In fact, with the exception of Damu and Rahid, it seemed every one of the bandits had gone slack. Ekon straightened.

Themba.

"Get moving!" Damu shouted. "What's wrong with you all?"

"Sir," said Rahid, rubbing his eyes. "There is a daraja here."

Ekon froze, trying to keep his expression composed. How did he know that? How could he possibly know that?

Damu stiffened. "You're certain?"

"It's been some time since I felt the presence of another one of my kind," said Rahid. "But I do feel it." He pointed toward the members of the Enterprise. "It's not the boy, which means it's one of the others."

Damu brought the knife to Ano's throat. "Whichever of you is controlling my men has ten seconds to lift whatever curse you've placed on them. If you don't, I'll cut your leader's throat. Ten ... nine ... eight ..."

He didn't get to six before Themba released her hold on the men. They blinked and stared around at one another, confused. Damu continued to hold the blade to Ano's throat.

"Now I want you to show yourself," he said. "Step forward."

Neither Themba nor any of the other members of the Enterprise moved. All of them merely glared at Damu. He pressed his blade harder against Ano's neck, and Ekon saw a trickle of blood slide down her throat.

"Seven ... six ... five ..."

"Stop!"

Ekon's eyes went wide as one of the members of the Enterprise got to her feet and stepped forward, a middle-aged woman with her hands raised in surrender. He knew her, of course. Obioma was the Enterprise's tongue; she spoke multiple languages and helped them deal with traders and buyers who didn't speak Zamani. She was a heavyset woman, with short curly hair and large brown eyes that made her look doll-like, but the resolve in them now was clear.

"Don't hurt her," she said quietly. "*I'm* the daraja."

Ekon jolted as he realized what the woman was doing. She was lying, she was sacrificing herself, for Ano.

"No!" Both Ano and Themba said it at the same time, the horror on their faces identical. Themba, who was sitting next to Obioma, jumped up and tried to pull the woman back, while Ano strained against Damu's hold.

"Sir, she's lying," Ano said quickly. "She's not the daraja, I am—"

"Stop it, both of you," said Themba. "*I* am the real daraja. Do not harm anyone else, take me."

Ekon watched as Damu's eyes flitted between the three of them, deliberating uneasily. He brushed something away from his face.

"Take the first one."

"No!" Ano's cries grew frantic as two of Damu's men grabbed Obioma and dragged her to him. They brought her to her knees before Damu grabbed her under the chin and forced her to meet his gaze.

"I've heard tales about your kind," he said. "They say some darajas can sing songs that drive men mad, that others can make bargains with stars." He bent lower so their faces were inches apart. "I've also heard that the skin of some darajas doesn't even burn, which leads me to wonder if—" He stopped short, looking up in confusion. Ekon followed his gaze, as did everyone else at the camp. In the night sky, there was movement. It came from the trees of the Lesser Jungle, a small twinkling cloud, barely visible in the night. For one fleeting second, Ekon thought they were stars, but . . . no, they were the wrong color, a reddish orange. He thought of the splendor, the kind he'd seen Koffi once summon, but that didn't seem right either. These were insects, slightly too big to be fireflies. Their collective buzzing was low, like bees. When he looked closer, he thought they might be beetles. Ekon turned back in time to see Damu's and his men's expressions had completely changed. They looked horrified.

"No," Damu whispered. His whole body began to tremble like a leaf left in a storm. Ekon didn't understand it. The cloud of firefly-like creatures was moving toward them slowly, almost lazily. One of the men let loose a scream, turned to run, but it was too late.

Without warning, the swarm surged forward.

Ekon's head filled with a buzzing as the beetles descended. In the darkness, he hadn't realized how many of them there were, but when they descended, the entire camp seemed to be overrun by them; there had to be thousands. He dropped to his knees as they filled the air around him, crawled across his skin, and flew into his face. It was impossible to see anything now; the beetles were everywhere. He heard someone scream, but it was impossible to tell who. A deep shudder overtook him as he felt the beetles' many legs creeping across any exposed skin they could find. His arms still bound, he could do nothing to fend them off, so he curled himself into as small a ball as possible. The beetles—whatever they were—hovered around his ears, their buzzing was growing unbearable, and it reminded him of another encounter, one he'd had with spiders in the jungle. His breath grew shorter, his mouth dry, and panic seized at his lungs as a new darkness crept into his vision.

"Boy!"

Someone was calling his name; he could just hear it over the buzzing. He felt that same someone grab his upper arm, hoist him to his feet. Ekon blinked several times. The beetles were still flying through the air, but he tried to see through them. Themba was standing next to him, her hand hooded over her eyes.

"Come!" she said, trying to move her mouth as little as possible. Ekon kept his own mouth shut as more beetles buzzed by his lips. He heard another scream, a terrible shriek as Themba pulled out a knife and cut his binds. She gestured, and they started to run toward the wagons. Only then did Ekon dare to look in the direction of those screams. His heart jolted in his chest.

Several figures were doubled over by the place where the camp's fire had been. At first, Ekon didn't understand what he was seeing, didn't understand the lurid red aura that seemed to glow around them. Then he did. Those figures were Damu's men, covered from head to foot by the beetles. They flailed as though they were burning, screamed into the night, but the beetles did not relinquish them. They seemed to be clustered especially thickly near certain parts of the men's bodies, their hands, wrists, and necks. Ekon saw a glint of yellow on one of the men, saw as he tried with all his might to pull something from his body. It clicked in Ekon's mind with horror.

Gold, he realized. The beetles wanted the gold. They were eating it, and eating the men's flesh right along with it. Ekon's stomach turned as he saw flecks of blood, the pink of raw skin, and a white flash of bone.

"Ekon!"

He turned his head. Themba was pulling him toward the wagons, trying to cover her face. Through the haze of the beetles, Ekon saw that Thabo had managed to hitch the mules to the wagons and that all of the members of the Enterprise were loaded onto them, swatting desperately at the air.

"Go!" Ekon shouted as they ran. One of the beetles flew into his mouth and he spat it out, fighting revulsion as he thought he tasted blood. "Go, we'll catch up!"

Thabo didn't hesitate. He grabbed the reins and ordered the teams of mules forward. Ekon and Themba picked up their pace.

"I'll help you on first," he said, covering his mouth. Themba nodded as they closed the distance between themselves and the last wagon. Some of the members of the Enterprise had torn open its back cover and were holding their arms out. Themba leaped, and Ekon moved to help her up. She groaned as her body slammed against the back of the wagon, but the Enterprise members held on to her. Ekon pushed while they tugged, and eventually they pulled her into the wagon. He braced himself.

"Jump!" Safiyah shouted. She extended one of her arms. "We'll pull you in!"

Ekon braced himself a moment, then he leaped too. There was a terrifying moment when he felt himself falling, then arms caught him fast. He winced as his ribs slammed against the wagon, pain ricocheted up his body, but Safiyah held him fast.

"We've got you!" she said. "Hold on!"

Slowly, they pulled him in. The beetles seemed to be thinning in the air now. Ekon felt more arms grab the back of his tunic as the members of the Enterprise tried to pull him into the wagon the same way they'd pulled in Themba, his knee scraping against the wood as it found purchase, as he started to push himself upward.

And then Ekon felt something warm and slick wrap around one of his ankles. He looked over his shoulder at the thing pulling on him, and bile rose in his throat.

Damu was holding on to him.

The man was now nearly unrecognizable, the beetles covering all but his eyes. They clustered on his neck, on his fingers, on the place where a golden earring had once been looped into his ear. His mouth was open wide, and Ekon saw they'd even covered his two front teeth, the ones he'd cast in gold. He moaned.

"Leeeease." The word was garbled. "Hellllmeeeee!"

A chill ran up Ekon's spine. The other members of the Enterprise were still trying to pull him in, but Damu's added weight was too much. Ekon could feel himself slipping backward. More of the beetles were coming back. Ice-cold fear fettered at his throat.

"No!" Safiyah was pulling, leaning now, so that most of her body was outside the wagon. "Come on!"

Ekon didn't understand how he still had the strength to hold on. He kicked as hard as he could, but Damu only clawed at him, flicking blood and gold and dead beetles across Ekon's clothes. They were going to fall, all three of them.

"Heeeelllmeeeeee!"

The wagon hit a hard bump in the road. Ekon felt a terrible lurch as he went flying through the air.

And then everything went dark.

CHAPTER 15

The MOST BEAUTIFUL THING

Koffi spent the next few days training with Thornkeep's darajas.

She'd learned first that there were six daraja orders; now she was discovering that, within those orders, there was a significant amount of room for variety.

She spent one day with a stocky boy named Izem, a daraja in the Order of Maisha. He showed her how, with a single touch, he could make a flower bloom or wilt on command. Another day, she met Onyeka, a tall, limber daraja in the Order of Mwili, with an affinity for mending broken bones. Some of the darajas were what Makena privately called "loyalists," those who were sympathetic to Fedu and supported his plans, but there were plenty of others, she found, who wanted to leave as desperately as she did. The darajas in that group took time to help her with the splendor when they could, coming up with exercises that helped her practice using it in secret. It was, she realized, the first time in her life that she had some semblance of a real community.

In her spare time, Koffi still ventured to the library too, though her progress there was far slower than her progress in working with the splendor. She still hadn't found any books that even mentioned the Order of Vivuli, let alone any details about other darajas in that order. She already knew—from her lessons and from Badwa—that being a daraja meant it was in her blood, a trait she'd inherited from a direct family member, but she had no idea who that family member might be. She thought hard about Mama, wondering now if she'd ever shown Koffi something by mistake. She was good with animals; perhaps she was in the Order of Maisha. If that was true, though, it still beggared the old unanswered question: Why hadn't she spoken with Koffi about any of this? A thought came to her, one that stung. Maybe her daraja blood hadn't come from her mother's family at all; maybe it'd been Baba. That would make a lot of sense. Baba had died years ago, and in his death left she and Mama with so many burdens that weren't theirs to carry. Maybe Mama had associated being a daraja with him, with all of his bad choices. It was plausible, but Koffi still couldn't quite justify it in her mind. She decided then that, when she did get back to Lkossa, it was a question she would ask. Thinking of Lkossa, of course, made her think of Ekon, and Koffi felt a pang as his face filled her mind. Ekon had been hardest to think about during her time at Thornkeep, mostly because she was least sure of what had happened to him when she left. Had he been arrested? Had he escaped? Had he moved on with his life? Those were unanswered questions too, but Koffi wasn't sure if she was ready for all of the answers to them.

When Makena came to her bedchamber to retrieve her the following evening, Koffi was dressed and ready. Her lesson tonight was with Zain, and she was more than a little curious about what it might entail. An anticipation bubbled through her as they walked to the study where he'd asked to meet, though Koffi couldn't discern why.

"You okay?" Makena asked when she noticed Koffi walking faster than usual.

"Yeah," said Koffi. "I guess I'm just nervous."

Makena threw her a sly look. "I'd say, when it comes to Zain, that's normal."

Koffi's cheeks warmed. "What do you mean?"

"Just that Zain's affinity is . . ." She paused look for the right word. "Strange."

"Strange?"

"I say it lovingly," added Makena.

"What is Zain's affinity?" Koffi asked.

"Trust me, it's easier for you to see it for yourself."

Finally, they reached a door Koffi had never seen before. Like most of Thornkeep, its wood was dark. Makena knocked twice, and her fist was still raised when Zain swung the door open. Tonight he wore a plain blue tunic.

"Good evening, ladies," he said cheerfully. "Makena, I see you're in better spirits tonight."

"Zain," Makena said in a clipped tone. "I've brought Koffi for her lesson with you. I will return for her in one hour."

"Great!" Zain rubbed his hands together. "Well then, in that case, we'll just—" He stopped as Makena raised her index finger, pointing it inches from his nose.

"I haven't forgiven you for that stupid stunt you pulled at the stables," she said in a low voice. "I want you to know that if so much as a single hair on my friend's lovely head is out of place when I come back, if she has so much as a scratch, I will *personally* put my foot—"

"Say no more, Kena," Zain said quickly, wincing. "I promise, we'll just go over the basics tonight." He looked over the top of her head so that his eyes met Koffi's. "She's in good hands."

Koffi didn't know why the way Zain was looking at her made her stomach swoop.

"Oh, she'd better be," said Makena testily. "Or you will certainly *not* be." She gave him one more reproving look before turning to head back down the hallway. Zain watched her go with a kind amusement mixed with real wariness.

"You've got yourself a very good friend there."

"Yes." Koffi smiled because she knew it was true. "I do."

"Well, if we only have an hour, we'd better get started." He moved aside and held the door open. "After you."

Koffi stepped inside the study, and Zain closed the door behind them. Like the library, it wasn't particularly big, but it was neat in the extreme. A tall bookcase was placed in one corner, and the room's only other furnishings were a chair and a desk with a pitcher of water and some goblets.

"Is this your study?" she asked.

"Eh, sort of," said Zain. "I commandeered it for myself some time ago. It's got the best view in all of Thornkeep."

Koffi glanced out the window involuntarily. Zain's study faced the north garden, and in the dusk, its red flowers looked set ablaze. It was, admittedly, a great view.

"So," he said, sitting on the edge of the desk. "Let's start with the easy things. How much do you already know about the Order of Akili?"

"Not much," Koffi admitted. "Just that it's the Order of the Mind."

Zain nodded. "Besides the Order of Vivuli, the Order of Akili is probably the hardest to conceptualize, because it's cerebral." He tapped the side of his head. "The mind is a complicated place."

"Sure."

"Now, like the rest of the daraja orders, there are subgroups within the Order of Akili. There are some within my order who are simply very intelligent; they're able to recall things at inhuman speeds. Some within my order are telekinetic; they can move things without touching them. And still, there are the rarities—like the polyglots, who can fluently speak any language they hear. Anyway, you get the picture."

"So what's your affinity within it?" Koffi asked.

"I'm what's called an illusionist," Zain explained. "When I summon and channel the splendor toward a certain person or people, I can make them see what I want, for as long as I want. I can conjure a person's sweetest dreams, or most wretched nightmares. I can also make people see things that aren't there, or vice versa."

"Really?" said Koffi. "That's . . . sort of terrifying."

Zain's eyes danced. "Watch." He pulled one of the books from the shelf and placed it on his desk. Koffi stared at it a moment, wondering what he was going to do with it, and then she found herself wondering why she was staring at an empty desk. She looked up at Zain, mystified.

"It's . . . it's still there, isn't it?"

Zain nodded, and when Koffi looked at the desk again, sure enough, the book had not moved.

"That's incredible."

"Oh, please." Zain fanned himself with a hand, pretending to be embarrassed. "Flattery will get you everywhere."

"Could I see what it's like," she asked, "when you create illusions in dreams and nightmares?"

Zain's brow rose instantly. "Eh, I don't think so."

Koffi frowned. "Why not?"

"Firstly, because it's much harder for me to work on a person who's awake. I have to summon more of the splendor, which makes the illusion much more intense," he said. "And second, because I just told Makena that we were only going over the basics tonight. You do recall what she made me promise her?"

Koffi huffed. *"Zain."*

"Look, *you've* never seen Makena when she's really pissed off," he said seriously. "*I*, on the other hand, have. Trust me, an intimate bubble bath with a *porcupine* is more pleasant."

"We don't have to tell her." The words tumbled out of Koffi's mouth, surprising her. She flushed as Zain looked at her with new interest.

"Ooh, secrets." He wiggled his fingers, and a devilish smile pulled at his lips. "Well, in that case, I'm in." He rose from the desk, then pointed to the chair behind it. "All right, you're going to need to sit down for this."

Koffi tempered the hum of excitement that coursed through her as she made her way around the desk and settled in the chair. It was made from a soft, worn leather and smelled of pine.

"Okay, so some ground rules," he said. "I'm only going to keep you in for a few minutes. It'll feel longer, trust me. If I start to see you react badly, I'm pulling you out, no questions asked, and we will *never* speak of this to Makena. Deal?"

"Deal," said Koffi.

The smile returned to Zain's face. He moved in front of the chair and bent so that his arms were on either side of her. She made herself keep breathing as her heart began to pound.

"I don't need physical contact," he explained. "But it's easier for me if I have it. That said, I'm all about respecting boundaries, so . . ." He met her gaze and held it. "*Can* I touch you?"

A sudden heat pooled somewhere below Koffi's navel. "What?"

"To do the exercise," said Zain. She didn't like the amusement in his eyes now. "Can I touch you?"

"Ah . . ." Koffi swallowed. "Yes."

"Excellent." Zain covered her hands with his own. "I'll just need you to *look into my eyes* . . ."

Koffi did, and the world around her went black.

In her dreams, Koffi was in a jungle.

She'd never seen this particular one before, of that she was certain, and yet it was a familiar place to her too. Its air was thick, humid; she watched beads of condensation collect on the massive leaves, large enough for her to lie on. When she closed her eyes, she heard the melody of cicadas, and when they opened again, beetles with wings of deep violet and silver passed before her, chased by butterflies of every color and imagining. She breathed in the smell of fresh flowers. *Home.* This strange place felt like home.

"Koffi."

Her heart jolted in her chest at the thrum of a voice she knew, quiet but warm. Slowly she turned, and the breath left her body in an exhale. Mama stood before her, smiling.

"Mama!"

"You made it, little ponya seed." She murmured the words into Koffi's hair as they embraced. "After all this time, you made it home. I knew you would."

"Mama." Koffi tried to find the words as she blinked hard once, twice, then let the tears slick her cheeks. Mama smelled the way she remembered, felt the way she remembered. "Mama, I missed you. But where's—?"

"Koffi!"

Koffi and her mother looked up at the same time, and Koffi's throat tightened as Jabir stepped out from behind one of the jungle's trees to offer a small wave.

"I hope you don't mind if I join you."

Mama held out her arm, welcoming Jabir as he folded into them. Koffi cried harder as he let his head rest against hers; he was taller than she remembered.

"We're going to be all right," Mama said in a voice only loud enough for them. "Just us three. We're together now. We're going to be all right."

Koffi believed that, more than she believed in anything else. This was her home, this place in the arms of the two people who loved her most. This was home, and she would stay.

"*Koffi.*"

Koffi stiffened in her mother's and Jabir's arms. The third voice she'd heard in the jungle didn't belong to either of them, and it sounded wrong. They kept their arms locked tight around her, but she turned and peeked over their shoulders. Then she froze.

Another boy was standing a few feet from them, and this one was not smiling at all. He had tightly coiled hair and full lips. The last time she'd seen him, he'd been wrapped in a linen death shroud, but now that was gone. His body was covered in horrible gashes, lacerations. Koffi knew him.

"S-Sahel?" Koffi stammered.

The silvery Sahel faltered, as though surprised she'd actually spoken to him. He stared at her, curious.

"Sahel, it's me. It's Koffi," she said. "From the Night Zoo."

She watched as his expression twisted into a grimace.

"Give it to me." Sahel's voice was wrong. It was thin as an evening breeze, hushed. "Give it to me."

"What?" Koffi tried to pull out of Jabir's and Mama's arms, but they were still holding her. "Give what to you?"

"The payment," he said softly, like a lover. "I cannot go to the godlands without it." He took a step forward, his gait stilted and uneven. Koffi's eyes wandered down to the rest of his body and noted the wounds, the bite marks and scratches. It had been bad enough when Koffi thought those wounds had been inflicted by the Shetani, a *monster*. To know now that Sahel had in fact died at the hands of warriors made them impossibly more chilling.

"Sahel." Her voice barely carried above a whisper. "What are you talking about?"

"Give it to me." The boy was closing the gap between them, a strange, hungry gleam in his eyes. She recognized that hunger; she'd felt it herself. "Perhaps he will accept your hair, your eyes, your blood. Perhaps I'll pay him that way."

A chill skittered up Koffi's arms. "Sahel, stop!" Again, she tried to pull herself from Mama's and Jabir's grasp, but they held her tight. Too tight.

"Let go of me, Mama." Koffi pulled away with all her might. "Jabir, please. You have to let—" The rest of the words died in her throat. When she turned and looked at her arms, she was not in her mother's arms.

She was in Fedu's.

A scream rose in her throat as she tried to pull away from the god, but his fingers dug into her flesh. He smiled.

"Come now, Dull Knife," he said softly. "Do not resist."

More people were beginning to emerge from the woods, but Koffi understood now what they were. The Untethered. She saw men, women, the old, and the young. She saw weeping mothers carrying their stillborn babies, men with gaping wounds earned in battle. Emaciated children wandered toward her with distended bellies and hollowed faces. None of them had eyes.

Give it to us. Their voices were one horrid chorus. *Free us.*

A mist was rising from the earth, and the sky above was green. Koffi looked down at her feet and watched as thorns snaked around her ankles to hold her in place, to hold her as the Untethered drew nearer.

Free us ... Free us ...

Sahel was approaching again, his mouth open in a silent wail. One of his transparent hands was outstretched, reaching for her. Any moment now, he would ...

"Koffi!"

Koffi's eyes shot open, and then they burned. Zain was kneeling before her, his brown eyes wide with fear. It took Koffi a second to reorient herself. She was not in the jungle now, she was in Zain's study. None of it—Mama, Jabir, Fedu, and the Untethered—had been real. For several seconds she could only stare at Zain, breathing hard.

"Here." Zain stood and grabbed the pitcher of water from the desk, as well as one of the goblets. "Drink this."

Koffi accepted the goblet without a word and tipped it to her lips. As soon as the cool water touched her lips, she felt herself calming. Over the rim, she could see Zain was still watching her, shaking his head.

"I'm sorry," he murmured. "That was foolish."

Koffi wanted to contradict him, to tell him that—as scary as that had been—she was glad to know what he could do. She wanted to say that aloud, but she couldn't. Her tongue wouldn't work, and her body felt unbelievably heavy. Every time she looked at Zain, she was struck by the contradiction of it. How could a person who looked so kind create something so monstrous?

Zain put his head in his hands, looking positively forlorn. "Oh, I might as well get my affairs in order," he lamented. "Makena is going to end me."

"She's . . . not . . . We're not going to tell her."

Zain looked up from his hands, confused. It took more effort than normal, but Koffi forced herself to sit upright in the chair.

"Thank you," she said. "For showing me that."

Zain stared at her in disbelief.

"What we're planning to do, leaving Thornkeep, is going to be dangerous," said Koffi slowly. "It's going to be difficult." She sighed. "I can't keep having these lessons where all I do is play with the splendor. At some point, I have to push myself harder, or I won't be ready."

Zain's expression changed, softened. "You don't want to push yourself too hard, though, Koffi. The splendor—"

"I don't want you to go easy on me." She met his gaze and hoped that she looked stronger than she felt. "Promise me that."

A beat passed before Zain nodded. "I promise."

"Thank you. How much time do we have left before Makena comes back?"

"A good amount," said Zain. "But I really think you've done enough for one lesson."

Koffi didn't argue. "Fine. But can we at least talk about the plan, how I'm actually going to get us out of here when the time comes?"

"Sure." He crossed the space between them and sat on the desk again. "We don't know where Thornkeep is situated in relation to the rest of Eshōza," he said. "Fedu is able to bring us here without going through the Mistwood because he is a god, able to travel in ways a mortal cannot."

"Of course he can," she said bitterly.

"So we're not exactly sure in which direction we should leave," he went on. "But we think our best bet is to go north."

"So we'd go through the north garden," said Koffi. "And then into the Mistwood from there."

Zain nodded. "Njeri is still doing some reconnaissance, trying to figure out which darajas are actually loyal to Fedu and which ones are pretending but secretly want to leave. As of now, there are fifteen darajas in our group, counting myself, Makena, Zola, Amun, and Njeri."

Fifteen. It wasn't a huge number, but Koffi was daunted by it.

"What you're going to do is use your splendor to create a path much like the one you created when you and Makena were trying to get out of the Mistwood the first time," said Zain. "But instead of trying to get back here, you would direct the splendor to show you a way home. We'll just follow you from there. I'm sure she's already told you, but Zola's engineering weapons that can be fortified with the splendor. We can use those if we run into the Untethered."

Koffi took a deep breath in.

"What's wrong?"

"Whenever I've used the splendor to guide me to something, I've always had a very specific target in mind," she explained. "The first and second time, I was looking for an individual person. The third time, I was just trying to get back to Thornkeep. I don't . . ." She faltered. "I don't know if the splendor will show me a path forward if I don't even know what I'm looking for. What if I get tired in the middle of the Mistwood, what if I get lost, what if the splendor doesn't work? What if—?"

"Koffi." Zain's voice was gentle. "Trust yourself."

She shook her head. "It's not about trusting—"

"It is," he insisted. "I'll show you." He moved to stand by the window, gesturing for her to come over too. Slowly, carefully, Koffi rose. Her eyes wandered past the flowers and fountains, until they found the start of the Mistwood. Even from here, she imagined she could feel its chill.

"I want you to try to summon the splendor again," said Zain. "Obviously, we can't repeat exactly what you did when you saved Makena, so tonight, just focus on the most essential thing, summoning it, getting used to the feel of it."

Koffi took a deep breath. Zain made that sound so easy, but she didn't know whether she could do it. The remnants of the nightmare still lingered in her mind, and she wasn't sure she could clear her head enough. But he was looking at her with an expectation now.

"All right." She took a step back from Zain, giving herself some space. "I don't know if this will work, but I'll try."

She closed her eyes and tried to clear her mind, tried to do what Badwa had taught her. One by one, she acknowledged her emotions. She was tired, sometimes still sad, but hopeful, and she clung to that. She took a breath, once, twice, a third time, and then reached for the splendor. There was a pause as she waited for it, for that tingle to start in her feet, but it didn't come. Koffi screwed her eyes shut tighter. *Come on,* she urged. *Please.* The splendor did not answer. It wasn't going to come. Koffi bit down on her lip hard, until she tasted blood. She had more power in her body than the other darajas in this place, and the splendor still didn't deem her fit enough to answer her when she called. She felt the cold press of doubt as it began to seep into her consciousness, all the voices in her head that told her to give up.

You're weak. You're stupid. You're a coward. You're not worthy of this power.

No. Koffi pushed against those voices. They're weren't real, and she reminded herself of that. She reminded herself that she didn't have this power by chance, she had it because Adiah had given it to her, entrusted her with it. Adiah has deemed her worthy of this power, because she was worthy of it. She was not weak, she was strong.

She called the splendor again, and this time it came in an onslaught. She felt it rush through her, building in her chest until it strained against her rib cage. *Too much*, a new voice in head warned. *Too much*, but she didn't pay attention to it. Instead, she opened her eyes and saw that the study was now full of tiny flickering speckles of light. They floated lazily around her, casting a golden luminescence on everything they touched—the books, the desk, Zain's face. He was staring at her now, in shock. Koffi took a deep breath and called the splendor back to her. One by one the flickering lights dimmed, but Zain hadn't taken his eyes off her.

"Was that . . . okay?"

It took Zain a moment to respond. He looked transfixed. "That," he said quietly, "was the most beautiful thing I've seen."

Koffi felt a new heat in her core that had nothing to do with the splendor. She was suddenly keenly aware of how close Zain was. She watched the way the dying light accentuated one side of his face, the curls in his hair and the curve of his jaw. She found herself wondering what would happen if she took one small step closer. She did, and Zain's eyes dropped to her lips. When she looked up again, there was a question in his eyes. She nodded. Zain's fingers encircled her wrists, tugging her closer still. He bowed his head, and Koffi closed her eyes. She held her breath then, waiting, wondering what would happen next, wondering if—

There was a loud bang, and Koffi and Zain sprung apart. For a moment, Koffi didn't understand what she was seeing. Amun was standing at the door, his eyes wide. Not Makena, Amun. Something clicked in Koffi's mind. That wasn't right, Amun wasn't supposed to be here. His face was shiny with sweat, his breathing labored. He looked as though he'd been running—running for his life.

"We need to get outside," he whispered. There was tremble in his voice. "Something bad has happened."

CHAPTER 16

The MATRON of the MARSH

Ekon knew well the stink of blood.

It was a distinct coppery scent, and one he'd quickly learned to recognize at the Temple of Lkossa. As a boy, sometimes he'd smelled it coming from the butcher room, where the cooks went to chop meat for the meals that would be served to the temple's brothers, warriors, and other staff. Other times, it had come from less savory sources, like the injured and sick who stood outside the Takatifu District's gates and shouted pleas for help from the Kuhani. It was a smell Ekon had long ago memorized, one he knew he'd never forget as long as he lived. It was a smell thick in his lungs when he awoke.

He opened his eyes, then immediately squinted, blinking in the morning light. Slowly, he turned on his side, wincing as something pressed into his cheek. When he pinched it away with a finger, he saw that it was grass, stained an ominous dark reddish brown. He counted to three, then pushed himself up, trying to reorient himself.

He was in an open grassland, flat as far as he could see and only interrupted by the long line of trees to his right. The Lesser Jungle. Suddenly everything from the night before returned to him—memories of Damu and his bandits, the Enterprise running away. His gaze panned around him. There was no trace of the members of the Enterprise anywhere. He got to his knees and started to brush something off of his legs, then froze.

A few feet from him, more of the grass was dark red.

Goose bumps spread across his skin as he neared it, poised on the balls of his feet. The sounds of flies buzzing in the air gave him pause, but he kept drawing nearer to the spot until he could see what it was. His stomach turned.

Damu was lying on the ground, dead. A few feet from him were the remnants of other bodies, all horribly contorted. If Ekon hadn't known for a fact that a few hours ago these men had been alive, he would have sworn their corpses had been there for days. Flies were buzzing around the carcasses, different from the glowing red beetles that had actually killed them, but Ekon still found them disturbing.

"Ekon? Is that you?"

Ekon whirled. The sun was still hovering on the horizon as it rose, making it difficult to look directly east, but he could make out a familiar silhouette approaching. He stepped forward and raised a hand.

"Safiyah?"

By the time Safiyah was close enough, Ekon could see her face was a mixture of annoyance and disbelief.

"How'd you get here?"

"Same as you," she said irritably. "I fell off the wagon with you when that oaf pulled you down."

"I barely remember it," said Ekon. "I fell hard."

Safiyah looked over his shoulder. "Speaking of which, please tell me Damu didn't get away. I've got a bone to pick with him."

"He didn't get away, but as far as the bone picking . . ." He gestured at the bloodied field. "I think you've already been beaten to it."

For the first time, Safiyah seemed to really notice their surroundings. She shuddered. "I didn't think the Walaji came this far south."

Ekon frowned. "The what?"

"The Walaji. The Devourers. There are all sorts of stories about them," said Safiyah. "The most well known is about a king who loved gold more than anything else, so much so that he sprinkled it into his food and wine until it drove him mad with an insatiable hunger for it. He spent the rest of his days devouring any gold he could find, until his body broke into a million tiny pieces. Those pieces grew legs and turned into beetles, and the descendants of those beetles still crave gold centuries later."

Ekon's eyes widened. "That's . . . an incredibly macabre story."

Safiyah shrugged. "That's the south."

Ekon looked around the grasslands again. "The Enterprise is gone. I'm not sure how we're going to find them again."

Safiyah rolled her eyes. "*Well*, we could start by following the road." She pointed. Ekon's cheeks warmed as he saw the dirt path cutting through the grass. "I've run enough routes with Ano to know how she thinks," she continued. "She won't want to take any more risks with the spices, so they're probably going straight to Bandari. That's where we'll meet them. Now come on." She turned on her heel, heading for the path. "With any luck, we'll get there by late tonight."

Ekon had taken note of the scenery around him as he'd traveled with the Enterprise before, but on foot beside Safiyah, he felt like he was seeing everything differently.

The land seemed to be changing before his eyes as he watched the warm tropical lushness of the Zamani Region give way to something cooler, something with a slightly starved quality to it. As the hours passed, the grass around them seemed to thin and lose its color, transforming into a pale amber. The ground underfoot grew wetter, reminding Ekon that they were heading into the infamous marshlands that so distinctly characterized southern Eshōza. But the hardest change was in the temperature. The sun was high in the sky overhead, its light beating down directly on them, but Ekon couldn't feel it through the chill of the breeze that seemed to be wrapping itself around him. A particularly strong gust hit him directly in the face, and he groaned with discomfort. The marshlands were encroaching now; brown puddles of stagnant water were growing more frequent; in the mud, it was less and less easy to follow the tread marks the Enterprise's caravan had left.

They reached a long clearing with grass as far as the eye could see. It rained heavily enough here that several small creeks cut through the grass. Safiyah stopped just at the edge of it, then swore.

"Well, this isn't good."

"What?"

"The road." She pointed, and when Ekon followed her finger, he saw that, up ahead, the path they'd been on was submerged in an inch of water. "This has happened to us before, when the rains are particularly heavy. Ano's practical, she'll have told Thabo to take the detour path, which is a little longer, but that road stays entirely above water. For us on foot, it'll probably add a few extra hours, but we should probably take it too."

Ekon's heart plummeted. He looked down the old path, frowning. It was still visible beneath the surface. "Couldn't we just keep following that path, though?" he asked.

Safiyah looked at him as though he'd grown another head. "Are you missing the whole inch of water over it? That's not good for shoes."

"So we can take them off," said Ekon, trying to keep the irritation out of his voice. "This path could get us to Bandari tonight, maybe around the same time as the Enterprise."

Safiyah frowned. "We could also get bitten by whatever lives in these marshes," she said. "It's not safe."

Ekon gritted his teeth. When he was honest with himself, a small part of him knew that Safiyah was probably right, that the detour was the safer bet, but it was hard to resist such a clear path literally set directly before them. For her, getting to Bandari a day late wasn't critical—it was, after all, the destination for her and the Enterprise—but for him and Themba, every day of travel counted. Even now, they still didn't know exactly where Fedu was keeping Koffi, what he was doing to her. One day could make all the difference. He decided then.

"I'm going through," he said resolutely. "If you want to go the long way, that's your business. I'm getting to Bandari tonight."

Safiyah rolled her eyes. "Don't be dumb."

Ekon scowled. "Look, last night, I saw a bunch of men get eaten by carnivorous beetles. I'm tired, I'm hungry, and I've had mud in my toes for hours." He shuddered. "What I want is to get to Bandari before one more bad thing—"

A crack of lightning suddenly tore the sky, startling them both. It was followed almost immediately by thunder, and a downpour of rain. Heat rose in Ekon's cheeks as Safiyah stared daggers at him.

"Before one more bad thing happens? Is that what you were going to say?"

Ekon grimaced. "If you have a better plan—"

"Wait!" Safiyah was no longer looking at him, but out toward the marshes. "What is that?"

Ekon followed her gaze. For a moment, he didn't understand what he was looking at. In the rain, it was difficult to discern anything in the marshes. Then, slowly, a shape came into focus. At first, it looked like a person, standing impossibly in the middle of one of the creeks, but the closer they drew, the better Ekon could discern their details. It was a person on a raft. He tensed.

"Careful," he said to Safiyah in a low voice. "They could mean trouble."

"Oh? What are they going to do," said Safiyah dryly, "steal our nonexistent money?"

They watched together as the figure drew closer, and Ekon was finally able to make out the stranger's face. To his surprise, it was a woman. She wore a brown burlap cloak and a large conical straw hat atop her head that seemed to be blocking out most of the rain. Strings of cowrie shells hung about her neck, swaying as she pushed her raft forward with a long paddle, and the bone-white dreadlocks tied behind her back fell well past her waist. She waved as she neared.

"You children all right?" she called out.

"NO!" Ekon yelled at the same time Safiyah yelled, "Yes!" They exchanged glares.

"It's chilly," said the old woman. Her voice was thin, reedy. She guided her raft until it banked in the mud. "You shouldn't be out here in weather like this without proper cloaks."

"We got separated from our group," Ekon explained. "We're trying to get back to them."

"Oh dear." The old woman's eyes widened in a concern that sounded genuine. "I'm sorry to hear that. If they're traveling by wagon or mule, they'll have taken the detour path." She gestured west. "This one's been flooded for about a week, it's no good."

Beside him, Ekon could practically *hear* Safiyah's smirk.

"Of course . . ." The old woman scratched her chin. "If you're trying to get to them quickly, I could get you across on this?" She indicated the raft. "It isn't anything fancy, but it is an efficient way to get around in these marshes."

"Yes, please!" said Ekon at the same time Safiyah said, "No, thank you." He massaged the bridge of his nose and offered the old woman an apologetic look. "Excuse us a moment." He and Safiyah moved away from the woman. "What—is—the—problem?"

"Rule number one when traveling through the marshlands," said Safiyah with narrowed eyes. "Do not take rides from strangers. It's bad luck."

Ekon rolled his eyes. "You're making a decision based on superstition?"

"I'm making a decision based on common sense," said Safiyah coldly.

Ekon shook his head, unable to believe what he was hearing. "Look, you're banking on the fact that the Enterprise will be in Bandari by the time we get there. What you don't know is how much extra time that detour will take us on foot. What if it ends up taking several more days, and Ano thinks we've perished? She might not wait around in Bandari."

Safiyah looked scandalized. "Of course she would—"

"You said yourself that she's practical." Ekon shrugged. "How long exactly do you think she'd wait for us?" Before Safiyah could answer that question, he added, "Do you really want *me* as your traveling buddy for the foreseeable future?"

That particular point seemed to resonate with Safiyah. She shifted her weight from foot to foot, looking uneasy, then: "Fine."

"Excellent." Ekon was already turning to the old woman.

"Auntie?" he said. "We don't have any money to pay for passage."

The old woman smiled. "That's quite all right," she said. "And you may call me Auntie Matope. Come, I'll get you across soon enough."

Ekon stepped aboard the raft, and after a pause, Safiyah did too. Auntie Matope picked up her paddle and pushed off from the mud bank, and they were on their way. The marshlands' chill didn't abate as they floated out into one of the creeks, but Ekon could at least appreciate the scenery. The grass on the marshlands varied between shades of gold and green, occasionally interrupted by blossoms of aquatic wildflowers. He sat down and peered over the edge of the raft. The water wasn't perfectly clear, but transparent enough for him to make out schools of fish, frogs.

He leaned closer, trying to make out one of the more brightly colored species, when suddenly something large and dark swam by. He reeled back.

"Um." He tried to keep his voice calm. "Auntie, I don't want to alarm you, but I think there are crocodiles in this water."

Safiyah stiffened at once, but Auntie Matope only cackled.

"They're not crocodiles," she said. "They're nanaboleles, water dragons."

"Knew we should have walked," Safiyah muttered under her breath.

Auntie Matope's expression was wry. "Nanaboleles are only dangerous to those who offend their mother," she said.

Ekon's brows rose. "Their . . . mother?"

"The Matron of the Marsh," said Auntie Matope. "The guardian of this region."

Now Ekon was very confused. "The . . . Matron of the Marsh?" he repeated. "I've never heard of her."

"Just as well," said Auntie Matope. "She is called by any number of names—Sovereign of the Seas, Ruler of the Rivers, the Water Witch."

"Wait," said Ekon. "You're talking about the goddess Amakoya."

The woman inclined her head and continued to paddle. "So you know the faith," she said as her smile widened. "Do you have a favorite, among the six?"

The question gave Ekon pause; he didn't think he'd ever been asked that before, and had to think about it. "Well," he started, "I was always taught not to have a favorite god or goddess, but . . . when I was little, I liked Atuno."

"The oldest god," the woman said sagely. "A fair choice."

"My older brother always like Tyembu." Ekon didn't know what made him say that aloud. "I think because he liked to pretend he could shoot fire from his hands, like him."

"And what about you, girl?" The woman nodded toward Safiyah, who was sitting on the edge of the raft, hugging her knees. "What god or goddess do you favor?"

"None," said Safiyah flatly. "I'm . . . not really religious."

"Not religious?" The woman stopped rowing for a moment. "You don't worship any god, not even the great Amakoya?"

Safiyah scoffed. "Tuh. Even if I was devout, I wouldn't worship her."

No longer did the woman look curious; her mouth was drawn in a long straight line. Something in her eyes had changed too. Ekon couldn't quite put his finger on it, but he didn't like it. His eyes panned and he became all too aware that they were now in the middle of one of the creeks, with no solid land in sight. He tried to meet Safiyah's eyes to communicate his concern, but the girl sat back, looking amused.

"You would speak ill of the water goddess?" The woman's words were clipped.

"I don't speak ill of her," said Safiyah, shrugging. "I just don't think she's very nice. I've heard stories. Once, she cursed a village with a hundred-year drought, simply because there was a girl within it who was said to be more beautiful than her. Sailors pray to her before they board ships, but if she doesn't like the prayers or think they're long enough, she sends sea monsters to devour them. If you ask me, she doesn't sound like the kind of goddess I would want to worship."

Ekon flinched. It was true, of the six gods, Amakoya certainly

272

wasn't known to be one of the most benevolent. He looked from Safiyah to Auntie Matope. The old woman now had a very different look on her face; there was an intensity in her gaze. She'd stopped paddling, and she was too still.

"Tell me your name, girl," she said. "I don't think I caught it before."

Safiyah jutted out her chin. "Safiyah."

"Safiyah." The paddle clattered noisily as it slipped from the woman's hands. Ekon watched in horror as it fell into the water and disappeared, but the woman seemed to take no notice. She was standing.

"You are a bold girl," said the woman. The raft was swaying now. "To insult me as you cross my waters."

The words registered a second too late. There was a crash, and Ekon's eyes shut of their own accord as an explosion of marsh water sprayed his face without warning. He heard a great rush, what sounded like a wave, and felt another massive splash of water so powerful, he had to turn away from it. Somewhere distant, he thought he heard someone—Safiyah—scream, but he couldn't be sure. He blinked several times, caught his breath, and looked back to where the woman had been standing. His lungs constricted.

Auntie Matope was gone. In her place stood someone else. The woman before him had deep bronze skin that seemed to shimmer, braids as black as night. The dress on her body looked to be made of some iridescent blue fabric that rippled and moved like an ocean's rolling waves. She was easily the most beautiful woman Ekon had ever seen, and also the most terrifying. He knew at once who she must be.

"Amakoya . . ." Even whispering her name made him tremble. "You're Amakoya." He automatically bowed low before raising his head again.

The goddess's brown eyes snapped in his direction, and for a moment Ekon thought he saw a flash of lightning streak across them. She tilted her head in regal regard, and when she smiled, Ekon saw she had the finely pointed teeth of a crocodile.

"Very good, boy."

Ekon's heart hammered in his chest. All around him, he could still hear the ripples of the marsh water, but he couldn't take his eyes off the goddess. She wasn't the first one he'd met, but something about her felt different. It took him a moment to name the thing he felt radiating from her: power.

"I offer kindness," she said coolly. "And you dare repay me with disrespect and blasphemy. I should feed you to my children."

"We're—we're sorry." Ekon turned, remembering for the first time that Safiyah was still there. She was on the raft's edge, soaked. "W-we didn't know—"

"Mortals," she said, cocking her head with amusement. A coarse laugh bubbled in her throat. "Always begging, always pleading, always desperate to prolong their short, little existences." She seemed to grow with every word, looming over them. "You think, because you beg, that I will feel something for you, perhaps pity or guilt. You are grossly mistaken. I have long since shed the inconvenience of emotion; it serves me no purpose. Understand this, you are but a second in my centuries. I will kill you, and I will think nothing of it. And when you are but dust in the wind, I will still live on."

"Wait," said Ekon. The words left his mouth before he had time to reconsider them. "I know your sister!" He raised his hands, knowing it would do nothing if the goddess decided to turn her wrath on him. He watched as Amakoya processed his words and her eyes narrowed.

"My sister?" she repeated.

"Badwa," said Ekon quickly. "I met her in the Greater Jungle, a short while ago. She helped a friend and me when we were in trouble."

The skepticism in the goddess's eyes did not lessen. "I don't believe it," she said. "My sister would never seek out or help mortals. It is beneath her."

"She wasn't the one who found us first," said Ekon. "It was the yumboes, they brought us to her."

Slowly, Amakoya's expression changed. The anger softened, and in its place Ekon saw sadness. The goddess placed her hand on her chest.

"I have not seen my sister in many years." She seemed to be speaking more to herself now. There was a distance in her eyes, a faraway look. Ekon took advantage of the moment to press on.

"While my friend and I were in the Greater Jungle, we spoke with Ba—er, your sister. There's something you should know." He hesitated. "It's about your brother Fedu."

Amakoya snapped from her reverie at once. "What of my brother?"

"He's plotting something," said Ekon. "He wants to cleanse the world of all non-darajas and create a new one. But the only time he'd have enough power to do so would be during—"

"The Bonding." Amakoya's eyes widened. She looked at Ekon now with new appreciation. "If what you've said is true, mortal, my brother must be stopped."

Ekon nodded. "He took my friend, a daraja, back to his realm in the south. I'm on my way there now to get her."

The goddess tilted her head, appraising. "Tell me your name."

"Ekon. Ekon Okojo."

She took a step closer, studying him. "East and west," she murmured. "One sun rises in the east. One sun rises in the west."

Ekon went cold. Those were the same words Sigidi had said to him back in Lkossa. The exact same words.

"Ekon Okojo," Amakoya repeated. "I will not impede you in your mission to find your friend and stop my brother."

Ekon breathed a sigh of relief, but the goddess's eyes had already turned to Safiyah.

"There is, however," she said, "no need for *you* to live."

Ekon didn't have time to process what the woman had said before there was a lurch. He scrambled to grab something as the raft tipped, then capsized. Somewhere distant, he heard Safiyah gasp before she plunged into the water. There was a crash of waves, a split second in which Ekon felt himself flung into the air, and then he was underwater too.

The world instantly silenced as he sank below the depths. Ekon turned his head and found that everything was slowed. He hadn't known the creek was this deep. The world around him was a blur of browns and greens, murky shapes that refused to come into focus. His lungs strained, and he tried to keep himself calm and thinking rationally.

Find Safiyah. Swim to the surface. Get to some kind of solid land.
Three tasks. He made himself count.

One. Two. Three.

Task one, find Safiyah. Ekon looked around again; this time, he had a stroke of luck. A few feet away, he could see Safiyah's blurred form kicking in the water. He pushed himself forward with all his might, ignoring the thing his foot bumped against. It seemed to take years for him to reach her, but he took hold of her wrist and tugged. She turned around, and when their eyes met, Ekon pointed upward.

Find Safiyah. Check. Now swim to the surface.

Safiyah seemed to understand as Ekon pointed up; slowly, the two of them made their way toward the creek's surface. It seemed so much farther away than Ekon remembered, and he was dismayed to see that, even with sunlight shining through, there was no sign of the raft.

Just a little farther, he told himself. *Just a few more feet.*

His grip on Safiyah's wrist tightened as he kicked his legs upward. Their heads broke the surface at the same time with a tremendous crash, and Ekon gasped as his lungs took in greedy gulps of fresh air. Beside him, Safiyah was sputtering too, but otherwise looked okay. She blinked several times before catching Ekon's eye.

"Remind me to never piss off a goddess again."

"Will do," said Ekon. He glanced left, then right. Several yards away, he could make out a riverbank. He nodded toward it.

"Can you get to those mud banks?"

Safiyah followed his gaze, then nodded.

"Good," he said. "Once we get to them, we can—"

A low roar filled the air, cutting off his words. Slowly, Ekon turned in the water, and a scream rose in his throat.

The creature that had risen just above the water's surface looked like a crocodile, but it was much larger, and skeletal. Wet, glistening scales the size of a grown man's head covered its entire body, and when it opened its mouth, Ekon saw rows of yellowed teeth.

It was a water dragon. A nanabolele.

"Safiyah." Ekon kept his voice low. The nanabolele was creeping toward them. "I'm going to count," he said. "When I get to three, swim as fast as you can to the banks."

"What?" Safiyah barely moved her lips. "Ekon, have you lost your—?"

"I'll distract it," said Ekon. "It can't go for us both at the same time. Just wait for my count."

Safiyah looked like she wanted to argue more, but when the nanabolele shrieked again, she clamped her mouth shut and nodded tightly. Ekon braced himself.

"One, two . . ."

On three, he let his hand slap against the water as hard as it could. The sound was satisfyingly loud, and Ekon was half terrified and half relieved to find that he was right; the nanabolele thrashed, its yellow eyes locking on him. In his periphery, he saw Safiyah dive below the river's depths again, presumably to prevent splashing. He barely had time to think about it before the nanabolele lunged at him, and then he too was ducking down beneath the waves. The creature went after him, and he realized his mistake a second too late. Underwater, in its natural habitat, it was stronger, more savvy. He watched in slow motion as the beast whipped its long, muscular tail so that the tip of it slammed into Ekon's chest. An explosion of pain slashed across his body and knocked him back. He opened his mouth and took in water. Fear set in as the corners of his vision began to blur, not from a panic attack, but because he was drowning.

One-two-three.

He would be okay if he could just get back to the surface. The problem was that no matter how hard he kicked, his body continued to sink. The blackness that had started in the corners of his vision had now encroached so much that he felt as though he were looking through a tunnel; the sunlight was getting farther away, dimmer. He closed his eyes.

I'm going to die.

Four words.

He was counting, waiting for his body to succumb to the creek's darkness, when he felt a hand encircle his wrist and tighten. He opened his eyes again. Safiyah had taken hold of him and was swimming as quickly as she could to the surface. Ekon tried to help, to kick his legs, but his body was fatigued, and he didn't have enough air in his lungs. When they broke the surface, he gasped.

"Come on!" she shouted. "Try to kick!"

Ekon focused, fighting a haze at the edges of the vision. Safiyah was half towing, half dragging him to one of the mud banks. A surge of relief flooded him as he found purchase in it, as she helped him to his feet, but then he heard her scream. They both backed away from the creek.

The nanabolele was emerging from the water too, and Ekon now had a true appreciation for its size. It was longer than his whole body; its head alone was longer than his arms. It moved on short, clawed feet that slightly elevated it as it lumbered toward them, so much like a crocodile. Ekon was suddenly struck by an idea.

"Stand back," he said. "I'm going try something."

"What are you—?"

He ran at the beast before he could give himself time to be afraid. The nanabolele hissed, clearly surprised by the sudden move, and swung its head left. Ekon went right. There was a fractional second in which the creature wasn't looking in his direction, and he took it. He leaped, threw his whole body on the nanabolele's scaled back. It smelled like fish and marsh water, its scales were slick, but he held on. It shrieked.

"EKON!" Safiyah screamed. "Have you lost your mind?"

"Help me!" Ekon shouted. The nanabolele was bucking, thrashing, desperately trying to get to him. "Help me flip it over!" He couldn't see Safiyah, but he heard what sounded like a groan, and then he felt her body behind his, also tugging at the beast. A feral rasping noise emitted from the nanabolele as it snapped its massive jaws, but Ekon could tell it was getting tired. Its movements were getting slower, and there was more time between each one.

"The next time it stills," he said to Safiyah, "throw your weight to the right!"

Safiyah didn't have time to answer. The nanabolele turned violently left, throwing its head so that it was able to look Ekon in the eye. He saw the beast's nostrils flare, heard it roar, before it stilled.

"Now!" Using every bit of momentum he had, he threw his weight; behind him, Safiyah did too. The world turned on itself; Ekon's back slammed against the ground. He had the sense to scramble out from underneath the nanabolele and pull Safiyah with him as the creature made a horrible shrieking sound, then abruptly went stone still. They both leaped to their feet and, for a moment, did nothing but stare.

"Is it . . . is it dead?" asked Safiyah. There was confusion in her voice.

"No." Ekon shook his head. "It's unconscious."

She turned to him. "How did you possibly know to do that?"

"It was a guess." Ekon was still watching the nanabolele. "It may not have been a crocodile, but I figured it at least belonged in the same family. All crocodilians can be dismantled by tonic immobility."

Safiyah stared at him. "Tonic what?"

"It's a physiological phenomenon in which—"

"In plain Zamani, please."

Ekon sighed. "If you can get a crocodile on its back, it will become catatonic and basically useless."

They both stared again at the nanabolele. It was, certainly, still alive—Ekon could see its scaled chest inhaling and exhaling—but its eyes were dilated, and it was completely still.

"Tonic immobility," Safiyah repeated. "I'll have to make a note of that for future reference."

"Hopefully not in the immediate future," said Ekon. He looked around them. It seemed Auntie Matope—Amakoya—had gotten them about halfway across the marshlands. He sighed.

"We're not going to be able to get back to the roads," he said. "We'll have to stay along the banks."

Safiyah sighed. "I was afraid you were going to say that."

"Come on." Ekon took a deep breath, then started up the mud banks. "We've got a long walk."

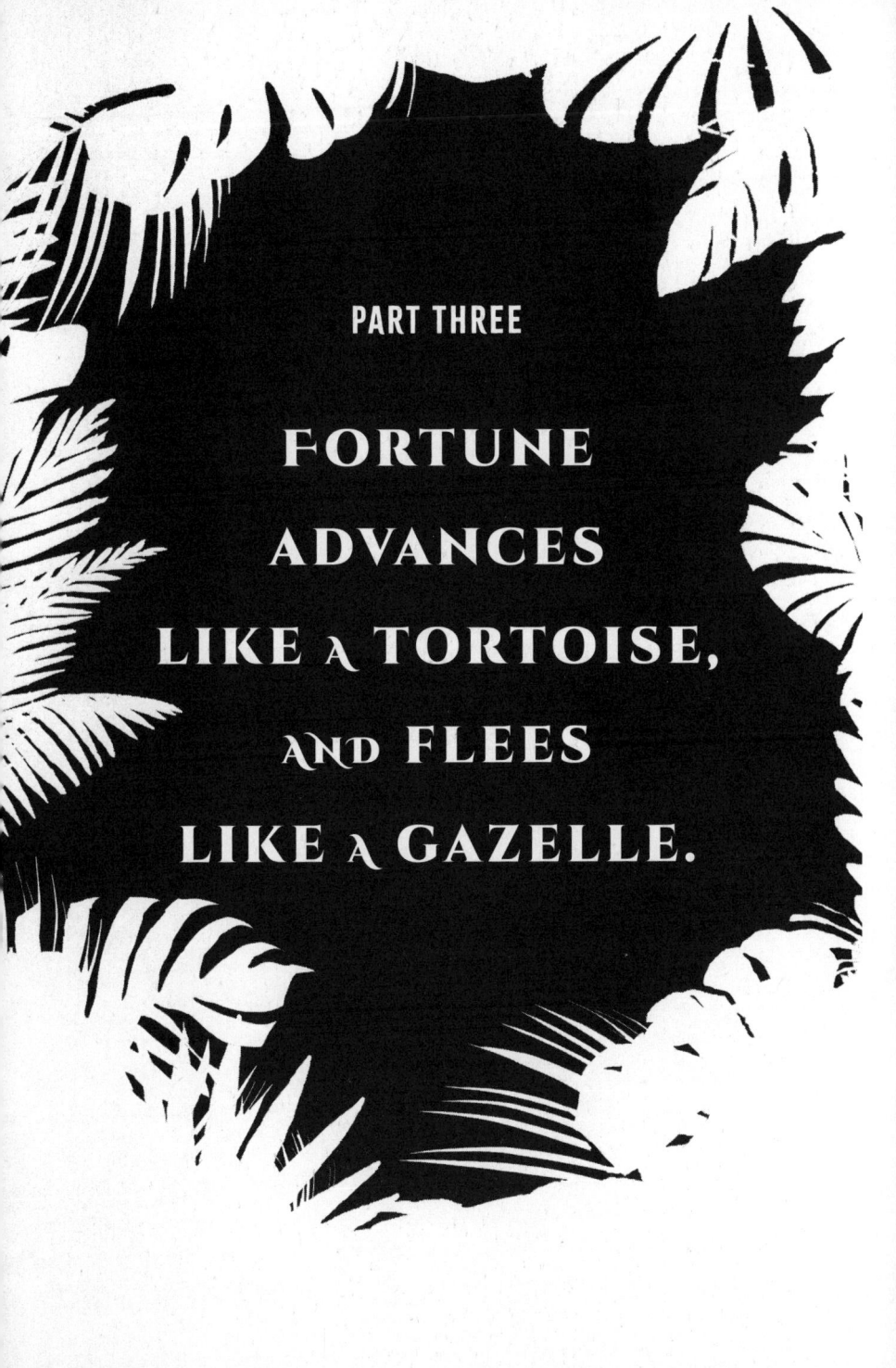

PART THREE

FORTUNE ADVANCES LIKE A TORTOISE, AND FLEES LIKE A GAZELLE.

A TERRIBLE SIN

BINTI

Mama says that lying is a terrible sin.

But tonight, it is a necessary one.

I tighten my grip on Nyah as we stroll together through Lkossa's crammed streets, stifling giggles with each step. The air around us is sweetened by the scent of Nyah's heavy perfume—some blend of jasmine and citrus. I can't tell if it's that smell or the palm wine we snuck earlier that's made my head feel a bit dizzy, but I find I don't actually mind the warm sensation. Still, through my pleasant haze, there *is* a point of concern.

"Are you—" My words are interrupted by a hiccup. "Are you sure we'll be allowed in? Neither of us are technically of age . . ."

"I'm sure," Nyah assures me, nudging me around another corner. She's wearing an easy smile, the kind I've learned to be instantly suspicious of. "Trust me," she goes on. "It's an open bonfire, no one's going to be sober enough to ask questions."

It's not exactly the most comforting answer, but it's the one I'm forced to accept. As if on cue, we pass a man who's clearly had more than a few drinks. He beams, wishes us both a happy Bonding Day, and presses shaba coins in our hands. Nyah smirks.

"Fine," I concede. "You've made your point."

The sun set hours ago, but Lkossa's streets are still full. It's a happy product of the occasion: Bonding Day, a religious holiday that gives everyone in this city a rare occasion to be united in festivity. I think of all those years ago, when Mama and I used to wander through these crowds, not enjoying the celebrations but picking for scraps. It feels like a distant memory now.

"We're here," Nyah announces, pointing ahead. I look up and see several stakes driven into the ground, all lit at their tops with torches. Streamers of blue, green, and gold flutter from them, and they've been arranged to form a crude kind of enclosure. There are people inside of it.

"Ready?" Nyah throws a look my way, a look that tells me there's no more time for second-guessing. No backing out now. I swallow the lump in my throat.

"Ready."

We approach the large man standing in front of the entrance to the enclosure—some sort of guard—and the minute his gaze finds us in the darkness, it narrows.

"Good evening, sir," Nyah says in a singsong voice. "We'd like to pay for two entries, please." She holds out the admittance fee, one fedha each, but the man doesn't take it. He is still looking us over with skepticism.

"How *old* are you two?" he asks slowly.

"Old enough." Nyah's lie comes out of her mouth with impressive ease, and she flutters her long black eyelashes for good measure. After a moment, the guard softens.

"I see . . ." His tone has now changed completely. "What's your name?"

"Daya," she says simply, and even though I know better, I

almost believe her. She turns to me with expectant eyes. "And *this* is my friend . . ."

"Rashida." I no longer have to practice saying the name; it comes to me easily now. The moment I speak it aloud, I feel a thrum. It's the thrill of being someone else, *something* else, if only for a few hours. Tonight, I am Rashida, no longer the daughter of the infamous Cobra, and no longer the girl so poor she had to borrow the dress on her back.

The guard gives us both a final once-over, but I can already tell the battle is won. A second later, he steps aside and nods for us to enter the enclosure without taking the coins Nyah offered.

"Just let me buy you and your friend a drink before the night is over," he says with a wink. Nyah takes my arm again and pulls me forward.

"You're going to *love* this," she says under her breath. I hear the excitement in her voice.

We enter the enclosure, and at once something seizes in my lungs. I begin coughing as a strange smell fills them, hard to describe, but almost . . . fruity . . . saccharine. The air is opaque, with tendrils of something wisping through and making it impossible to see much farther than a few feet in front of me.

"What . . . *is* this?" I wave my hand through the smoke with a mixture of bewilderment and wonder.

"It's called matunda," she says, putting an accent on the second syllable. "You smoke it from a pipe. It feels a little weird at first, but don't worry, you get used to it."

I'm still deciding if matunda is something I'm interested in "getting used to" when Nyah spots a group of people sitting on logs that have been moved to make a smaller circle. They're waving us over, and I'm relieved to see that most of them look my age at least. It makes me feel a little less alone here.

"Come on!"

Nyah guides me over to the group—two boys, and three other girls—and introduces them to me in turn as we settle on the large floor pillows. I don't hear the names of any of the girls, but I do hear when she introduces one boy as Kibwe. I recognize *that* name; she's been talking to me about him practically nonstop for the last two weeks. Almost as soon as she sits next to him, she's engrossed in a conversation with him, which leaves the second boy as the only other person to talk to.

"Hi." He offers a small wave. "I'm Lesego." He has to shout over the loud music, and offers a sheepish half smile in apology.

Rashida, I mouth.

"What's your poison?"

"Sorry?"

He picks up what looks to be a silver pipe connected to a hose. There are several of them, I now realize, and I figure that *this* is how matunda is actually smoked. Lesego seems to read the look on my face.

"I like strawberry," he shouts over the noise.

"What?"

He opens his mouth to try again before thinking better of it, then just scoots closer to me. He smells like the spiced soaps I've sometimes seen for sale at the market.

"Strawberry," he repeats. "But if it's your first time, you might like something a little lighter, like mint."

I watch him set up the matunda in silence, trying to ignore the sudden tightness in my chest that has nothing to do with the smoke around me. Mint flavor makes me think of mint leaf, which makes me think of Mama. Thanks to Nyah's mother, we've finally found a sort of home with an old innkeeper who needs help. The pay isn't much, but it's a roof over our heads. Mama promised things would get better, and they have, but . . . I still lied to her tonight. She knows I'm spending the night with Nyah; she definitely doesn't know that we're at a party. Guilt pricks at me like a thorn.

"Hey!" I startle from my thoughts as Lesego leans closer, looking concerned. "Are you okay?"

"Yeah." I nod quickly. The bonfire casts a harsh red-gold light over everyone; in that luminance, I can appreciate that Lesego is handsome. His skin is chestnut brown, and his short curly hair is as black as a crow's wing. Two matching dimples form in his cheeks when he smiles again.

"Okay, just take it slow," he directs, handing me one of the pipes. I don't want to look like a fool, so I bring it to my lips immediately and suck in a hard breath.

My lungs instantly feel as though they've been set on fire, and I start coughing so hard, I'm sure I'm going to bring up a lung.

"Whoa, whoa." Lesego pats my back. "Easy."

"Sorry." I'm grateful for the dimness now, it at least hides some of my embarrassment, but Lesego waves a dismissing hand.

"It's no big deal," he says. "No one's first time is great. It's really something you've got to ease into."

"Honestly," I say between coughs, "I think I'll be okay never trying it again."

"Fair enough." His smile widens. "So, what do you do?"

"I help out at an inn," I say carefully. "With my mother."

"Really?" There's surprise in his voice. "But you speak so well!"

When my brows knit, he raises his hands, alarmed. "Wait, no—that's not I meant! Just, you sound like you're educated, I mean, like you read books. I mean . . . sorry."

Now a pleasant flush heats my skin. I'm almost eighteen, so I've certainly had to deal with boys—and men—changing the way they look at me, but no boy or man has ever looked at me the way Lesego is looking at me now. He isn't looking at my body, undressing me with his eyes, or saying things that make me want to roll mine to the heavens. He's flustered, looking at me now with admiration, even respect.

"How come I've never seen you around before?" he asks. "Nyah comes to these kinds of parties all the time."

I'm careful to consider my answer. I don't want to say that, truthfully, I rarely have a night off like this. "I guess I'm just busy most nights."

Lesego nods solemnly. "That's good. I stay busy too."

"Really?" I ask, eager to shift the focus of the conversation. "What do you do?"

"Entrepreneurship, mostly," he says at once. "I've got some great business ideas. I just have to find some financial backers to get me started."

A smile sneaks across my lips, pulling at the corners of my mouth. After years on the street hustling with Mama, it's unreasonably refreshing to hear someone talk about a legitimate business venture.

"I hope you find a financier to make one of those ideas happen."

"Me too." He looks down at his hands for a moment. "Then I could afford to . . . maybe take you out sometime?"

"Oh." There's warmth in my cheeks again, but this time I don't mind. My hands feel clammy and my heart is pattering in my chest like a drum, yet none of it feels bad. I've never really been asked out before by any man, properly or not.

"Thank you," I reply. "That would be . . . really nice."

I don't know if the new buzzing in my head has anything to do with the way Lesego is looking at me now, or with the smoke still clouding the air, but suddenly everything around us seems to quiet and fade to something distant. A sea of blurred faces floats around us, but none of them are discernible.

"Rashida . . ." Lesego's not looking at my eyes, but my mouth. I don't mind so much now; I'm finding it easy to look at his. I want to know what comes next, what he's going to say, what he's going to do in these next precious few seconds.

Then I hear it: a scream.

Everyone turns as a second one pierces the air, and then a wail. My eyes search the crowd until I see it, and my heart sinks. There's a Son of the Six here, made distinct by his uniform. He has a small squashed nose, wide-set eyes, and a face twisted into what looks like a permanent scowl. His presence here alone would put me on edge, but what has struck fear into me isn't him, but what he has in his grasp.

A boy.

He looks to be eleven or twelve, still young enough to be called a child despite his lanky arms and legs. He dangles limply in the warrior's grasp, and I can already see a line of blood trickling from his lip. I stiffen as my eyes drop to his wrist, to the tarnished silver bracelet he's wearing. I've, of course, seen a bracelet like that before, on my own mother.

"I'll ask you again," says the warrior. His voice is full of cold menace. "What were you doing here?"

The boy glowers. "I told you, none of your business."

It's the wrong thing to say. The words have barely left his lips when the warrior withdraws the hanjari dagger from its hilt. He points its tip just below the boy's eye.

"Watch how you speak to me, boy," he says, "or you won't be watching anything at all."

The boy's remaining courage slips from him as the tip of the warrior's dagger pierces skin, drawing a garnet-red drop of blood that bears an unsettling resemblance to a tear.

"Now," says the warrior. "What were you doing here? This party's private. Darajas aren't welcomed."

"I just wanted some food." The boy speaks quietly, but in the silence his words carry. "That's all."

Several bystanders scrunch their faces in disgust, and the warrior's eyes narrow to slits.

"You are, in fact, confirming that you knowingly trespassed into an area restricted under DANAH law with the intent to steal?"

The boy flinches. "I . . . I didn't really think of it as stealing, I was just going to take the scraps—"

"By the authority granted to me by the highest authority in this city," says the warrior in a new proclamatory voice, "I find you guilty of trespass and theft, and sentence you to ten bullwhip lashes, to be received consecutively, and without delay."

"No, *please*."

There is no hope for the boy or his pleas as the warrior withdraws the crop from his belt. The metal embedded in the leather glints in the firelight. I look away as his hand rises, but it does nothing to stop me from hearing the sharp crack when that leather meets flesh.

Crack.

I flinch.

Crack. Crack.

The boy screams.

"Rashida?"

I jump. Nyah is standing over me, her face stricken. "I just remembered, my mama needs me at home. You're staying with me tonight, right?" There's a tremble in her voice, tears glistening in her eyes. She cringes as another crack of the warrior's whip splits the night.

"Yeah." I keep my voice steady as I rise, pretending to smooth the front of my dress. My palms feel sticky with sweat and my throat is dry. The smell of the matunda smoke isn't pleasant anymore; it just makes me sick to my stomach.

"Rashida!" Lesego rises too, looking concerned. "You're already leaving?" He looks sad, and I don't know whether to be glad that he's sad I'm leaving or upset that *that* is what's bothering him, not the boy being beaten just a few feet away from us.

I feel Nyah slip her hand into mine and tug. I only have time to say "It was nice to meet you" to Lesego before she pulls me away and through the crowd. Already, some people have returned to their drinks and conversations, while others are still watching as the warrior metes out the boy's punishment. Nyah and I don't speak as we pass the guard at the entrance to the corral and head back into the night. Her breath comes quick, panicked, and I don't have to ask her why. We both know how close a call that was, *too* close. That boy is a reminder: We may be able to pretend, but we will never truly be a part. We walk in silence until the bonfire is long gone, but I hear the crack of the whip long after.

CHAPTER 17

ICHISONGA

Koffi's heart thundered in her chest.

Each ragged breath seemed to rattle her bones as she fought to keep pace with Amun and Zain as they bolted out of Thornkeep. Both boys were sprinting ahead of her, and past them she could see a circular assembly of darajas already gathered in the north garden. A massive bonfire had been erected, and Fedu was standing beside it. Dread unfurled in the pit of her stomach as she took in his expression, the eerie calm in his face.

"Over here," said Zain. Koffi let him take her hand and lead her around the circle until they found Makena. She saw her own worry mirrored in the girl's eyes.

"What's going on?"

Makena shook her head. "I don't know." She looked from Koffi, to Zain, to Amun. "He wouldn't tell us anything. He just told us all to come here."

Amun's face grew stricken, and the muscles in Zain's jaw feathered. "Could he know?" he asked in a barely audible voice. "About the plan?"

"I'm not sure how," Makena whispered. "No one's said anything."

Koffi's eyes roamed over the darajas in the circle. There were enough of them here that the likelihood of Fedu overhearing them was slight, but she was still on edge. She searched, trying to pick out faces in the crowd. She couldn't tell if anyone was missing. Once again, her eyes went to Fedu. He stood perfectly still, his hands folded, as he seemed to be waiting for something. Without warning, he cleared his throat.

"My children." He opened his arms in welcome, as though this was a party. "I have summoned you all this evening with a bittersweetness." He turned his eyes up to the night sky, the bonfire's flames casting his face in eerie relief. "On nights like this, I am reminded of how beautiful Thornkeep is, of how truly unique it is. In an age where darajas are hunted like dogs in some parts of this continent, Thornkeep is a commune, a safe harbor. In a flawed world, it is the closest I have ever known to a utopia."

Koffi exchanged a glance with Makena, and then with Zain; both of their eyes were fixed on the god, their expressions full of the same confusion and uncertainty. A chill lingered in the air. Try as she might, Koffi couldn't shake the feeling that something was wrong, that something bad was about to happen. She turned back to Fedu as he bowed his head.

"Alas," he said with a sadness, "a true utopia can only remain as such when its inhabitants abide by its rules." He folded his hands again, as though in deliberation. "The rules I have instated at Thornkeep are few, but some are absolute. When those rules are broken, I am forced to act."

He looked above the heads of the darajas in the circle and

signaled. Everyone turned their heads at once. In the dying light, it was difficult to see, but Koffi thought she discerned three figures making their way toward the crowd, two walking quickly, the one in the middle much slower. The dread intensified, and Koffi's breath grew shallow as she, Zain, Amun, Makena, and the rest of the darajas waited for those three figures to step into the firelight. When they finally did, Koffi nearly choked on a scream.

Zola stood between two male darajas from the Order of Kupambana. Her usually neat black dreadlocks were disheveled, her yellow tunic was ripped, and her bottom lip was swollen. Koffi barely recognized her. Gone was the cheeriness she'd seen in the girl's eyes; in its place was raw fear. Beside her, Koffi heard Makena's soft gasp.

"Come forward, Zola." From the center of the circle, Fedu's voice was unnervingly pleasant, warm.

Koffi's eyes went from him to Zola. At first, she half expected the girl not to move, to run as soon as the darajas released her from their gasp. But when they did, Zola did not run. She hung her head so that her hair fell in front of her eyes as she trudged forward, and Koffi thought she'd never seen someone look so utterly defeated. The circle of darajas parted slightly to let her through, so that now it was only she and Fedu in its center. There was a long pause before the god spoke again.

"Many of you know Zola," he said. "She is a daraja from the Order of Ufundi, one of Thornkeep's most talented blacksmiths."

Zola didn't move, didn't so much as acknowledge her name being called. Her eyes were trained determinedly on the grass, and Koffi thought she looked as though she was steeling herself for something.

"I remember the day I found Zola," Fedu went on, his lips touched by a smile. "She was a small child then, perhaps only five. It was unusual to see a little girl in a forge, wandering among grizzly old men, but she seemed to be enjoying herself. She has always had a natural gift for ironwork."

Next to her, Koffi felt more than saw Zain stiffen. It was clear that whatever unease she felt about this was shared. Fedu sounded nostalgic; the longer he went on, the more he sounded like he was speaking of someone in the past.

"Zola's parents were reticent the first time I invited her to apprentice with me here," Fedu continued. "They were protective, and I imagine they weren't fond of the idea of sending Zola away. But Zola's father—a non-daraja, I might add—possessed in him a selflessness that allowed him to understand the value of sacrifice. He eventually agreed to send Zola to Thornkeep with me. You all would agree that she has had quite the home here."

None of the darajas in the circle dared to agree or disagree.

At the mention of her father, Zola lifted her head, her eyes glittering with tears, though she still did not speak. In the wake of Fedu's words, Koffi shuddered. She hadn't asked Zola exactly how she'd come to be at Thornkeep. She knew from Makena that the darajas here had been taken, but hearing Fedu's story now painted a chilling image in her mind. She saw Zola as that little girl Fedu had described, a little girl with her own family, with her own careful set of hopes and dreams.

"It was brought to my attention recently," Fedu went on, "that Zola has been working on projects, projects that are banned at Thornkeep." He pursed his lips, looking troubled. "Would you care to speak about those projects, Zola?"

The girl didn't answer.

"Perhaps you require something to refresh your memory." He held out his hand, waiting. After a moment, Koffi saw one of the yellow-clad darajas break from the crowd, a young man. He trembled from head to toe as he approached Fedu holding a thin box. A nausea rose in Koffi. She recognized that box; Zola had shown it to her the first time she'd visited the forge. When Zola saw it, she stiffened, but Fedu's smile only grew. He took the box from the daraja and inclined his head.

"Let us examine this," he said lightly. "Zola, if you would do the honors. Unless someone else would like to volunteer?"

Koffi's stomach twisted violently as Zola looked up, searching the crowd for help. No one stepped forward. Slowly, she took the box from Fedu and opened it. In the firelight, the papers within glowed a yellow-orange.

"Would you care to tell us what these papers are?" he asked softly.

Zola only stared at them. She looked far away, numb. After a moment, Fedu went on.

"These are drawings—very good drawings, I might add—of weapons," he said. "The problem is, Zola, you are not supposed to be making weapons. You are forbidden."

Zola stared up at the god, stammering silently. She seemed to be trying and failing to find words to speak. More tears welled in her eyes.

"Shh." Fedu cupped Zola's face with one hand. She shuddered under his touch. "There, there, child. Be at ease. Even the most innocent lambs sometimes wander from the flock."

Zola closed her eyes, and Fedu brushed her tears away.

"I understand if you've made a mistake." His voice was a murmur, but it carried. "And you can rectify that mistake now, there's still an opportunity. All you have to do is tell me what the weapons are for."

Zola opened her eyes. Koffi watched as, again, she looked up at the god. A lump in her throat bobbed as she swallowed hard. When she spoke, her voice was little more than a rasp.

"I drew them . . . for myself. For fun. I wasn't going to make them."

Fedu's eyes flashed. "Now, now, little Zola." He shook his head, looking like an indulgent parent. "Let us not insult each other. You are a clever girl, and I am an old god. Some of your drawings were, indeed, fanciful sketches, but some of them were not. Some of them were detailed, contained notes, material lists, precisely the things one might include for weapons they *did* intend to make." He pulled his hands away from her and clasped his hands. "And so, I ask you again: *What are the weapons for?* Perhaps there are comrades among you who are planning something foolish—a coup, a rebellion of sorts?"

Zola dropped her head.

"If you tell me the name or names of your co-conspirators, Zola, I might be able to help you," Fedu coaxed. "I do not wish to see you in any more pain."

A chill rocked through Koffi as the gravity of his word sank in. *Any* more *pain*.

"I will give you one final chance to be truthful with me." Fedu had not raised his voice once, but now there was an edge to it, a sharpness like a knife's blade. "Tell me what the weapons you planned to make were for, and who they were for."

Koffi expected to see more tears when Zola raised her head again. Instead, what she saw in the girl's eyes was plain: defiance. It blazed in her eyes and pronounced itself in the way she set her jaw, held her lips together firmly. Her answer was clear. Fedu shook his head.

"Regrettable," he said. "It is truly regrettable." He turned then, and for the second time held out his hand. A daraja dressed in green stepped forward, a girl. She had to be from the Order of Maisha. Koffi had never met her before. The girl's eyes were hard as she glared at Zola, looking distinctly betrayed. From her tunic's pocket, she withdrew something small and handed it to Fedu. Koffi couldn't see what it was until the god held it between his fingers: a tiny silver whistle. Cries went up around the crowd of darajas as they saw it, and the defiance Koffi had seen in Zola's eyes flickered out like a candle as she laid eyes on it too.

"No." She shook her head. "No, no, no, no!"

"I am grieved to do it, Zola," Fedu sounded contrite. "It hurts me, truly. But you have left me with no choice. If the lamb wanders too far from the flock, if the lamb refuses to return to her shepherd, she must be left to the wolves."

"No!" Zola howled, an inhuman sound. She dropped the box of papers as she fell to her knees, grabbing fistfuls of her hair. "No, no, please—"

Fedu brought the whistle to his lips and blew.

A heavy silence fell upon the garden, descending with all the blunt force of an ax. It was followed by a loud bang.

Koffi started to turn, to look around, and then she felt it: a deep rumbling underfoot. It sounded like approaching thunder, but in the clear night sky, she knew that wasn't right. Something was charging forward on massive, pounding feet. It was coming from the stables, and vaguely Koffi remembered something from her first visit there. A stall with a closed door. She recalled now what Amun had said when she'd asked what was behind that door.

Something you hopefully never have to see.

Beside her, Makena shuddered, and a single word escaped her lips. "Ichisonga," she breathed. "Ichisonga."

Koffi didn't have time to ask what an ichisonga was; in seconds, she had her answer. From the darkness, a creature emerged. At first glance, her instinct was to call it a rhinoceros, but that wasn't what this animal was. It ran on four legs, carrying a hulking body covered in rough gray skin that reminded her of armor. Thin reddish hair gathered around its ankles, and its eyes were flat and black. But that wasn't what scared Koffi; it was the massive white horn protruding from the beast's skull. It was twice the length of her arm, its point congealed with a reddish-brown crust. She knew what it was.

The darajas scattered as the ichisonga ran forward, but its dull gaze was focused, heading toward Zola. In a half beat, she was on her feet, running. The ichisonga roared, a deep, guttural sound, as it picked up its pace.

No. Koffi clenched her teeth together. A fear she'd never felt the likes of before clawed up her throat as she watched Zola tear across the north garden. Her steps were clumsy, impaired, but she ran as hard as she could. The ichisonga picked up speed, snorted as it lowered its head. Its blood-crusted horn was getting closer to Zola's back, closing in. It would run her through. Zola turned abruptly, barely missing the horn, but it lacerated her arm.

Dark blood sprayed through the air, she cried out but didn't stop. Koffi tore her gaze away from the daraja to look at Fedu. He was watching them both with a faint intrigue, the lazy way one might watch a passing butterfly.

The ichisonga picked up speed and, with a sudden burst of energy, knocked into Zola. She went flying, then landed face forward on the grass. For a second, Koffi though she wouldn't rise, but she did, this time looking pained. The ichisonga rounded on her, pawing at the grass. It lowered its head, and abruptly, Zola's eyes met Koffi's.

I'm sorry. She mouthed the words, but no sound escaped. *I'm sorry.*

Without warning, she took off again. The ichisonga bellowed in fury, but this time, Zola didn't look back. Even from a distance, Koffi could see her eyes held a purpose they hadn't had in them before. She was no longer running away, but toward something. Koffi understood a second too late what was about to happen.

She watched with horror as Zola ran into the Mistwood.

There was a hush, a sudden new silence, and every daraja in the garden stood perfectly still. Even the ichisonga seemed to understand that its chase was over. Koffi stood, watching the Mistwood's fog swirl in the quiet, betraying no sign that Zola had been there at all. Seconds passed, though for Koffi they could have been years. A shrill note broke the quietude: Fedu's whistle. Several darajas from the Order of Maisha rushed forward to subdue the ichisonga and take it back to the stables. Fedu watched. When he spoke, his voice was gentle.

"Let this night serve as a reminder," he said, "of the graces I offer to those in Thornkeep who abide by my rules, and of the punishment that awaits those foolish enough to break them. You are all dismissed."

One by one, the darajas dispersed. At they passed her, Koffi saw that some looked shaken, others were sobbing outright, and some didn't look bothered at all. A breeze lifted, carrying with it the smell of the garden's flowers, the richness of burning firewood, and the lingering stink of old blood. Koffi didn't move, nor did Makena, Zain, Amun, or Njeri. The five of them stood there in the silence, until they were the last ones left in the garden, alone with the dying bonfire.

"It's my fault." Zain spoke first, his voice little more than a whisper. "I told her to begin work on the weapons. She drew those more detailed sketches because of me."

"We shouldn't talk about that here," Njeri cautioned. "Someone might hear—"

"I don't care!" Zain erupted, a wildness in his eyes. His voice was strangled. "It shouldn't have been her." He shook his head. "It shouldn't have been her."

Without a word, Makena pulled Zain into her arms. She was shorter than him, but he collapsed against her. Amun joined them, tears wetting his cheeks as he bowed his head. Njeri pulled Koffi in. The five of them simply stood there, drawing ragged breaths beneath a quiet moon.

"I'm getting us out of here," Koffi whispered. She wasn't sure who the words were for—her friends or herself—but she said them like an oath to the stars, a vow. "I am going to get us out of here, and we are going home."

CHAPTER 18

THE ZAMANI QUICKSTEP

Ekon had never cared for geography.

It was, for him at least, too ambiguous a subject, too unpredictable. Unlike numbers—which were, of course, inherently trustworthy and consistent—geography could change, maps could be manipulated, and cartographers could lie. The books he'd once read in the Temple of Lkossa, for example, had described Kusini—Eshōza's southern region—as mild, moderately aquatic, with occasional temperate winds.

Every one of those descriptions was a falsehood.

After their encounter with Amakoya, he and Safiyah had walked through the marshlands for the better part of five hours. Five hours and thirty-six minutes, to be precise. Ekon had hoped that, sometime in that interval, his wet clothes would dry, or that they'd find a source of fresh water to drink, but it was to no avail. The marsh water seemed desperate to cling to every bit of skin it could slick, adding a certain sliminess to his steps. He gazed up at the setting sun, watching as it dipped ever closer to the earth, and fought the chill seeping into his skin.

"H-h-how many more miles to Bandari?" he asked.

Beside him, Safiyah shook her head, shivering. Her clothes were soaked too. "At least five," she said through chattering teeth. "We're not going to make it there tonight."

To himself, Ekon swore. The longer it took them to get to Bandari and find Themba and the rest of the Enterprise, the more nervous he felt. "So what do we do now?"

"There." Safiyah squinted at something in the distance. "Is that a village?"

Ekon narrowed his gaze. Up ahead, he could see a collection of lights and buildings interrupting the dusk. "Looks like it."

Safiyah rubbed her arms aggressively. "We should stop there. It's only going to get colder, and we need to change out of these clothes."

Ekon opened his mouth to argue, then stopped, instead glancing at the purpling sky overhead. Safiyah was right; in less than an hour, the sun would truly be gone from the marshlands, and he had no desire to see what an evening with its residents entailed. He quickened his steps, keeping his eyes trained on the village ahead. It took shape as they neared it. If he had to guess, it was likely a fish or rice town; more than one fisherman's longboat was propped near it. Most of its buildings were elevated on stilts, and beneath some of them there was water. He and Safiyah passed through its modest front entrance, and he was overwhelmed with the smells of fried rice, fufu, and spicy fish stew, if his nose was correct. His stomach rumbled in protest.

"Up there," Safiyah said, pointing, "there's a sign for an inn."

Ekon followed as they hiked up the narrow side street, stopping at a white-painted building with a wooden INN sign swinging just above its door. Safiyah knocked, and a middle-aged man answered the door. He looked haggard, but laugh lines crinkled his eyes. He gave Ekon and Safiyah a once-over, then smiled.

"I see you two have gotten well acquainted with the marshlands."

"That's one way of putting it," said Safiyah, her voice full of fatigue. "Uncle, we wondered if you might have a room, just for the night?"

The innkeeper looked them over again, considering. "I have one room," he said after a moment. "It's got two twin beds. Will that be suitable?"

Ekon sat up straighter. "Um, actually—"

"That'd be perfect, except . . ." Safiyah faltered. "We got separated from our group and don't have money, but we're willing to work for our keep."

The man waved his hands. "The gods are merciful to the merciful," he recited, and Ekon was surprised to hear the proverb from the Book of the Six. "Come in, come in," said the man. "It's cold out. Let's get you two warmed up."

Iyapo, the innkeeper, kept good on his word. In a matter of minutes, he'd shown Ekon and Safiyah to separate bathrooms and given them fresh clothes to borrow while theirs dried by the fire. Once changed, he led them back to the inn's main floor, which seemed to serve as a tiny pub. There were only a few rickety tables crammed into the space, but the waxy candles at the bar gave the place a cheerful—if not homely—ambience.

"My husband's the barkeep," he explained. "He'll be out with food and drinks for you in a minute."

Ekon almost sighed aloud when, minutes later, a grizzly-looking man with a kind smile came over to their table with two steaming plates of fish on a bed of rice. Ekon closed his eyes as he took the first bite, relishing the blend of savory tastes. He didn't even remember the last time he'd had a meal this filling, this good. Moments later, the barkeep appeared again with two large glass mugs. Ekon eyed the frothy contents warily.

"Cheers." Safiyah picked up her glass. "To a day getting acquainted with the marshlands."

Ekon fidgeted. "Cheers," he said. "I'll, uh, wait for some water."

Safiyah's brows froze. "What's wrong?"

"Nothing," said Ekon quickly. "I just, as a rule, don't really . . . That is to say, I've never . . ."

"Hold on." Safiyah's eyes were wide. "Is this your first drink? I thought you were seventeen or something?"

"I am." Ekon nodded. "But in the Temple of Lkossa, consumption of alcohol is forbidden."

Safiyah's eyes danced. "You're in luck, then. This is banana beer—cheap, but frothy and sweet. Try some."

Ekon eyed the glass. He didn't really have any real reservations about drinking the stuff, it just felt odd, another step away from all he'd done. He counted to three, then picked up the glass and downed it. Safiyah gave him an amused look.

"You're definitely going to feel that the next time you stand up."

"I'll be fine," said Ekon, though he could already feel his belly warming.

A fiddler suddenly stepped into the room. Ekon watched him sit on one of the stools in the room's corner and begin to play a jaunty tune. For several minutes, the two of them just sat there and listened to it while they ate. Eventually, Safiyah spoke up.

"So, this girl you're after," she said between quick sips of her own drink. "She's Themba's granddaughter, but you never actually said how you know her, what she is to you."

"Uh . . ." Ekon tapped his fingers against the table. He had no idea how best to describe all that had happened with him and Koffi in a succinct way that made any sense.

"I heard what you said to Amakoya," she added. "Sounds like you two had quite the adventure in the Greater Jungle. I hope she's okay."

Ekon made himself smile, though he knew it didn't reach his eyes. "I'm sure she's fine." He forced himself to put that out into the universe. "Knowing her, she's probably already kicked her captor at least a few times. She's . . . fond of kicking people."

"Sounds like a pretty cool girl."

"She is," said Ekon. He was surprised how much better it made him feel to talk about Koffi. "Except for when she's being bossy, crude, and not listening to me."

"Now, that sounds like a girl I'd be friends with." Safiyah grinned for a second, but Ekon saw something flicker in her eyes. "And so, you and her, were you . . . ?"

"Ah, no," said Ekon quickly. "I mean, no, we . . . we weren't together or anything."

Safiyah's expression was inscrutable a moment, and then abruptly she stood.

"Do you dance, Okojo?"

"Dance?" Ekon hated the way his voice cracked on the word. "You mean, like, with choreography?"

Safiyah rolled her eyes, but the gesture was half-hearted. Ekon felt a jolt as, abruptly, she took his hand and pulled him to his feet. Sure enough, his head instantly felt slightly fuzzed.

"Here's an easy one," she said, tapping her foot in time to the fiddler's tune. "It's called the Zamani quickstep." She daintily hopped twice on one foot, letting her heel just barely touch the ground, then bent her knee so that her toe skimmed the ground instead. She repeated the move with the other foot, then did a quick pirouette and nodded. "See? Not so bad."

Ekon shook his head. "There is no way I'm graceful enough to do that."

Safiyah threw him a rueful look. "Fine, we can just do a two-step."

Ekon didn't have time to object as Safiyah pulled him toward the middle of the room, grabbed one of his hands, and put it on her waist. The other she interlaced with her own. Ekon's pulse leaped.

"Wait a second—"

"This one's simple," she said. "Just two quick steps to your left, then a slow one to your right, and you're doing the two-step."

Ekon frowned. "But that's three steps."

Safiyah snorted but said nothing else as she continued to dance. Ekon surprised himself by falling into step with her. At first, he had to focus on the counting, making sure his feet moved at the same time as hers, but he found that, gradually, his body naturally fell into the cadence of the fiddler's tune.

One-two-three. One-two-three. One-two-three.

"You're leading," he said after a moment.

Safiyah made a face. "Am not." She guided them into a turn, then pursed her lips. "Okay, I might be leading."

"It's all right." Ekon smiled. "It's not like I know how to."

Safiyah smiled back at him then, and he was caught off guard by how pretty she looked. The bar's candlelight caught in the center of her dark eyes, threw half of her face in its golden light while casting the other in soft relief. She closed her eyes a moment, and Ekon's heart began to pound harder in his chest. He was hyperaware now of the place where Safiyah's fingers rested on his shoulder, the careful spot on her waist where she'd put his hand. Without warning, he started to panic. What if his palms got sweaty? What if she noticed?

"Uh . . ." Ekon made himself look around the room. "Safiyah, I think . . . We should . . ."

"Hm?" Safiyah's eyes were still closed.

"I think we should probably call it a night," he said quickly. "We're going to need plenty of sleep if we're planning to get up early tomorrow."

Safiyah's eyes shot open, and she took an abrupt step back. Ekon felt something like cold in her absence. "Right." Her voice was strangely tight as she ran her hands down the front of her tunic, as though unsure of what else to do with them. "Right," she said again, unnecessarily. "Let's ask the innkeeper for our key, then."

Ekon and Safiyah got their key and two pillows from Iyapo, then made their way up the stairs he'd indicated to get to their room.

With each step, Ekon felt his body grow heavier. The adrenaline rush he'd gotten from their encounter with the nanabolele was well and truly gone by now, and it was all he could do to make it up the stairs. Safiyah inserted the key in the door's lock and pushed it open.

"Oh."

Ekon looked over her shoulder and felt something plummet in his chest.

The room before them was small and neat, furnished with two nightstands, a window, and a complimentary trunk Ekon could only assume was meant for long-term occupants to keep their things in. It also had one bed in the middle of the room. Singular.

"What . . . ? We . . . ?" he sputtered. "I thought he said the room had two beds?" His heart began to race. He tried to keep the alarm out of his voice.

Safiyah entered the room and kicked off her sandals with a shrug. "Looks like he made a mistake."

Ekon looked from Safiyah to the bed, then back again. "Well, what are we going to do?"

Safiyah's back was to him now, but at his words, she glanced over her shoulder. "Well, I'm going to bed. What you do with the rest of your night—"

"I *mean*, what are we going to do about the sleeping arrangement?" Ekon was feeling increasingly panicky. He and Koffi had slept next to each other in the Greater Jungle without issue, but . . . He eyed the bed again. *This* felt decidedly different.

Safiyah snorted. "Well, you can always sleep with—"

"On the floor, then," said Ekon quickly, his voice a few octaves too high. "Right. Sounds like a plan." At once he dropped to the

311

ground at the foot of the bed, lying on his back with his hands neatly folded across his chest. He realized he likely looked ridiculous, but he didn't care. If he was here, on the floor, he wouldn't have to think about what lying in a bed with Safiyah would—

Nope. He shook his head. Nope, not letting his mind go there.

"All right." Safiyah looked down at him, lips pursed for a second, before she stepped over him and blew out the candle on the nightstand. In the darkness, Ekon heard the gentle sigh of the old bed as she settled on it. "Good night, Okojo."

". . . Good night."

The floor of the inn's room was cold, hard, but Ekon relished it. He didn't want to be comfortable. If he was comfortable, he'd start thinking about Safiyah a few feet away from him, about the way she'd looked downstairs under the bar's candlelight. He'd start thinking about the place his hand had rested on her waist, the way she—

"Okojo."

Ekon sat up abruptly. His eyes had adjusted to the dark, and he could just barely make out Safiyah's silhouette. She was sitting up too. "Huh?"

"Your teeth are chattering, loudly. It's going to keep me up all night."

"Oh." Ekon breathed a sigh of relief. She could only hear his chattering teeth. But of course, it wasn't like Safiyah could hear his thoughts. Thank the gods. "Sorry about that. It's just a little cold. You got an extra blanket you can throw me?"

"No." Ekon couldn't see Safiyah's face, but he heard the exasperation in it. "Honestly, Okojo, your honor won't be compromised if you sleep in the bed."

Ekon stiffened. "I . . . I can't," he stammered.

"Why?"

He searched his mind, frantic. "It's . . . it's improper."

"Okojo, name one single thing about me that's proper in any way."

Ekon swallowed, continuing to rack his mind.

"Come on." He heard a smile in her voice. "We've had a long day. That floor can't be comfy." She sighed. "I promise it'll be a perfectly honorable night's sleep."

Ekon hesitated a second longer, then: "Fine."

He stood with his pillow, very carefully moved to the other side of the bed, and lowered himself into it. He couldn't see Safiyah well in this darkness, but he felt her wriggle beside him and stiffened.

"Stop moving."

"Relax, it's not like I bite." She paused. "Unless . . ."

The blood drained from Ekon's face. "Safiyah!"

"Kidding! Only kidding!"

"You promised." In the dark, Ekon's voice sounded more serious than he really meant it to. At once, Safiyah stopped moving.

"Fine, fine." She yawned, and Ekon felt her turn so that her back was to him. "I'm calling it a night. See you in the morning, Okojo."

Ekon nodded, though he knew she couldn't see it. "Good night, again."

In Ekon's dreams, the Temple of Lkossa was still beautiful.

He moved down its halls in a gentle sort of glide, taking in its polished floors, the mastery of its architecture. When he breathed in, he could smell the cedarwood, the smell of home, thick in his lungs, and somewhere in the distance, he thought he could even hear the morning chants of the temple's brothers. An idea occurred to him. It was still early enough that he could get to the library to do some reading before his lessons with Brother Ugo. It would be cutting it close, but—

"Ekon."

Ekon turned in the direction of the voice that had called his name. When he saw who it belonged to, his heart skipped a beat. There was a man sitting on one of the temple's stone benches. He had a full beard, dark skin, and kind eyes that crinkled in their corners.

"Baba?"

How Ekon had missed seeing his father as he'd initially passed the bench, he did not know, but he also didn't care. Baba was here. Baba was whole. His father stood as he approached, embracing him, and Ekon realized he'd forgotten how tall his father was. Even now, he seemed too large for the hall.

"It's good to see you, son," he said in his thunderous voice. "Your mother will be here soon."

"Mama?" Ekon started. "She's coming to the temple?"

"Yes," said Baba. His eyes shot up to Ekon's head. "And if I were you, I'd find a brush before she gets here. You know as soon as she sees you, she'll be onto you about a haircut . . ."

Ekon heard his father's words, but he was too lost in his thoughts to respond. Baba was here. Mama was here. Both of his parents were together, in the same place.

"Where will we meet her?" he asked.

"Out on the front lawns," said Baba. "Come, we'll walk there."

Anticipation coursed through Ekon's body as he and his father walked in step through the temple's hall. Every so often, a Son of the Six would pass, smile, and nod in deference to them both. Ekon shook his head. "I can't believe this."

"Can't believe what?" Baba asked, one brow raised.

"I can't believe that you're here," said Ekon. "Can't believe that Mama came, that—"

"Traitor!"

Ekon and his father both whirled around at the same time, tensed. Ekon's eyes traveled down the hall and landed on someone. Kamau. His brother was standing with a spear in hand, fury contorting the expression on his face. His eyes were locked on Ekon, and his teeth were bared.

"Kamau?" Baba looked alarmed. "What is the meaning of this?"

"Traitor!" Kamau banged his spear against the floor, so hard it rattled Ekon's teeth. "Blood traitor!"

"Kamau." Now Baba's voice was severe. He turned to Ekon and clapped him on his shoulder. "Clearly something has upset your brother."

Ekon's mouth felt dry. "Baba, there's something I need to tell you—"

"Don't worry, son. I'll speak with him." Baba sounded so calm, so sure, as though every problem could be resolved with a cool head and rational words. "You just head to the front lawns and find your mother. I'll be . . ." Ekon watched as his father looked up, eyes catching on something over his shoulder. A slow horror spread across his face, and when Ekon turned, he saw why. A scream rose in his throat.

Where Kamau had been standing, there was no longer a man, but a beast. It had greenish scales, a long mouth full of teeth, honey-gold eyes. Ekon knew what it was. A nanabolele. The creature hissed as it eyed Ekon and Baba, a low sound rumbling from the back of its throat as its muscles coiled like a set spring.

"Ekon," Baba whispered. "You go to your mother. I'll fend this creature off."

"What?" Ekon felt a chill. "No, Baba. I won't leave you."

"Go, Ekon," Baba insisted. "It's all right, I'll catch up to you. I'll—"

The nanabolele sprang without warning, lunging though the air. Ekon watched as the beast sailed past him with a terrible slowness and instead caught Baba in its jaws. He heard a sickening crack, a scream of pain.

"Baba!" Ekon yelled. He grabbed the nanabolele by its tail, heaved with all his might. It was no use. The thing was devouring Baba. Ekon heard the crunch of its powerful jaws, his father's moans. Tears streamed from his eyes now.

"Baba!" he yelled. "I'm trying, I'm trying!"

The nanabolele stopped its attack abruptly, and to Ekon's surprise, it turned to meet his gaze. The beast opened its mouth, but this time no roar escaped it, only a voice. Kamau's voice.

"Traitor," he whispered. "You are a traitor."

Ekon scrambled back on his hands, terror rising in him. "No." He shook his head. "No, I'm not."

"Traitor." The nanabolele had turned around entirely now, abandoning Baba's body as it advanced toward Ekon instead. "Traitor. Traitor. You are a filthy blood traitor."

"No!" Ekon screamed. "No. No. No."

"EKON!"

Ekon's eyes shot open as he was ripped from the dream. He sat up.

It took several seconds for his breathing to steady, for his fists and jaw to unclench. He looked around in the dark, trying to find his bearings. He counted, fingers tapping on his knees. He was in a room, an inn. There was a window to his left, one window. It let in a sliver of moonlight, which traced the silhouette of Safiyah beside him. She was sitting up too, watching him with concern. One of her hands, Ekon noticed, was on his shoulder. He took several deep breaths, in and out, as his heartbeat steadied.

"What happened?"

"You were having a bad dream," said Safiyah gently. "You were moving around a lot, talking to yourself."

The reality of everything hit Ekon suddenly. He'd been talking in his sleep. His cheeks grew hot as he imagined what Safiyah might have heard, and he was grateful that his dark skin hid the blood rushing to his face.

"I'm sorry," he said after a moment. "I didn't mean to wake you."

It was difficult to see Safiyah's expression in the dark, but he thought he saw her frown. "Sorry?" she repeated. "Ekon, that's not something to apologize for. We can't control the things that scare us."

"I'm scared all the time." The words escaped Ekon before he could stop them. "And I wish I wasn't. I wish I was braver."

For a long time, Safiyah said nothing, then: "I don't think

being brave means you're never scared," she whispered. "I think being brave means you're always scared, but trying anyway. And I think you're really brave, Ekon, whether you see that or not."

A small smile touched Ekon's mouth. He fell back against his pillow and tucked his head under one arm. "So, you think I'm brave, huh?"

Safiyah lay back down too. Her heard her blow out a breath. "Well, don't let it go to your head."

"Too late. The damage has been done, and it's irreparable."

Safiyah laughed then, and it was a musical sound. Ekon found that he liked it. He turned on his side, propping his head with one hand.

"Thank you," he said sincerely. "For saying that."

In the dark, Safiyah's expression grew serious. She turned on her side too. "You're welcome," she said softly. Ekon was aware now of how close they were, close enough that he could practically feel the sheets between them shift as her chest rose and fell with each breath. The moonlight illuminated one of her plaits, and without thinking, he reached out and curled a finger around its end, once, twice, three times. He pulled his hand back suddenly.

"Sorry, was that okay?"

Safiyah smiled. "That was okay." His breath hitched when her thumb traced along his jaw, her touch feather light. "And is that okay?"

Ekon's voice lowered. "That is . . . very okay."

"Good." Without warning, she closed the gap between them. A current like lightning coursed through Ekon's entire body as her lips found his. It was a quick thing, over before it had even begun. Safiyah pulled away, and squeezed Ekon's hand in hers.

"Good night times three, Ekon."

Ekon paused. "Good night times three, Safiyah." *Three, a good number.*

Ekon focused on the warmth of Safiyah's hand in his until, at last, he descended into dreams.

CHAPTER 19

LITTLE KNIFE

Strike. Parry. Guard.

Standing inside her bedchamber, Koffi blinked the sweat from her eyes, ignoring its sting, as she tried to hold the practice sword in her hands upright. She didn't much care for the thing—it was old, heavy, and dull—but she gritted her teeth as she watched Njeri across the room. The girl was sitting on a divan with her hand raised, signaling for her to wait.

"Go."

Koffi closed her eyes at once, summoning the splendor with a practiced ease. She opened her eyes and watched as the practice sword's blade took on an illuminated, golden quality, as though she'd dipped it in sunshine. She felt the thrum of energy as it moved through her, flowing in a perfect cycle from her hands to the wooden blade and back again. She looked up at Njeri and nodded.

"Advance."

Koffi needed no further prompt. She lunged forward, ready to execute her first combination with the sword.

Strike. Parry. Guard.

In her hands, the splendor in the wood flickered as she executed each move, but Koffi ignored it as she transitioned to her second combination.

Strike. Parry. Pivot.

The sword flickered again, but Koffi gritted her teeth, running forward. There was one more combination, one more to get this right.

Strike. Parry—

The blade in her hand went dim as the splendor faded suddenly, and Koffi shuddered as the energy left the wood and returned to her. For several seconds, she just stared at the dulled sword—furious, speechless.

"You're not concentrating." From the divan, Njeri shook her head. "You're too focused on the way you think you look when you move. It's like you're trying to appear as though you know the steps instead of just . . . knowing the steps."

The assessment stung, but Koffi tempered her embarrassment and returned to the middle of the bedchamber. "I want to go again."

"All right," said Njeri. "Take your position."

Koffi automatically spread her feet apart and bent her knees, bracing herself.

"Go."

This time, Koffi was quicker. She barely had time to think about it as she summoned the splendor and felt an onslaught of it run through the bones in her arms to illuminate the sword. She took a deep breath as she prepared to repeat her first combination.

Strike. Parry. Guard—

The wood dimmed again, this time without the warning flicker.

When Koffi threw the sword to the ground with more force than strictly necessary, Njeri's brows rose.

"I didn't teach you that move."

"It's hopeless." Koffi crossed the room and let herself flop onto her bed. "I can't do this." When she looked up, Njeri was standing over her with her arms crossed.

"So that's it?" the girl asked. "You're going to give up on everything, just like that?"

"I'm not getting it," said Koffi angrily. "I'm getting worse, not better."

Koffi and Njeri had been working in her bedchamber for the better part of the last three hours. Koffi still wasn't able to use splendor blades, to push her own splendor through an empty hilt, but she now knew how to push the splendor into an existing blade, so she'd made do with what she had. Now, though, she pressed the heels of her palms into her eyes.

"I don't understand," she heard Njeri say. "You've not even had the chance to train that long—why are you putting this unreasonable amount of pressure on yourself to be perfect?"

"Because I have to be!" Koffi sat up again. There was more anger in her voice than she intended, but she couldn't temper it. She lowered her voice, but only slightly. "Because every day that I don't get this right is a day we're still here. It's a day when one of us could be caught by Fedu. I won't let that happen."

Something shifted in Njeri's eyes. "Koffi," she said softly.

"I have to get this right," Koffi said, deliberately speaking over her. "I'm tired of being weak, I'm tired of not being able to do anything, I'm tired of—"

"Koffi." Njeri raised her voice slightly. Her tone had become

322

more severe. "Listen to me," she said firmly. "What happened to Zola . . ." She trailed off a moment. "You can't blame yourself for that."

Koffi heard the words, but she couldn't absorb them. It had been three days since Zola's death, since the night of the ichisonga, but the memories from it were still painted in Koffi's mind with too-vivid color. She saw that terrible beast, Fedu's smile, Zola's face . . . Something in her broke all over again when she thought of the way Zola had run into the Mistwood, into her own death.

"If I had learned more quickly . . ." Her voice was thick when she spoke. "If I'd gotten us out of here more quickly—"

"No." Njeri shook her head. "The fault for Zola's death starts and stops with Fedu. Don't carry that guilt, it doesn't belong to you." She moved to sit down beside Koffi on the bed. "I'm going to tell you something," she said, "something I've not told anyone before."

Koffi looked up. "What?"

"How I came to be in Thornkeep," said Njeri softly. "It's . . . not a nice story." She picked at several loose threads on her sleeve before speaking again.

"You guessed right the first time you met me. I'm Baridian, but I'm not from any of the big cities. My family lived in a rural town, in the Ngazi Ranges." She stared past Koffi, as though remembering it. "It wasn't a very big community, but it was tight-knit, so everyone knew each other. We all looked out for one another. Life was good." She frowned. "Until the Shaman came."

"The . . . the Shaman?" Koffi repeated.

"That's what he called himself." Njeri's mouth twisted, as though she'd tasted something bitter. "It was clever. No one in a village like mine had heard of such a person. In he comes with his sweeping robes and painted cowrie shells on his neck, talking of gods and power. He was like a colorful new bird everyone wanted to look at.

"At first, it was harmless enough. He helped people, made ointments and salves for the afflicted, crafted toys for the children. Over time, people came to accept him, but I never did. I never trusted him. My parents didn't understand it, but I always felt there was something off about him. He made me uncomfortable. Then I started getting sick."

Koffi watched as the girl who always looked so strong hugged herself and shivered. Her eyes were far away, remembering. "I've never felt so bad in my life. I was feverish every day, achy, hallucinating. I even lost my sense of smell and taste. My parents were convinced that I was going to die. But the Shaman said that he could help me. He offered to take me to a city far away, where there was medicine that could cure me. I begged my parents not to let him take me, pleaded, but they thought it was best. I suppose they truly thought it was the selfless thing to do." She blinked and seemed to come out of a trance. She met Koffi's gaze and held it. "I never saw them again."

Koffi felt numb. "And you never tried to leave? To escape?"

Njeri threw her a cynical look, somewhat returning to her normal self. "Of course I did," she said. "In the early years, I must have tried a hundred times. He caught me every time. And once he realized that I wasn't strong enough to aid his great endeavor, he didn't mind punishing me either." She held up her arms, and for the first time Koffi noticed her scars. They were striped across Njeri's dark skin, pink and shiny in the candlelight. Koffi recognized them instantly: only a whip or crop could leave that sort of permanent mark. She shivered.

"I did give up eventually," Njeri went on.

Koffi's heart fell. "I'm so sorry, Njeri."

Njeri shrugged. It was a casual gesture, but one that didn't quite meet the daraja's eyes. "My story isn't unique," she said resignedly. "And it probably isn't even the worst. You ask most of the darajas in Thornkeep, and they'll tell you similar stories of a mysterious stranger showing up in their city or village and luring them away. It's how he got most of us."

Koffi thought back to something in the jungle. Adiah. There'd been a moment, right after they'd found each other, in which Adiah had told her some piece of her truth, about how she'd been tricked into creating the Rupture that destroyed Lkossa because of Fedu's trickery. The thought made her ill. How many innocent children had Fedu taken over the years, destroyed the way he'd destroyed Adiah?

"I'm sorry." She wanted to say more, but it was all she could think to say.

"Don't be sorry," said Njeri. There was a new ferocity in her voice. "Be angry. Not for me, but for the other darajas, for Zola, for all the ones like her that we don't know about." She poked Koffi hard in the chest. "They're the reason you can't give up. You're the first real chance we've ever had of leaving this place forever. You're the best of us."

Koffi winced. "I don't feel like the best of anything."

Njeri paused for a moment. "I want to show you something." She rose and crossed the room again to get something from her bag, looking over her shoulder conspiratorially. "Close your eyes."

Koffi obeyed. She listened as Njeri's footsteps returned to her, as she sat down on the bed again and put something in Koffi's hands.

"Okay, you can open them."

Koffi looked down, and her heart started in her chest. She recognized the simple hanjari dagger. It wasn't fancy or jeweled, but there was a name carved into its hilt: ASAFA OKOJO. Okojo. Ekon had given her his dagger back in Lkossa. She'd woken up in Thornkeep without it, figured it had been discarded. Now . . . She held the blade up. It looked the same, but she could tell it had been refurbished, carefully cleaned and sharpened. Tears welled in her eyes.

"I found it in the forge," said Njeri, "the day before yesterday. It turns out, Fedu had given it to Zola to destroy, but she'd kept it, cleaned it. I think she'd planned to give it to you."

Koffi thought back to the first time she'd met Zola in the forge. The girl had mentioned then that she was working on a surprise, but Koffi had forgotten. The tears fell freely now.

Njeri put her hand over Koffi's, and for several seconds, the girls sat there, not saying anything at all. Eventually, it was Njeri who broke the silence.

"I want you to know something, Koffi," she murmured. "Fedu gains his power by making others feel small, by making them forget that they are powerful. Don't let him do that to you. I don't care what he calls you, you are not his little knife, you are no man's tool. You are your own weapon."

The words reverberated through Koffi in a swell. She heard the echo of them in her mind, the start of a mantra.

I am no man's tool. I am my own weapon.

"Come on." At once, Njeri was on her feet. "I want to show you something else."

Koffi rose with her. "Is it another drill, because I *really* don't think I can—"

"We're done with drills for today," said Njeri, shaking her head. There was a glint in her eyes. "I'm going to teach you something new."

※

Koffi had had every intention of going to sleep after Njeri left her that night, but she didn't. Instead, she went to the library.

She did her best to walk on the balls of her feet as she made her way there, keenly aware of how quiet Thornkeep became when the sun descended and its daraja residents retired for the evening. For the first time, she realized she did not know where Fedu slept—if he slept at all. She brushed away a shiver at the thought of how he might occupy *his* nights.

Soon enough, the library's doors rose to meet her, and a feeling like relief passed over her as she carefully cracked one door and walked through. A part of her almost found it funny; growing up, she'd never really like reading or books, a fact Ekon had been mortified by, but now that had changed. Fedu's library—macabre as it was—held answers, information, things she needed. Besides that, there was a peace about this place unlike any other on these grounds. She sighed. She'd been coming to this library for weeks now, looking for anything she could find about her order, the Order of Vivuli, without luck. There was no reason to think tonight's search would be any different, but Njeri's words stayed with her.

I don't care what he calls you, you are not his little knife, you are no man's tool.

If she was going to be her own weapon, the person to lead the darajas out of Thornkeep once and for all, she couldn't give up, even on something as small as this. As always, she moved to the shelves on her right first, the ones about Eshōzan history, and began to run her fingers along the old books' spines. It was unlikely that she'd find anything useful here, but she had to exercise her due diligence and look over every one of the library's sections. She carefully skimmed the next one, volumes on medical science and anatomy, then another, botany and complex biology. She was about to move on to the biographies when she stopped short. Something on the very bottom shelf of the biology section caught her eye: a book, touched just right by a beam of moonlight shining through one of the library's windows. It was sticking out slightly from the others, as though it had been jammed in somewhere it didn't really fit. Without thinking, Koffi pulled it from the shelf to examine it. She saw now why she'd missed it, why anyone browsing these shelves would have missed it. The book was small, colored a dark, fading blue, and the writing on both its spine and cover was illegible. Carefully, she opened it, flinching when its binding crackled. The ink on its title page was nearly translucent, but she could just discern the words, penned in a neat calligraphic font.

THROUGH THE AGES: An Account of Historic Darajas

Koffi's mouth went dry as she stared at the words, as they sunk in. With trembling fingers, she flipped the first yellowed page, and on the next found a table of contents. In bolder words she read ORDER OF AKILI, followed by a list of about twenty names. She skipped several more pages, until she stopped on one featuring more of the meticulous typeface beside the printed image of a woman. She wore her hair short and had a jovial look about her eyes. Koffi read the text beside her.

Name: Cyrah
Status: Deceased
Order: Akili
Affinity: Able to read minds
Notes: None

Koffi's heart skipped a beat as she turned more pages, stopping on another face and name. This time, there was a young boy named Kafele pictured, another daraja from the Order of Akili. Per this book, he was dead, but he'd been a powerful illusionist like Zain, able to hypnotize masses. One by one, Koffi browsed the pages. There was a section here for notable individuals within each of the five noble daraja orders. Koffi knew she shouldn't have been surprised, but her heart fell when she got to the end of the book and saw there was no section for the Order of Vivuli. But of course not. Zain had said himself that the Order of Vivuli wasn't even formally recognized by most scholars. She was just about to return the book to its place on the shelf when she noticed something else: a dog-ear on its last page, bent as though to bookmark it. Slowly, she cracked the book open again, squinting in the dark. The handwriting on this last page was different from the rest, roughly scrawled, but she stiffened as she read its words:

ORDER OF VIVULI
Lest they be forgotten.

There were no pictures next to the names on this single page, but Koffi read them hungrily. Her eyes skimmed over the first one. It read:

Name: Mansa, Stormbringer
Status: Deceased
Order: Vivuli
Affinity: Able to summon lightning and thunder at will
Notes: Favored by the god Atuno

Koffi read over the text once, twice, a second time. It was almost a surreal feeling. She'd desperately wanted to know about other darajas like her, and now she had proof of not just one, but several. She kept reading, so fast the words blurred on the page. After Mansa's name was a passage about a daraja called Ona'je, who'd been able to speak to the dead; he was no longer alive, nor was the next daraja, a woman called Winta, who'd been able to see into the past using objects taken from it. Koffi sighed. These people, these *darajas*, were long gone now, but seeing their names reminded her that they'd once existed, and that made her feel less alone.

Her eyes dropped down to the last two names on the list, and she read them over slowly. The first was a daraja named Sigidi, a seer with the ability to see the future. His whereabouts were unknown, but his status was listed as *Alive*. She started. Below his name was the last daraja on the list. Koffi read her note twice:

Name: Akande
Status: Unknown
Order: Vivuli
Affinity: Able to use the splendor as a compass
Notes: Last seen in Chini

Koffi's mouth popped open. She couldn't believe what she was seeing. *Able to use the splendor as a compass.* That sounded almost exactly like her affinity. She sat back a moment, wrapping her head around the implications of it. Was it possible there was another daraja somewhere out there, someone with the same affinity as her? Someone like that could teach her, better than anyone else. She read the passage again. *Status: Unknown. Notes: Last seen in Chini.* There was no guarantee Akande was still alive, but . . . there was no guarantee they were definitely dead. If, once she got out of Thornkeep, she could find this Akande person somehow, she might be able to—

She froze when she heard a sound several yards away from her, near the library's doors—footsteps—and panic flitted through her body. She had not closed the door, only cracked it, and now she could distinctly hear two sets of nearing footsteps. She silently swore. On the one hand, she wasn't *technically* doing anything wrong. If she was caught here, there wasn't much anyone could do except send her back to her bedchamber. But on the other hand, it was very likely that her whereabouts would be reported back to Fedu if the wrong person caught her. She didn't need the god scrutinizing her actions any more than he already was. Slowly, she rose, hugging the little blue book to her chest as she crept forward. A sliver of yellow light permeated the darkness from the doorway, and she moved toward it as quietly as she could manage. She had a few options from here. She could try to close the door before anyone came close enough to notice it was open, then wait for them to pass. Or, if she was quick enough, she could slip out entirely and make a run for it. Neither option was ideal. She was inches from the doors now, but the two sets of footsteps were louder, closer. She tensed as she reached the library's doors and peeked with one eye out into the corridor.

Two male darajas were walking away from her down the hall. She couldn't see their faces, but from their respective purple and red tunics, she gathered that one was from the Order of Kupambana, and the other from the Order of Mwili. They were chortling, distracted. *Good.* They would be down the hall in a few seconds, and she'd have time to leave the library unnoticed. In the hall's quiet, their voices carried.

"You're sure?" the one in the red tunic asked. "You heard him?"

Koffi watched as the daraja in purple nodded. "I didn't hear it myself, but Gamba did. He said Fedu will be ready to move forward soon."

At once, Koffi froze.

"I thought he was waiting for Koffi," said Red Tunic, "waiting for her to figure out her affinity or something."

"I don't think Fedu cares," said Purple Tunic. "I heard him talking the other night. He's getting impatient."

"Well, I won't be sorry when he does decide it's time for us to leave," said Red Tunic. "I've been ready to go. I'm sick of seeing the same girls."

Their chortles echoed down the hall well after they'd turned the corner and disappeared, but Koffi stayed where she was. Her heart was thundering in her chest, so hard her rib cage ached. One boy's words echoed in her mind.

Fedu will be ready to move forward soon.

She knew it then.

It was time to leave Thornkeep.

CHAPTER 20

BANDARI

It was a curious thing, to compare a city's sketch on a map to the image it presented in reality.

Ekon had certainly read about Bandari; at some point in his schooling, he'd even studied some of its history and architecture. But when he was honest with himself, he knew that—as he and Safiyah hiked up the final crest leading to its front gates—the books and missives written by Lkossan scholars hadn't done the old city justice. It was slightly smaller than Lkossa, distinct for the light gray stonework that seemed to comprise most of the city. The occasional bunch of creeping vines hung from some of its taller structures, and the way buildings were clustered together in a line along the Eastern Ndefu River reminded Ekon of the molars of some mythic creature of old.

He and Safiyah joined the crowds pouring into the city, and as he traversed its roads, the differences between it and Lkossa grew more and more distinct. With its proximity to water, there were far more fishermen stationed in the markets, and a larger variety of fresh fish in the vendor stalls. The Kusini Region's ever-cool breeze seemed to linger here, and consequently, the merchants that moved through these streets wore clothes of heavier fabrics. As soon as they'd entered the city, Safiyah had directed them away from the heavier foot traffic and down a less busy set of roads. According to her, the Enterprise's business often took place away from the main markets and closer to the ports. Ekon was glad for the excuse to sightsee.

"Tourists always go to the market for fish," Safiyah was saying, "but the best fishermen hang out by the east docks. If we have time, I'll take you."

Ekon smiled but said nothing. It was rare to see Safiyah in such high spirits. She wasn't from Bandari, but it was abundantly clear she had an affection for the city. He studied her, the way her eyes closed when she was taking in a pleasant smell, the way her brows pinched when she found something strange. In his mind, he couldn't help but go back to the night before, to what had happened.

He'd kissed her.

It had been a quick, fleeting thing, but . . . it had also been a nice thing. Ekon had woken up thinking about it, but he hadn't known what to say to Safiyah. She hadn't said anything to him either, which made it all the more confusing. Were they supposed to talk about it? Were they not? A pang of guilt lingered in his mind, too, as he considered something else.

Koffi.

Not so long ago, in the Greater Jungle, he'd kissed Koffi too, and he'd liked it. He frowned as he walked. He'd gone from kissing no one to kissing two people in a short amount of time. Was that allowed? He thought of Safiyah's question in the inn, when she'd asked if he and Koffi were together. They weren't, but . . . what they'd gone through together meant something. She was, at the very least, his friend, someone he cared about, but . . . Safiyah had become a friend too. He didn't want to hurt either of them, but he had the uncanny feeling that he was hurtling toward something, a decision.

You'll have to choose eventually, said a voice in his head. *You can't pick both.*

Ekon suppressed that thought miserably as he kept walking.

Safiyah led them down a narrow road, this one canopied with bright fabrics. In the sunlight, they cast bright squares and triangles on the ground, giving the street a magic, otherworldly look and feel. Some vendors were sitting at stalls as they passed, while others who couldn't afford as much were on the ground. They passed a young woman displaying beads on a tattered blanket, holding what looked to be a deck of cards on her knee. Ekon tried to walk past her without stopping, but she caught his eye and smiled.

"Tarot readings!" she called out. "Free tarot readings! Pick three cards and peek into your future!"

Ekon looked to Safiyah, expecting to see a laugh in her eyes, but to his surprise—and dismay—Safiyah looked intrigued.

"What do you think?" she asked, raising one brow. "Could be fun."

"Uh . . ." Ekon glanced from Safiyah to the woman, uneasy. "I'll pass."

"Oh, come on," she said, and Ekon felt a rush of heat course through his body as she took his hand, pulled him along with her, and approached the woman. They both settled down on her blanket, and she smiled.

"Which one of you will I read for first?" she asked in a kind voice.

"I'll go," said Safiyah. "My friend is a little shy."

The woman obliged, and began to shuffle her cards with practiced hands. They made a pleasant sound as she passed them between her fingers, and Ekon found himself trying to count how many were in her deck. Eventually the woman stopped and spread a handful of cards on the blanket, nodding.

"Pick three, dear."

Safiyah deliberated and then picked one card from the middle and two on each side. She handed them back to the woman, who took her time inspecting them.

"Mm," she mused. "Your first card is the running jackal, which means you will go on a perilous journey."

Ekon and Safiyah exchanged significant looks.

"Your second card," the woman said, "is the golden swallowtail, which can mean prosperity or riches."

"I'll take either," said Safiyah cheerfully.

"And for your last one . . ." Her expression softened. "The elephant shrew."

"What's that one mean?" asked Safiyah.

"Love," said the tarot card reader. "Elephant shrews are among the rare creatures who mate for life. They symbolize a great, lasting love. When we put your cards together . . ." She slid all three of them toward Safiyah. "The cards tell us that you will go on a dangerous but prosperous adventure, at the end of which you will find your true life mate."

On the blanket, Ekon fidgeted, suddenly feeling very uncomfortable. Safiyah smiled at him.

"And what about you, young man?" To his discomfort, the tarot card reader had now turned her full attention to him. "Would you like your cards read?"

Ekon stammered. "Well, I mean . . . it isn't strictly necessary . . ."

"You might as well," said Safiyah, nudging him with an elbow. She was rising to her feet and dusting her clothes off. "I'm going to get water from one of the wells. I'll be back." She was gone before he could object, and Ekon turned to find the woman was now looking at him expectantly. He sighed.

"All right," he said with resignation. "I'll do it."

The woman's smile broadened as she grabbed the deck and immediately began to reshuffle it. Once again, Ekon found himself staring at her hands, trying to memorize the cadence with which she moved the cards with her fingers. It was almost hypnotizing. She stopped a few seconds later and, just as before, spread the cards out on the blanket between them facedown.

"Pick three."

Ekon hesitated. Safiyah had been very strategic in her selections; she'd picked one from each side and then one in the middle. He decided to try the same tactic. One by one, he picked his cards, and then slid them back to the woman. She picked them up, eyes crinkling, but when she flipped the cards, the smile slipped from her face. In its place was an expression Ekon could not read. The woman was holding on to his three cards, staring at them now in open confusion. A new wave of anxiety rose in Ekon as the seconds stretched.

"Is . . . is something wrong?"

The woman looked up slowly, meeting Ekon's gaze with a wariness she had not had before. Her eyes looked blank, distant, and when she spoke, her words were barely a whisper.

"East and west."

"What?" Ekon leaned closer, unable to stave off the panic that'd just spiked through him. "What did you say?"

"One sun rises in the east. One sun rises in the west," she said in a flat voice. "East and west."

A chill shuddered through Ekon. *East and west. One sun rises in the east. One sun rises in the west.* Those words were specific. Sigidi had said them to him in the alley, then Amakoya had said them verbatim in the marsh water.

One sun rises in the east. One sun rises in the west.

Why did people keep saying those words to him? What did they mean? He stood, backing away from the woman, disturbed, at the same time Safiyah returned. One look at his expression, and her smile slipped.

"Hey, what's wrong?"

"Nothing," Ekon said, more curtly than he meant to. "It's getting late. We should find the Enterprise." He turned on his heel without waiting for her, feeling slightly sick.

"Okay?" Safiyah ran to catch up with him. "But I don't understand, what happened back there?"

"I told you, it was nothing." Ekon brushed her off. "Just some kooky card reader. She's probably a con artist anyway."

"Ekon." There was a sternness in Safiyah's voice that made him bristle. "If something happened back there—"

"Nothing happened!" Ekon whirled on her, feeling a new anger licking at his skin. "Look, Safiyah, I know we've spent the last few days together, but that doesn't mean you know me. And it doesn't give you the right to pry into my business after I've said I'm fine."

Hurt clouded Safiyah's face. "Ekon—?"

"Just leave it, Safiyah," Ekon said coldly. He didn't recognize his own voice. "This was fun, but now I need to find Themba. She and I have a real mission that we haven't even started. We have to find Koffi. She's the most important thing right now, the only reason I'm here at all."

Ekon watched as his words landed like arrows loosed from a bow, one by one. Safiyah's brows knitted together, her eyes narrowed as though—if she looked at him long enough—she could pull something from him, maybe truth. When his face stayed blank, her expression changed. There was a sadness there, a moment of real pain, and then nothing. Safiyah smoothed her face so that it betrayed nothing.

"All right, then." Her tone was clipped. "We'd better find the Enterprise." If his voice had been cold, hers was glacial. She turned away, walking quickly down the street. Abruptly, Ekon felt a tremendous wave of guilt.

"Safiyah, wait!"

But Safiyah's steps did not slow, did not falter as she disappeared into Bandari's crowds and left Ekon standing alone in the middle of the street.

BAGGAGE

BINTI

I've never been so nervous in my life.

I survey the tiny, threadbare room before me, trying to temper the anxiety churning in my belly. It's stuffy in here, and despite my best efforts, sweat is already dampening my underarms. It makes me feel sticky.

There isn't much to look at: Three overturned boxes serve as makeshift chairs and are pushed around a rickety old table with a cloth thrown over it to cover the stains. I wanted to add a candle as the centerpiece, but had concerns that with the room's low ceiling and lack of ventilation, we might end up choking to death, so we're going without.

"Mama!" My voice cracks with nerves, rising several octaves as I look over my shoulder at the doorway. "Hurry! It's almost time!"

A few minutes later, Mama enters the room holding a wooden tray of food. I want to be annoyed at her—she's taken her good, sweet time all evening—but then she starts uncovering the food and my mouth waters instead. There's a huge bowl of jollof rice, and another full of savory egusi soup. Beneath a plain cloth, several banku rolls are steaming beside a tiny jar of black pepper sauce. It's a surprisingly impressive arrangement.

"You made all this?"

Mama throws me a scathing look. "Don't be ridiculous. Auntie Lota said we could have the inn's leftovers, she's getting soft in her old age and she likes you, so she's agreed to indulge this nonsense." Abruptly she sticks a finger into the dipping sauce, then pops it into her mouth. "Oh! That's got a good kick!"

"*Mama.*"

"Stop all that noise." Mama frowns. "You're too old to be whining like that. If you want something, you speak like an adult."

I sit up straighter, chastened. Even though I'm loath to admit it, I know she's right. Tonight is a big deal, and if I want to be treated like an adult, I need to act like one. I take a calming breath, then start again. "Mama, I would very much appreciate it if you didn't start eating until Lesego arrives," I say politely. "I really want things to go well tonight. I . . . I really like him."

"Why?" says Mama, her gaze shrewd.

"He's kind, smart, ambitious—"

"You don't find it *odd* that his family isn't joining us for this *oh-so-special* dinner?" Mama asks as she begins setting out plates and utensils. "Or *strange* that he says he doesn't have any other family in this city?"

I fidget. The truth is, I do think those things about Lesego are a little weird, but I definitely don't want to admit it right now. "The last few years have been hard on a lot of people, Mama. Who are we to judge someone else's circumstances?"

"Smart."

I give her a look, and she tuts.

"I still think this is a lot of trouble and fuss for a boy you've only known for, what, a couple of weeks?"

"Months," I correct, unable to entirely keep the slight bite from my tone. Mama notices it anyway and purses her lips.

"A good, decent boy should be taking *you* to dinner," she says. "Not the other way around. If you ask me, the boy's just looking for a free meal."

I swallow, feeling guilty. Mama doesn't know that Lesego and I have been seeing each other far longer than I've indicated, that he has—in fact—been courting me. In truth, Lesego has been more than just "decent," he's now treated me to several meals and even bought me a few gifts. I hadn't expected it; I was sure that, after my abrupt departure from the Bonding Day party, he'd never want to see me again, but it's been just the opposite. After that first night, Nyah helped us meet again. It's been wonderful ever since. Lesego grew up in this city, just like me, but his outlook on life is so different from mine. Whereas I usually only walk places when I have to, when I'm with Lesego we wander the city, taking detours and roads neither of us have ever been down just to see what's at the other end. With Lesego everything is an adventure waiting to be discovered. He's fully let me into his world. In a way, this dinner is my chance to let him into mine—at least in part.

"I *really* like him, Mama," I repeat.

In answer, my mother sucks her teeth. "Well, then, I certainly hope he's worth it. I haven't seen you put this much work into something in a long time."

She's right; it took a lot of work to make this night happen. Mama and I still work for Auntie Lota, the innkeeper, but we don't make much money at all. It took promising to work several nights for free to convince the old woman to let us use this spare storage room for the occasion—after hours, of course. I'd have personally preferred to meet Lesego at one of Lkossa's cheaper restaurants, or even one of the food stands closer to the central markets, but we can't afford that sort of luxury, so this is the best we can do. I don't want Lesego to know how hard Mama and I actually live.

"We should probably go out to the front of the inn," I say. "He'll be here soon."

Mama quirks a brow that lets me know I will be the sole member of Lesego's welcoming party. Fine by me. I leave her to pretend to rearrange plates and napkins on the table, and head down the narrow hallway. Outside, the sun has already set, and the sky is dotted with the first stars of the night. Even though I'm not entirely sorry Mama didn't come with me, I'm a little sad she's not here to see these stars with me. We used to love looking at the stars together. I miss that version of my mother; she's changed lately. It started the first time I mentioned Lesego, and it's only gotten worse. Mama's more irritable, her temper is shorter. I wish I understood why.

"Hey!" A voice pulls me from my thoughts. "Rashida!"

My heart skips a beat. Lesego is coming toward me in the starlight, dressed in what I know are his best tunic and sandals. His gait somehow manages to be both casual and confident; just like everything else, he makes it look easy. I wish I could make things look easy. In a way, I wish I was more like him.

"Hi."

Lesego is beaming, and suddenly, I feel strangely self-conscious. When he bends down to kiss me, I turn my head just slightly so that his lips brush my cheek instead of my mouth. He pulls back, looking perplexed.

"Should I . . . *not* kiss you?"

"No! I mean yes! I mean . . ." I tug nervously on one of my twists. I like when Lesego kisses me, and normally I would want him to, but I don't know how to explain to him how I feel right now. "It's just that, with my mother . . ."

"Oh, right!" Lesego straightens up instantly, and I appreciate that he makes a visible effort to look more serious before offering me a tiny wink. "Best behavior from now on, promise. Lead the way."

We duck inside the inn and head to our makeshift dinner parlor. Just before we enter, I look over my shoulder.

"So, about my mother," I whisper. "Don't take anything she does personally, okay? She's nice, but she can be a bit . . ." I pause for a moment, searching for the right word. "Odd."

Lesego shrugs. "She can't be *that* bad," he says in earnest. "She made you."

My cheeks warm at the compliment. Lesego always knows what to say to make me feel better, more at ease. This time, I don't overthink as I take his hand and open the door. Mama is already sitting at the table. Her eyes instantly flit to our interlaced hands, and she frowns before glancing at Lesego.

"You must be Masego."

The blood drains from my face, but Lesego doesn't miss a beat. He moves to stand beside me and inclines his head. "Good evening, Auntie. My name's actually *Le*sego, and I'm so grateful and honored to share your table this evening. If you don't mind, I brought you a small token of my gratitude." He reaches into his sack and withdraws something wrapped in tissue paper. Mama and I both watch—with what I suspect is equal surprise—as he unwraps it to reveal a small stalk of what looks like lavender wrapped in white ribbon. When he offers it to my mother, she looks utterly flabbergasted.

"What's this?"

"Rashida told me that you're a horticulture enthusiast," Lesego says with another small bow. "I saw these at the market earlier today, and the seller said they were fresh, so I picked some up for you. Please consider it a gift, a thank-you for opening your home to me tonight."

My heart swells in my chest. I hadn't known Lesego was going to do that, but I also can't say I'm totally surprised. This is the kind of person he is—impulsive but thoughtful.

My mother rises from the table slowly and takes the lavender from him, bringing it closer to inspect.

"*Rashida*"—she pauses, giving me a significant look—"is correct."

She rubs the stalk between two fingers, and holds it up to her nose for a long, deep whiff. After a moment, she looks up at us both, unsmiling.

"I certainly hope you didn't pay much for this," she says. "It's average quality, but you'd have found far better in the outer villages."

Just like that, the joy in my proud heart sputters out, replaced by anger. I know Mama is just putting on a show; even *I* can tell that the lavender is not only expensive, but of excellent quality. She's goading Lesego, seeing how he'll react. To his credit, Lesego's bright smile only falters for a moment.

"Thank you for that advice. I will keep that in mind the next time I bring you a gift, Auntie," he says kindly.

"*If.*" Mama's brows arch. "*If* there's a next time."

"Okay!" I clap my hands, probably louder than necessary. "Who's hungry? Because *I* am starving!"

"Me too," says Lesego. He gestures for me to sit down first, then takes a seat last. "What's on the menu tonight?"

"Rashida," says Mama. "Before we begin, I need to borrow you for a moment in the kitchen."

Dread pools in my stomach as together we rise, leaving Lesego alone at the table. The minute the door to the storage room closes, Mama whirls on me.

"I don't like him."

"Mama!" I throw up my hands. "He's only been here for *five minutes!*"

"He called you the wrong name," she says with a scowl. "He called you Rashida."

"That's not the wrong name," I say, trying to ignore my rising embarrassment. "It's the name I've *asked* him to call me." I want to kick myself now for forgetting to tell her what I wanted to be called during Lesego's visit, but I've compartmentalized my life so thoroughly that Binti and Rashida feel like two separate people.

Mama blinks several times. "*What?* Why would you *ask* to be called the wrong name?"

"It's not the wrong name, it's just a different one," I counter. "The one I prefer. I like it better than Binti, it sounds stylish."

"It sounds *foolish.*"

"It makes me *happy,*" I insist. "Please, Mama."

My mother gives me one more impassive look before shaking her head and making her way back toward the storage room. When we reenter together, Lesego is still sitting at the table, looking none the wiser.

"I believe we are ready to eat," says Mama in an all-too-sweet voice. My suspicions grow as she sits back down and begins ladling food onto plates. "We have a delicious meal before us. Masego, have you had banku before?"

"Oh, absolutely, Auntie." Lesego nods fervently as Mama offers him one of the rolls. "I grew up on it. My mother used to make an excellent recipe, though these might be even better."

"Your *mother*?" Mama sits up straighter, showing real interest. "Rashida told me previously your parents weren't in the city. If it turns out they're here, I'd love to meet them."

I don't say aloud that I think Mama meeting Lesego's parents is a *horrible* idea, but before I say anything, Lesego shakes his head. For the first time this evening, he actually looks a little sad.

"I'm afraid that won't be possible," he says. "My parents don't live in Lkossa. They moved south, to Bandari, several years ago."

Mama folds her hands. "Your mother and father decided to move away and leave their own son behind?" She doesn't keep the incredulity from her voice.

Lesego shrugs. "My parents and I disagreed, discussed it, and in the end decided to go our separate ways—literally. It was an amicable parting, and I still write to them as often as I can."

Mama cocks her head. "And what, if I may ask, did you disagree with your parents about?"

"Actually, it was about Lkossa," says Lesego between bites of food. "My father and especially my mother got more and more concerned about the city's safety, what with more attacks near the jungle's border being reported and the rise in daraja crime."

I nearly choke on my rice, and Mama's eyes instantly narrow

into slits. I notice her bracelet is concealed under a sleeve, which she tactfully tugs down her arm.

"I'm sorry, I don't think I heard you. Did you say . . . *daraja* crime?"

"Yeah." Lesego goes on, completely oblivious to the change in the room's mood. "My mother's convinced that darajas are dangerous, unstable, and that the city needs to go back to stricter measures to keep them regulated and separate from the rest of society."

My heart is thundering in my chest. Lesego and I have talked about his family before, but never this. Sweat gathers on the back of my neck, and I don't dare look at my mother. Her rage is practically emanating from her; I feel its heat.

"And," she says in a thin voice, "what are *your* opinions on daraja crime, young man?"

Lesego shrugs. "Well, I don't know any darajas personally," he says. "But they seem like all right people. I mean, so long as they stay in their place, I don't really see any problem with living alongside them."

Stay in their place.

Finally I chance a look at my mother. A thousand emotions are flitting across her face in rapid succession—anger, humiliation, fear, and, worst of all, grief. I can see the exact moment in which she realizes what I've done, and what I *haven't* done. Lesego doesn't know she's a daraja because I haven't told him that, because I don't want what comes with it. I don't want the baggage.

"Ah!"

I look up in time to see Lesego put his head in his hands, pained. His eyes close briefly, and when they open again, he's squinting at his plate as though trying to see something small.

"Lesego!" I stand. "Are you okay?"

"Yes, Lesego," Mama croons. "You look quite *unwell*."

"Oh no, I'm fine." Lesego begins rubbing his temples hard. "I just . . . I seem to have some sort of headache. It's strange . . . came out of nowhere."

My blood cools as I glance from Lesego to my mother. She's still staring at him, unblinking. A terrible understanding dawns on me.

"Perhaps you should send your friend home, Rashida?" she says silkily. "He doesn't look well at all."

"No, no." Lesego waves a hand, trying to fight through the pain. "It's just a migraine. I'm sure it'll pass in just a few—ugh." He screws his eyes shut tighter and winces. "On second thought, I'm sorry, but . . . I think it's probably best for me to go."

"Yes," says Mama. "I think it most certainly is."

I'm at a loss for words as I help Lesego to his feet, then carefully lead him out the door and down the hallway. There are any number of things I *want* to say, but only two words come to me as we step out into the night.

"I'm sorry."

"Don't worry about it, Rashida." Lesego blinks a few times and rubs his eyes. "We'll do this again some other time, okay?" That's Lesego, always kind, always hopeful.

"Okay."

He gives me a swift kiss—this time deliberately on the cheek— before heading into the night. A part of me worries about him walking these streets with a headache, but I suspect that as soon as he gets far enough from my mother, all traces of it will mysteriously disappear. I wait until I can't see him anymore before

349

barreling back into the inn. By the time I'm in the storage room, I'm seething.

"How *could* you?"

Mama is still sitting at the table, dipping a piece of banku into her pepper sauce. She looks up at me with wide eyes I don't believe for a second.

"I'm sure I don't know what you're talking about?"

"You ... you ..." I'm so angry I can barely speak. "You used the splendor on him, to *hurt* him!"

"A fair trade for the things he said," Mama snaps, all pretense instantly gone. "Did you even *hear* him?" She stands too, shaking with a fury that matches mine. "He spoke of daraja crime, of darajas knowing their place. He's no better than the Kuhani, or the Sons of the Six, or the rest of this city's bigots!"

"He's *not* a bigot! He is kind, and compassionate, and . . . he doesn't know better."

"Because you've lied to him," Mama says quietly, and I hear real hurt in her voice. "Because he doesn't even know that he is in love with the *daughter* of a daraja." Mama comes around the table and takes my hands in hers. "They're our people, Binti," she says. There's a desperation in her voice. "When people disparage darajas, they are disparaging us, me, *you.*"

This isn't the first time Mama has said something like this to me; in fact, she's been saying it to me all my life. But something about it feels different tonight. Before I can say anything else, she folds me into her arms and weeps.

No, Mama, I want to say as she squeezes me tight. *Not our people. Your people, Mama. I am not a daraja, and I never will be.*

CHAPTER 21

HOME

In Koffi's dreams, she visited the Mistwood.

The acacia trees always appeared first, rising from the mist itself like so many spindly men with crooks in their backs, their ash-gray bark cast to silver in the moonlight. Their thorns, long as a finger, did not touch her as she moved among them, and no sound came from her feet as she padded across the wood's dirt. When she inhaled, the scent of pinewood sap filled her lungs; when she exhaled, the voices came to her.

Help us.

Like a chorus, they sang the words in a whine, in a growl. Only two words, but they were touched with a hungered quality, a desperation.

Help us.

"Who are you?" Koffi asked the trees, but they did not answer as their trunks swayed in the quiet breeze. She closed her eyes and reached for the splendor resting in her body, pulled it to the surface until it thrummed through her core, and those familiar speckles of golden light appeared in the air around her, twinkling, waiting. She turned slowly, taking in all that was the Mistwood. She had to be at the heart of it, though she had no recollection of deciding to come here. Such was the nature of dreams. Her muscles coiled and tensed as she waited for the voice—the voices—to call out again, but when her gaze panned the trees a second time, she caught a glimpse of a face instead. The face of a little girl.

The thick black braids on her head were unraveling at their ends, and her torn clothes hung loose off her bony frame as she cautiously approached Koffi with one hand in her mouth. She tilted her head with uncertainty, and instinct prompted Koffi to lower to her knees so that she was level with the little girl.

"Are you all right?" She tried to speak softly, but in the Mistwood's perpetual quiet, her voice reverberated like the pluck of a kora's string. The girl stopped walking, flinched.

"I wanna go home." Her voice, in contrast to Koffi's, was paper thin, a mere whisper nearly lost in the wind. Koffi watched as tears filled her eyes, replaying the little girl's words in her own mind.

Home. I wanna go home.

"It's all right." Koffi extended her arms, and the girl took a few steps forward. "It's all right, I won't hurt you."

The girl considered a moment. There was a wariness in her eyes that didn't look right in a body so small. Koffi wondered at that. The girl stood perfectly still for one second, two seconds, three, then she seemed to come to a decision. In careful steps, she closed the gap between the two of them until she was standing within arm's reach of Koffi.

"I wanna go home."

"It's all right," Koffi repeated. "We'll get you home." She looked around again, then stood. The speckles of splendor were still floating around her, throwing fracturing golden light against the trees.

I know what to do, Koffi thought. *This is something I can help with.*

"I have a special gift," she told the little girl. "And I can use it to get us out of this place, okay?"

The girl nodded, and when Koffi reached out again, she offered her free hand. It was cold to the touch as Koffi took it in her own, like a dress that'd been left out on the laundry lines overnight, but Koffi only squeezed it. The Mistwood was a scary place; who knew how long this little girl had been lost here. She called to the splendor and it came back to her, hovering around her arms and legs and face, still waiting.

Show us the way out of here, she asked it, *the way home.*

Without hesitation, the splendor began to move. Like golden pearls strung along an invisible necklace, they formed a line, one that seemed to stretch on forever. She looked down again and found that the little girl's eyes had gone wide, though the emotion behind them was still difficult to discern.

"That light will lead us home," said Koffi. "We just have to follow it, okay?"

This time, the girl didn't answer. She seemed transfixed by the splendor now, watching the speckles of light with a kind of awe. Slowly, she took her fingers out of her mouth and made to touch them, but they danced out of her reach. She frowned.

"I wanna go home."

"Come on," said Koffi, giving her other hand a gentle tug. "Let's go."

The Mistwood held its quiet as they walked.

One step after another, Koffi followed the golden light. With each stride, she felt a growing sense of relief, of confidence. This was her gift as a daraja, her affinity. It was an unusual one, but useful. After all of this time, after all of this practice, she'd mastered it.

We're going home.

There was power in those words, Koffi felt the strength of them down in the soles of her feet. Home. She could see it now, the streets of Lkossa as they unwound themselves before her, its sounds, its smells, its people. She'd been robbed of the chance to truly get to know Lkossa—she'd been locked away at the Night Zoo for so long—but when she finally returned, when she got home, everything would be different. She would find Mama and Jabir, and they would sew together a life from the scraps they'd been given. It wouldn't be grand, but it would be beautiful; it would be theirs.

Home.

The lights of the splendor were twinkling now; up ahead, Koffi saw that they were leading toward an opening in the trees, a paler light. She saw the first hints of stars in an inky sky, a low-hanging moon. Koffi quickened her steps.

"Come on," she said, pulling at the little girl. "You see that light up there? We're almost out of the Mistwood, we're almost home." She was surprised to feel a sharp tug on her arm. When she turned, the girl had stopped walking. Her eyes were wider now. Her lips trembled.

"I wanna go home."

Koffi tempered the slightest touch of irritation. "We are going home," she said gently. "See, right there up ahead? That's home."

The girl shook her head. "No, I wanna go home."

They were close, so close. Koffi took a deep breath, lowering so that again she was on her knees before the girl. She tried a different tactic.

"Where is home for you?"

The little girl tilted her head, as though confused, and Koffi sighed. Perhaps this child didn't really know where her home was.

"You understand me, which means you speak Zamani," she said. "Are you from the Zamani Region?"

The little girl did not answer. Instead, she reached out and touched Koffi's cheek, her hair.

"Home," she whispered. "I wanna go home."

"We are." Koffi now had to make an effort to keep the frustration from her own voice. "We're going home, it's just up there." She looked over her shoulder and pointed again to that light. "It's just a few more . . ." The words turned to ash on her tongue as she turned back around and looked at the little girl. She'd changed, in a hundred tiny ways. No longer was her skin brown, like Koffi's; it was gray, flaked in places. Her unraveling braids were no longer thick, but stringy and thin, white. Worst of all, where the girl's brown eyes had been, there were only two fathomless black holes. Koffi shuddered, tried to pull her arm away.

"Let go of me."

"I wanna go home." When the little girl spoke, her voice was no longer singular and fragile; it was that same chorus—cold and demanding. "Take us home."

"Who are you?" Koffi felt the start of a new terror begin to nibble at her edges, its teeth tiny and sharp as it grew hungrier. Chills broke out over her skin. She was cold, too cold, and the little girl was not relinquishing her grip. Pain lanced through her arm as that grip tightened, as the muscles and joints in her shoulder protested. There was a hunger carved into the girl's face, into the lines around her gaping mouth.

"She has two eyes." The voices came from the girl's mouth, but Koffi heard them all around her, echoing among the trees. "But she does not need both, she could give us one. All we need is one, for the payment, and then we can go home. We want to go home."

"No!" Koffi yanked her arm from the little girl's hands, ignoring the snap of pain she felt in doing so. She stood and backed away quickly, doing her best not to trip on the acacia trees' roots. Their long white thorns scratched at her bare skin now, warm blood trickled down her arms, her legs. She glanced over her shoulder yet again. To her dismay, the light up ahead was getting dimmer, the speckles of splendor were fading, but if she could get to them, if she could run . . .

She started toward that opening in the trees as fast as she could. It was still several yards away, but if she could get close enough, if she could make it . . .

Her body lurched as an ice-cold hand caught hold of her ankle, sending her crashing toward the ground. Her mouth filled with the taste of earth, grit crunched between her teeth. She tried to rise to her elbows, to get back to her feet, but something still held her. When she turned, the little girl was still there, lying on her belly as she held on to Koffi with both hands. She grinned.

"Let go of me!" Koffi tried and failed to keep the fear from her voice. "Let go—let go of me!"

But the girl did not acknowledge her, and when Koffi's gaze lifted, she saw that they were no longer alone. Others moved between the trees now, emaciated people with skin the color of sludge and cavernous holes in the places where eyes belonged. Their toothless mouths pulled into slackened smiles, their fingers bent like claws primed to tear into flesh.

"NO!" Koffi screamed and thrashed, but it was no use. The thorns were growing longer, the faces of the Untethered seemed to surround her on all sides. They would—

"Koffi?"

Koffi opened her eyes with a start. It took her several seconds to recalibrate, to get a sense of her bearings. She was, she realized, no longer in the Mistwood; she was in Zain's study. Understanding came back to her slowly. She was sitting in Zain's armchair and he was kneeling before her, hands hovering just above the backs of hers. She met his gaze.

"How did I do?"

"You did better," he said. "That was about a minute longer than before."

A minute, only a minute. Koffi slumped in her chair, frowning.

"That's good, Butter Knife," said Zain, rising. He moved to sit on the edge of the desk. "You're getting better, little by little, every time you try."

Koffi said nothing, but tried to temper her annoyance. She was still training with the darajas of Thornkeep during the day, but her nights had taken on new purpose. If she was going to lead everyone through the Mistwood, she needed some way to practice, to get used to being there. It had been Zain who'd agreed to help her simulate it in preparation.

"We're running out of time." Koffi closed her eyes and massaged her temples. "I have to get this right. I can't keep freezing up and panicking every time I see the Untethered." Doing it in dreams was one thing, but she didn't want to think about what would happen if she did it in real life, when everyone was following her, counting on her. These people were putting their lives in her hands. Every time Koffi truly thought about that, her stomach twisted.

"Why don't we try something else, like working with the splendor?" Zain's gaze lifted to the study's vaulted ceiling. "We don't have much space in here, but we can try some exercises?"

Koffi sighed. "Okay."

"Right." Zain looked around. "I want you to pick out three things in this room, any three things."

Koffi's eyes settled on the goblet on the desk, a bright-red-spined book on the shelf, and a green apple Zain had been holding earlier. She told him the three she'd picked.

"Now," Zain continued, "close your eyes and count to ten. I'm going to hide those three things in different parts of the room. When you get to ten, I want you to call the splendor. Think about those three items, finding them, and see if the splendor will show you where they are."

Koffi pursed her lips. "So, hide-and-seek?"

"Essentially, yes."

She stared at him, but when one of his brows quirked, she shrugged. "Fine."

"Close your eyes and start counting," he said with a smirk. "As you do, try to think about your three items. Think about them with as much detail as you can."

Koffi obeyed, closing her eyes and taking deep breaths in and out. Behind her eyelids there was nothing but blackness, but she tried to do what Zain said.

One, two, three...

She pictured the goblet first; it was small, copper, with gold around its brim.

Four, five, six...

She thought of the book on the shelf, its spine red as blood; there'd been fancy white letters on it, but she hadn't been close enough to discern what they said.

Seven, eight, nine...

She pictured the apple last: light green, small, slightly dented on one side.

"Ten." Koffi opened her eyes. Zain was standing in the middle of the study, looking triumphant.

"Good luck," he said. "You'll need it." There was a taunting in his voice, but it didn't reach his eyes.

Koffi closed her eyes again, and this time she tried to focus. Njeri had been teaching her breathing exercises, and now she practiced holding breaths in both her chest and her diaphragm. With each exhale, she felt herself becoming more centered, more aware of her body's intricacies, the way everything worked together like a carefully crafted machine. When she called the splendor to her now, she didn't ask, she commanded.

Come to me.

In a rush, the energy coursed through her, hot on her bones

and against her skin. She imagined it leaving her, forming tiny dots of light in the space around her. Once again, she pictured the copper goblet.

Find it, she ordered. *Show me where it is.*

She opened her eyes and watched as the speckles of light wound and twirled in the air like leaves picked up by a breeze. Slowly, they reoriented themselves to form a loose sort of line leading from her to a spot on the bookshelf's top shelf. She followed it, dragging a footstool so that she could reach it. It had been some time since the books on this shelf had been touched, a thin layer of dust covering each one. There was no evidence at all that Zain had moved them, but the speckles of light floated to a space behind them. Carefully, Koffi slid two or three of them forward, grasping at the air. Her fingers closed around a cool metal stem, and when she withdrew the goblet, she felt a thrill. She glanced over her shoulder and grinned at Zain.

"Nice," he conceded. "Now the book."

Koffi carefully stepped down from the stool and placed the goblet on the desk. Once again, she closed her eyes and tried to picture what she wanted the splendor to see too, the pages of the old book, the crease in its leathery binding.

Find it, she commanded. *Help me find it.*

The speckles that had hovered by the goblet rose in the air, twinkling like tiny stars a moment, before moving to create a new line. This time, it led to the desk. She felt Zain's eyes on her as she walked around it once, twice . . . and then to one of its drawers. Koffi tugged it open, and felt another surge of excitement as her eyes landed on the little red book. She held it up, victorious. Zain opened his mouth to speak, but she held her hand up. She knew what he was going to say: the apple. Where was the apple? Her eyes roamed the room. In truth, there were few hiding places left. A small throb had started at the base of her head, and she felt the smallest bit of dread as it grew more intense. That throb was her body's first signal, a warning that she was approaching her limits. She gritted her teeth.

No. She wasn't sure who she was talking to, her body or herself. *No, not now. I'm finding that apple.*

With a low groan, she pushed past the pain and tried to quiet her mind again. The splendor was still in the air, still waiting for her to address it. She closed her eyes and raised her hands.

The apple. She didn't speak the words, but they sounded thunderous in her mind. *Show me where the apple is, lead me to it.*

There was a long, terrible moment in which the splendor began to flicker out, in which she wasn't sure if it had heard her at all. She wondered if it might be abandoning her; perhaps it sensed her fatigue. She raised her hands slightly higher.

Show me, she commanded. *Now.*

Without warning, a new blaze of energy erupted somewhere in her ribs, hotter than she'd ever felt before. It was like swallowing a coal; a pressure built in her throat, behind her eyes, in her pores. She heard a small pop, and then the world seemed to mute itself; in its place, a dull roar filled the air. The golden speckles of light were growing now, trembling as they moved to form a line for the third time. She watched as they bobbed in the air, lowering, until they led her straight to Zain. He hadn't moved from his spot in the middle of the study, and now his eyes were wide as they locked on Koffi. Koffi felt like it took ages to reach him, to close the small space between them. This time, she was the one who smirked as she pulled the apple from his pocket and held it up. As though it understood its job was done, the splendor began to fade.

"And that's three items." Koffi beamed. "I've got to say, that felt pretty—" She stopped as she watched Zain's expression change. He looked bewildered. "What?"

"Koffi, you looked . . ." He seemed at a loss for words. "You looked really different when you did that."

Koffi frowned. "Different?"

"Your whole body was glowing," he said quietly. "Even your eyes."

The words caught Koffi off guard. She'd pushed herself, yes, felt that last vestige of the energy come to her when called, but she hadn't felt so different from usual. The way Zain was looking at her made her feel odd. There was awe and appreciation in his gaze, but there was also something that looked uncomfortably like fear. She watched the corner of his mouth pull down, saw the slight pinch between his brows.

"Koffi, I know that you're feeling a lot of pressure right now, more pressure than anyone else at Thornkeep," he said carefully. "But you have to remember that you're still holding the splendor you took from Adiah within you. That much energy makes you powerful, but . . ." He hesitated. "Don't let it consume you, okay?"

Koffi wasn't immediately sure what to say. There was real concern in Zain's eyes, a concern she herself had never seen before. After a moment, she nodded.

"I'll be careful," she said. "I promise." With her free hand, she took Zain's and squeezed. He jumped at her touch, but didn't look unhappy about it. His eyes softened, and every muscle in his body seemed to relax.

"I think you've more than proven yourself for one night," he said kindly. "Come on, I'll walk you back to your room."

Koffi let him take her from the study without a word. She was grateful when its candles extinguished, letting them both fall into new darkness. A darkness in which she didn't have to admit what she'd just felt when she'd called the splendor to her.

A hunger.

Koffi spent most of the next day with Makena, and when dusk fell, they made their way to the den where Njeri, Amun, and Zain were waiting. From the moment she entered it, she could feel a palpable excitement crackling in the air. Zain and Amun were sitting in chairs, but Njeri was on the floor sitting cross-legged before a large piece of parchment. At first Koffi didn't understand what she was looking at, but when she moved to stand over Njeri's shoulder, she recognized it—it was a crude map of Thornkeep's grounds.

"We've come up with a plan," said Njeri, using her palms to smooth out the sketch. "I've talked with the last of the darajas I trust, and it looks like we have eighteen coming with us—that's just shy of ten percent of Thornkeep's darajas."

Koffi tempered the knot in her stomach. Eighteen wasn't a huge number, but it felt big to her.

"The plan itself is simple," Njeri went on. "We'll go through a normal day, and that night eat dinner." Her eyes flashed. "Or at least, we'll pretend to." At Koffi's confused gaze, she lowered her voice and went on. "Izem is going to be adding a special ingredient to everyone's food and drink, a concoction of lavender. It won't harm anyone, but it will make everyone sleep very deeply. No one will hear or notice us leaving.

"I'm going to gather all of the girls from their quarters, Amun will gather the boys. We're split pretty evenly. Meanwhile, Makena and Zain will escort you to the north garden. We'll meet up there, and..."

"And then we'll go," Koffi finished, "into the Mistwood."

Makena nodded. "We don't know how thick the Mistwood actually is, so we'll need to pack. We can't travel heavy—Fedu will notice too much food stored up, but if we start rationing small amounts of nonperishables now..."

Koffi let Njeri's words fade as she went over the rest of their plan's logistics. After some back-and-forth, it was decided that they would leave in four days. That gave them enough time to prepare, but not so much time for anyone to get cold feet and alert Fedu. Koffi said nothing as, one by one, the darajas left the den. She even waved Makena off. Eventually, only she and Zain were left in the room.

"Are you okay?" He was still sitting in his chair, watching her intently.

"Yeah." The lie came easier than Koffi cared to admit to herself, but that didn't stop her from saying it. "Just nervous, I guess."

"You're going to be fine," he said. "You've practiced almost every day. We've been doing the simulations—"

"Simulations aren't the same as the real thing, though," she said, shaking her head. She knew as soon as she said the words that they were the ones that had been sitting in the back of her mind, gnawing at her. "Zain, no matter what, I'm not going to feel ready to do this unless I know that I can be in the Mistwood for a long amount of time without falling apart." She paused. "Which is why . . . I need to ask you for a favor."

At once, Zain pursed his lips. "Why do I have a feeling I'm not going to like what you're going to say?"

"Because you're probably not," Koffi admitted. "But I have to ask."

Zain pinched the bridge of his nose. "Go on."

Koffi braced herself, then spoke. "I want to go back to the Mistwood, tonight."

CHAPTER 22

REGRETS

Ekon tried to talk to Safiyah.

He'd tried exactly three times—he'd counted. But no matter how he constructed the words in his mind, they fell apart every time he looked at her.

They'd found the Enterprise exactly where Safiyah had said they would be; their wagons were arranged near the edge of East Bandari, in the section of town where grocers and merchants operated. Ekon recalled now the looks on the Enterprise members' faces when they'd seen them coming down the road. He'd expected them to be happy to see Safiyah, but what he hadn't been prepared for were the whoops and cheers. He hadn't expected Thabo to pull him into a hug, or Abeke to start clapping and shaking her fist. *They're not just happy to see Safiyah,* he realized, *they're happy to see you.*

"We thought you two were gone for sure," said Thabo, almost looking guilty. "How did you make it here on foot?"

"It's . . . a long story," said Ekon, but when the other members of the Enterprise continued to stare at him, he looked to Safiyah. "Ah, Safiyah can probably tell it better than I can."

Safiyah gave him a cutting look, before addressing the Enterprise. She recounted everything that had happened after the Walaji's attack—their encounter with Amakoya, the nanabolele, their trek through the marshlands. Ekon noticed she was careful to skip over the night in the fishing village, and a refreshed guilt pricked at his side as he remembered the softness of her hand in his, the way her face looked when she was truly asleep. When she was finished, Kontar clapped him on the shoulder.

"Any man who gets through all of that and still makes it back to us is a man I want at my side," he said. He turned to address the rest of the Enterprise. "I'd like to call a formal vote," he announced. "A vote to make Ekon a permanently employed member of the East Eshōzan Trading Enterprise, effective immediately."

A cheer went up among the other members of the Enterprise even as Ekon started. He looked around at all of them. "You . . . you want me to permanently work with you guys? All the time?"

"It wouldn't be anything too glamorous," said Abeke. There was a twinkle in her eye. "But you've been a real help to me with the inventory and accounts; you've really got a natural knack for number crunching. We could use a junior accountant on the payroll."

Junior accountant. Ekon played with that title in his mind. Junior accountant. His job, his *paying* job, would be to work with numbers. He let himself imagine it, a life on the road with the rest of the Enterprise, traveling from city to city. At the Temple of

Lkossa, he'd spent hours in its library reading books about the rest of the continent; he'd never dreamed he might someday have the opportunity to see it for himself.

That's the life this offer comes with, said a voice in mind. *That's the real offer, freedom.*

In all his years at the Temple of Lkossa, with its brothers and the Sons of the Six, he'd never been praised for the things he was good at, the things he loved. A good recitation of verse from the Book of the Six? A victory on the sparring lawns? Those had been the things that had been valued and praised. To consider now a life wherein he might get to be valued and praised for doing the things that made him happy was almost too much. Something bloomed in his chest, warm, like sunshine erupting. The members of the Enterprise were still smiling at him, waiting. His gaze panned, and then stopped on someone else sitting by one of the wagons. Themba.

At once, the sunshine feeling in his chest cooled.

The old woman wasn't smiling at him like everyone else, but she wasn't frowning either. Her expression was pensive, curious, as though she too was waiting to hear what his answer to the Enterprise's proposal might be. She didn't need to speak a word; in those brown eyes Ekon heard a single name.

Koffi.

Her face burned through his mind, along with everything else. He remembered the cruelty in Fedu's laugh, Adiah's scream as she'd fought him to her last. With a twinge of pain, he remembered what he'd promised Koffi in own mind—how many times had he sworn that he'd be the one to find her, to save her? He knew then what his answer would be; he was shaking his head before he said the words.

"I'm sorry," he said quietly. "Your offer is generous, but I can't accept it."

There was a long pause in which no one spoke. Ekon wanted to look at the ground, at the sky, anywhere but here. A voice eventually interrupted the silence.

"Very well, then."

Ekon looked up and locked eyes with Ano. She was standing near one of the wagons, holding a teakettle. Her expression was utterly indifferent. "It sounds like a decision is made. Ekon will not be joining the Enterprise." Her voice was flat. "Now that that bit of business is resolved, we can get back to the real work. Let's have lunch and then determine which merchants we have time to set up appointments with this afternoon . . ."

Another moment passed before the members of the Enterprise seemed to snap from a reverie. One by one, they walked away to join Ano for lunch or otherwise busy themselves with duties around the camp. Safiyah gave him one more impassive look before going to join the others. Ekon went to sit with Themba. She said nothing as he eased beside her, buried his head in his hands.

"That went well," she said mildly.

"Why didn't they ask you to join them?" said Ekon between his fingers. "You're the Cobra, you're supposed to be infamous or something." When he lowered his hands, Themba was giving him a shrewd look.

"As a matter of fact, they did ask me, a short while after we got away from those bandits," she said. "I turned them down too, not that I think they really expected me to say yes. With you, though, it seems they might have been more hopeful. They seem more disappointed."

"You're not making me feel better."

Themba shrugged. "You know, if you wanted to go with them, I wouldn't blame you."

"What?" Ekon sat up, glaring at the old woman. "How can you say that?"

Themba raised her hands. "Apologies, boy, I meant no offense. I know you care deeply about my granddaughter. In fact, in many ways you know her better than I do."

Ekon relaxed, suddenly feeling a bit bad. As much as he cared about Koffi, he understood that the way Themba looked at her would always be different. They were of the same blood. When he spoke again, his tone was softer.

"You should know that I'd never, ever abandon Koffi. I'd never leave her with Fedu. I—"

"Love her?" Themba's brows shot up, and the expression on her face was just short of amused. "Are you sure? From what you've told me, you and Koffi spent a matter of days together in the Greater Jungle. I have no doubt the two of you got to know each other in a special way—it was an intense situation—but can you really say you know her, that you love her?"

Ekon opened his mouth, but Themba went on.

"You do not owe me an answer to that question, boy," she said, holding a hand up. "The only person you owe an answer to is yourself, and"—she made a point of meeting Ekon's eyes and then looking across the campsite, to the place where Safiyah was sitting with the other members of the Enterprise—"to those who may be affected by that answer."

In spite of himself, in spite of everything, Ekon laughed. "This seems like the kind of conversation a mother would have with her child."

At this, Themba frowned. "What happened to your mother?" she asked. "I don't think I've heard you mention her."

"She left our family when I was really little." Ekon said the words quickly, as though that could make them hurt less. "I really don't even remember her anymore."

Themba nodded, rocking back and forth on the ground. "I'm sorry to hear that, Ekon."

"I'm not." Ekon shrugged. "I'm better without her anyway."

Themba offered a smile, but it didn't reach her eyes. "Tuh. Now you sound like my daughter," she said.

Ekon looked up, temporarily distracted by this new piece of information. "You're talking about Koffi's mom?"

"Yes," said Themba sadly. "My only child."

Ekon sat up. For a moment, he recalled the first time he'd ever seen Koffi. She'd been running across the burning Night Zoo's grounds with another woman, one with a blurred face he couldn't envision clearly. He winced as he remembered what had happened that night. Shomari, his former co-candidate, had taken the woman down with his slingshot. He could still see it, the jolt as the rock had hit the back of her head and she'd toppled down the zoo's border wall. Neither he nor Shomari had stopped to check on her, to see if she'd . . . He shuddered.

"You and her don't . . . uh, get along?" Ekon waited a beat before adding, "Sorry, you don't have to talk about it. I didn't mean to pry."

Themba rocked from side to side for a moment in silence. "I suppose I owe you that truth as much as anyone," she finally said. "After all, in a way, what happened between Koffi's mother and me is the reason we're here. The reason you're here."

Now Ekon was fully intrigued. "What do you mean?"

Themba sat back. "The first thing to know about Koffi's mother is that she's stubborn as an ox. I suppose I can't fault her for that—she probably got it from me—but . . . it made her childhood difficult, and harder still when she grew older. I'd thought that things would change once Koffi was born, but . . ." Emotion was beginning to creep into her voice now. It wasn't quite anger, but something sadder, an old frustration, a fatigue. "It's my fault," she murmured. "All of it."

Ekon had a thousand questions all teeming in the back of his mind. He wanted to ask every single one, but something told him to bite his tongue, to wait. He observed Themba rocking and rubbing a thumb over the medallion she never took off. For several seconds, the air was filled with nothing but heavy silence. Then she looked up sharply.

"Koffi does not know that I exist," she said brusquely. "But that's not her fault." She rubbed her temples. "The first few decades after the Rupture were an incredibly uncertain time. There was violence, poverty, no one trusted anyone, and it got worse. By the time Koffi's mother was born, anti-daraja sentiments were strong. The laws were strict. Darajas became completely segregated from the rest of society. We could not eat, sleep, or otherwise dwell alongside non-darajas."

Ekon swallowed. "Was Koffi's mother a daraja too?"

Themba shook her head. "No, but she might as well have been. Different cities had different rules, of course, but in Lkossa, it was decreed by the Kuhani that anyone related to a daraja would share the status of a daraja, and be subjected to the same second-class status unless they publicly renounced all ties to the daraja or darajas in question." She gave him a skeptical look. "Well, you can imagine how well that went."

"What happened?" Ekon asked.

Themba pursed her lips. "Of course, people held strong in the beginning. No one wanted to renounce their own family members because of something they'd been born with and couldn't help. Those 'mixed' families tried to create communities of their own to circumvent the laws, and it worked, for a time.

"But then the Kuhani and the Sons grew more stringent. They banned congregations of more than three at a time, forced us to wear identification bangles. Then there were the night raids. People's homes were ransacked, entire streets of daraja-owned businesses burned down mysteriously in the night with no follow-up investigation. It was nothing short of covert warfare. And it destroyed us like a disease from within."

Ekon cringed. He'd already done the math and figured that his father definitely would have been alive when some of this likely happened. He didn't want to think about Baba doing such a thing. "What did you do?" he asked quietly.

Themba rocked forward and back. "Koffi's mother and I survived, persisted in spite of it all. Even when some people, the weaker ones, gave in and renounced their own family members, we stuck together. She was a resourceful girl, never complained when we had to move, always taking up extra jobs to help me with money." Themba looked off into the distance. "We didn't have much, but we had each other." She shook her head.

"But eventually, it did become too difficult to bear, and one day she asked me to never speak to her again, to pretend I essentially wasn't her mother at all." Tears glistened in the old woman's eyes. "I did warn her." She seemed to be saying the words more for herself than Ekon. "I warned her that she could pass on the daraja blood to a child, and if she did, she would need me or another daraja to help teach them how to manage their power." She hung her head. "My daughter did not listen. Instead, she married a nondaraja and likely hoped for the best. And I stayed back, as promised. I watched as the optimistic young man she married started venture after venture, and took out loan after loan. I watched as he spent every coin they had on dreams, and left my daughter to pick up the tab." Her gaze met Ekon's and now there was real anger there. "I didn't have money to help her, and I suppose she wouldn't have taken it even if I did. But things got bad, in the end. Her husband, Lesego, Koffi's father, got involved with bad people, then got tricked into signing indentured servant contracts for himself, my daughter, and their child in order to pay back his staggering debt. They've been trapped in those contracts ever since."

Ekon frowned. He didn't know how to process the way he felt. In the few weeks he'd spent with Koffi, he'd thought he knew her—or at least had started to get to know her. But listening to Themba made him realize that he barely knew her at all. He remembered the story Koffi had told him one night by a fire, after she'd treated his wounds. She'd told him a little about her parents and how they'd ended up in the Night Zoo, but that had only been a fraction of the story.

"Why didn't you help them?" The question left him before he could stop it.

Themba hung her head. "Because I swore an oath, an eternal vow. It is the most powerful kind of promise a daraja can make."

"A vow?" he repeated. "You didn't help your daughter and granddaughter because of a vow?"

Themba's eyes flashed. "I regretted it as soon as I did it, and I've regretted it every single day and night after. At the time, I thought it was the right thing, I thought it would make her happy, to give her the freedom she always wanted. In the end, I think the only thing I managed to give her was the one thing I didn't want to: a life full of regrets."

"I'm not sure that's entirely true," said Ekon before he could stop himself. When Themba looked up at him, he shrugged. "I've never met your daughter, obviously, but I do know Koffi, despite what you think."

"What's she like?" asked Themba. The question was casual enough, but Ekon heard the edge in it.

"Predictably stubborn," Ekon said with a laugh that surprised him. "Sometimes she's frustrating. She doesn't plan anything ahead, and she tends to kick people when they make her mad." He pursed his lips, thoughtful. "But she's also kind, funny, and loyal to the end. She's a good person." He nodded to her. "And I suspect at least a part of that is because of you, in a way."

Themba pressed her lips together for a long time, staring at her hands. Her voice was soft when she spoke again. "That's very kind of you to say, boy." She patted his shoulder as she rose and started back toward the camp. "I'm glad my granddaughter can call you a friend. I hope she always does."

"Yeah," said Ekon quietly. "I hope so too."

The rest of the afternoon with the Enterprise passed without many words exchanged. Every other hour or so, Ano and Kontar would take spices or herbs to Bandarian merchants to trade or sell; the rest of the camp busied themselves preparing for the next leg of their journey. From Bandari, the Enterprise would take a ship west along the Ndefu River, until they ended up in the capital of the Kusini Region, a city called Chini. Ano agreed that Ekon and Themba would spend the night, and then the groups would go their separate ways in the morning. Ekon didn't sleep much that night. When he tried to sleep, his dreams and nightmares tangled like thread. He saw visions that he wasn't sure were real or from his imagination, and just as quickly those visions gave way to grotesque images of monsters—first the nanabolele, then the Walaji. In the end, he opted to stay awake through the night listening to the crackle of the fire. By dawn, he was already awake and dressed. He and Themba had one final meal with the Enterprise before Ano handed them traveling cloaks.

"You'll need them," she explained. "It only gets colder from here." She looked between them. "I hope you find your friend."

"Thank you," said Ekon in earnest. "For everything."

One by one, he and Themba bid the rest of the Enterprise farewell, and Ekon was surprised to find each goodbye was sadder than the one before it. Traveling with the Enterprise hadn't been luxurious or even easy most of the time, but in hindsight Ekon realized that it'd been the first time in his life in which he'd truly felt like he'd belonged, like he'd been accepted. He looked up and realized Safiyah was the last person standing before them waiting to say goodbye. She gave Themba a quick squeeze before the old woman made a point of excusing herself so that the two of them were alone. Uncomfortable seconds passed as neither of them was quite able to look the other in the eye. In the end, Ekon made himself speak first.

"I was a jerk." He didn't bother dressing up the words with any fluff. "I'm sorry."

Safiyah nodded, though Ekon thought there was a sadness in the gesture. "I forgive you," she said, "and I hope you find what you're looking for in the south. If you change your mind, the Enterprise is around. I'm sure that offer to join us will always stand."

"Tuh, I doubt it," said Ekon. "I'm pretty that Ano is more than happy to see me go."

One of Safiyah's brows rose. "Don't be so sure," she said. "I spoke with Kontar yesterday. He may have been the one to formally invite you to the Enterprise, but he got the idea from Ano. She told him she thought you'd be an excellent addition to the Enterprise."

"Really?" Ekon frowned, genuinely surprised now. "Why would she say—?"

"Ekon?" A few feet from them, Themba was standing with their bags in hand. "Are you ready?"

Ekon looked between the old woman and Safiyah. "I—"

Safiyah closed the gap between them before he could say another word, kissing his cheek so quickly, he wasn't sure if he'd imagined it. His skin burned in the place her lips touched.

"Until we meet again, Ekon," she said as she turned and made her way back to camp. "Gods be with you."

The traveling roads seemed different now, and Ekon couldn't tell if it was because he and Themba were now traveling on their own or if something intangible had changed.

At least in his mind, it seemed there were far fewer people on the road, and where before it had been well trodden and wide, it seemed to be getting narrower and more twisty as they went on. As he'd traveled south with the Enterprise, in the intersection where the Zamani Region became the Kusini Region, the landscapes had shifted by the day, alternating back and forth between marshland and grassland. But after he and Themba boarded the ferry to take them across the Ndefu River, there was no more ambiguity; they were now truly in southern Eshōza.

A near-constant mist hung in the air now. Sometimes the clouds of it grew so thick that it looked like a mass of cotton on the road, waiting to consume them. Other times, it was silvery and thin, so inconspicuous that he didn't even realize they'd been walking through it until they emerged and found proper sunlight again. The mist wasn't the only new element to contend with either; a chill had also set in almost as soon as they'd left Bandari, and hours later, Ekon felt it in his bones. He and Themba had muttered about it at first, making little jokes to lighten the mood, but as the hours passed, they'd stopped talking altogether and moved closer so that they could conserve at least some body heat as they walked. Finally, Themba squinted at the sky. The sun was blotted out by clouds, casting it in a dark iron gray.

"Look." She pointed. "Up ahead."

Ekon narrowed his own gaze and tried to follow her finger to where she was indicating. It was barely discernible in the distance, but he thought he saw something that looked like a sentry tower up ahead. They looked at each other, then back at it.

"If it's a tower, it could give us a better vantage point," Ekon noted.

Themba nodded, and they started toward the tower. With each step toward it, Ekon's heartbeat pounded harder in his chest. The tower was still shrouded in mist, still far off, but something about it both repelled and pulled at him. If he could just get to it . . .

"Ekon." Themba's voice snapped him from his reverie. "Stop."

Ekon obeyed, but hesitantly. "I thought we were going to check out the tower."

"We were . . ." Themba's eyes were now wary as she panned the space around them. "But we've been walking toward it for more than ten minutes now, and we're no closer than we were ten minutes ago." She pursed her lips. "I think that it's an illusion, created by a very skilled and very powerful daraja."

Ekon looked from Themba back to the sentry tower. He realized that she was right; the tower had not moved at all. He shivered. "So what do we do?"

"Go back," said Themba, already turning. "We'll figure out our location and work from there to try to find—"

"Themba."

"Not now, Ekon. I'm trying to think—"

"Themba!"

The old woman opened her mouth to argue, then stopped short. Her eyes had found the same thing Ekon's had: a massive white wall of mist as high as the eye could see. The longer Ekon stared up and into it, the colder he felt.

"This is it." Even as he said the words, he knew they were true. "This is the realm of the dead."

CHAPTER 23

T̶ʜᴇ UNTETHERED

"For the record, I don't like this."

Koffi walked alongside Zain in silence. Around them, the air was cool and fragranced slightly with the florals of the garden. She breathed them in, calming herself.

"I'll be fine, Zain."

The trees of the Mistwood loomed higher and higher as they approached, as though watching, waiting. Koffi thought of the first time she'd seen the Mistwood from Thornkeep's windows, the fear it had drawn from her. So much had changed.

Koffi's eyes shot to Zain as, together, they stopped several feet away from the first tendrils of mist. He had a resolute expression she didn't like.

"So . . . ," she started. "You'll wait here and make sure no dara-jas spot me, and I'll—"

"Don't even try it, Koffi." Zain was giving her an impatient look. "You really think I'm just going to sit out here while you go into the Mistwood by yourself?"

Koffi tensed. "Zain." She tried to keep the fear out of her voice.

"The whole point of me going into the Mistwood right now is to see if I can handle being in there, to see if the splendor will actually hold up when I call to it. If I fail . . ." She very deliberately let the words trail off, but in answer Zain only shrugged.

"We're all going to die someday. If my day is today, I'd rather die doing something interesting."

He said the words casually, with a hint of a joke in them, but Koffi didn't laugh. Before them a breeze slightly lifted the mist so that its translucent white curls danced against the trees. She swallowed.

"You're sure?"

"I'm sure, Koffi."

She nodded, sucked in a sharp breath, then made her way forward. She didn't mind when Zain's long strides fell into step with hers, and she didn't pull away when he grabbed her hand. He squeezed it as they came within the final few feet of the Mistwood. They were now so close Koffi could see the acacias' thorns, and it took everything she had not to shirk away from them as she neared.

"Steady, Butter Knife," Zain breathed.

Steady. That was what Koffi focused on in those last few inches. She kept her feet steady and her breath steady as they stepped into the mist, as a hush fell over everything around them.

And then they were inside the Mistwood.

The chill came first, as Koffi had known it would. She was prepared this time, and pulled her cloak closer with her free hand. Around her, there was nothing but mist. She knew the acacia trees had to be around—she remembered all too well the way they'd cut into her the first time she'd come here—but she couldn't see them now. Beside her, she barely saw Zain, and suddenly she was grateful he had taken her hand.

"You okay?" she asked.

In the opacity, she saw Zain nod, only a fractional movement. "This place is worse than anything I imagined," he said. "I can't imagine how Makena would have felt, being alone in here."

Koffi nodded. The Mistwood, it seemed, was impossibly creepier at night.

"How far in do you want to go?" Zain asked.

"Not far," said Koffi. "I just want to know that I can summon the splendor. I'll ask it to show me the way home, and then the way back to Thornkeep."

"Simple," said Zain. Koffi thought she heard a tremor in his voice.

"I have an idea," she said. "But . . . I'll need both hands."

"Oh." She was surprised when Zain dropped her hand immediately, looking embarrassed. "Yeah, of course."

In the absence of his touch, Koffi felt a new chill cool her blood, but she focused on the task at hand as she stopped. "Stay close," she said to Zain quickly, and then she closed her eyes. In the new darkness, she tried to remember everything she'd learned from the darajas of Thornkeep. She inhaled and exhaled slowly, tried to listen to her body, acknowledged each emotion.

I am afraid. There is no use in denying that truth. I am afraid I'm going to fail. But I am hopeful too, hopeful that this might work.

When she summoned the splendor, she didn't call it aloud or in her mind. She simply reached for it, from a place lower than her heart. She felt its rise, the warmth that crept into her as it filled her body. Her eyes opened, and she watched as not many, but one single ball of golden light formed between her hands, a perfect sphere. Beside her, Zain let out a small gasp.

"I didn't know you could do that."

"Neither did I."

She looked at Zain in time to catch his narrowed eyes, but there was a smile in them. "Always full of surprises, Butter Knife."

With the new light before them, they ventured farther into the Mistwood. Around them, it was still difficult to see far ahead, but they could now at least avoid the branches and thorns. Eventually, they reached an area where the trees thinned slightly, and Koffi stopped.

"Here," she said. "This is where I want to try."

Zain nodded. "You can do this," he whispered. "I know you can." He stepped back to give her space.

Koffi's eyes resettled on the orb of light still hovering between her hands. It was light, she understood that much, but it was something else: a living, pulsing energy. Adiah's energy, the very energy that had lived in her body for ninety-nine years, the very energy that had turned her into the Shetani. When Koffi had heard that, she'd imagined some vile, horrible entity possessing Adiah like a demon; this golden energy was much harder to vilify. She felt its heartbeat, in sync with hers, waiting. Slowly, she spread her hands farther and farther apart, praying that what she had in mind would work. She closed her eyes again and tried to imagine that single orb of light breaking, splintering, forming the smaller speckles of light she was used to. When she opened her eyes, the orb was shuddering violently.

Come on, she prayed, watching it. *Come on ... Work ...*

Without warning, the orb of light erupted. It was soundless, but Koffi still jumped as an explosion of light filled her eyes. From somewhere beside her, she heard Zain yelp, and automatically she shielded her own eyes. When she lowered her hands, her heart was pounding.

What looked like thousands of tiny speckles of light now filled the space around her. Some danced between the branches of trees, others swirled in the air just before her eyes. She exhaled.

"Koffi!" Zain's voice echoed in the mist. "Koffi, you did it!"

"Not yet." Koffi held up a hand. She was still staring at the splendor. It was here, it had listened to her up to this point, but . . .

"There's one more test," she said, "one more thing I have to do to be sure." She looked around her, at all the speckles of light, and thought a single word.

Home.

It hummed through her, gentle, but Koffi felt the power in that word. *Home. Show me the way home.*

The splendor around her began to descend, then moved into a line. Koffi's breath caught as the line led well into the mist ahead of her, toward home.

"Yes!"

The breath left Koffi's body as she felt herself being swept into a huge hug, as Zain picked her up off the ground. He swung her once, twice, then set her back on the ground, beaming. "You did it, Koffi," he breathed, touching his forehead to hers. "I knew you'd be able to, knew you'd—"

Koffi went cold as the words died in Zain's throat and she watched his expression change. He was looking over her shoulder, horrified. Koffi knew what she would see when she turned to follow his gaze, but that still didn't prepare her for the image.

An Untethered man was standing between the trees, several yards away. His skin was gray and translucent, and his curly hair was white. He did not speak as he stared back at them, as though processing.

"Koffi." Zain only breathed her name. "Don't panic."

Koffi heard the words, but they sounded far away; her eyes were fixed on the Untethered man. Like the rest, he had no eyes, but she still felt his glare. He took a step toward her, and several of the splendor's lights flickered. She felt her blood cool.

"Koffi!" Zain was shouting now. "Don't lose focus, don't—"

But it was too late. The Untethered man was coming closer now, and each step seemed to pull something from her. Around her, more of the splendor's lights were dimming. Zain moved closer to her as they fell into darkness. In seconds, the Untethered man would be upon them; he was moving faster now. Koffi braced herself.

And then she heard it: a war cry.

It was different from a scream, there was power in it. Koffi opened her eyes in time to see that, from the opposite end of the trees, someone else had joined them in the clearing: a woman. She looked older than Koffi by several years, with short curly hair the color of clouds, and a plain gray tunic. Koffi had never seen her before, yet something about her felt familiar. It took a moment for her to name the thing that felt different about her: The woman's skin wasn't gray like the Untethered man; it was brown. When she moved in the light, she was certainly translucent, but . . . Koffi squinted. The woman looked normal, but she also looked Untethered. Koffi and Zain watched as she circled the Untethered man, holding what looked to be an iklwa spear in hand.

"Go!" she ordered, eyes flashing. "Leave this place!"

The Untethered man turned his gaze so that his empty eyes faced the woman instead. He advanced a small step forward, but when she jabbed her spear in the air again, he flinched.

"Go!"

Koffi watched in wonder as, abruptly, the Untethered man turned and left the clearing as quickly as he'd come. The woman watched his retreating back, unmoving, for several seconds, before facing them.

"Are you two all right?"

Both Koffi and Zain nodded.

"Be at ease." The woman lowered her spear. "I mean you no harm."

"Who are you?" Koffi asked. Beside her, Zain shifted.

"I am called Ijeoma," said the woman. "It means 'good journey.'"

"Ijeoma," said Zain. "How did you come to be here?"

Ijeoma smiled. "I suppose that depends on what you mean when you say 'here.' I have been in the Mistwood for decades." She nodded to Koffi. "But I am here before you now because of you."

Koffi frowned. "Me?"

Ijeoma stood straighter. "There is immense power in the ties of blood, bone, and soul," she said. "I thought you might have learned as much when you communed with the goddess of the jungle."

Understanding struck Koffi with the force of a lightning bolt. "Wait." She hesitated. "Are you saying you're one of them? One of my foremothers?"

Ijeoma smiled. "We are separated by several generations, but yes. My blood is yours, and yours is mine."

Zain stepped forward, glancing between them. He looked shocked. "If you and Koffi are related, does that mean you're a daraja too? Are you Order of Vivuli?"

"Yes to your first question," said Ijeoma, "but no to your second. In my life, I was in the Order of Maisha."

"I don't understand, though," said Koffi. "If you live here, it means you're . . . dead."

Ijeoma nodded her head, solemn. "I am."

"But you're not like that Untethered man. You're not gray, and you still have eyes."

Ijeoma sighed, and for the first time Koffi believed the woman when she said she'd been in the Mistwood for decades. There was nothing intangibly aged about her. She looked off into the distance for a moment, then met Koffi's gaze.

"Come with me," she said softly. "I want to show you both something."

Koffi and Zain exchanged a look. In the boy's eyes, Koffi saw the emotions she was sure were reflected in her own—wariness, residual fear, hesitation, but also curiosity. They came to an unspoken agreement then, and Koffi turned back to Ijeoma.

"Okay, lead the way."

There was an eerie silence as they walked through the mist, Ijeoma just steps ahead of them. Koffi didn't understand, but the woman walked with a determined purpose, only occasionally batting at the wisps and tendrils of mist as they got in her way. Ten minutes went by before she finally faced them again. Koffi realized they'd stopped in another clearing, and people were gathered there in a small huddle. People with gray skin. At once, she tensed, but Ijeoma put up a hand.

"It's all right, they will not harm you either."

Koffi watched as Ijeoma moved among the Untethered, offering soft greetings and waves, until her muscles slowly relaxed. She now saw that—counting Ijeoma—there were five of them: a small boy, an old man, a middle-aged woman, and another man lying on his back, who Koffi could not see well. They looked up as she approached, apparently as surprised to see her and Zain as she was to see them.

"These people are like me," Ijeoma explained, settling among them. After a moment, Koffi sat down too, and so did Zain.

"I still don't understand," said Zain, looking around at them. "You're not like the man that was going to attack us."

"Or the people our friend Makena described," said Koffi. "I saw them, they tried to pull parts of her body—they were monstrous."

New sadness crept into Ijeoma's features. "It is an easy thing, to turn men into monsters," she said. "If you know how to do it."

"What do you mean?" asked Koffi.

Ijeoma gestured widely to the Mistwood. "The souls who occupy the Mistwood are stuck in a purgatory. We are the ones Fedu has not and will not allow to pass on to the godlands for our afterlife. Some of those souls, upon realizing they are stuck here, lose their minds and become the creatures you have encountered." Her eyes gleamed. "But there is a smaller, second group of us, those who still believe there is hope for us, and any other soul who is cast here by misfortune or malice. By holding on to that hope, we retain a small piece of our humanity, and that is what keeps our bodies and minds whole."

Koffi opened her mouth to respond but was cut off by a low moan. She jumped, then realized the sound was coming from the man lying on the ground. Upon closer inspection of him, she cringed. It was immediately clear—by his uniform and by the terrible old wounds across his body—that he'd been a soldier, lost on a battlefield.

"He is in constant pain," Ijeoma explained in a hushed voice. "But he still holds on to the hope that, someday, he will make his way to the godlands."

A new emotion bloomed in Koffi's chest as she watched the Untethered man continue to moan, watched the labored breath in the rise and fall of his chest. It took her a moment to name that emotion, but it was sadness. The warrior looked young; he might have been a few years older than her. In some ways, he reminded her of Ekon. Without thinking, she touched his chest; at once, the warrior quieted, his breathing calmed.

"I'm sorry," Koffi whispered to him. "I'm sorry." And she was. She was sorry that this young man was suffering, sorry that he had not found the peace he deserved in death. An idea came to her suddenly. She didn't know if it would work, but she wanted to try. She closed her eyes and pulled some of the splendor to her, directing the speckles of light so that they hovered over the warrior's body. At once, he went still, so still Koffi worried that she might have harmed him. Without warning, his closed eyes suddenly opened. Like Ijeoma, his were not gone, but they were certainly devoid of color. He looked around at the golden speckles of light in awe for a moment, then slowly he sat up. When they began to rise, he got to his feet, then—to Koffi's shock—he stepped into the air. Like climbing invisible steps, he ascended, following the light into the mist above until his body was no longer visible. Koffi stared up at the place where she'd last been able to see him, speechless.

"Koffi." Zain was still sitting on the ground, looking back and forth between Koffi and the sky. "How did you do that?"

"I—I don't know." A fresh panic was seizing at Koffi's insides as she looked at the ground where the man had been lying. She turned to Ijeoma. The woman looked equally stunned. "Where did he go?"

Ijeoma's gaze lifted to the sky too. "Unless I'm mistaken," she said slowly, "I believe he's gone on to the godlands."

The gravity of the words took a moment for Koffi to process. She stared at Ijeoma in confusion for several seconds. The godlands. "How would that even be possible?" she asked. "I don't know how to send anyone to the godlands."

"Koffi," Zain said slowly. He was looking down at his hands, and the skin between his brows was pinched, as though he was trying to work through a difficult math equation. "I think . . . I think I may have gotten it wrong when I told you what your affinity is."

"What do you mean?"

He looked up. "I thought your ability allowed you to use the splendor to guide you to the things you most wanted," he said. "But . . . what if it's deeper than that? What if the splendor works as a compass, something that helps you find the things you want, but also helps others find what they want?" He pointed to the empty space where the warrior had been. "That man wanted to go on to the godlands. You gave him a bit of the splendor, and it guided him from there, but it was because you helped him. You helped him move into the next world, like a bridge, a connector."

"If that's true," said Ijeoma, "you'd be the first daraja of your kind, in my recollection. You'd be the Dira, the compass, the answer to every hope we've held on to here in the Mistwood."

Dira. The compass. Koffi considered the words, replayed what she'd just seen the splendor do. Excitement unfurled within her. "I could help the rest of the Untethered," she said, "the same way I just helped that warrior, couldn't I?"

Ijeoma nodded.

Koffi turned to Zain. "All this time, we thought we had to prepare to fight the Untethered," she said. "But we had it wrong. They're not the monsters we thought they were at all, at least not all of them. I can help them."

"And we can still leave Thornkeep," Zain added.

They both got to their feet. "We need to go back," Koffi said to Ijeoma. "But I promise we'll return. Will you be here?"

Ijeoma stood too. "I will stay in the Mistwood until the last Untethered soul is free from it."

Zain nodded. "We will come back," he said. "I promise."

Ijeoma bowed her head. "Then for now, I will say goodbye."

Koffi and Zain bid Ijeoma farewell before making their way back to Thornkeep. Whereas the first time, Koffi had been nervous about calling the splendor, she found it easy now to follow its little flickering lights until the two of them were passing through the mist again and stepping onto Thornkeep's lawns. It was strange to see the place unchanged in spite of all that had just happened. Koffi fought to catch her breath, to stay calm.

"I can't believe we just saw that," she said.

"Neither can I." Zain's eyes were alight. "It changes everything."

"Since getting here, all I've wanted to do was get out," said Koffi. She walked back and forth across the grass. "But now I have the chance to make a difference, not just for myself and the darajas here who want to leave, but maybe for all of the Untethered." She paused. "I need to tell Makena."

Zain inclined his head. "And I need to tell Amun."

"We can meet up tomorrow, in the den, and figure out a new plan." She took his hand in hers again and squeezed it gently. "Thank you for coming with me."

She was surprised when he lifted her hand and gently kissed it.

"At this point, Koffi, I think I'd go just about anywhere with you."

Koffi beamed, then tore across the north garden, back to Thornkeep. She raced through its halls, for once not worried about anyone seeing her. All she could think about was Makena, what she'd do and say once she told her what had happened. She reached her bedroom door and crashed through it in a rush.

"Makena," she started. "You'll never believe—"

She stopped cold.

Makena was sitting on her bed, tears streaming down her face. Beside her sat Fedu, who had one hand fettered around her upper arm.

"Hello, Koffi."

Koffi didn't know what to say. This didn't make sense. Why was Fedu here? His lips curled into a smile that cooled her blood.

"It is the most curious thing," he said softly. "Just a short while ago, as I gazed out onto Thornkeep's grounds, I saw something peculiar in the north garden." His eyes flashed at the same moment a dead weight dropped in Koffi's stomach.

"I saw two people who appeared to be coming out of the Mistwood that borders these grounds," he said, "which, of course, should be impenetrable and impossible." His eyes narrowed. "And yet, there you were. How did you do it?"

Words pressed against the back of Koffi's teeth, but she kept her mouth shut. If she told Fedu what her affinity with the splendor was, their plan was done before it'd even started. There'd be no leaving Thornkeep at all, and no doubt several of the darajas who'd helped plan with her would face punishment. But if she didn't speak . . . her eyes met Makena's, desperate.

"I know you are fond of barters, Koffi," said Fedu. "So I will make you yet one more: You have until midnight tonight to come to me willingly and tell me what your true affinity is." Without warning, Fedu rose, yanking Makena to her feet. "If you do not, Makena will die."

CHAPTER 24

The VALLEY of DEATH

Ekon stared up at the vast wall of white before him, motionless.

For a few seconds, as he studied it, he felt a strange sense of familiarity that he didn't understand; he'd certainly never been to this place before. Slowly, though, the recognition dawned on him. The wall before him looked like an enlarged version of the wall he'd once scaled at Baaz Mtombé's zoo the night he'd gone after Koffi. He remembered it so vividly, the determination he'd had to get over it then.

That wasn't at all what he felt now.

Themba took a few steps forward so that she was only feet away from the mist. Ekon wanted to pull her back, to tell her to get away from it, but he didn't know why. So far, the mist had done nothing at all but loom before them in a swirling mass of white. In a way, it was almost beautiful, but Ekon didn't trust it. He watched as Themba crept closer, her hand raised.

"What do you make of this?" he asked.

"I'm not entirely sure," she said. "This mist . . . it isn't natural. It's been created—but by what, I do not know."

"This is the best lead we have to get to Koffi," he said. "So how do we get past this wall?"

In answer, Themba pursed her lips. "I don't think we get past it at all," she finally said. "I think . . . we're going to have to go through it."

Ekon swallowed. He'd been afraid she might say that.

"Listen, boy," she said. "I don't know exactly what will happen when we do, but whatever does, *don't* let go. Keep your eyes straight ahead, and don't stop for any reason." She held his gaze. "No matter *what* happens, do you understand?"

"Yes." He shook her hand for emphasis. "I'm ready."

Themba took a deep breath before closing her eyes. Slowly, the hand that was holding Ekon's started to warm.

"How are you—?"

"Shh," she chided. Without warning, she took a step forward, now inches from the mist. Like before, it seemed to reach for her, silvery-white wisps dancing around her face, but she paid no mind as she took another step into the mist, pulling Ekon with her. The minute it touched his skin, Ekon shivered. It was colder than anything he'd ever felt before. Every one of his pores seemed to scream as he and Themba took yet another step forward, and this time, Ekon was nearly submerged in the mist. He resisted the urge to turn around, to get one last look at the open fields behind them, before Themba took another step forward and he was immersed completely. At once, the world went quiet.

"Themba?" he murmured. "Are you . . . okay?"

"Shh." With her free hand, she raised a finger to her lips. She was still standing beside Ekon, but in the mist she was getting more and more difficult to see. "Keep your eyes forward."

Ekon obeyed. Before them, he saw nothing but whiteness, swirling and coiling through the air in transparent ribbons. It was unnerving. The two of them were alone here, but he couldn't entirely allay the feeling that they were being watched, that something could be waiting just a few feet ahead. Ekon reached out, trying to feel his way through the opacity.

And then a hand grabbed at his wrist.

Ekon screamed and reeled back as a person seemed to float toward him through the mist. The figure before him was horrifying. He couldn't tell if it was male or female. Their skin had a slightly grayish tinge to it, and the place where their eyes should've been was hollow and empty. They did not move as they stared, slack-jawed, at him; they only stood with their arms extended, reaching for him. He thought he heard a low, wispy moan escape the figure's mouth.

"What the—?"

"Back away!"

Ekon felt a different hand, warmer, snatch his upper arm and pull him back. Themba. Her eyes had opened again and she was staring at the figure warily. "And be quiet."

Ekon lowered his voice. "What is that?"

"Something we don't want to upset," she said tersely. Slowly, she and Ekon maneuvered around the creature, which was still staring off into the nothingness as though it had forgotten they were there. A few steps forward and it disappeared into the mist again. Ekon fought a shiver.

They continued their walk carefully, moving in a quiet shuffle. Gradually Themba closed her eyes again.

Just keep moving straight, he thought to himself. *Just keep moving straight.*

The problem was, it was impossible to discern any sense of direction in the mist; they could have been moving in a straight line or circles and he wouldn't have known the difference. The longer they walked, the more uneasy Ekon felt. He stopped short when he thought he saw a slight movement a few feet ahead of them, a large ripple.

"Themba..."

"Hush, boy." Themba still had her eyes closed.

Ekon started to speak, then stopped. He'd just seen another movement, this time to his immediate left. In the distance, he heard a shrill keening sound, like a hawk or an eagle.

"Themba," he said as quietly as he could, "I really think we should—"

His words were cut off by a scream, and then Ekon saw them.

A mass of people were approaching them. At least, Ekon thought they were people—or had been at one point. Like the figure he'd seen before, these people were devoid of color, washed-out. They did not appear to be running, but Ekon was still unnerved by how quickly they seemed to be closing the gap between them. He jerked his arm, and Themba opened her eyes. Her mouth opened in horror.

"Ekon, run!"

Ekon needed no further prompt as he let go of Themba's hand and tore away. He felt more than heard Themba move with him, turning back the way they'd come. He raised his arms to cover his face as the gray people fell upon them, cringing as their hands began to grab at him. Something wasn't right about their touch, their fingers felt hard and stiff like bones, too cold. One of them grabbed at the back of Ekon's tunic with a surprisingly strong grip and yanked, throwing him off-balance. Ekon heard moans rising from the crowd. He heard hissing, the gnashing of teeth, and a constant wailing sound in the distance. He felt himself being whirled around as the one who'd grabbed him turned his body so that they were face-to-face. To his horror, he found himself looking not at a man, but at a child. The little boy couldn't have been older than twelve, but there were bags under his eye sockets. He wore no clothes, and his belly was swollen and distended. He bared his teeth as he stared at Ekon with gaping holes where his eyes should have been.

"No!" Ekon tried to pull away, but the boy's grip was unrelenting. Other figures were closing in now, they'd be upon him in seconds . . .

"Away!"

Ekon's head snapped to the right. Themba was running toward him with her arms out wide, as though she were pushing against something invisible from either side of her body. There was a sheen of sweat on her brow.

"Stay next to me!" she said, panting. "Come on!"

The gray figures raised their arms as Themba and Ekon ran, shielding themselves. Ekon guessed that whatever Themba was doing—something with the splendor—was repelling the figures and keeping them at bay. He ducked behind her and tried to stay on her heels as she charged through the crowd. It was difficult to do; Themba was both shorter and slower than him, and every few feet Ekon had to force himself to slow down to avoid running into her. He looked over Themba's shoulder and did a double take. He couldn't tell if he was imagining it, but up ahead the mist looked to be changing in color; it was getting lighter and less opaque. He thought he could see something beyond it, the start of what looked like green grass. They were almost through.

Just a little farther, a voice in his head encouraged. Themba was still pushing through the crowd, and the gray figures were still staying back. A little farther.

Ekon let his fingers tap at the air, trying to find a count. He could measure the distance between them and that opening. *Thirty feet . . . twenty-seven feet . . .*

"Ekon."

Ekon stopped short at the voice that had called his name. Themba kept running, and he felt whatever shield of protection she had created fading from him as they grew farther apart, but he couldn't make his feet move. That voice, the one that had called his name, was distinct and familiar, even if he didn't want it to be.

Impossible, said something in his own head. *It's not possible.*

But when Ekon turned, he saw the face that he knew he would. The man was standing in the midst of the gray figures, his skin the same faded quality as theirs. His beard was neatly trimmed, and the clothes he'd worn—now torn and covered in brambles— had once been regal. He wore the uniform of a warrior. Ekon stared at his father's ghostlike figure.

"B-Baba?"

The figure didn't answer, only stared. In his periphery, Ekon saw the other figures circling him, watching to see what he would do. He knew he should run, catch up to Themba again, but he still couldn't move. He couldn't even count. He could only stare. The figure that looked like Baba slowly raised his hand, pointing at Ekon. He opened his gaping mouth and in a horrible, rasping voice said:

"You ... killed ... me."

"No." Ekon shook his head emphatically as he felt the empty gazes of the other gray figures turn on him. There seemed to be a palpable change in the air as some of them licked their lips, others inclining their heads and taking a step forward. "No!" Ekon repeated, louder. "No, Baba, I didn't kill you. The Shetani didn't either. It was—" But the words abandoned him as the figures pressed in. Baba's face contorted, and Ekon watched as his eye sockets grew larger, as his open mouth elongated. His skin turned waxen, and the rasp from his throat grew louder as he stepped forward. This time, none of them needed to grab Ekon to keep him still. He sank to his knees.

"Killed me ...," the Baba figure said. "You killed me."

I didn't, thought Ekon. It wasn't me. He knew it was true, but that didn't seem to matter now. The mist was growing thicker and darker; he couldn't see anything but the gray figures all around him. His breath grew short as he felt his mouth pop open. Suddenly the air didn't feel as cold anymore.

"Ekon!"

Someone else was calling his name from far away, but Ekon didn't move. It was easier now to be still, to be like Baba.

"Ekon! Get up!" Themba was standing over him, a plea in her eyes. She was drenched in sweat, and her headwrap was askew. She bent over and tried to pull him to his feet. "Get up!"

The gray figures were pressing in again, but this time, Themba wasn't conjuring a shield to keep them back. Maybe she couldn't. Ekon let her pull him to his feet again. She stared around at the gray figures, breathing hard.

"I understand you can't let us both go." She raised her voice so that it would carry, but Ekon still heard the tremor in it. "But I offer you a barter. Let the boy go on, and take me instead."

Ekon snapped from his reverie at once. "Themba, no—"

"Hush, boy," Themba snapped. She looked straight ahead now, at the figure that looked like Baba. Ekon followed her gaze and saw the figure was looking at her with a curious expression, as though considering. Themba jutted out her chin.

"Do you accept it?"

A long pause passed before the Baba figure slowly nodded. He lifted one hand, and as though he'd given some kind of silent command, the other gray figures backed away from Ekon and descended on Themba. She shivered violently as their hands found her, grabbing on to her arms and legs and neck, but she did not move. Ekon watched in terror.

"Themba!" he shouted. "Don't—"

"*Go*, Ekon." Themba was closing her eyes now, and there was a disturbing resignation in her voice. "Go."

"But—"

"Find my granddaughter," she said calmly. "*Find* her, and take her home to . . . to her mother."

Ekon started to shake. "There has to be another way to do this. There has to—"

"The barter is struck, boy," said Themba. She winced as the gray figures began to tug at her clothes, her hair, but she remained still. "It's all right, *go*."

Ekon felt himself backing away, even though everything inside of him wanted to stay. He watched Themba get smaller, lost in a sea of gray as the figures continued to swarm her. He made himself turn and run when he heard the first scream.

He ran until he could hear the wails and moans no longer.

Themba is dead.

Three words, and Ekon felt each of them drop into the pit of his stomach with heavy finality. He shuddered as each one embedded itself into the walls of his mind and laid down roots that couldn't be ripped out without pain. He felt them pollinate and grow, spreading until they consumed his thoughts.

Dead. Themba was dead.

Ekon couldn't erase the last image he had of Themba's face. There'd certainly been a calm there, a determination he'd grown used to seeing in the old woman, but he knew there'd been other emotions there too—fear, pain, agony. He didn't know what those ghostlike beings had done to Themba, and selfishly he didn't want to find out.

Coward, said a voice in his mind.

Ekon ignored it and pressed on, hurrying. This deep into the mist, he could barely see his own hands in front of him. It was unnerving, and too similar to another kind of mist: the one he remembered from his time with Koffi in the Greater Jungle. On that particular occasion, he and Koffi had been knocked unconscious and had woken up to find their things stolen by a giant spider. Ekon hurried his steps, counting each one as he went on.

One-two-three. One-two-three. One-two-three.

The air was cooling with each step, raising goose bumps on his skin and sending his teeth chattering. In a matter of minutes, the feeling in his fingertips was gone, and his nostrils began to burn. He shook his head until the temptation to sit down and curl up in a ball subsided.

Koffi was somewhere in this strange place, and he would find her, he just had to keep going. *One-two-three.* With each step forward, he imagined himself getting closer and closer to her. He would find her, then take her to the Kusonga Plains, just like they'd planned. He would find her, he had to.

But what if you don't? asked a sinister voice in his head.

You have failed so many people, so many times, said that voice. Ekon heard the vitriol in it, the mocking. *You failed Koffi when you didn't stop Fedu from taking her. And now you've failed Themba. She's dead because of you.*

The voices, the monsters in his head were all he could hear now, all he could feel as they tore at his insides. In this mist, in this desolate place, it would be all too easy to give in to them. His breathing slowed, and he felt himself begin to surrender.

And then he saw light up ahead.

At first, he wasn't sure if it was real or one more illusion, but no . . . the closer he got, the closer he could discern it; the trees and mist around him were beginning to thin, and he thought he saw the barest hint of a green lawn up ahead. He quickened his steps, breaking into a full-fledged run. He crashed through the last of the trees, bracing himself for whatever might be on the other side of them, and then he stopped. He was standing at the edge of a garden.

Its flowers varied, but they were all some shade of deep crimson red. To his right he saw a building that looked similar to the stable found at the Temple of Lkossa, and way past them—straight ahead—he saw a large black stone building, its many windows set aglow in shades of yellow and orange.

What was this place?

"Stop."

Ekon jumped as a sudden voice speared through the silence. It was low, rich, and there was a hint of a growl in it, but it wasn't Fedu's at least. Slowly, he raised his face to the voice's speaker. It was a young man who looked to be about his age, with brown skin and dark hair. He was frowning.

"Who are you?" There was a tremble in the young man's voice as his eyes shot from Ekon to the trees he'd just emerged from. Ekon didn't understand his fear—he was the one without a weapon in this situation. Slowly he raised his empty hands.

"My name is Ekon Okojo," he said slowly. "I'm sorry, I didn't mean to trespass. I was just looking for my friend. I thought she might be here."

This seemed to catch the young man off guard. "Friend?" he asked incredulously. "Who's your friend?"

"Koffi," said Ekon. "Her name is Koffi."

Ekon watched as the young man's eyes widened. Something seemed to be dawning on him slowly.

"Look." Ekon stepped forward. "No disrespect, but I really, really need to find my friend. I think she may be in some kind of danger—"

"Koffi is in danger."

New fear climbed up Ekon's throat. "You know her? You know Koffi?"

The young man nodded, and Ekon thought he saw fatigue in his eyes, a matching fear.

"My name is Zain," he said. "Come with me."

PART FOUR

LOVE IS A CROCODILE IN THE RIVER OF DESIRE.

The Night Zoo

RASHIDA

I look into my daughter's eyes, and I hate them.

It's not because they're not beautiful; they're colored a lovely deep brown, and when the sunlight catches them just so, I see flecks of gold. No, I don't hate them because of their color, I hate them because they don't belong to me, or to my husband. Those eyes are unmistakably, undeniably the Cobra's. No doubt if I stood my daughter beside her, some might even think Koffi was *her* child.

"Mama!"

My heart skips a beat as I catch Koffi grinning at me. There is an admiration and a love in that look I never want to lose a single piece of. "Can we go?"

There was a time when I was like her, when I looked forward to market days. I cast around our tiny home, at the welcome mat that's too worn and the curtains that are too tattered. Koffi doesn't see any of those things, she just sees home. She doesn't know that it won't be our home for much longer.

"One minute, little ponya seed," I say as sweetly as I can. "Just a moment." I pop my head into my bedroom and eye Lesego. He is sitting in the room, surrounded by boxes. When he feels my gaze, he looks up at me and offers a small smile.

"This is just about it," he says with a sigh. "The new buyers have agreed to take everything here, so we won't have to worry about carrying anything. We'll stay the night, then leave in the morning."

So we won't have to worry. He speaks as though we have a choice in leaving our things behind. I bite back the words I want to say, and nod instead.

"I'm going to take Koffi to the market with me. I still have a few last-minute errands to do before . . . our appointment."

"All right, I'll be here." He stands and, in the length of a few strides, crosses the room to take my hand in his. He kisses the back of it and meets my gaze.

"I love you, Rashida."

"You too."

His eyes dim just slightly, and a familiar guilt pools in the pit of my stomach, but I ignore it. I still love Lesego, but there are days I'm not so sure I'm *in* love anymore. I don't know how to say those kinds of words aloud, so I say nothing at all.

"Mama!"

We look up as Koffi's voice brings us back to the present. I peck Lesego's cheek a final time before forcing a smile and going to find Koffi. She's standing in the front door's frame, looking impatient.

"Let's go, Mama!"

I take her hand and leave the house, closing the door quietly behind us.

Koffi doesn't keep hold of my hand for long. I remember how, when she was first learning to walk, she used to take hold of the hem of my dress when she was trying to stand. She squeezed the worn fabric tight in her fist with a determination I admired, but she doesn't do that anymore. Now she walks and runs on her own, looking over her shoulder less and less. It's a beautiful thing, and a terrifying thing, watching her become an entire person before my eyes. I was so scared when I learned I was carrying her, but I'm starting to believe that was the easy part. When Koffi was inside me, we were inextricably attached, her heart beating alongside mine. Now she is outside in the world, feeling, growing, living, and so too a piece of me is out in the world—exposed, fragile.

"Mama, look!" Koffi stops her funny waddle-run to look back at me. Her tiny pink tongue protrudes from her lips as she squints in concentration and wiggles her fingers. I tense as I see tiny flickers of light hover around her hands.

"Koffi!"

The smile drops from her face as I run to close the gap between us and close my hand over hers. "Don't do that again, do you hear me?"

Koffi frowns. "Why, Mama?"

"Because . . ." I pause, searching for the right words. "Because it's a bad thing."

Koffi cocks her head, and the gesture is so reminiscent of my mother that I have to resist cringing. "But it doesn't *feel* like a bad thing?"

"It is." I snatch her hand again and lead her down the road.

It'll go away, a voice in my head assures me. *It's just a phase. It won't last. She's not like Mama. She's not a daraja. She can't be.*

I repeat those words to myself until my heartbeat steadies again.

She's not a daraja. She can't be.

I don't want to think about what it means if I'm wrong.

Koffi tugs at my arm as we move through the market's winding streets, but I keep her close to me.

This place used to bring me so much joy when I was a little girl, and even when I was a young woman, but that's gone now. I pass one of the shops I used to visit as a teenager, one of the ones Nyah introduced me to when were younger. Grief stabs in my chest when I think of my old friend.

It's been a year since her body was found along the Greater Jungle's edge, since she was killed by the creature they call the Shetani. I know she wouldn't have wanted me to, but I pushed two shabas into her palms before they wrapped her in her shrouds, tokens for her to pay her way into the next life. I miss her all the time.

We move through the market quickly and carefully. People are murmuring that there's been another attack by the Shetani, and the news fills the streets with a palpable sense of anxiety. I've heard some say that darajas are to blame for it, that the few who remain in the city are the ones summoning it from the jungle. Even though I know it's not true, I don't correct them anymore. There are barely any darajas left in Lkossa; the ones who used to live here are gone, hiding, or dead.

Koffi skips and stumbles beside me as I near the grocer's cart. In my head, I'm preparing a speech.

We don't have the money for you this time, but Lesego has a potential new job. He'll have the full amount soon . . .

I swallow a lump in my throat as we approach the grocer, and draw myself up to full height. He is a wizened man with a nose that reminds me of a squashed tomato. As soon as his eyes find me in the crowd, they narrow. I stop before him.

"Do you have the rest of the money?" he asks.

I take a deep breath. "Not yet. But I wanted to let you know that it's coming really, really soon. Lesego might have a new job offer—"

"Pfft." The grocer is already shaking his head. He waves my words away with a dismissive hand. "Don't bother with yet another excuse, girl, I know I'm never getting that money back. I should never have loaned it to your good-for-nothing husband in the first place. I trust Lesego as far as I can throw him."

The insult isn't for me, but I wince anyway.

"Wait." I open the flap of my shoulder bag and dig around. "I . . . I can't cover Lesego's full debt today, but I can put something toward it." My fingers search the contents of the bag until they reach the cloth at its very bottom, and my heart sinks to my stomach. My coin purse is gone. I look around, wondering if in my distraction I was pickpocketed. But no, as soon as that thought comes to mind, I know the truth. My bag and my coin purse stay in my house under the slip of my pillow, and only one person knows that.

Lesego.

He wouldn't see it as stealing; he probably hadn't even meant to. He forgets to tell me things sometimes, borrows money for his

business and doesn't remember to tell me, but . . . but he's my husband. What's mine is his, what's his is mine. We're married, which
means we share everything. But that now means I have no money
at all, not even for stale bread.

"What's wrong, Mama?" My heart pinches at Koffi's wide,
worried eyes. The grocer watches us, waiting.

Tears burn in my eyes, but I blink them away before she can
see. "Nothing, ponya seed." I don't meet the grocer's eye as I mut-
ter, "We'll come back later." It takes every bit of control I have to
stay calm as I steer her away from the grocer and into the moving
crowds of people.

This day can't get any worse.

We're almost to the end of the market when I hear it. At first,
I'm sure it's in my imagination, but then . . . no. I hear it again. My
name.

"Binti!"

No. It can't be, not here. I swivel, looking over my shoulder
while simultaneously trying to herd Koffi forward, but then my
eyes lock on her face.

Mama.

My mother is pushing through the crowd as fast as she can,
moving against the waves of people.

"Binti! Binti, wait!"

No. A memory returns to me, a day not so long ago when I let
my mama meet Koffi. It took minutes for her to start badgering
me, to start warning me that Koffi could be a daraja like her. I
cannot allow Koffi to hear things like that, I cannot allow them to
meet again.

"Binti!" My mother is dangerously close now. She probably

can't see my daughter, who's too short, but she will in a moment. I do the only thing I can think to do: I turn and kick the leg out from one of the fruit stalls. A cascade of melons tumbles out into the street, and people move and shuffle to get out of the way as the vendor bemoans his ruined produce. It's the momentary distraction I need. Quickly, I haul Koffi away. I can still see my mother, neck craning as she tries to find us, looking in the wrong direction. My heart pounds like a drum with each step we take away from her, and I imagine what she could do to me if our eyes met. Maybe she'd make me stop walking, make me give Koffi over to her. A worse thought crosses my mind—what if she uses her powers against Koffi, makes her leave me? I hurry my steps.

"Mama! Mama—ow! You're hurting me!"

"Huh?" I look down, dazed. My grip around my daughter's arm is viselike, painfully tight. She is scowling up at me with a ferocity that reminds me so much of my mother that I want to back away from her. Immediately, I release her.

"Sorry, little one." I force myself to smooth her hair, to sound calm. "I just didn't want to get caught up in all that mess."

"That's okay, Mama," says my daughter breezily. She's already forgiven me, and I don't deserve it.

"I forgot my money," I lie. "We'll have to do our shopping another time."

"All right, Mama." My daughter looks over her shoulder, visibly puzzled. "Mama, who was that woman calling us?"

I stiffen. "What woman?"

"The nice lady," my daughter presses. "The one who followed us?"

I grab hold of her hand. "There was no woman, Koffi."

"There was!" Koffi struggles to keep up with me. "Why did she call you that name, Mama?"

"She confused me with someone else." I say nothing more as I pull her along, trying to keep my face smooth. Sweat dampens the neckline of my dress, a dizziness threatens my vision, and I want to vomit. I keep imagining my mother coming toward me. My mother, who's never met my daughter, my mother, who I haven't seen in four years.

"Who was she, Mama?"

"Nobody," I whisper. "Nobody at all."

By the time we return home, Lesego is waiting outside the door.

He waves, and I return the gesture, careful not to look at the sign nailed to what was once our front door: SOLD. That single word makes it all feel that much more real.

"How'd your errands go?" Lesego asks.

Koffi looks to me, uncertain, but I shake my head.

"Fine," I say as I let go of her hand and let her run to her father. "It was fine."

"Good." Lesego turns his focus from me to Koffi. He crouches down so that they are level with each other before giving her a serious look.

"Are you ready, Koffi?"

"Ready for what, Baba?"

"Me, you, and Mama are going on a little adventure," he says. A string in my heart tweaks as she lets him take her hand and squeeze; she trusts him entirely. "It's going to be lots of fun."

"What kind of adventure?" Koffi asks.

I watch Lesego carefully then. He has yet to tell me how he plans to explain things to Koffi, but Lesego meets my gaze only for a moment before, without warning, he lifts Koffi up and plops her onto his shoulders. She shrieks in delight.

"That's the surprise!" he says, pretending to tickle her sides. "Let's go!"

※

Lesego leads the way, with Koffi on his shoulders, until we reach the start of the Kazi District. My heart pangs as I look up and down its streets. The time in my life in which my mother and I lived here is so long ago now that sometimes it doesn't even feel real anymore. For a moment, I have the strangest temptation to keep going up the road and follow the path back to what was once our home. I stamp it out as Lesego stops before one of the smaller and shabbier buildings on the main road. Judging by the dimness of the windows, it's empty. I look to Lesego, confused.

"Are you sure this is the right place?"

Lesego nods. "He told me to meet him here after noon." Lesego shrugs. "That's now."

A few more minutes pass before I discern a figure coming toward us from down the road. His features are difficult to see against the afternoon sunlight, but I'm immediately sure that this man is bigger than any I have ever seen. His robes swish around his ankles as he lumbers forward. When he catches sight of us, his steps falter.

"Can I help you?" His voice is gruff.

"Uh . . ." Next to me, Lesego suddenly sounds unsure. "Uh, hello. My name is Lesego. You and I met a few days ago, you told me to come here to discuss . . . employment opportunities?"

The man takes a step closer, and now I can see him more clearly. He has blond-dyed dreadlocks that fall to his elbows, and paunchy brown skin that has almost certainly seen better days. He stares between us a moment, frowning, as though trying to recall such a conversation. Then:

"Ah yes, Lesego. Of course. Please forgive my momentary lapse, of course I've been expecting you." He looks up at Koffi. "And this must be your little one, and"—he turns to me—"your lovely wife, Bashida."

"Rashida."

"My name is Baaz Mtombé," he says quickly. "Right this way. Sorry, if you'd just allow me to get around you . . ." He squeezes past us and pulls a key from his pocket to open the door of the building we're still standing in front of. There's a bit of maneuvering, and then he gestures, welcoming us in.

The interior of Baaz's shop isn't much more promising than its exterior; in fact, I'm not even sure it is his shop at all. The room Lesego and I enter is sparsely furnished with only a small round table and chairs in varying states of disrepair set in the middle of the room. Baaz takes a seat first, and I notice he takes the best of the three chairs for himself.

"Please," he says, "sit."

Carefully, Lesego lifts Koffi from his shoulders and hands her to me. Koffi looks nervous now, but I take her and hold her in my arms. Then Lesego and I both sit.

"Now," Baaz begins. "I appreciate you both coming to speak with me today. I've already had some introductory conversations with Lesego, and he tells me that you—"

"Poo-poo head!" Koffi shouts, glaring at Baaz.

Lesego and I exchange a look of horror before I turn to my daughter.

"Koffi! What is wrong with you?"

"Apologies, sir," Lesego says quickly. "She's only five, still learning."

"Quite all right, quite all right," Baaz says. He offers Koffi a smile, but I notice it doesn't quite reach his eyes. "Children will be . . . children."

In answer, Koffi gives him a withering look so reminiscent of my mother that I nearly choke. Even Baaz seems unsettled for a moment before he addresses both of us again.

"Lesego, Bashida, I want to get right to the point," he says. "I know that the two of you are facing financial hardship, and I do feel for your situation."

Financial hardship. When he says the words aloud, there is no longer a place for me to hide from their reality. I feel myself getting smaller by the second.

"What I'm offering you is fairly straightforward." Baaz withdraws a slightly wrinkled bit of yellow parchment from his bag, straightens it, then places it on the table before us. Text covers most of the page in a tiny font, but my eyes fix on the bolded words written in swooping red calligraphy at the very top:

BAAZ MTOMBÉ'S LEGENDARY NIGHT ZOO

"The arrangement is simple," he says. "First, I will give you the money you need to pay off your debts in full."

I look up sharply. "In full?"

"In full," Baaz repeats. "Lesego tells me your debts total to about fifty thousand dhabus at present. That's a sum easy enough to make disappear."

My heart is pounding now, and even Lesego looks visibly excited.

"In exchange, you will sign agreements promising to pay back the debt I have resolved on your behalf. You will not have to pay me monetarily, but through fair labor at my zoo. I'm in need of maintenance workers, sometimes called 'beastkeepers,' to maintain the grounds and occasionally tend to the animals I keep there."

I pause. "Are the animals at the zoo . . . safe?"

"Oh, *absolutely*." Baaz offers me a smile that I'm sure is supposed to be friendly, but all I can focus on is the too-bright glint of his golden incisors. "These are generally tame, domesticated beasts. If you've ever looked after a dog or cat, you'll have all of the expertise you need."

When neither Lesego nor I immediately answer, he adds: "Additionally, we offer on-site training and support for new employees."

Lesego nods, but now I have questions. Before I can go on, Baaz continues.

"I always want to ensure that those who work for me feel valued, and so, in addition to employment, you'll be provided with lodging and three meals each day—provided you complete each day's minimum work requirement."

"What about our daughter?" I cut in. "She's five years old. I . . . I want her to have an education, not just work all day."

Baaz gives me a placating look. "Of course, of course, Bashida, I understand your concern. You certainly will have time, after work, to give your little one as much education as you'd like."

It's not the answer I was hoping for, but Lesego gives me a re-assuring pat on the small of my back.

"We really appreciate your offer, Bwana Mtombé," Lesego says. "It sounds like a promising opportunity. If my wife and I could just have some time to consider—"

"Oh, I'm afraid that's not possible." Baaz smiles again. "There are other applicants who are just as interested as you and your wife. I can give you a few minutes to discuss, but you'll need to make a decision this afternoon."

"Oh." I watch Lesego falter. "I see . . . Well, then, could we just have a moment to discuss?"

"Of course!" Baaz clapped. "I'll give you five minutes to your-self." He rises and moves to the other end of the room. I realize it is as much privacy as we can expect, and lean in to Lesego.

"My love, I don't know about this," I whisper at a volume I hope Baaz can't hear. "We haven't had much time to read over this." I ges-ture to the contract again. The print somehow looks even smaller and harder to read now. "It seems like a lengthy commitment."

"It won't be." Lesego smiles. "Just until we pay off the debts. When you multiply the hourly wage by the hours in a day, we'll have that paid off in no time at all."

I look down at Koffi in my arms. Her eyes are barely open now, and something pulls in my chest at the sight of her so vulnerable. I look up and meet Lesego's gaze. "Are you *sure* this is the right thing to do?"

Lesego nods. "This is the fastest way to pay off the debts, Rashida," he says. "The only other options are . . . not exactly aboveboard." He doesn't have to say more for me to understand. There are, of course, other ways to make a lot of money fast, but none that are legal. I've spent my whole life trying to separate myself from things like that; I won't stop now.

"All right." I nod slowly. "Then let's do it."

Lesego stands, takes my head in both his hands, and kisses my forehead. "This is our fresh start," he murmurs against my skin. "You'll see. Things will get better."

With all my heart I want to believe his words. I just can't explain the sinking feeling as Lesego turns to where Baaz is standing.

"Baaz!" Lesego calls. When Baaz turns around to face him, he corrects himself. "Um, Bwana Mtombé?"

"Hm?"

"My wife and I . . . we've made our decision. We accept your offer."

"Excellent," Baaz says, approaching us with a quill and ink. "Just sign here."

We rise the next morning at dawn.

There is a quiet in the air as we prepare the last of our things, tying up boxes we will not take and folding clothes we will never wear again. As of today, this house is no longer ours; this is our last morning in it. I start to gather the last remnants of our food—a few scraps of bread and some fruit that hasn't quite expired—but Lesego puts his hand over mine.

"We won't need it," he says brightly. "Baaz said three square meals a day."

I hesitate, then put the food down.

"Mama." Koffi stumbles as she walks from our bedroom to me, still rubbing sleep from her eyes. "Where are we going?"

I brave a small smile and scoop her up into my arms. "Do you remember how yesterday Baba said we were going on an exciting new adventure?" I take a deep breath. "Well, it's finally time for that adventure to start."

"Oh." For several seconds, Koffi says nothing. She rests her head against my shoulder, and I can't see her face. Another moment passes before she says, "Mama, I'm sleepy."

"I know, ponya seed."

"Can I go back to sleep?"

"Not right now, sweetie."

Since we are not taking any of our possessions, per our contract, we are ready to leave in just a few more minutes' time. Outside, Lesego leaves the key to our home under the front door's mat, then turns to me. There is excitement in his eyes, the look he always gets before he begins any new venture.

"We should head off," he said. "Baaz says work begins at sunrise." He treks ahead of me, walking down the road in quick, jaunty steps. I'm less eager to go. I have the uncanny feeling that it will be some time before I walk this road again. In my arms, Koffi squirms against my chest.

"Will it be fun, Mama?" Her head tilts to meet my gaze as she asks her question. "The new adventure?"

"The *most* fun." I once thought there was no taste worse than that of hunger; I understand now that lying to my daughter is far worse.

Satisfied, Koffi tucks her head back under my chin and nuzzles into my neck. I feel her heartbeat fluttering against my own. Perhaps she is as nervous as I am.

Lesego and I do not speak as we leave Greater Lkossa, but I feel its buildings watching my passage. The air is dry even now, the prelude to a day that I'm sure will be full of relentless heat. It occurs to me that, as much as Baaz told us about our jobs, I have no idea what his premises actually look like—I hope there is some shade.

"We're almost there," says Lesego, pointing. We're out of the city now, and up ahead, on a hill, I make out the bleary image of what looks like a walled brick fortress.

"Mama." Koffi's tiny voice hums against my neck. "That place looks *scary*."

"I know, sweetheart." I comb my hand over her head. "But I promise it'll be fine. You're going to like it."

She doesn't say anything as we keep walking.

"We'll have fun, you'll see." I'm not sure if I'm saying the words for her or for myself. "And we'll be safe there."

Safe. I wrap that word around me like armor as my steps quicken.

Safe. I cling to that word like it's my last hope, because in truth, it is.

Safe. I sheathe that word like a weapon as I square my shoulders and approach the towering front gates of the Night Zoo.

CHAPTER 25

A NEW PLAN

When Koffi closed her eyes, she saw Makena's face.

It seared in her mind, burned each time she remembered the raw fear she'd seen in the girl's eyes as Fedu had dragged her away. The god's words echoed in her thoughts.

You have until midnight tonight to come to me willingly and tell me what your true affinity is. If you do not, Makena will die.

Koffi sat on the edge of her bed, pulled back to another moment from early in her time at Thornkeep, the time Makena had been taken into the Mistwood. The words from that day came back unbidden.

This is your fault. Your fault.

That time, she'd been able to rally, to go after Makena, to *do* something. Not now. The choice was clear-cut. Fedu had given her a mere hour to make her decision, and either one she made would end in loss. If she confessed to him what her affinity was, if she showed it to him, Fedu would know that his work could begin, he'd use her, and this continent would be upended. She thought back to the elders from the Night Zoo, the way they talked about the Rupture. Utter destruction. Utter chaos on a tenfold scale. That was what waited for her if she told Fedu what she could do. But if she did not . . . Makena would die.

Tears stung Koffi's eyes now. She tried to hold them in, but they fell and streaked her cheeks anyway. More terrible thoughts flooded her mind the longer she sat in the quiet. If Fedu knew that she'd gone into the Mistwood, who was to say he wasn't already rounding up other darajas she'd been seen with to ask questions? She thought of Njeri, Amun, and the darajas they'd recruited to join them in their plan; some of them had only just agreed to leave Thornkeep. *This* was the reward for their bravery.

Her thoughts were cut off as a jingling sound filled the air. Koffi looked again to the bedroom doors, tense. It wasn't midnight already, was it? Her breath hitched as one of the doors swung open, revealing the silhouettes of two people. She barely had time to register it before they were stepping inside. Light illuminated both faces, and Koffi's mouth went dry.

"Koffi?" Ekon was standing before her, his eyes wide.

Koffi tried to open her mouth, but whatever words she thought to say abandoned her as Ekon closed the space between them in three strides. In seconds, she was enveloped by him, lost in his arms, in all the smells she'd forgotten—shea butter, leather, and cedarwood. Fresh tears welled in her eyes as he squeezed her so hard, she thought her ribs would break, but she didn't care.

Ekon. Ekon was here. *Ekon.*

Ekon withdrew from her, his hands still on her shoulders. A smile tugged at his lips, but it didn't reach his eyes. There was a somber quality to them.

426

"You're okay," she whispered.

"And you're in prison, *again*," he said ruefully, casting a glance around the room. He shook his head. "We've really got to stop meeting like this."

"How?" The word escaped Koffi in a choked sob. "How did you do it? How did you get here?"

Ekon tapped his fingers against her shoulder three times. *One-two-three.* And the simple gesture made her want to cry all over again. He held her gaze as he spoke.

"Koffi, I've been looking for you," he said quietly. "From the second you disappeared."

It took a moment for Koffi to process those words, the weight of them. "You have?"

Ekon nodded. "I found someone—your grandmother."

Koffi started. "What?"

"It's a lot, I know." Ekon's fingers tapped faster against her skin. "She . . . she was a daraja, and she *knew* about you, knew who you were, and she wanted to find you too. We got a lead that you might be here, and then we joined this illegal spice-trading gang, and . . ." He stopped, probably in response to the look on Koffi's face.

"You joined a *gang*?"

Ekon smiled again, and this time it did reach his eyes. "I'm full of surprises."

Koffi went back to something else Ekon had just said. "My grandmother," she began. "You said she *was* a daraja. Is she . . . ?"

Some of the light left Ekon's eyes. "Her name was Themba. She helped me get through that mist to find you," he murmured. "But she didn't make it out. I'm sorry."

A snarl of emotions tangled within Koffi then. Confusion.

Loss. Grief. She didn't know how to truly grieve someone she'd never really known, and yet . . . the ache was still there. All this time, she'd wanted to know how she'd come to be a daraja, where that missing piece had come from. Now it was gone.

"Koffi."

She looked up and found Ekon was watching her, his expression serious. "I came here to get you out, to get you away from Fedu. I'm not sure if there's any other way to do that except by going back through the mist, but—"

"Hold on."

Koffi and Ekon both looked up. Zain was still standing at the bedchamber door with his arms crossed, and Koffi started. In the midst of everything, she'd completely forgotten he was there. It was hard to read the look on Zain's face at the moment. The usual laughter in his eyes was gone, but he didn't look angry either. His gaze was trained on Ekon.

"Shouldn't you maybe ask Koffi before you just presume to spirit her away?"

Koffi watched Ekon's face twist into a scowl as he whirled around to look at Zain. "What are you talking about?" There was a growl in his voice. "I'm not *presuming* anything. Koffi never wanted to be here. I'm taking her, and we're leaving." His face turned stormy. "If you try to stop us—"

"Wait." Koffi hated to have to say the word, hated how small her voice sounded. Ekon turned again, confused. "Wait a minute." She moved so that she was standing between Zain and Ekon. It was a strange, uncomfortable feeling, watching the way they eyed each other, their expressions full of uneasiness, distrust. She reached for Ekon, then thought better of it.

"You're right, Ekon," she said slowly. "I *do* want to leave Thornkeep—sooner rather than later—but . . ." She looked to Zain. "But I can't just go, not without the other darajas. They're being kept here too, against their will. And there's something else." She took a deep breath and told them about Makena, about Fedu's ultimatum. Horror spread across Zain's face, and though Ekon had not been in Thornkeep long enough to know any of the other darajas, he seemed to appreciate the severity of the situation. When she'd finished telling them both, Ekon sat down on the bed while Zain leaned against the wall. For several seconds, neither of them spoke, but it was Ekon who broke the silence first.

"Is there any other way?" he asked. "Any other way to get out of Thornkeep?"

Koffi nodded. "There's something else you should know," she said, "about my affinity with the splendor. It's . . . not what you or I initially thought." Quickly, she explained what had happened in the Mistwood the first time she'd gone into it and what had happened tonight when she'd returned to it with Zain.

Ekon's eyes widened. "Well, that changes things, doesn't it?" he said. "We could still get everyone out, if someone can find Makena."

"If Fedu has Makena, it'll be almost impossible to get to her now," said Zain, shaking his head. He started to pace. "He'll want to make sure there's no way for us to save her except to do what he wants."

"But even still," Ekon pressed. "If we could get to her, and if we could get out of Thornkeep with Koffi leading us, how would we go about doing that?"

"Originally, we planned to walk," said Koffi. "We had a plan to leave under the cover of night, when everyone was asleep, but that's obviously no longer an option."

Ekon frowned thoughtfully. "So the only way to get out of Thornkeep is through that mist?" He asked the question aloud, though he didn't seem to be waiting for an answer. "I mean, there are no tunnels or passageways that lead under it, and we can't exactly fly over it—"

"Hold on a second." Zain had straightened, his eyes wild. Ekon looked at him, surprised, but Zain's eyes were on Koffi. "*We* can't fly ourselves over the Mistwood, but . . ." He trailed off, and at once Koffi understood. She breathed the single word.

"Kongamato."

"Congo-*what*?" Ekon was looking between them, confused now.

"Never mind." Koffi took a deep breath, looking between them. "I have a new plan, but I need you to trust me."

Ekon and Zain glanced at each other as though seeing who would answer first.

"I trust Koffi," said Zain. "Let me know what you need."

"Same here," said Ekon.

Koffi nodded. "All right," she said. "Here's what we're going to do."

When the two darajas came to Koffi's bedroom, she was ready.

She kept her head down as they opened the door, did her best to look dejected as they forcibly dragged her to her feet and frog-marched her through Thornkeep's halls.

"Don't try anything funny," said one of them, a short daraja from the Order of Mwili. Dumi. Koffi had trained with him once; he'd shown her how he could clean and refresh a person's blood, and he'd been kind, but not anymore. His eyes were set forward, with a coldness in his gaze. The other daraja was from the Order of Akili, Zain's order, but Koffi didn't know her. She bowed her head.

"Of course." Carefully, she dared a glance over her shoulder, back at her bedchamber, empty now. Zain and Ekon had long since gone to take care of their parts of the plan. Koffi closed her eyes.

Please, Koffi prayed. *Please let this work.*

The walk to the north garden felt much shorter than Koffi remembered. One minute, it seemed she was being led out of her bedchamber; in the next, they were walking across the immaculately kept grass. Another bonfire had been started, but this time there was something else beside it: what looked to be a long pole stuck into the ground. Her heart thundered as she laid eyes on Fedu, half-bathed in the roaring fire's light. The darajas of Thornkeep had been summoned again—from here, Koffi couldn't tell which ones. Just past the darajas' circle, in the shadows, she thought she saw the black silhouette of something large and horned, waiting. She shuddered.

"Koffi." Fedu stepped forward, his voice pleasant as ever. "So glad that you could join us."

The two darajas marched her to the center of the circle, then pushed her to her knees before Fedu. The god's eyes twinkled, but there was no warmth in them.

"The midnight hour is upon us," Fedu announced. "I have made Koffi a barter, and now the time has come for her to make

431

her choice. She will tell me what her true affinity to the splendor is, or . . ."

He gestured, and Koffi was finally forced to look at the pole next to the fire. Makena was tied to it, her mouth painfully bound. Dried tear tracks stained her cheeks, and when her eyes found Koffi's, she shook her head subtly. Koffi understood the implicit message in that little movement.

Don't. Don't tell him.

"But before you make your decision," said Fedu, eyes gleaming, "there is another matter I would like to address. It appears that there is an intruder at Thornkeep."

Koffi looked up. "What—?"

She whirled around as, from the shadows of the garden, two more darajas appeared, pinning Ekon's arms down so that he couldn't struggle. His eyes were wide, frantic, as they met Koffi's.

"Koffi, I'm sorry—"

"Silence!" Fedu's voice cracked through the air like a whip. When he turned back to Koffi, there was no laughter in his eyes anymore. "Did you really think a *mortal* could enter my realm without my knowledge?" His voice was little more than a low hiss. "You truly thought it was a matter of hiding him? Yet again, you underestimate me." He nodded to the two darajas still holding Ekon.

"Bring him to me."

CHAPTER 26

A GOOD WARRIOR

Ekon felt the god of death's eyes boring into him as he was marched forward. Still, he kept his head bowed.

"Ekon, it has been too long."

He stole a glance upward after a moment and found that Fedu was staring down at him with a look that might have been called affectionate. It made his skin crawl. The darajas holding on to him stopped several feet before the god and then moved back so that it was only Ekon and Fedu standing in the middle of the lawn. To his right, Koffi was being held on either side by two other darajas. Her eyes were wild as they flitted back and forth between Ekon and Fedu, but the god seemed unbothered.

"You traveled all this way for Koffi?" he asked, voice full of intrigue.

"Yes." Ekon said the word as boldly as he could manage, but even still, he could feel his hands—pinned at his sides—begin to move of their own accord. His fingers tapped a slower, more careful rhythm than usual.

One. Two. Three.

Fedu was standing before him donned in a solid white dashiki and pants, the gleam of his gold chain catching in the bonfire's light. He looked nothing like the old man Ekon knew and remembered from the Temple of Lkossa now, the man who'd called himself Brother Ugo. The god before him stood tall, unblemished, unwrinkled. And yet, Ekon thought he still caught a hint of the old mirth in Fedu's eyes, the same twinkle he'd had when he'd disguised himself as an old man. Conflating the two utterly different characters was disarming.

"I am impressed," said Fedu, massaging his chin. "I always knew you were a head above the other candidates you competed against, the boys you called your peers, but this . . ." He gestured widely. "This determination, this *tenacity*. It is why I picked you so long ago, Ekon. You have always been a good warrior."

Ekon had looked up briefly, but at the words he lowered his gaze again. He was embarrassed to feel tears pricking at his eyes now. *A good warrior.* The words were far too close, too reminiscent of the last conversation he'd had with Fedu in the sky garden.

You were the perfect combination. Keen, desperate for approval. It made you easy to mold into what I needed.

Fedu moved to stand closer to the pole where a girl was tied. Ekon had never seen her before, but he knew from what Koffi had told him that this had to be Makena. She was a slight girl, with large eyes and dark, springy hair. She only had a half second to glance at Ekon before Fedu was upon her. Ekon watched as the god pinched her chin and forced her head up so that she was looking at him. Dread pooled at the base of Ekon's stomach as a cruel smile sliced across Fedu's lips.

"Makena," he said softly. "You see that boy just over there? I want you to pay close attention to him. *He* is going to decide tonight whether you live or die."

Chills broke out over Ekon's skin. Somewhere in the crowd, he thought he heard someone scream.

"What?"

"At first, I thought I might leave it to Koffi." Fedu stepped away from Makena as fresh tears streamed down her face. "She is, after all, Makena's friend. But then you showed up here, and a more interesting idea came to mind. The valiant warrior, come to save his heroine, but forced to do the unthinkable to achieve his mission. I've already made a deal with Koffi, Ekon. Now I will make a deal with *you*." His eyes flashed. "Kill this girl, and I will free Koffi."

"NO!"

Ekon turned in time to see Koffi trying to step forward, straining against the two darajas still arresting her arms. "No, Ekon, don't do it—he's lying!"

"*Am* I?" Fedu tilted his head, as though pondering an entertaining riddle.

"You wouldn't let Koffi go so easily," said Ekon through his teeth. "You still need her."

"True." Fedu nodded. "But I have a feeling Koffi will prove useful to me whether she is in my custody or not."

Ekon frowned. What did he mean, whether she was *in his custody* or not? The god didn't give him any more time to consider the words.

"Make your choice *now*, Ekon Okojo. Her life"—he pointed to Makena—"or *her* freedom." He nodded to Koffi.

Ekon looked from Makena and Koffi again, panicked. Then he swallowed.

"All right, I've made my choice."

Fedu's eyes danced at the same time Makena's eyes widened with terror, but he did not look at the girl.

"*Come,*" said Fedu. "Bow before me."

Ekon's eyes traveled the length between him and Fedu, counting.

One-two-three. One-two-three. One-two-three. Nine steps.

He ignored the frantic beating in his chest and focused on the numbers. Numbers had always made sense. Numbers would always make sense. He took one final breath, then began the walk.

One-two-three. One-two-three. Six steps.

In his imagination, he heard Fahim's voice, a different plea. *You need to come home.*

If that offer had ever really been on the table, it was gone now. Ekon's throat tightened. Even after everything, the Sons of the Six hadn't expelled him from the ranks; they'd offered him one last bridge to redemption. He'd burned it. He could never go back. There was only one path left for honor.

One-two-three. Three steps.

Ekon took the last few steps until he was before Fedu. As an old man, as Brother Ugo, he'd been much shorter; now the god of death was exactly his height. Ekon's eyes shot to the creature still waiting in the shadows. The ichisonga. Koffi had told him about it, told him what it did to people. He eyed its horn and tried to temper the nausea roiling in his gut.

"Your choice?" asked the god.

"I need a knife." Ekon spoke quietly, but he sensed that the entire garden and all present could hear him. From far away, he thought he heard a dry sob, but he didn't look to see who it'd come from.

Fedu grinned, his white teeth gleaming wickedly. He nodded to one of the darajas nearest to him, a young man wearing yellow. When he stepped forward, Ekon saw he had a knife in his hands. He bowed as he gave it to Fedu, who in turn offered its hilt. Ekon looked from it to the god several times, deliberating.

"You wish to kill me?" Fedu murmured. He was still grinning. "You could try. Remember, though, that I am immortal. It will take far more than a common knife to end me."

Ekon had known it was true from the moment he'd asked for the knife, but he still felt something in him deflate as he heard the words aloud. He accepted the knife without a word, feeling its new weight in his palm. He rotated it in his hand, watched its blade glint golden and then orange in the garden's firelight. He looked to Makena and found her eyes were already on him, waiting. They were only a few feet apart. He could get to her in a matter of strides. Six strides, maybe five . . .

"Do it," said the god.

Ekon turned so that he was facing Makena and breathed in, counting slow.

One-two-three. One-two-three. One-two-three.

His grip on the knife tightened as he ignored the sweat slicking his hand now. A breeze brushed his face, cooling against the bonfire's heat. With his free hand, he tapped his fingers and counted one more time.

One-two-three. One-two-three. One-two—

"What are you doing?" Fedu asked. "I told you to—"

Without warning, Ekon pivoted. The movement was effortless—he'd done the duara a hundred times—and yet it seemed to happen slowly. He watched as his blade sliced through the night air in a perfect circle, felt the world blur as he spun around. He caught a glimpse of Fedu's face, a fractional moment of shock, before he buried the blade in the god's chest, in the place his heart should have been. Fedu gasped.

"Zain!" Ekon looked over his shoulder. "NOW!"

A blade wouldn't kill the god of death, but Ekon hadn't needed it to; he'd just needed it to stun him long enough. Already, Zain was running forward, hands raised. Ekon didn't see the splendor as the daraja abruptly stopped, but he felt the wave of it as Zain's eyes widened, as he raised his hands. One by one, darajas around the bonfire fell to their knees, screaming, hands pressed against their ears as though to block out a terrible sound as they screamed. Ekon had known that he was planning to do it, had expected it, but that made it no easier to see. For several seconds, he could only stare at the darajas on the ground—bewildered, transfixed.

"EKON!"

Ekon jolted from his stupor. Koffi was running past him, toward one of the darajas on the ground.

"Makena!" she shouted. "Help her!"

Ekon needed no other prompt. He whirled around and saw Makena there, still tied to the stake. Her eyes were wide with horror. Ekon rushed to her, closing the gap between them and pulling the gag from her mouth as gently as he could. She coughed.

"Sorry," he said sheepishly, moving to the back of the stake to undo the ropes.

"Wait." Makena was still coughing, gasping. "You"—*cough*—"weren't going to"—*cough*—"kill me? That whole thing was an *act*?"

Ekon pursed his lips. "Koffi thinks my acting skills leave a lot to be desired," he said, pulling at the knots. "But I for one think *that* performance deserved several awards."

In the end, it had been Koffi's plan; Ekon just hadn't known if it would work. He gave the knots one more tug, and they loosened enough to fall around Makena's ankles. She stepped away from the stake and rubbed her arms.

"Sorry again," he said, "about the whole pretending-to-kill-you thing."

"It's all right," said Makena mildly. "I'm sure we'll get better acquainted another— NO!"

Ekon followed Makena's terrified gaze, new dread clawing up his throat. Across the lawn, he saw Fedu slowly rising from the ground, pulling the dagger from his chest. He tossed it to the ground, not seeming to notice as the blood oozed from the wound. Not red blood, Ekon noted. Fedu's blood was golden. It soaked his shirt as he stood, but his eyes were set on something ahead of him: Koffi. She had knelt down beside one of the screaming dara-jas and seemed to be looking for something, not aware of Fedu.

"*Koffi!*" Ekon shouted. "Look out!"

Koffi looked up, then flinched. Fedu had already started toward her. He wasn't walking normally—for its simplicity, the knife Ekon had stabbed him with seemed to have had some effect—but he was advancing with a single-minded focus. Ekon's eyes shot back to Koffi, and he was surprised to see she hadn't moved. Why? Fedu was getting closer to her, stumbling, but with a look of that same eerie hunger. Koffi glared back at him, stayed crouched down until he was within only a few feet of her, and then abruptly stood. She gave Fedu one final, withering look, and brought something to her lips—something small and silver. Ekon had seen her withdraw it from the pocket of the daraja she'd been searching and hadn't given any thought to it; now he saw it was a whistle of some sort. Fedu stopped short as he saw it, stricken.

"No!" he said, looking around. "No—"

Ekon watched as Koffi narrowed her eyes, took a deep breath, and blew.

A low rumbling filled the air, and Ekon felt the ground shake underfoot. A chill skittered over his arms as the ichisonga charged forward, but the beast did not have eyes for him or anyone else on the lawns, only Fedu. The god turned as the creature approached, tried to make a run for it, but he was nowhere near fast enough. It happened in seconds. The ichisonga charged, its great gray head lowered as it accelerated into a gallop. It reached Fedu, and a wet, squelching sound filled the air as the creature's long horn impaled Fedu, the tip erupting from his chest. The god let out a terrible scream of pain, but the ichisonga did not slow its charge. Ekon felt another wave of nausea as it tossed its head back and forth, Fedu's limp body still skewered by it, and knocked into the fire. A shower of sparks flew into the air, and the bonfire's towering logs came crashing down, its flames licking hungrily at the garden's green grass and beginning to spread. Ekon backed away, watching for one horrid second before he screamed a single word into the darkness.

"*Run!*"

CHAPTER 27

BEASTS OF RUIN

There was something both frightening and calming about fire.

Perhaps because it was indiscriminatory in what—and who—it consumed. From her place on the north garden's lawns, Koffi watched as the bonfire's flames leaped higher and higher. Around her, the darajas under Zain's illusion were still screaming, and from somewhere even farther than that, Koffi could hear the rough snorts of the ichisonga, the moans as it ran away with Fedu into the darkness. She heard Ekon's shout, an order to run, but she couldn't move. She found herself transfixed as the red-orange flames began to spread past the boundaries of the bonfire in which they'd been contained. The acrid smell of smoke filled the air, burning her lungs and reminding her of another time, in the Night Zoo. There'd been a fire there too, screams like the ones she was hearing now.

"Koffi!"

Koffi started as someone called her name, grabbed her arm. She braced herself, but relaxed when she saw it was Amun next to her. He was as beautiful as ever, but there was terror etched into every detail of his face.

"We have to go," he shouted over the noise around them. "Now! Zain can't hold the darajas loyal to Fedu for much longer."

Zain. The name brought Koffi back into focus. She looked to her right and saw that he was standing in the exact place he'd been before. Koffi realized now that, in all of their practice sessions together, she'd always been the one he'd been creating illusions and delusions for; she'd never actually seen what he looked like when he was using the splendor himself. Zain's face was the picture of calm; he could have been sleeping. Still, when Koffi looked closer, she saw it: Zain's jaw was trembling, and a sheen of sweat glistened on his brow. None of the muscles in his body were tensed, but he looked as though he was under enormous strain. Koffi looked around them. There were at least twenty darajas on the ground, still under his influence. He'd explained before that keeping even one person in an illusion was exhausting; she didn't want to know what doing this might cost him.

"We have to get out of here," said Amun, looking from Zain to her. "Njeri's gathering the darajas who want to leave. Do you have a plan?"

A plan. The word jarred something in Koffi's mind. A plan, yes, she had a plan. She glanced over her shoulder one more time, then shouted, "This way!"

She didn't wait to see if Amun was following before she tore in the direction of Thornkeep's stables. In her periphery, she saw Ekon and Makena running to fall into stride with her, and behind her she heard more footsteps that she hoped belonged to Amun or Njeri. The stables loomed as she drew nearer to them; even at a distance, she could hear the panicked cries and bleats of its inhabitants. The animals' collective sound was a stab between her ribs. She stopped before the stables' doors and turned. Ekon, Makena, and Amun were with her, but no one else. Her heart sank, but she stood straighter when she spoke.

"I don't have the strength or confidence to get everyone through the Mistwood on foot right now," she said. "So our next-best bet is to take the kongamatos."

The reactions she got were exactly what she'd expected. Amun nodded, grave, while Makena stared at her in horror. Ekon looked confused.

"Is anyone going to tell me what a kongo—?"

"Koffi, it's not safe!" Makena cut in. "Thornkeep's kongamatos aren't trained. Who's to say they'll even know what they're doing, where to go?"

"They'll know if I take the lead," said Amun. He didn't look happy about this plan, but there was a resolution in his expression. "I can ride Mjane. She's oldest, and they respect her. Coupled with my affinity . . . I think I could persuade them to follow her through the Mistwood."

"We have to try," said Koffi. She looked off into Thornkeep's grounds. The fire still raged near the bonfire, but the other gardens were still dark, shadowed. "And we need to leave quickly."

"Right," said Amun. "I'll get the kongamatos ready." He disappeared into the stables without another word.

"Find Njeri and any other darajas who want to leave," said Koffi to Makena. The girl nodded and headed toward Thornkeep, leaving Koffi and Ekon alone. In their silence, the distant bonfire's roar was a soft crackle. Koffi turned to Ekon and found that he was smiling at her.

"What?"

"You've changed," said Ekon. "You're more confident now."

Koffi considered that idea. She hadn't necessarily felt different from before, but it occurred to her that maybe she had changed. The last time she'd seen Ekon, she'd known so little about being a daraja, about her affinity to the splendor. She hadn't been at all comfortable with the idea of leading anyone else. But maybe that was the point, maybe no one ever felt truly *ready* to lead, maybe it was something that one just had to *do*. In spite of everything, she met Ekon's gaze and held it.

"Thank you, Ekon."

"You're welcome, Koffi."

A sudden bang made them both jump: Amun was coming through the stables with one of the kongamatos on a lead. Koffi hadn't seen this one the first time she'd come to the stables; it was colored a deep blue like the sea, and its scales sparkled alternately in the distant firelight and the moonlight above. Beside her, she heard a gasp.

"*That's* a kongamato?" Ekon was staring up at the creature in horror.

"More specifically, this is Wingu," said Amun, smiling. "He's not as old and mature as Mjane, but he's big, so he'll be able to carry several people without any trouble."

Koffi looked over her shoulder. Across the north garden lawns, there were two different groups of people running toward the stables, and she recognized both. Njeri was sprinting with darajas in her wake, a group of about twelve from the looks of it. Slightly to the left, Makena was running too, but more slowly, as she helped hold someone upright. Zain. He must have lifted his illusions on the darajas loyal to Fedu, which meant . . .

"GO!" Their time was finite now; Koffi didn't want to be around when those darajas who'd been under Zain's influence finally came to and understood what was happening. "We need to go now!"

Amun dashed back into the stables at the same time Njeri and the others reached them. Koffi's eyes roamed over the faces of the darajas she'd brought with her; they looked terrified.

"Come on!" She led them into the stables. "We don't have a lot of time." Her feet seemed to carry her of their own accord through the winding hallways and stalls until they reached its rear and the kongamato paddock. She slid the doors open and heard a collective gasp.

"Everyone follow Amun's instruction and pick a kongamato!" she ordered. "We'll be following him to get out of Thornkeep."

There was a pause in which no one seemed able to move, and then Njeri began ushering darajas forward. Koffi watched, counting to herself, as Amun allocated darajas to different kongamatos based on their size and weight. There were more than enough kongamatos here to get them out. Relief flooded her.

"Koffi!"

She turned and saw Makena and Zain limping through the stables' doors too. Makena was out of breath, and Zain's eyes were barely open.

"He overdid it," Makena explained. "Holding off all the darajas."

"Ride with him," said Koffi, trying to temper the fleeting pain in her chest at the sight of Zain that way. She watched as Amun directed them toward an older-looking kongamato, trying to stay calm.

"What about you?"

Koffi looked up and saw Ekon still standing by the stables' doors. He looked wary.

"You're going to ride with me," she said.

"Over here, Koffi!" Amun was waving her down now. Together, Koffi and Ekon made their way across the paddock. Most of the darajas had boarded their kongamatos now, and Koffi's eyes widened as they fell upon the one Amun was standing beside now. Its scales were a golden yellow, its eyes the color of amber; even under the night sky it looked brilliant.

"This is Njano," he said. "She's younger, but fast, and she likes to fly."

Koffi stood before the kongamato, awed. "She's beautiful."

"She's *huge*," Ekon whispered.

"I'm going to get on Mjane," Amun continued. "We're ready when you are."

Koffi watched him go before turning to Ekon. He was still eyeing Njano. "*I'm* ready," she whispered. "Are you?"

Ekon's eyes were still trained on the kongamato. "As ready as I'll ever be."

It would have to be enough. Koffi approached Njano slowly, her head bowed. The creature regarded her with a look Koffi almost would have called amusement in other circumstances before lowering to the ground. Even on her belly, her back came up to Koffi's chest.

"Come on."

"Where exactly did these things come from?" Ekon asked as he helped Koffi up, then pushed himself onto Njano's back.

"We'll have to talk about that later." Koffi cast one more look around the paddock at the other darajas. Every one of them was looking at her, waiting, and she felt like she should say something, but she didn't know what.

Something inspiring, a voice in her mind encouraged. *Something motivating.*

"Once we head into the Mistwood, there's no turning back," she said aloud. "Stay together, no matter what."

They weren't the words she planned to say, she wasn't even sure if they were the right ones, but they were the only ones she had. She took one last steadying breath before she leaned in and breathed the command, loud enough only for Njano to hear.

"Kapunda."

A shriek erupted from the kongamato's body, there was a sharp lurch, and then the world around her blurred as they were catapulted into the air.

There was a sharpness in the wind as it lashed against her skin and tore through her hair, but she relished it as Njano soared higher and higher. She stole one final glance over her shoulder, watching Thornkeep grow small. From here, she could no longer see the golden-lit windows or the gardens' trees and flowers. The farther away from the grounds she got, the more alive she felt. A small smile touched her lips.

Home. We're going home.

Ekon's arms tightened around her as Njano dipped, and Koffi tried to remember the way Zain had moved when he'd taken her on her first ride. It was simple enough; she just had to lean slightly in the direction she wanted to go in, or lean forward to pick up speed. She was still getting used to the feel of the commands when something whooshed past her in a large blur of black: Mjane. Amun was on her back. He turned the kongamato in mid-air so that they were facing her.

"If you create the path, I'll lead," he said.

Koffi nodded, then closed her eyes. It was much harder to focus, to block out what was happening around her, but when she reached for the splendor, it answered. She felt it move through her body, forming fragments of light around her hands.

Home, she commanded it. *Show me the way home.*

She no longer wondered if the splendor would obey her; she knew now that it would. In a surge, the bits of light multiplied to form lines in the sky. Behind her, she heard Ekon gasp, but Koffi focused on that light. It passed Amun and Mjane and disappeared into the clouds.

"Follow the light!" Koffi shouted, and Amun nodded. She watched as other darajas on their kongamatos passed her in flurries of colors, one by one. She waited until she was at the back of the group to move forward again. The breath left her body as she leaned forward, and Njano shrieked again, tearing into the night sky.

"It took me hours on foot to walk through the Mistwood," Ekon shouted behind her. "At this speed, we'll be through in a couple of minutes!"

Koffi heard him distantly but focused on the light. Several yards ahead, Amun was still following it, so she had to keep the splendor's path bright. Past him, she could see the mist beginning to thin, the stars of a different night's sky twinkling in the distance.

"Koffi," said Ekon. "We're almost there!"

Koffi could see it now: The mist was lifting. Cheers went up from the darajas all around her as they saw it: freedom, hope, home. Up ahead, she watched as Amun began to guide Mjane down.

"We're going to land," she said to Ekon, and now Koffi leaned forward. It was all too easy to remember what had happened the last time she'd descended on a kongamato with Zain, but this time she was ready. She braced herself, tightening her knees' grip on either side of Njano as the kongamato's body plummeted sharply. She heard Ekon yelp, but Koffi kept her gaze trained on the ground, focused. Already, she could see grass, not the manicured green of Thornkeep's lawn, but a wilder yellow kind. She braced herself, closing her eyes and preparing for the impact in those last few seconds, but when Njano landed, she felt only a gentle thud. And then, like that, it was over.

"We made it!" Ekon jumped off Njano and whooped, punching the air. "We made it!"

Around her, Koffi heard other darajas cheering as she watched the last glimmers of the splendor path flickering out. She cast her eyes and saw that the mist was now behind them; they were standing in an open plain that stretched for miles in every direction.

"Where are we?" she asked.

"The Kusini Region in the south," said Ekon. "By wagon, Lkossa is a few weeks' journey north."

Lkossa. Even hearing the city's name made something in Koffi's heart thrum. Lkossa. *Home.* She could go home.

"Hey!" One of the darajas was pointing to something in the

distance, and Koffi tensed. It was difficult to make out, but she could just barely discern what looked to be the wagons of a caravan coming her way.

"We need to leave," she said quickly. "Everyone, back on the kongamatos—"

"Wait." Ekon held up a hand, squinting. He looked to be in disbelief. "Hold on. I think I know that caravan—they're friends."

Friends. Koffi relished that word. They'd need all the friends they could find now, to get home, to figure out how to remove the splendor from her body. She was watching the caravan draw closer when she heard a scream. She whirled, and her blood went cold.

A figure was coming out of the mist behind them, slow and deliberate. She recognized its frame, the confident way it walked forward, but nothing prepared her to see Fedu as he emerged from the wisps of white like a ghost. His clothes were torn and bloodied, and his eyes were wild.

"Hello, Koffi!" he said with a manic grin.

Koffi didn't see the other darajas retreat, but she felt their abandonment, heard their footsteps as they moved away. A fear like she'd never felt before shuddered up her body as she took the god in. There was a horrid gaping hole in the middle of his chest, so large she could see straight through it. He followed her gaze, and his smile lengthened.

"A grievous injury," he said, indicating toward it. "But it will take more than that to kill me, *far* more. I will heal in a matter of time, and when I do, I will resume my work, whether you comply willingly or not."

"Koffi." Next to her, Koffi heard Ekon whisper her name.

Ekon. He'd been the only one to stay beside her when Fedu appeared. Her eyes cut to him, and she saw he was staring at the god, his expression stricken. "I want you to run. I'll try to hold him off."

Fedu's eyes flitted to Ekon, as though for the first time he'd noticed him there. "Ah, Ekon Okojo." There was almost an affection in his voice. "It seems I misjudged you. I didn't think you capable of what you just did. I admit, I'm impressed."

"Run," Ekon said through his teeth. "It's you he wants. You need to get out of here."

"Yes, Koffi." Fedu's eyes danced, eerily bright in the starlight. "*Run.* Run, and I will catch you, like I caught Adiah, like I caught the rest of my darajas. You will spend the rest of your life *on the run.*"

It was true. Koffi knew it. Ekon would try to protect her, and maybe she could escape Fedu tonight, but he would always chase her; she'd spend the rest of her life running. He would terrorize her, ensure that she always lived in fear. She met the god of death's eyes, and he smiled as though he knew what she was thinking. A sudden white-hot anger erupted in her chest at that. He found this, *all of this*, amusing.

Her fingernails dug deep into the meat of her palms as a renewed anger rose within her like an evening tide. She felt the splendor in her body growing, swelling, and imagined the things she could do with it. It boiled her blood, drew sweat to her brow, made her overwarm all over. She felt like a breathing inferno, a living tempest. And in that moment, as new power surged through her and crashed against her bones, she knew what she could do, what she wanted to do. Distantly, she thought of what Amun had once told her, about kongamatos. He'd called them "beasts of ruin," creatures of war that could only destroy. Very well, then. Perhaps that was what she would become. She opened one of her hands and imagined what she wanted. The splendor poured from her, forming and fusing until she held a spear in her hand, entirely cast in golden light. Its energy hummed when she lifted it.

Destroy, a new voice within her urged as the splendor in her body grew. *Destroy him.*

"Exquisite," said Fedu tenderly. His eyes—still focused on Koffi—were bright with elation. "Absolutely exquisite."

The wonder in his voice made Koffi even angrier. She let loose the spear with perfect aim, watching with satisfaction as it struck him in his middle and split like so many bolts of lightning. Fedu screamed, and Koffi smiled.

Destroy, that new voice said again. *Destroy him.*

She summoned more of the splendor from her body now, more than she'd ever summoned before. A longer spear formed in her hand, and she threw it toward the god with relish. This time, it skewered his thigh, and Fedu howled in pain as he fell. He started to pull himself on his elbows toward the Mistwood.

He says he is immortal, whispered the strange voice. *Let us put that to the test.*

Fedu was nearly obscured now, still backing into the Mistwood's shelter. Koffi opened her hand again, feeling the heat of a third spear as it warmed her skin.

This one, this will do it. This will kill him.

Fedu was no longer visible, he'd disappeared into the mist, but Koffi found she didn't care anymore. She felt, for the first time, truly powerful.

Destroy. The strange voice was no longer singular, but a gleeful chorus. *Destroy, destroy, destroy it all . . .*

"Koffi!"

Another voice, a familiar voice, silenced the chorus instantly. Koffi blinked, feeling the splendor recede from her as quickly as it'd come as she turned in that voice's direction. She found that Ekon was staring at her, but she didn't recognize the expression on his face. He looked shocked, terrified.

"Come back," he said quietly. "Come back."

Come back. Koffi heard the words, but they sounded faint. She felt the splendor that had torn through her body continue to fade, but with it, so did something else. A dull roaring filled her ears, a sound that made it impossible to hear the rest of the words forming on Ekon's lips. Her knees trembled as she tried to step forward, and she felt herself falling. In the distance, she thought she heard someone shout, but she couldn't be sure. From the ground, she stared up at the stars above, a thousand tiny diamonds speckled across a black blanket of night.

She watched them until the world darkened, until she felt nothing at all.

CHAPTER 28

EAST AND WEST

Ekon was counting again.

One-two-three. One-two-three. One-two-three.

He sat before a fire, beneath the stars, watching the glittering fragments of its red-gold flames leap and dance against the night sky. It had been an hour since he'd moved, and in his mind, he only saw one face.

Not nine, not six, not three. Just one.

Koffi.

Even now, his heart still raced with a palpable fear when he remembered what she'd done, what she'd looked like as she'd faced down Fedu. He'd seen a new kind of anger in her eyes, a hate. He'd watched the glowing spears form in her hand, watched as she'd thrown them with an eerie delight. In that moment, Koffi hadn't looked like herself at all. She'd looked like someone else. *Something* else.

He cast an involuntary glance over his shoulder at a tent the members of the Enterprise had set up a few feet away. Daraja healers had been running in and out of it from the moment he'd brought Koffi, unconscious, there, but she hadn't woken up. New fear roiled in Ekon's gut. What if she didn't wake up? No. He wouldn't let himself consider that. Koffi had to wake up. She would, and when she did, they would figure out what to do next. His eyes cast around the fields surrounding them.

Camp looked different now.

He counted thirty in their group now, a mix of Enterprise members and darajas. The differences between the two groups were stark. Most of the darajas were still clustered together, eyes wide, as they seemed to be trying to find their bearings. They'd have to figure out what to do with them too. He tapped his fingers against his knee.

One-two-three. One-two-three. One-two-three.

At the sound of footsteps, he looked up, hopeful, then tensed as a shadow fell over him. Zain. The boy eased onto an adjacent log, slightly close for Ekon's personal comfort—but he said nothing. After a moment, Ekon broke the silence.

"How's she doing?" He didn't need to say her name.

"Nothing new," said Zain. "She's still unconscious. They don't know what's wrong with her."

Ekon made himself count, and he made himself breathe. *One-two-three.* For every problem, there was a solution. This would be no different.

"So what now?" Ekon asked, gesturing. "Where are you and the other darajas going to go from here?"

"I can't speak for them," said Zain. "They're all free to go wherever they want from here, but . . . I want to stay with Koffi. The

Bonding is getting closer." He gave Ekon a meaningful look. "And she still needs to get to the Kusonga Plains and deposit it before then."

Ekon nodded. "Before she was captured and brought here, we'd had . . . a similar plan."

Zain looked over his shoulder at the tent that held Koffi and the healers. "If Koffi wakes up—"

"*When* she wakes up." Ekon barely kept the hostility from his voice.

Zain offered an insufferably patient look. "*When* Koffi wakes up, we'll need to move out quickly. We can't stay here."

In the midst of the fear, the anxiety, and the fatigue, a new hint of anger touched Ekon as Zain's words sank in. He stared, incredulous. "You can't be serious. We just left the mist, and Koffi's hurt. She needs time to recover—"

"Yeah, and you know who won't wait?" Zain's eyes flashed. "Fedu. She dealt him a good blow, but he's a god, and he won't be incapacitated forever. As soon as he's able, he'll come after us, *all* of us. We can't let him have Koffi."

Ekon stared at the ground for a long while before speaking again. "Fedu was able to travel from Lkossa to Thornkeep in seconds," he said, more to himself than to Zain. "There's no way we can hide from him."

Zain shook his head. "We have gifted darajas among us who can help keep our group hidden for a little while. It's not a permanent solution, but if we're lucky, we can last long enough to get to the Kusonga Plains."

Ekon was quiet, still counting on his fingers. "And what happens . . . if we *can't* move fast enough?"

Zain took a deep breath. "From what Koffi told me, Adiah held on to the splendor for nearly a century, and by consequence, it disfigured her, turned her into a monster. Koffi is stronger than Adiah, but what she's doing still takes a tremendous amount of strength. If she can't sustain that self-control, we may have to consider . . . other options."

Every muscle in Ekon's body went rigid. "What *exactly* are you saying?"

Zain turned slowly and met his gaze. "I'm saying that Koffi is like a ticking bomb, Ekon. It's not a matter of *if* she'll explode, but when. If she has the choice herself—"

"*No.*" Ekon shook his head. "You can't be serious."

"Lower your voice," Zain said. There was a new frost in his words. "It's not safe for anyone else to hear this."

Ekon bit down hard on the inside of his cheek, considering a moment. "You—you can't mean what I think you mean." He forced himself to keep the words to a whisper. "Tell me you're not saying that Koffi has to die, or . . . or *sacrifice* herself?"

"If she can't hold on to the splendor in time for the Bonding ceremony, that may be what happens." Zain's tone was flat, matter-of-fact.

"She's not a martyr," said Ekon through his teeth. "Or some weapon to be used and discarded."

One of Zain's brows rose. "You're right, she's not a weapon," he said. "She's *the* weapon, one Fedu has made it clear he will happily deploy. And if you think Koffi wouldn't be saying the exact same thing if she was conscious, maybe you don't know her as well as you thought." He left without another word.

Ekon started to shake. Because he was tired, because he was

hungry, because Koffi was in a tent a few feet away and he didn't know if she would live. But mostly because of what Zain had said. The words echoed in his mind over and over, like a snake's low hiss.

Maybe you don't know her as well as you thought.

"Ekon?"

For the second time he looked up, fists clenched and ready for a second round with Zain. This time, though, it was Ano staring down at him. She looked tentative.

"May I sit?" Her face was obscured, but her voice was soft.

"Go ahead."

For several long minutes, neither of them spoke as they stared into the flames. Ekon broke their shared silence first.

"You followed Themba and me."

Ano nodded. "We knew almost as soon as you left us that we'd made a mistake. We took a vote, and then we came." She looked around them, her face somber. "Themba is not with you anymore."

"She died." Ekon said the words more harshly than he meant to. "In the Mistwood."

For several long seconds, Ano said nothing. "I'm sorry. She was . . . an exceptional woman, and I know she cared for you."

"*She* did." There was a bitterness in Ekon's voice. "But *you* didn't."

Shock registered on Ano's face. "What?"

"I want to know the real reason," said Ekon. "I want to know why you agreed to come here, to come after us. You made it clear that you never wanted me to travel with you, and now I'm supposed to believe that you had a change of heart?" He shook his head. "I don't believe it, and I want to know the truth."

There was a long pause. When Ano spoke again, her voice was thick. "We came back," she said slowly, "because I couldn't let anything happen to you. I couldn't abandon you again."

"Again?" Ekon stiffened. "What are you talking about?"

"You asked for the truth, Ekon," she murmured. "And you deserve it." She sighed. "The first truth is that my name is not Ano."

Ekon stilled.

"My name is Ayesha Ndidi Okojo. I am your mother."

"No." Even as he said the word, he knew that what she had said was true. It had been thirteen years, but the longer he stared at Ano's face, the more certain he now was. The short black hair he remembered was different, there were faint lines in places where there had not been any before, but it was her.

Mama.

"I'm sorry." She wrapped her arms around herself, and Ekon was struck by how small she looked, how frail. "I'm so, so sorry," she repeated. "But you have to believe I never wanted to leave you."

In the midst of the shock, it took a moment for the anger to come, but then Ekon felt it. It was a great, constricting thing, filling all the space between his ribs. He tried to find the words—the cruel words, the desperate words—to explain the emotions coursing through his body. He found he could only muster three.

"We needed you." His voice cracked on the last word. "Kamau and I . . . after Baba died, they tried to . . . they were going to split us up, send us away."

"I was trying to protect you," she said. "I swear it. If I knew of another way—"

"Protect me from what?" Finally, Ekon erupted. He'd repressed all of it, the anger, the grief, the hurt, for thirteen years; now he had no strength left. "What was *possibly* dangerous enough to leave us?"

Ano lowered her head. "East and west."

Ekon froze. "What?"

"You wouldn't remember it," she said. She was still staring at the ground. "The night I brought you to Sigidi."

Sigidi. Ekon felt a chill as he remembered something, a man leaving the apothecary, a friend of Themba's, a daraja.

"Why did you go to see Sigidi?" His voice sounded hoarse even to his own ears, choked.

"I did not intend to do it," said Ano. "I was planning to take you to a midwife. You were crying incessantly, and I thought it might be colic. Your brother had had the same affliction. I took you to the woman who treated him, but when I went to her, she told me there was someone else waiting for me, a man who already knew my name, though we'd never met before." Her eyes turned distant then she closed them and shuddered. "That night, I met Sigidi for the first time, and he told me that he could see into the future. He relayed to me a prophecy: 'East and west. One sun rises in the east. One sun rises in the west. One sun sees only triumph. One sun sees only death.'"

Ekon shook his head. "I don't understand—that's talking about two different suns rising. It has nothing to do with—"

"You do not speak the language of prophecy," said Ano. Her smile was sad. "You are too literal. The suns mentioned in that line do not refer to suns in the sky, but male children—*sons*. One son rises in the east. One son rises in the west. It is a reference to you, and to your brother."

"But . . ." Ekon frowned. "No, that still doesn't make sense. Kamau and I were both born in the Zamani Region, in the east—"

"Too literal, again," said Ano, shaking her head. "Kamau was born in the morning when the sun rose in the east." Her eyes grew somber. "But you, I labored with you for nearly a day, from sunrise to sundown. By the time I'd delivered you, it was dusk, and the sun was in the—"

"*West.*" Ekon said nothing as a lump rose in his throat, as a fear he'd never felt before gripped him. "What else did Sigidi's prophecy say?"

Ano stared at Ekon a long time before she spoke again. "'One son rises in the east, one son rises in the west. One son will know glory, one son will know death.'" She paused, visibly hesitant. "I asked Sigidi if he could tell me anything else about the prophecy, anything else that might help me understand. He only told me that, in the end, one of my sons would grow up and kill that which he loves most." She shook her head. "I was vain; I thought perhaps it might mean that one of you would kill me, so I left. But now . . ." She trailed off. "I see the way you look at her."

"Her?" Ekon started.

Ano said nothing, but looked purposefully to her right. Ekon followed her gaze. Together, they stared at the tent where Koffi lay.

AUTHOR'S NOTE

When I sit down to begin a new story, I rarely know at its inception what themes I will find within its threads as I weave it. In the case of *Beasts of Prey*, I hoped to write a story that celebrated the rich and nuanced history from which my heritage and identity stem. I hoped to do that again in *Beasts of Ruin*, but I also hoped that—perhaps in the confines of this story's metaphorical walls— I might have the opportunity to write about harder things, more challenging ideas. Thus, this is again the story of two people on very different adventures, but it is also the story of two people contending and persevering in spite of betrayal, fear, and uncertainty at every turn. It is a narrative that examines, sometimes uncomfortably, the fraught relationship a person can have with their heritage when that heritage has been deliberately erased or vilified. To that end, I want to acknowledge two books that partially influenced the creation of Binti's point of view specifically: Nella Larsen's *Passing*, and Fannie Hurst's *Imitation of Life*.

Within *Beasts of Ruin*, there is a character named Sigidi, who I named after Sigidi kaSenzangakhona (1787–1828), a formidable Zulu warrior and king who is credited as the founder of the Zulu people of South Africa. More often known in history as Shaka

Zulu, Sigidi is universally considered to be one of the world's most brilliant military tacticians, and is credited with popularizing the use of the iklwa, a short spear. Though accounts surrounding his childhood are inconsistent, it has been suggested that a prophetess named Sithayi prophesied that he would be a great warrior. She was right.

I've made no secret of the fact that I love animals, mythical and otherwise, and I love having the opportunity to write stories that feature ones some readers may not have heard of before. I want to use this space to share a bit of information about the creatures you've met within *Beasts of Ruin*.

You'll be pleased (or horrified) to know that the deathstalker scorpion referenced in this book is quite real, and quite venomous. Their scientific name is *Leiurus quinquestriatus*, and they are most often found throughout northern Africa and in parts of what is often referred to as the Middle East. While the venom from their telson (their stinger) isn't always lethal, a child, an elderly person, or an immunocompromised person could be killed by it.

In Swahili, the word *walaji* (wuh-LAH-gee) means "devourers." While the Walaji mentioned in this book—and the creepy legend behind them—are fictional, part of the idea for them was inspired by bees and butterflies. Most people don't know that, although both insects are known to eat pollen and nectar, bees and butterflies will also drink blood, tears, sweat, and even the fluids from carrion.

The nanabolele (nah-nah-boh-LAY-lay) mentioned in this book was inspired by a creature of the same name whose origins can be traced to the Basotho (or Sotho) people of southern Africa. Sometimes called "water dragons," they are described as luminescent predators, and some accounts claim they wear the spots of a leopard. The most well-known Basotho myth about nanaboleles is the story of a princess named Thakané, who was sent to retrieve the skin of one. In *Beasts of Ruin*, I altered the nanabolele slightly to make them more crocodilian, in keeping with Amakoya's known affinity for crocodiles.

On a related note, it's worth mentioning that the tonic immobility that Ekon and Safiyah use to defeat the nanabolele is based on real science. Biologists know little about why tonic immobility causes crocodilians to become catatonic. This usually lasts for fifteen to twenty seconds in nature, but for this story, I extended it just slightly to give our brave heroes time to escape!

Likewise, the kongamatos (KONG-ah-MOT-ohz) mentioned in this book are inspired by a creature of less certain origins, but they are referenced in the folklore of several African countries, including Angola, Zambia, and Congo. Notably, their name translates to "breaker or destroyer of boats"; they were truly beasts of ruin and known for their legendary devastation. Scientists have suggested that the kongamato may have originated from the order of pterosauria, which encompasses all flying reptiles (dinosaurs) who lived within the Mesozoic era more than sixty million years ago. While few have heard of the kongamato, far more are familiar with pterodactyls, which are another species within the pterosauria order.

The ichisonga (itch-ee-SŌNE-guh) referenced in *Beasts of Ruin* comes from the mythos of the Lamba people in Zambia. Described as a formidable water beast with a large horn on its head, it is said that the ichisonga hates hippopotamuses and protects elephants. I took some liberties with its characteristics in this story, but needless to say, it is a very fearsome creature.

Keep reading to see where the adventure began

CHAPTER 1

GOOD SPIRITS

The hut reeked of death.

It was a nauseating smell, both fetid and sickly sweet, thick in the dusk as it filled Koffi's lungs. A quarter hour had passed since she'd last moved; her legs were stiff, her mouth dry. Every so often, her stomach twisted, threatening revolt. But it was no matter; she kept still as stone. Her eyes were fixed on what lay mere feet from her across the worn dirt floor—the victim.

The boy's name was Sahel. Koffi hadn't worked with him in the Night Zoo long, but she recognized his bare face, mahogany brown like her own, framed by tight black curls. In life, he'd had a crooked smile, an obnoxious braying laugh not unlike that of a donkey. Those things had abandoned him in death. She studied his lanky frame. As was Gede practice, most of his body was shrouded, but dried blood still stained the white linen in places, hints of the gruesome wounds beneath. She couldn't see them, but she knew they were there—the scratches, the *bite marks*. From the darkest corners of her mind, a chilling image grew vivid. She imagined Sahel stumbling through a jungle, clumsy, oblivious to what waited for

1

him among the vines. She envisioned a grotesque creature stalking forward in the moonlight, tongue darting between serrated teeth as it eyed easy prey.

She heard the scream.

A violent shudder racked her body then, despite the muggy heat. If the rumors she'd heard earlier were true, Sahel's manner of death had been neither a quick nor a painless affair.

"Kof."

Across the stuffy hut, Mama was on her knees beside Sahel's body, staring at the tattered blanket before it. On it were six crudely carved wooden figurines of animals—a heron, a crocodile, a jackal, a serpent, a dove, and a hippo—one familiar for each god. The oil lamp to her right bathed one side of her face in lambent light; the other was cast in shadow. "It's time."

Koffi hesitated. She'd agreed to come here and offer parting rites for Sahel, as Gede custom called for, but the thought of getting any closer to the corpse unnerved her. At a sharp glance from Mama, however, she moved to kneel with her. Together they let their fingers brush each of the figurines before folding their hands.

"Carry him." Mama whispered the prayer. "Carry him to his ancestors in the godlands."

Their heads were still bowed when Koffi asked the question in a murmur. "Is it true?"

Mama cracked a wary eye. "Koffi . . ."

"Some of the others were talking," Koffi went on before her mother could stop her. "They said others were killed, that—"

"*Hush.*" Mama's head snapped up, and she swatted the words away like tsetse flies. "Mind your tongue when you speak of the dead, lest you bring them misfortune."

Koffi pursed her lips. It was said that, to pass into the next life, one of the gods' animal familiars—represented by the figurines before them—carried each soul to the god of death, Fedu. Each soul then had to pay Fedu before being carried on to paradise in the godlands. A soul with no money to pay for passage was doomed to walk the earth as a lost spirit for all eternity. Like Koffi, Sahel had been a beastkeeper indentured to the Night Zoo, which meant he'd had little money in life and likely had even less in death. If faith held true, this meant his misfortunes had only just begun, whether she minded her tongue or not. She had started to say so when the hut's straw-thatch door opened. A stout woman with salt-and-pepper cornrows stuck her head inside. Her simple tunic was identical to theirs, gray and hemmed just below the knee. At the sight of them, she wrinkled her nose.

"Time to go."

Mama gestured to the figurines. "We're not finished—"

"You've had ample time for this nonsense." The woman waved a dismissive hand. She spoke Zamani, the language of the East, like them, but her Yaba dialect gave her words a sharp, clicking quality. "The boy's dead, praying to toys won't change that, and there's work yet to be done before the show, which Baaz expects to begin on time."

Mama gave a resigned nod. Together, she and Koffi stood, but once the woman had left again, they both looked back to Sahel. If not for the bloodied shroud, he could have been sleeping.

"We'll return and finish our prayers later, before they bury him," said Mama. "He deserves that much."

Koffi tugged at her tunic's frayed neckline, trying to temper a moment's guilt. Everyone else in the Night Zoo had already offered prayers for Sahel, but she'd begged Mama to wait. She'd blamed chores, then a headache, but the truth was, she hadn't wanted to see Sahel like this, broken and hollow and devoid of all the things that had made him real. She'd built her own kind of walls to protect herself from the near-constant reminders of death's presence here, but it had crept in anyway, intruding. Now the idea of leaving Sahel to lie here in the dirt, as alone as he'd been in the last grisly seconds of his life, unsettled her. She thought again of what she'd heard other beastkeepers whispering earlier in the day. People were now saying that Sahel had waited until late last night to make a run for it. They said he'd gone into the Greater Jungle hoping to find freedom and instead had found a creature that killed for amusement. She winced. The Shetani's murderous reputation was frightening enough, but it was the fact that the monster had evaded capture for so many years that set her on edge. Misunderstanding the look on her face, Mama took Koffi's hand and squeezed.

"I promise we'll come back," she whispered. "Now come on, let's go." Without another word, she ducked out of the hut. Koffi glanced back at Sahel's body a final time, then followed.

Outside, the sun was setting, cast against a bruised sky curiously fractured by strange black fissures amid the clouds. Those fissures would fade to a gentler violet as monsoon season drew nearer, but they'd never truly disappear. They'd been there all Koffi's life, an indelible mark left by the Rupture.

She hadn't been alive a century ago when it had happened, but elders deep in their palm wine still spoke of it on occasion. Drunk, voices slurred, they recalled the violent tremors that had splintered the earth like a clay pot, the dead who'd strewn Lkossa's streets in the aftermath. They talked of a relentless, blistering heat that had driven men mad. Koffi, and every other child of her generation, had suffered the consequences of that madness. After the Rupture, her people—the Gedes—had been dwindled down by war and poverty, easy to divide and regulate. Her eyes traveled along the cracks in the sky, weaving overhead like thin black threads. For a second, she thought she felt something as she surveyed them . . .

"Koffi!" Mama called over her shoulder. "Come now!"

Just as quickly, the feeling was gone, and Koffi kept on.

In silence, she and Mama whisked by mud-brick huts crammed along the Night Zoo's edge; other beastkeepers were getting ready too. They passed men and women dressed in shabby tunics, some nursing freshly bandaged wounds from encounters with beasts, some marked by more permanent injuries like old scars and missing fingers. Each carried a quiet defeat in their hunched shoulders and downcast eyes that Koffi hated but understood. Most of the Night Zoo's workers were of the Gedezi People like her, which meant the show would go on this evening, but Sahel's absence would be felt. He hadn't had real family here, but he'd been one of them, bound to this place by bad luck and bad choices. He deserved more than quick prayers in a run-down hut; he deserved a proper burial with token coins placed in his palms to ensure he made it to the god-lands. But no one here could afford to spare any coin. Baaz made sure of that.

A chorus of shrieks, roars, and snarls filled the eventide as they reached the crooked wooden post marking the end of the beastkeepers' huts, trading red dirt for an expanse of green lawns filled with cages of every size, shape, and color. Koffi eyed the one nearest her, and the eight-headed nyuvwira snake met her gaze, curious. She followed Mama's lead around cages of white pygmy

5

elephants, chimpanzees, a pair of giraffes grazing quietly in their paddock. They passed a dome-shaped aviary full of black-and-white impundulus, barely mindful to cover their heads as the birds beat their massive wings and sent sparks of lightning into the sky. Baaz Mtombé's Night Zoo was rumored to hold over a hundred exotic species within its confines; in her eleven years of contracted service to it, Koffi had never bothered to count.

They moved quickly between other enclosures, but when they reached the grounds' border, her steps slowed. The blacksteel cage kept here was separate from the others, and with good reason. In the dying light, only its stark silhouette was visible; what it contained within was veiled in shadow.

"It's all right." Mama beckoned even as Koffi instinctively faltered. "I checked on Diko earlier today, and he was fine." She approached the cage at the same time something in its corner shifted. Koffi tensed.

"Mama—"

"Come now, Diko." Mama kept her voice low as she withdrew a rust-speckled key from her pocket to insert into the massive padlock. In answer, there was an ominous hiss, slick as a blade. Koffi's toes curled in the grass, and from the cage's shadows a beautiful creature emerged.

His body was reptilian and sinewed, entirely adorned by iridescent scales that seemed to hold a thousand colors captive each time he moved. Clever citrine eyes danced back and forth as Mama tinkered with the lock, and when the beast flicked his forked black tongue between the bars, a smell like smoke tinged the dry air. Koffi swallowed.

The first time she'd seen a jokomoto, as a little girl, she'd thought they were creatures spun from glass, fragile and delicate. She'd been wrong. There was nothing delicate about a fire-breathing lizard.

"Get the hasira leaf out," Mama directed. "Now."

At once, Koffi pulled three dry, silver-veined leaves from a drawstring pouch at her hip. They were exquisite, shimmering with white resin that left her fingertips sticky when she pinched them. Her heartbeat hammered as the door to the jokomoto's cage swung open and his head swiveled. Mama covered her nose with one hand, then raised the other in warning.

"Steady . . ."

Koffi went stock-still as the jokomoto bolted from his cage and slunk toward her on long clawed feet. She waited until he was within a few yards of her before tossing the leaves high into the air. Diko's eyes caught them, and he lunged, impossibly quick. There was a flash of pointed teeth, a merciless crunch, and then they were gone. Koffi stuffed her hands back into her pockets quickly. Jokomotos weren't native to this part of Eshōza; they were creatures from the western part of the continent, said to be children of Tyembu, the desert god. At roughly the same size as a common monitor lizard, Diko wasn't the largest, fastest, or strongest animal kept in the Night Zoo, but he *was* the most temperamental—which also made him the most dangerous. One wrong move and he could set the entire place ablaze; it was all too easy to recall the nasty burns on beastkeepers who'd forgotten that. Her heartbeat only settled after the hasira leaf's power took effect and the lurid yellow glow in his eyes slightly dimmed.

"I've got it from here." Koffi was already moving behind Diko with a leather harness and leash snatched from a nearby post. She stooped down, and the moment she fastened its worn straps under his scaled belly and tightened them, she relaxed. The flimsy binds were a silly thing to take comfort in—they'd do nothing if Diko's mood soured—but he was subdued, at least for now.

"Make sure those binds are secure."

Koffi looked up. "Done."

Pleased, Mama bent to give Diko's snout a demonstrative pat. "That's a good boy."

Koffi rolled her eyes as she straightened. "I don't know why you talk to him like that."

"Why not?" Mama shrugged. "Jokomotos are spectacular beasts."

"They're dangerous."

"Sometimes things that seem dangerous are just misunderstood." Mama said the words with a strange sadness before patting Diko again. This time, as if to affirm the point, he gently nudged her palm. This seemed to cheer her back up. "Besides, just look at him. He's in good spirits tonight."

Koffi started to argue, then thought better of it. Her mother had always had a strange empathy for the Night Zoo's inhabitants. She changed the subject.

"You know, that was the last of the hasira leaf." She patted her empty pouch for emphasis. "We're out until more is delivered." Even now, wisps of the leaves' cloying fragrance still suffused the air. Inadvertently, she caught a lingering whiff of it, and a pleasant thrum tickled the edges of her senses.

"Koffi!" Mama's voice turned sharp, cleaving through that

momentary bliss. She was still holding Diko's leash, but frowning. "You know better. Don't breathe it in."

Koffi shook herself, unnerved, then fanned at the air around her until the smell was gone. Plucked from shrubs along the Greater Jungle's border, hasira leaf was a sedative herb potent enough to knock out a mature bull elephant when consumed; it wasn't wise to inhale its fragrance at close range, even in small quantities.

"We should get moving." Mama's gaze had locked on an illuminated tent set across the Night Zoo's grounds; other beastkeepers were already heading toward it with animals in tow. From here, it was no larger than a candle's red-gold flame, but Koffi recognized it—the Hema was where tonight's show would be held. Mama glanced her way again. "Ready?"

Koffi grimaced. She was never ready for shows at the Night Zoo, but that hardly mattered. She'd just moved to stand on the other side of Diko when she noticed something.

"What's wrong?" Mama asked, noting Koffi's raised eyebrow.

"You tell *me*." Now Koffi squinted. Something was off about her mother's expression, but she couldn't quite tell what. She studied it harder. The two of them looked similar—shoulder-length black twists, broad nose and full mouth framed by a heart-shaped face—but there was something *else* about Mama tonight. "You look . . . different."

"Oh." Mama looked uncharacteristically flustered, there was no doubt about it. Then Koffi named it, that foreign emotion in her mother's eyes. Koffi was embarrassed to realize the thing she hadn't recognized was happiness.

"Did . . . something happen?"

Mama shifted her weight from foot to foot. "Well, I was going to wait until tomorrow to tell you. After what happened with Sahel earlier, it didn't seem right to discuss it, but . . ."

"*But?*"

"Baaz pulled me aside a few hours ago," she said. "He calculated our debt balance, and . . . we're almost paid off."

"What?" Something like shock and joy erupted in Koffi. Diko snorted at the sudden outburst, sending tendrils of smoke into the air, but she ignored him. "How?"

"Those extra hours we took on added up." Mama offered a small smile. She was standing straighter, like a plant coming into full bloom. "We only have two more payments left, and we could probably pay those off in the next few days."

Sheer disbelief coursed through Koffi. "And after that, we're done?"

"*Done.*" Mama nodded. "The debt will be paid, interest and all."

Koffi felt a long-held tension within her release as she exhaled. Like most things in the Night Zoo, the terms and conditions held by its indentured workers only benefitted one person. Eleven years of service with Mama had taught her that. But they'd won, beaten Baaz at his own wretched game. They were going to *leave*. It was so rare that beastkeepers managed to pay back their debts—the last one who'd managed it had done so at least a year ago—but now it was their turn.

"Where will we go?" Koffi asked. She could barely believe she was really posing the question. They'd never gone anywhere; she barely remembered a life outside the Night Zoo.

Mama closed the gap between them and took Koffi's hand in hers. "We can go *wherever we want.*" She spoke with a fervor Koffi had never heard before. "You and I, we'll leave this place and start over somewhere else, and we'll never, *ever* look back. We'll never return."

Never return. Koffi considered the words. All her life she'd longed for them, dreamed of them. Hearing them now, however, they felt strangely different.

"What?" Mama noted her changed expression immediately. "What is it?"

"It's just . . ." Koffi didn't know if they were the right words, but she tried. "We'll never see anyone here ever again."

Mama's expression softened with understanding. "You'll miss it."

Koffi nodded, quietly angry with herself for doing so. She didn't necessarily love working at the Night Zoo, but it was the only home she'd ever known, the only *life* she'd ever known. She thought of the other beastkeepers, not quite a family, but certainly people she cared about.

"I'll miss them too," said Mama gently, reading her thoughts. "But they wouldn't want us to stay here, Koffi, not if we didn't have to."

"I just wish we could help them," Koffi murmured. "I wish we could help all of them."

Mama offered a small smile. "You're a compassionate girl. You lead with your heart, like your father."

Koffi shifted uncomfortably. She didn't like being compared to Baba. Baba was gone.

"Sometimes, though, you can't lead with your heart," said Mama gently. "You have to think with your *head*."

A horn's brassy trumpeting split the air without warning, its summons rising from the distant Temple of Lkossa to reverberate across the Night Zoo's lawns in long, sonorous notes. They both stiffened as the sounds of newly agitated beasts filled the ground around them, and Diko bared his teeth in anticipation. The city's saa-horn had at last announced nightfall. It was time. Again, Mama's eyes flitted from the Hema to Koffi.

"It's almost over, little ponya seed," she said softly, a touch of hope in her voice. She hadn't called her that in years. "I know how hard this has been, but it's almost over, I promise. We're going to be okay."

Koffi didn't answer as Mama tugged Diko's leash to lead him toward the massive tent. She followed but kept a step behind. Her eyes cast wide, holding in their gaze the final remnants of a sky the color of blood. Mama's words echoed in her mind.

We're going to be okay.

They would be okay, she knew that now, but her thoughts still lingered on something else, *someone* else. Sahel. He wasn't okay—he'd never be okay again. She couldn't help but think of him then, of the boy with the crooked smile. She couldn't help but think of the monster that had killed him and wonder who it would take next.

ACKNOWLEDGMENTS

It is a magical thing, to create from nothing. It is another matter entirely to create from nothing within a finite amount of time, which is what writing *Beasts of Ruin* required. Simply put, this book would not exist without the many people who continue to lend their constant support, love, and encouragement. I won't possibly have the space to name each of them here, but the following is my valiant attempt.

To **Stacey Barney**, my truly dynamic editor: Thank you, first and foremost, for believing in me in the moments I doubted myself. Thank you for being patient with me, and thank you for your wonderful laugh, which always reminds me that everything will be okay. Also, thanks for teaching me about mugger money!

As always, I am so thankful for my literary agent, **Pete Knapp**, who remains my most ardent champion and advocate within the publishing world. Pete, thank you for being you, and for always smiling on the inside. My additional thanks to Stuti Telidevara, Emily Sweet, Andrea Mai, and the phenomenal Park & Fine team for their continued care, professionalism, and unparalleled industry acumen.

To **Olivia Russo**, my publicist and fairy godmother extraordinaire: Thank you for making so many wishes come true, for emails with many exclamation points, for your infectious kindness, and for being a friend throughout this journey. I'm so glad to know you.

To Kim Ryan, thank you for allowing Koffi and Ekon to travel farther than they ever could have imagined, and for allowing them to touch the lives of readers all over the world.

To my fantastic UK team: Natalie Doherty, Charlotte "Lottie" Halstead, Harriet Venn, Michael Bedo, and Rowan Williams-Fletcher, thank you so much for your support and passion throughout this journey. Thank you also to all of my publishers outside of the United States, who have worked so enthusiastically to give my books new homes!

I so appreciate the immensely talented creatives responsible for making *Beasts of Ruin* a beautiful book, inside and out. Thank you, Virginia Allyn, for yet again creating beautiful maps of Eshōza and Thornkeep that truly make them feel like real places. Thank you, Marikka Tamura and Theresa Evangelista, for your continued savvy in this book's interior and exterior design, respectively. Finally, thank you to Elena Masci for creating *Beasts of Ruin*'s brilliant U.S. cover and thus allowing Black kids to see faces like theirs on the cover of a fantasy novel.

A sincere thanks to the peerless teams at Penguin Young Readers and G. P. Putnam's Sons Books for Young Readers, who turn everything they touch into gold: James Akinaka, Kara Brammer, Trevor Bundy, Venessa Carson, Colleen Conway Ramos, Felicia Frazier, Alex Garber, Jacqueline Hornberger, Cindy Howle, Carmela Iaria, Todd Jones, Jen Klonsky, Misha Kydd, Jen Loja,

Lathea Mondesir, Shanta Newlin, Summer Ogata, Sierra Pregosin, Emily Romero, Shannon Spann, Caitlin Tutterow, Felicity Vallence, Chandra Wohleber, and the indomitable Bezi Yohannes ("in the bleak midwinter").

I am also so grateful to the Penguin Random House Audio team for so beautifully transforming my written words into audiobooks that can be enjoyed by an even larger readership: Heather Dalton, Katie Punia, and Julie Wilson. Thank you as well to the wonderful audiobook narrators who have breathed life into my characters by giving them voices: Keylor Leigh, Tovah Ott, and Ronald Peet.

I truly don't think this book could have been written without the support of Natalie Crown, who has had my back in every way over the last year. Natalie, thank you for all the voice clips and for letting me complain and work out all the messy knots until they made sense. Thank you for being the best friend and critique partner imaginable, and for always being on my side—you're the best. (*Forza Ferrari!*)

To say that finding lasting and meaningful friendships in your twenties is difficult would be an understatement; finding friends who understand the unique adventure of being an author is even harder. That said, I so cherish the friends who understand what it means to be a writer and who have provided me with an irreplaceable support system: Lauren Blackwood, Lane Clarke, J. Elle, Maiya Ibrahim, Emily Thiede, and Amélie Wen Zhao. I love you each to pieces. A heartfelt thank-you, too, to the friends I think of as extended family: Adrie, Robyn, Jarret, Kris, Kim and Michelle, Billie, Bricker and Ashley, FA'12, Brumett, and Bates.

I owe a genuine thanks to the authors who've been on this

road a little longer and offered guidance, compassion, and empathy while I wrote the Notoriously Difficult sophomore novel: Dhonielle Clayton, Brigid Kemmerer, Margaret Rogerson, and Samantha Shannon. In particular, my thanks to Renée Ahdieh, Sabaa Tahir, and Roshani Chokshi—I got through this past year largely because, in the moments I stumbled, they held me up. Another heartfelt thanks to Daniel José Older and Brittany N. Williams, for being there when it counted most.

Thank you to the wonderful friends I've made within the writing community who've joined me, stayed with me, and inspired me on this journey: Daniel Aleman, B. B. Alston, Rena Barron, TJ Benton-Walker, Ronni Davis, Alechia Dow, Brenda Drake, Kristin Dwyer, Namina Forna, Kellye Garrett, Adalyn Grace, Jordan Gray, Sonia Hartl, Isabel Ibañez, Taj McCoy, Becca Mix, Shelby Mahurin, Sarah Nicolas, Claribel A. Ortega, Molly Owen, Krystal Sutherland, Catherine Adel West, and Margot Wood. I'm so grateful as well for the educators, librarians, booksellers, social media influencers, and readers who have championed my books in the places I could not. Every day I get to do what I love for a living because of you—thank you. A special shout-out to two of *Beasts of Ruin*'s biggest advocates: Brittney Threatt and B. McClain.

As always, thank you to my family—Mom, Dad, Corey, and Ashley—for being my most spirited fans and the North Stars in my life when I find myself utterly lost. Thank you to my grandparents, my godmothers, and my Aussie family for an infinite amount of love and support. To Oscar H., and Elissa T.—your stories are just beginning, and it's my honor to be a part of them, even from across the sea. Much love always to my many beloved sisters of Alpha Kappa Alpha, who inspire me every day.

Last, but not least, thank you to my Puddin'. This world is much more beautiful and much more fun with you in it. Thanks for putting up with all the nights I fell asleep on the couch with my laptop on my knees, and for dancing with me even when the music stops.

(Just kidding, my very last thanks are to Dolly, for making my life many things, but never boring. I'll tell you a secret, little waffle: My best ideas for *Beasts of Ruin* were born from my walks with you.)